I0589609

WHAT HEALS
THE HEART

Karen A. Wyle

ISBN 978-0-9980604-5-3
Published 2019 in the United States of America
Oblique Angles Press

Cover design by Kelly A. Martin of KAM Design

Author photo by Holy Smoke Photography
Dedication photo by Karen A. Wyle

Dedication

To – who else? – my husband of thirty years,
Paul Hager.

Chapter 1

JOSHUA GIBBS felt sun on his face and thought about opening his eyes. He decided to wait. He had some blessings to savor that wouldn't need sight.

He was in a bed, a four-poster with a well-stuffed husk mattress, instead of in a tent on rough ground. He was in Nebraska, far from any of the towns he had passed through — or seen devastated — during the war. The sound nearest his right ear wasn't the whistle of a shell or the wails and screams of dying men, but the soft grumbly snore of his Irish Setter. And the dog's name might be Major (or, to give the full grandiloquent version, Reginald Phineas Major), but that was the closest to an officer he'd find for miles around.

And what Joshua smelled, when he took a slow, lazy sniff, was a mix of Major and almost-clean bed linen, and not . . . well, no need to sully a brand new morning with the memory of what he'd have smelled this time nine years ago.

But thoughts like these were not worth staying abed for. He opened his eyes and sat up, stretching out his arm and laying a hand lightly on Major's side for the warm breathing comfort of it. Major's eye twitched, and his tail, but that was all. A dog knew, without having to think about it, what safety meant.

Joshua levered himself out of bed. He'd shave, get dressed, and take a walk with Major before frying himself some breakfast.

As a boy, if he could have even imagined himself so

old as thirty-three, he'd have assumed he'd be leaving a
wife behind staying warm in bed or making breakfast, or
better yet, accompanying him on his morning amble. But
things change. War changes them. And solitude suited him,
these days.

Most of the latest — perhaps the last? — snow had
melted. It wouldn't take him too long to clean off his boots
after his walk. Joshua liked having clean boots when he saw
patients, even if some folk in town might think it affected of
him.

He headed away from the square to start, toward the
creek that had given Cowbird Creek its name. If he'd been
taking this road out of town to see a patient, he'd have been
riding his trotter Nellie-girl or using one of the livery stable
buggies. He wouldn't have had time or attention to spare
for the serviceberry bushes just starting to put forth their
lacy white flowers, or the sparrows with their thin high
chirps, stirring about on whatever business sparrows had.

He got as far as the buttonwood tree by the creek
before his hollow stomach reminded him to turn round. He
took a turn around the square and saw a light in the
laundry. Li Chang looked to be hard at work already. It
wasn't easy to get the Chinese fellow talking, as busy as he
kept himself, but his tales of the gold fields could cure
anyone of hankering after mining. Though he'd managed to
make enough of a stake to set up his business and even pay
for help — except the help had given up on America and
gone home a year since.

Turning the corner brought Joshua past the church.
Passing the church meant passing the churchyard. A few of
his patients were at rest there, though others were buried on
their farms. One or two of them wouldn't be there yet, if

he'd known then what he knew now. He paused, bowed his head, and sent them a silent apology, and a promise to stick to his books until he knew as much medicine as anyone could learn that way.

At least there were other folk, asleep in bed or about their chores, in town and outside it, who might have been sleeping colder in the ground if not for him.

He picked up his pace, more than ready for breakfast. He had bacon and eggs he'd got in payment from the farmer whose cough he'd dosed two days ago. Good thing he liked his eggs runny, because he hadn't left all that much time for cooking and eating before opening his office and seeing who sauntered or stumbled or limped in to be doctored.

By now, everyone knew that Doctor Gibbs saw patients in his office on Tuesdays, Thursdays, and Saturdays, unless someone in urgent need of him called him away somewhere. The town days, when he got them, gave Nellie-girl a good rest, not to mention Joshua himself. Sometimes things were slow, and he'd have time to read or even (out of sight of the street) practice magic tricks or nap a bit. And the stroll to the office — or rather, the long way around, ending up at the office — gave him a chance to watch the town come alive, as much as it ever did, and to greet a neighbor or two.

Joshua had by now lived in Cowbird Creek long enough to take particular notice of any new face. So when he saw a woman heading into the general store and realized he could not remember seeing her before, he stopped and took a second look. Besides her being unfamiliar, Joshua's first impression was that she was tall for a woman, and next, that she was thin, her plainly cut dress doing nothing to disguise the fact. As she turned into the store, he caught a glimpse of striking green eyes and a long dark braid hanging beneath her simple bonnet — darker than Joshua's own, almost black.

A farmer, one of Joshua's patients, was lounging nearby while one of his sons argued with the blacksmith's helper about how long it took to shoe a carthorse. Noting the direction of Joshua's glance, he spat some tobacco juice and said, "That'd be the daughter on that farm that changed hands last month. Skinnier'n you, ain't she?"

Given the farmer's girth, his view of what it meant to be "skinny" was somewhat skewed. Joshua would describe himself as lean. The farmer, meanwhile, added, "Owners gave up fighting the drought and went back east. I heard something about these folks renting land somewhere else and coming here to buy their own place. Got some kind of funny name, Crick or Stream or suchlike."

With that pronouncement, the farmer straightened up and went in to relieve his son in the dispute with the blacksmith's helper. Joshua pulled out his pocket watch and hurried along.

Two patients were waiting outside his door when he opened it, the sheriff and the blacksmith. That's why the blacksmith's helper had been manning the shop, then. Joshua steered the blacksmith, who seemed the steadier on his feet of the two, not to mention the one who wouldn't get ruffled about waiting, to a chair and took the sheriff into the back where he'd set up his exam table and instruments.

The sheriff hoisted his considerable bulk up onto the table. "My belly's been aching considerable."

Joshua noted the sheriff's flushed color and straining suspenders. "And just what have you been putting into that belly of late?"

The sheriff shrugged sheepishly. "You know Ma's pork chops and creamed corn, and her molasses pie. You had vittles like that waiting at home, you'd eat too much of 'em, I reckon."

"Well, roll up your left sleeve." Joshua picked up the lancet and gave the sheriff the pan to hold. He didn't hold with bleeding patients for many ailments, but this seemed like one of the times it might help. And most of his patients believed it would, which could make a difference in itself.

When the pan held a sufficient quantity of blood, he took it to throw away later and bandaged the arm. "Take it easy on that pie, now." He grinned. "You can bring some by my place, to remove temptation."

The sheriff snorted as he slid off the table and made his way toward the front of the office, swaying a bit as he went. Joshua followed him to make sure he stayed on his feet, then looked around for the blacksmith. But the chair was empty. Just then, his fugitive patient hurried back in. "Sorry, doc. Had to run to the outhouse, like I've been doing every few minutes for two days now. Can you fix me up?"

Joshua stroked his chin. "I just might have something that'll help you." He fetched a glass jar half full of powder, powder he ground up from the plant that Cherokee medicine man had shown him. The blacksmith watched, his forehead wrinkled and eyebrows lowered.

"What in tarnation is that?"

Joshua laughed. "Darned if I know what it's called, except in Indian talk. But it works better than anything I can say in English."

The blacksmith was shaking his big head. Joshua held up a hand, palm out. "Now before you go blustering at me, you should know those folks have some pretty good remedies. Living the way they do, they notice things. Tell me, how many people around here have got milk sickness lately?"

The blacksmith just looked confused. Joshua

suppressed a sigh. "I haven't had a patient with milk sickness since I came to town. And you know why? It's because a doctor who listened to Indians did some listening when a Shawnee woman told him —" It had actually been a lady doctor, Doctor Anna, but Joshua didn't think the blacksmith could swallow that idea when just the idea of Indian medicine was sticking in his craw. "This woman told him that milk sickness came from drinking milk or eating meat from an animal that fed on white snakeroot. And that doctor told people, who told people, and now most farmers know to keep their stock away from white snakeroot. Now do you want me to give you something that'll help you, or would you rather move into the outhouse and try to shoe horses there?"

Joshua made the blacksmith drink down the first glass of water and powder before he left with a pouch holding six more doses. Whether he'd keep taking it, well, that was the blacksmith's problem, for now anyway.

There was no one waiting, but before Joshua had time to do more than take a book down from the shelf, the door opened and a woman walked in. No, more like sailed in, a proud vessel, a four-master. She took off her coat to reveal a well-tailored dress, fitting snugly on her large, well-upholstered frame. Her graying, wavy hair peeked out from under a truly astonishing hat.

He hadn't met this woman, but he believed he'd heard about her. Another newcomer to town, from somewhere back east; a widow; and apparently Jewish. That'd make her the first Jew he'd met.

She held out her hand. "Doctor! I'm so pleased to be meeting you. I'm Freida Blum."

He shook her hand, studying her. He'd never heard

her accent before, or not quite. It wasn't as thick as the accent of that German he'd tended the last year of the war, when he'd turned medic; he could understand her without straining. But "Doctor" ended in a rough, husky sound, and "meeting" sounded more like "meetink." There was something different about her vowels that he couldn't put a word to. And her speech had a rhythm and a melody to it, almost like singing, or chanting anyway.

But here he was standing and gawking when he needed to be doctoring. "Please come through to the back and sit up on that table. Then you can tell me what brings you in today."

She strode after him, passed him, and got on the table with a little jump, the wood creaking as she landed. "Oh, I've just had some aches and pains, here and there. And I get tired by afternoon. My age, you don't expect to feel like a spring chicken. But I thought I'd stop in."

She was studying him quite as much as he'd studied her. Whatever she'd heard about him, he guessed it was her curiosity more than any medical need that had sent her his way. But he'd check her over. He picked up his stethoscope.

"So young, for a doctor! But that's just an old woman talking, I suppose." (He wouldn't call her old, exactly. Not quite. She might be in her middle fifties or a little older.)

Speaking of talking, she would need to stop. "If you could just take a deep breath, and then another, while I listen to your lungs."

"Of course, of course. How can you do your job —" ("yure chob") — "when I'm rattling on like a freight train? Samuel always said to me, Freida, the way you talk, when do you manage to breathe?"

"Mrs. Blum. Please."

Praise be, she stopped talking and took deep breaths as he commanded. Her lungs sounded good. But she winced as she took the third breath. And she put a hand to her back as if it was paining her. She might have her reasons for being there, at that.

Or she could be lonely. Lonely people without enough to do sometimes felt sicker than they really were. "What do you do during the day, generally?"

The woman beamed at him as if rewarding the question. "I sew for so many people! This dress, I made it. All I have to do is walk around town, it's as good as putting an ad in the paper. And I'm helping the minister set up a social library, so good for the children. And my little neighbor, she's like a daughter to me, I take care of her babies sometimes so she can get her rest."

Not idle, then.

He pressed the stethoscope to her ample chest, giving thanks once again to the inventor who had spared him the even more awkward necessity of putting his ear there instead. Her heart sounded good — or did it? There might be a faint suggestion of a galloping rhythm.

Laudanum would help her with those aches and pains. He reached for a bottle, but Mrs. Blum stopped him, exclaiming, "Oh, I have that at home! May I come to you for more when I run out?"

Joshua pointed next door. "I get mine from the pharmacist. You can do the same."

A shade of what might have been disappointment crossed her face. For whatever reason, she apparently found doctors more interesting than druggists. Her next questions suggested as much. "How did you learn so much about medicine? Did you go to one of those new schools?"

He shook his head. "I picked it up during the war, to start with." And that was all he was going to say about those years of floundering and failing, the lives lost all around him, the suffering he could do little to ease.

The bell on the front door jingled a welcome chance to escape more questioning. Maybe he'd be summoned to some nicely far-off homestead to attend a stolid farmer, someone who had less to say for himself. "Excuse me, Mrs. Blum." Without waiting for an answer, he stepped back into the front room to see a familiar face, a farmer's youngest son, shifting his weight from foot to foot, his hands clutched together in front. The boy's hair was wet — it must have started to rain since Joshua's sunny morning walk. Good news for the farmers.

"Please, doc, we need you to come see to Paw. He was sharpening the coulter for the plow, and it fell over on his leg. It's cut something awful."

Joshua's lips tightened, and he barely avoided a frown. That's what wishing brought you. You'd think he'd learn. "I'll get my bag."

Chapter 2

THE BOY had brought a wagon. That meant Nellie-girl could stay dry in her stall at the livery stable. Joshua could have huddled under a tarpaulin, but it wouldn't cover the boy, and it would have been rude to leave him unprotected. Joshua could cope with rain blowing sideways and sneaking under his poncho and running down his back. It would distract him from what might be waiting.

Arms and legs. He hated hearing that someone had an arm or leg injury. Just the words brought back the heaps of sawn-off limbs piled behind the medical tent. Sometimes he'd be seeing them through rain like this, as they slowly settled deeper into the mud.

He'd had to assist, handing over the bone saw, administering chloroform, holding the men down when the drug caused them to thrash about or on those horrible occasions when the surgeon ran out of it. He'd never had to do the cutting. Not then, and not after, not yet. But sooner or later the time would come. He knew fate wasn't kind enough to keep him from it.

Would it be today?

He had brought his bone saw in its leather case. And his white linen smock, the one he used to save his clothes when he had dirty work in store, and would have Li Chang wash and bleach after. An amputation would be the dirtiest work there was. He remembered the smocks the surgeons wore, layer on layer of red, dried blood darker under fresh red splashes, with the occasional white splinter of bone.

Joshua prayed as he rode, prayed hard and desperately, prayed that the smock in his bag would be clean and white when he turned homeward.

The leg wasn't as bad as the boy had made it sound. Joshua should have reckoned on that, on a boy's fear seeing his pa laid low. He'd be able to stitch up the wound and bandage it.

Joshua took the syringe of morphine from his bag, but before he could offer it, the farmer snorted and waved it aside. "I'll just take the usual, if you have it."

That was no surprise. Stoicism seemed to come with farming, from what Joshua had seen. He offered his whiskey flask instead. The farmer took only a couple of swallows before pushing it away. "Let's get this done, then. I have work to do."

Joshua gave the farmer as stern a look as he could muster. "No you don't, not today. That's what your good lads are for. You'll rest up and let that leg start healing."

He poured a little whiskey into the cap of the flask and dunked his needle in it, the way one of the camp doctors had always done. His patients didn't seem to get such bad infections, so whatever made it work, Joshua would follow suit. Then he got to stitching, the farmer grunting a little with each stitch.

Twenty-five grunts later, Joshua offered his patient the flask again. This time, the man took a longer drink. Then, his mouth twitching into a smile, he offered the flask to his son, standing pale at his side. "Here, boy. It'll help you look more like yourself before your ma gets home. Good thing she was at her sister's."

The boy stood up straighter and manfully gulped down

the whiskey, while Joshua contemplated how things would have gone if the farmer's wife had been home. Most likely she'd have kept her countenance better than the boy, and as well as her man. Wives had to be strong, out west.

Would the boy be sober enough to get Joshua home again? Well, Joshua could always take the reins if need be. And the boy could sleep it off in Joshua's bed, if he had to, before heading home.

* * * * *

Joshua closed the door behind the farmer's boy, holding the empty coffee cup, and leaned against the door. He'd made enough coffee for both of them, but hadn't ended up drinking any. Bone-tired as he was, he didn't have the strength to deal with coffee jitters.

He stumbled over to the dresser where he kept his nightshirt, pulled off his soaked frock coat and shirt and trousers, let them fall in a sodden heap on the floor, and pulled the nightshirt on. He'd take the wet, wrinkled clothes to Li Chang in the morning. Times like this, he was sorely grateful to his sisters back in Pennsylvania, who'd pooled their resources to send him a second set of clothes suitable for a doctor. He used almost his last strength to dig the bone saw in its case out of his bag and shove it out of sight on the shelf where he kept it.

Scratching at the door heralded Major's return from wherever he'd been wandering. Joshua grabbed a towel from the hook near the door and let the dog in. Rubbing the dog down warmed him up a little, but the sooner he was in bed with every quilt and comforter he owned on top of him, the happier he'd be. He moved to blow out the oil lamp.

Were those steps on the stairs up to his rooms?

And then, the door again, but this time a knock, or

maybe a kick, a dull thud, once and then repeated.

If he'd had the energy, he would have cussed a blue streak. Not now. Oh, God, not now. A knock this late meant an emergency. He would have to somehow find the wit and the strength to save someone, and he had none of either left.

"Doctor Gibbs!" ("Doh-ktor Kibbs.") A woman. He knew he should, but didn't, recognize the voice.

She didn't *sound* sick. Could it be one of her neighbors, or worse, a neighbor's child? But if it were childhood disease, he might be able to treat the fever, at least, or do something for vomiting. He could handle that. He opened the door.

There stood Mrs. Blum, her fur coat making her look like a friendly mama bear, holding a covered pot in her hands.

"I saw you come in, looking so wet and tired. I brought enough for the boy who was with you, but I see he's gone. May I come in? You won't leave an old woman standing outside on a staircase, will you?"

He stumbled back dumbly and let her pass, shoving the door shut with a weak thrust as she barreled toward the kitchen table. She put the pot down, dropped her coat in a corner, and pulled out his chair. "Sit, sit!"

He collapsed into the chair while she rummaged around, seemingly quite at home, finding a bowl and a spoon. She pulled a ladle from some pocket, then whisked the cover off the pot. Fragrant steam rose up out of it. He leaned forward, sniffing, and smiled weakly to see Major coming toward them to do the same. "What is it?"

"What is it? Chicken soup is what it is! What else, for warming you up and keeping you from catching your death?" She paused, almost coy. "Oh, here I am telling you your business. But if you don't already know about chicken soup, it's time you did, no?" (Though the "no" sounded more like "nu.")

She dipped the ladle in once, twice, three times, and then stopped and frowned at the bowl in frustration, looking ready to scold it for not having more room before pushing it toward him. "You start with that. I'll put the rest on the stove to keep warm."

The soup had hunks of carrot and big chunks of chicken, and some sort of strange, light dumplings. Joshua barely made himself use the spoon instead of picking up the bowl and pouring it into his mouth. As it was, his hand shook so that he spilled some of the soup on the table. Without missing a beat, Mrs. Blum tossed a dish towel his way before dragging a stool over to the table and perching on it, overflowing it on every side. When he managed to look up from his miraculous meal, he saw her beaming at him, clearly delighted at the way he was slurping the soup down with no sign of table manners. The moment the spoon clinked the bottom of the bowl, she grabbed the bowl and filled it back up to the brim. "Eat, eat!"

He was feeling full to the brim himself, but he thought it likely that if he dared to stop before the bowl was empty again, she would seize the spoon and feed him like an infant. He made his way manfully through.

Finally he was able to push the bowl away and sit back. She gave the pot one longing look before shrugging and abandoning any hope of stuffing him further.

He would have liked to let Major lick the bowl, but was not sure whether Mrs. Blum would be offended. Major weighed in by nudging Joshua's knee with his muzzle and whining. Joshua looked up at his benefactor. "I am sure my dog would appreciate the remaining traces of your excellent soup."

He was relieved at Mrs. Blum's low chuckle. "Why not? My chicken soup should be good for dogs, even."

Joshua put the bowl on the floor; Major looked up at Joshua for permission and then set to licking it out. Once Major finished, he inspected the bowl in case he had missed a drop and then trotted away.

Joshua picked up the bowl and contemplated the effort of cleaning it. Mrs. Blum, apparently reading his mind, grabbed the bowl and looked around for a water tap. Seeing none, she wrinkled her nose, opened the door, and let the rain rinse the bowl before setting it on the drainboard. She leaned against the wall and looked down at him, shaking her head. "Out in all hours and all weather, and he comes home to nothing!"

Joshua shrugged. He had a good idea where this was going.

"So where's Mrs. Doctor? You need to get married!"

Just as he'd thought. He'd fended off similar comments from a few ladies at church when he first arrived in town. He'd ignored them with as much dignity as he could muster, and after a while, they'd given up. But looking at the massive and motherly figure looming in his kitchen, Joshua felt suddenly uneasy. Something in her tone and expression showed considerable determination. Even zeal.

* * * * *

"Boot blacking, coffee, cornmeal, flour, soap. Put it on your tab?"

"Thank you kindly." The suggestion would, in fact, save him some embarrassment. His patients had lately been paying in roast chickens, bacon, cream, potatoes, even horseshoes — all welcome and useful items, but it left him short of coin.

"And you've got a letter."

This would take some juggling. Joshua picked up the envelope first, opening it and extracting the letter, tucking the envelope into his vest and laying the letter on the counter. Next, he grabbed the sack full of supplies in his left hand and picked up the letter in his right. That left him without a way to tip his hat, so he nodded his goodbye and walked out, glancing at the letter as he went. Major, idling in the street, jumped up to follow.

Joshua knew he had not been a satisfactory correspondent. The last letter to his mother in which he had mentioned anything of actual importance had been the letter he sent on his way west, trying to explain why he had felt compelled to leave his family and his home so far behind. Even as he sent that letter on its way, he had known it would fail in its mission. What he had been unable to say to her face, he had been equally unable to put into words on paper. Either would have required that he call to mind, and then stain her memory forever by recounting, the life he had lived as a soldier and a medic. Without that understanding, how could she understand how unreal and hollow the civilized life of Philadelphia had become for him?

His mother still wrote every two weeks, however, and he'd been awaiting her latest for several days. Now he saw what had kept her busy. His middle sister's baby had come — except it was twins! A boy and a girl. He could imagine his younger and oldest sisters knitting madly to deal with the surprise.

As for his father — what? He was writing a book?

Joshua had been paying just enough attention to where he was going that he didn't trip on the planks in the street or walk in front of any horses. But not enough, it turned out, to avoid walking smack into someone. He started backward, dropping his sack, and stammered apologies, while Major added to the confusion by circling the scene and barking loudly.

His victim, Joshua realized, was the tall green-eyed woman he had seen in the street the day he first met Mrs. Blum. She had managed to stay on her feet and now stooped to help him retrieve his groceries, whisking them away from Major's investigative sniffing. Her hands looked strong, with long fingers; it took her almost no time to fill his sack again. She stood up, neither smiling nor frowning, and handed him the sack. "I hope that isn't bad news in your hand."

He tried to pull himself together enough to answer her. "Uh, no, not bad news. Just news. Babies. Two of them. That is, my sister just had twins."

The woman's eyes widened. "Congratulations to your sister! I'm sure she'll cope splendidly."

An interesting way to put it. Was she speaking from experience, and if so, her own or someone else's?

Manners! What would his mother — or for that matter, Freida Blum — say? "I beg your pardon. I'm Joshua Gibbs."

The woman tilted her head slightly and nodded in what might, unlikely as it seemed, be approval. "The doctor. I've heard of you. People speak well of you."

Did they? He supposed they might. The comment left him feeling absurdly pleased. With some difficulty, he suppressed a foolish grin.

He was becoming curious about the woman's identity, but accidental assault was hardly the basis for him to ask about it. She took pity on him and volunteered the information. "My name is Clara Brook. We're recent arrivals. Our farm is a little over four miles to the southwest." He was not that good at accents, but thought she might have grown up in or near Kentucky.

Joshua had about an hour before he needed to be back for his afternoon office hours. How much money did he have on him? He'd grabbed a few coins in case he needed them at the general store. It *should* be enough, at least if he held himself to a single scoop without toppings. "May I buy you an ice cream? As an apology for my inexcusable carelessness?"

Miss Brook looked at him gravely. "Hardly inexcusable. I've seen —" She cut off the comment and said instead, "Thank you. That would be very nice." Not a fan of hyperbole, it seemed, in others or in her own speech. Joshua led the way, in case Miss Brook had not yet learned the ice cream parlor's location. Major had apparently decided to adopt her, trotting by her side rather than his master's. When they reached their destination, Miss Brook paused and gestured toward the dog. "Does he accompany us or no?"

Joshua shook his head, having decided previously that ice cream was unlikely to be a good addition to Major's diet. Miss Brook then startled Joshua by snapping her fingers toward Major and pointing to a position near the window. Major immediately sat.

The clerk at the ice cream parlor looked at Joshua with some surprise as they entered. Joshua asked Miss Brook's preference, ordered her single scoop of strawberry along with his own vanilla, paid — narrowly escaping the embarrassment of coming up short — and carried both plates to the little table next to the window.

Now what? Well, she knew he had sisters, one of them with new additions to her family. Surely he could ask after similar details, at least indirectly. "How have you and your . . . your family been finding Cowbird Creek? Is it what you hoped, when you decided to settle here?"

Somehow it failed to surprise him when she avoided a conventional response. "I wouldn't say we know enough, yet, to answer that question. Or perhaps I should say we didn't have very specific expectations. My parents wanted to buy land, to leave my brother someday, and there was land for purchase here. It's a deal of work for the four of us, but we're used to work."

A brother, but no sisters — at least none still at home. It was unlikely she'd lost sisters in the War of Rebellion, but she might have had more brothers before that long and bloody nightmare. All through his childhood, he had wished he had brothers instead of, or in addition to, three sisters. That wish, too, had died in the war.

It was Joshua's turn to say something, but nothing came to mind. Miss Brook did not seem to be one of those women who could set a man to talking. Or maybe she chose not to do so. He could think of only one inane question. "What are you growing, or raising?"

Her left eyebrow twitched upward. "The usual, I suppose. Corn, oats. I have some interest in planting winter wheat, but my father has not yet agreed. I have a vegetable garden, though I'm still getting accustomed to the weather and how it affects what I can grow. We raise hogs — and chickens, of course, but mainly for our own eggs and our own pot."

He might be carrying home some of those eggs, some day. They would be good eggs, he'd wager — he guessed she took good care of the hens.

Before he could come up with some other conversational gambit, she asked him, "What's the most surprising thing about Cowbird Creek? Something we wouldn't have had a chance to learn yet?"

There was a question he hadn't heard before. "Hmm. Let me think." Madam Mamie's establishment was tonier than some, but even if that counted as surprising, he could hardly mention it. And the presence of a Jewish widow was unusual, but he doubted Mrs. Blum would appreciate being held up as a local oddity. "Our Chinese laundryman struck it rich — well, maybe not rich, but close — in the California gold fields."

Miss Brook smiled, the first smile he'd seen from her, but quickly went grave again. "I don't think I'll mention it to my brother. He used to hanker after the gold fields himself, and I'd be sorry to remind him."

She had finished her ice cream, and he needed to be back for any patients needing him. He took a final spoonful of his own and stood up. "Miss Brook, it's been a pleasure, despite my regrettable way of introducing myself. I'm sure I'll be seeing you again."

That eyebrow twitched again. "I agree. Though I hope it won't be in your professional capacity."

Cursing his clumsy tongue, he bowed and escaped back to territory where he was less likely to put a foot wrong.

By the time he finished with his last office patient — the blacksmith again, who had burned his arm — it was close to dinner time. It might be rude to go see Mrs. Blum at such an hour, as if he was angling to have her feed him, but he'd been wanting to check up on her, and had already asked about and learned where she lived. As he approached the snug house two blocks from his office, he made up his mind to refuse any invitation and stick to his purpose.

Of course, she was determined to overwhelm that intention. "How am I? How should I be, an old woman, my feet tired of carrying so much of me? But I'll let you do your listening and poking if you eat something first, still so skinny, I'd make two of you at least."

She pushed him toward the kitchen, pointed imperiously to a chair, and brought a platter of beef ribs from the stove, then fetched a bowl of corn already shucked from the cob with big pats of butter melting at the top. He felt his mouth watering and knew she had won this tussle.

Over dinner, she asked him about his day, his patients, any amusements he had found time for. He admitted his clumsiness outside the general store, and the new acquaintance resulting from it. Her response was an emphatic sniff. "The brother, he's a nice young man, so polite. But the sister, I don't know, she walks around like she's too good to talk to anyone, not much in the way of social graces."

Joshua frowned. "I didn't see her that way. She's tall, so she's bound to carry herself differently from smaller ladies. And she may be shy, new to town as she is."

Mrs. Blum sniffed again and changed the subject. "I have pie, cherry, you'll like it." She sighed dramatically. "And then you can be the doctor and tell me everything that's wrong with me."

When he finally examined her, he was far from sure whether her lungs were as clear as before, and more certain than before that her heartbeat sounded irregular. Did she show signs of fluid retention? Her skirt covered her feet and ankles. Slyly, he ordered her, "Kindly kick your left foot in the air."

She tilted her head and regarded him with profound skepticism. He resisted the urge to retreat, saying, "If you would, Mrs. Blum. And then we'll be finished."

Mrs. Blum rolled her eyes and obeyed. As he had suspected, her ankle, as far as he could glimpse it, appeared slightly swollen. He would need to keep an eye on her.

Which did not have to mean sharing her opinions of any particular townspeople.

Two days later, when he spotted Miss Brook carrying a large sack of groceries toward a wagon, he saw his chance to repay a favor. He darted across the street, just behind the mayor's wife's fashionable buggy, and held out his arms. "May I assist?"

She stopped short, her expression suggesting an indignant retort on the way until she recognized him and relaxed, smiling. "If you like, Doctor."

He carefully transferred the sack from her arms to his and trotted along next to her, noting the length of her stride. The dust on her boots made him suddenly conscious of the perhaps unnecessarily polished condition of his own, but she showed no sign of noticing the disparity. When they reached the wagon, he followed her directions about where to stow the contents of the sack and then stretched his arms. It had been a pretty heavy sack for a lady to carry.

A thought appeared to strike her as he prepared to bid her adieu. She leaned into the wagon and extracted two long sticks of hard candy. Offering him one, she said simply, "You've had your chance to even one score. Might I offer you some refreshment?"

Courtesy and desire went hand in hand for once. "That's very kind of you."

Miss Brook gestured toward a wrought-iron seat in the corner of the town square, saying, "Shall we sit while we indulge ourselves?"

Joshua would not have presumed to suggest it; and he could not help reflecting that Mrs. Blum might come to hear about them once again spending time together. But then, that might be just as well. She should realize his social life was his own affair, her views and intentions notwithstanding. And if the weather was chilly for sitting, they both had coats on, and he would not be the one to complain so long as Miss Brook found it comfortable. "My tired feet and I thank you, ma'am."

They settled on the bench with their candy. Miss Brook made no attempt to hide her enjoyment of the sweet. But from time to time she turned to him as if studying him. He let her scrutinize him. Maybe she would discover something about him that he needed to know.

When she finally asked him a question, it concerned nothing at all profound. "What is the oddest thing you've ever eaten?"

A peculiar thing to ask, but it made a kind of sense. You could learn a lot about someone's life from the answer: how far they had traveled, how poor they had been or how wealthy. Or whether they had been to war. Feeling like a cheat, he evaded the question. "I'll tell you what seemed strangest to me when first I ate it, as a boy. Steamed clams. Or oysters, when I was older. Raw, slimy — I thought I'd choke on it. But it slithered right down. And yourself?"

"Rattlesnake. I was — in difficulties, at the time, and ready to try anything. I thought it might poison me. But here I am, so obviously it didn't."

She returned her attention to the candy. Joshua did the same, though the memory of that oyster haunted his tongue, combining poorly with the candy and making him queasy.

Maybe the rattlesnake was sabotaging Miss Brook in the same manner. She stood up rather abruptly and dropped the remains of her candy on the grass. "I'd best be getting home."

Joshua pulled out his pocket watch and gulped. He had barely enough time to go see the last of his day's patients before they would be having supper. "Thank you for the candy."

He could think of nothing more to say, so he gave her an awkward bow and hurried off to saddle Nellie-girl. A glance backward showed that Miss Brook had made it to her wagon and was heading out of town. And he had better stop looking after her, and be about his business.

Chapter 3

IT WAS a fine morning, unseasonably warm, and no one had summoned Joshua yet. If no one did, it would be one of his office Thursdays; but first, he and Major might have a little time to play. "Get your stick, boy!"

The dog grabbed the stick lying across the room from the fireplace and bounded over to Joshua, wagging his tail. Joshua grabbed his hat and overcoat, opened the front door, let Major run down the steps, and followed after. When they had both reached the street, Major dropped the stick at Joshua's feet, backed up a few yards, and assumed his "ready to play" position, front legs flat on the ground and hindquarters in the air. Joshua picked up the stick and hurled it around thirty yards. Major pivoted and scampered after it, soon returning with the stick in his teeth.

Joshua rubbed Major's head and took the stick. "What a good dog, what a good boy!" Major thanked him by jumping up, trying to lick his face. Joshua laughed, squatted, and let Major lick him before wiping his face with his sleeve. Standing back up, he threw the stick again, and they repeated the ritual four more times, except for the face-licking, which Joshua did not want to encourage unduly.

Five throws was plenty for Joshua. The last time, when he took the stick, he shook his head and said, "All done, Major." Major lowered his head and his tail drooped before he regained his good cheer and trotted under the steps to explore the shadowed corners.

Still no anxious patients to be seen. Joshua climbed up the stairs and went back inside to retrieve the small leather sack containing his pipe, tobacco, and tamper. Settling himself on the steps, he filled his pipe and tamped the contents of the bowl. He would need to buy more tobacco soon, such as it was. Joshua rarely dwelt on those creature comforts he had left behind in Philadelphia, but he could not deny that his family had been able to afford a better quality of tobacco.

At least the tobacconist, located so conveniently below Joshua's rooms, carried an inexpensive sweet blend. Joshua was determined not to be ashamed of his fondness for sweets, but he could hardly afford to visit the candy shop or ice cream parlor on a regular basis. And he could not, in conscience, wish illness or injury on their proprietors in the hope of receiving their goods in payment.

Joshua lit the pipe, let it go out, lit it again, and sat back to smoke. As he attempted without much success to blow a smoke ring, he noticed that Clara Brook, passing by with a basket on her arm, had stopped and was watching him with an appraising eye. He turned away to hide a blush before realizing how rude he must seem and turning back, lifting his hat to her. "I hope you're enjoying the morning, Miss Brook."

She hoisted her basket and replied, "Reasonably well, given the lack of interest I find in daily errands. I see you are enjoying a more entertaining pastime. But given the challenges of your own daily lot, I can hardly begrudge you a moment of relaxation."

He had certainly never met a woman with such an inclination toward frankness. It left him somewhat at a loss for words. Whether she recognized that fact or just felt the call of her duties, she said nothing more, but simply nodded to him and went on her way. He waited until she was some distance away before taking another puff.

Before long, one of his farmer patients approached, carrying a big sack of what must be flour over his shoulder. He was probably on his way back from the grist mill on the edge of town. The farmer spied Joshua sitting on the steps and called out, "Fine morning for a smoke, ain't it?"

Joshua lifted his pipe in acknowledgment. "That it is."

The gesture drew the man's attention to the pipe itself. "Say, Doc, why you smoke a clay pipe instead of one of those fancy soldier pipes? Or didn't you smoke during the war like all the others?"

"Oh, I smoked. And I made pipes, but I lost the only good one." Of course he had smoked a pipe back then. The odor of the tobacco masked the many fouler smells of camp and battlefield; and it was easier to forget hunger and fatigue with a pipe in hand.

And like everyone else, he had carved pipes from ivy root or hickory or whatever he could find. The first few efforts were crude enough, but at least they wouldn't break from rough treatment, like the clay pipes Joshua smoked now. He never did acquire the artistry of some of his fellows, with their pipe bowls in the likeness of a soldier's head or a cowboy's, but he'd felt some pride in his final effort, made the last year of the war: an eagle's head etched on the bowl and scroll work on the stem. He had meant to bring it home, a reminder that those years had their moments of comfort and even a kind of peace. But somehow, in the mad scramble of one of the last battles, it had disappeared. He could only hope someone had found it, cleaned it, possibly admired it. That man might even be holding Joshua's pipe, filling it or smoking it, at this very moment.

The farmer must have given up on further conversation while Joshua was lost in thought. He had walked on and was almost out of sight. Joshua took another puff, blew out the smoke, and hoped that other man somewhere down south had better tobacco.

* * * * *

Dovis Hawkins, the barber, had been in business in Cowbird Creek for some years longer than Joshua. He might have been one of the first settlers other than farmers, showing up around the same time as the blacksmith and Madam Mamie's predecessor. And as barbers did, he'd done his share of what he called doctoring, from bleeding to lancing abscesses to pulling teeth to setting broken bones. Whether those he bled got weaker from it, or the abscesses refused to heal, or the teeth were maybe the ones that didn't need pulling, or the bones healed crooked . . . well, Joshua mostly hadn't been there to witness. From what he'd seen, however, he could with a clear conscience consider himself an improvement.

Mr. Hawkins disagreed. He never took the matter up with Joshua directly. Instead, he used his status as (according to him) a pillar of the town, and his wide acquaintance, to plant as many doubts about Joshua as possible. Whenever Joshua met a patient in the street who seemed uneasy about seeing him, he had a pretty good guess as to why.

Should he finally have it out with the barber face to face? He wasn't especially good at knowing how to handle a quarrel with someone old enough to be his father. And he could easily come out of it looking like a bully. It might be prudent to imagine what others — not those most sympathetic to his feelings, like Robert, but people like Clara Brook, or Freida Blum, or Thaddeus Spencer, or the mayor — would think were they witnesses.

No, he would refrain from direct confrontation. Better to try Hawkins's tactics.

He felt up and down his farmer patient's arm, shaking his head and frowning. "It feels as if you broke this some time back and didn't have it set properly. Funny, I don't remember being out of town when this must have happened. Even if I was seeing to a patient, someone could have fetched me without too much delay. Well, I'm sorry I managed to miss you. This break could give you trouble off and on."

The big man hunched his shoulders and shuffled his feet on the floor. "I guess I might have stopped in to see Mr. Hawkins about it."

Joshua shook his head, aiming for a "more in sorrow than anger" demeanor. "There's not a lot I can do about it now — short of rebreaking it and setting it. If it gets to where you can't use the arm, we might have to try that. In the meantime, you can try willow bark tea for when it pains you." He sent the man off with a packet of the tea leaves, hoping he would gossip or complain enough to spread the word. And that Hawkins would do no serious mischief in the meantime.

He had barely had time to sit down at his desk before new footsteps approached. Joshua rolled the kinks out of his neck and arose to welcome the new patient. But when the door opened, Clara Brook stepped in looking the picture of health, her cheeks pink from fresh air and her bonnet slightly askew as if the spring breezes had been tugging at it.

He realized he was staring at her and made haste to adopt a more professional manner. "Miss Brook, how may I assist you?"

"In fact I need no assistance. I was passing and in less of a hurry than usual, and decided to satisfy my curiosity. I haven't had occasion to see the interior of a practice such as yours." She looked around his office with every appearance of interest. "I hope you'll pardon my indulging such an impulse."

"Of course." He waved her in. "Your visit is a welcome distraction."

She looked more closely at him. "I hope the concerns from which I'm to distract you are not too troubling. Is one of your patients in serious condition?"

Joshua shook his head and snorted simultaneously. "Only from his own poor judgment and the — the ignorant overconfidence of another."

Miss Brook laughed. He had not seen her laugh before. It brightened her face to a remarkable extent. "You cannot possibly say so much without saying more."

The prospect of sharing his frustration was certainly tempting. He asked her with some hesitation, "May I count on your discretion?"

The laughter fell away from her face. "You may, in fact. I have some practice at keeping confidences."

He was both sorry to have asked and intrigued by her response, but he went on without exploring the tangent. "There is a longtime resident of Cowbird Creek who considers himself well versed in medical matters, an opinion unfortunately shared with some of the people here."

To Joshua's dismay, Miss Brook nodded as at familiar knowledge, saying, "I would venture to guess that you refer to Mr. Hawkins."

Joshua grimaced. As he was about to confirm her statement, it suddenly occurred to him that she might be a source of new information. "If you would not consider it inappropriate, I would very much like to know what you have heard about Mr. Hawkins's attempts at providing medical treatment, and their results."

Miss Brook didn't actually laugh this time, but her face brightened again, and he felt a momentary absurd pride in having cheered her. She lifted a hand and ticked off items on her fingers as she said, "I've heard that he cured a farmer's rheumatic gout by bloodletting. And conversely, that he bled a young woman with female complaints to the point where her life was despaired of, though she recovered — a recovery for which he claimed credit. And there was one more, I believe . . . ah, yes. That he will willingly set a broken bone for no more payment than a bottle of whiskey."

Joshua found he was clenching his fists and forced himself to relax them. "I hope you believed only that he bled the farmer and the young woman, for whatever good or ill it did, and that he set a bone, if not competently."

Miss Brook pursed her lips and stroked her chin in an obvious mockery of deep thought. "After giving the matter prolonged consideration . . . ." She broke into a broad smile. "I did tentatively conclude that in case of any injury or illness, visiting the good Doctor Gibbs would be a better idea."

It was his turn to laugh, as much in relief as to share the joke. "If you or yours ever need such assistance, which I hope will not be any time soon, I'll humbly stand ready to provide it."

Miss Brook's smile died away, and she reached into her pocket for a rather plain-looking watch, one he suspected had previously belonged to some man in her family. "I see I've idled away quite enough time, and must be about my errands. A good day to you, Doctor." She looked around the office one more time, started to move toward the door, and then turned back around. "I'm glad I stopped in. After all, one knows a person better after seeing him on his own ground." And with that, she turned again and walked out his office door.

* * * * *

When some errand required Joshua to pass by the barber shop, he generally made a point of not looking inside. But as Joshua dragged himself home from a fruitless call on a consumptive farmer, he saw a familiar silhouette in the corner of his eye. He turned and saw Clara Brook, standing close to Hawkins and chatting with every appearance of animation.

His first reaction, little as he could justify it, was a feeling of betrayal. Miss Brook knew how he felt about Hawkins and Hawkins's presumptuous and unsound practices. Was she a friend of the barber? Had she been drawing Joshua out, gathering intelligence on the man's behalf? Amusing herself by witnessing Joshua's frustration?

He pulled out his pipe as an excuse to lurk nearby, fiddling with tobacco and tamper, until Miss Brook emerged with a cheery wave back to Hawkins as she stepped out into the street. Joshua hurriedly stowed away pipe and all, moving to intercept. She greeted him with a frank and guileless face, almost immediately shadowed with concern. "You look weary, Doctor."

Joshua at once felt a fool. How could he confront her with his suspicions, in the face of this sympathetic interest? And yet he saw no way to converse easily without clearing the air. He strove to appear neither hurt nor hostile as he asked, "Are you well acquainted with Mr. Hawkins, then? You did not mention the fact when we last discussed him."

Miss Brook's eyes widened for a moment before lighting with what could only be amusement. "No, the gentleman and I are not such good friends that I saw need to mention it. But when I have occasion to pass by, and both he and I have sufficient leisure, I will sometimes pay a short visit."

She paused, as if awaiting an impertinent demand for explanations, and then went on to provide one. "As much as he gives the appearance of having a wide acquaintance, and as much as he enjoys — may I say, the sound of his own voice? — he strikes me as after all being somewhat lonely. And I have found that he seems to take pleasure in the company of those considerably younger than he. I believe he and Mrs. Hawkins have no children."

The notion of Hawkins in need of compassion left Joshua momentarily speechless. Miss Brook stood patient for a minute or so before gesturing down the street. "My way is homeward. Do we walk in the same direction? Or are you bound for your rooms, and a well-deserved rest?"

Joshua cleared his throat and managed to say, "The latter. I wish you a pleasant evening." Too embarrassed to linger, he tipped his hat, turned tail, and strode away, her footfalls receding behind him.

Chapter 4

"YOU KNOW they won't use 'em. And what whores won't use, they won't buy." Robert, the town pharmacist, held the box of French letters in his hand and shook it like a warning rattle.

"May as well keep trying. I could talk them into it sooner or later. And 'til then, I'll need some for my own use."

Robert put down the box and wagged a finger. "Joshua, Joshua. What would the church ladies say? Or your new friend the widow?"

Joshua groaned. "My new self-appointed guardian angel would tell me to get married yesterday and make lots of babies. Fat ones."

Robert rummaged in his stores and pulled out several bottles of the mercuric chloride Joshua would need for his visit. "At least you've talked them into using this."

"I didn't have to. Soon as I got to town, my first time stopping by, they were on me asking about it."

Joshua counted out the coins for his purchases; Robert scooped them up, dropped them in the till, gave Joshua his change. "I think I'll go with you and get me a drink — at least. I always get first-class treatment in your company."

Madam Mamie's parlor house stood on the far corner of the square from the church, though local humor varied as to which one was supposed to be trying to pull away from the other. The second story balcony had scalloped trim in bright red paint, always kept fresh, and red lanterns hung in the windows facing the street. Downstairs in the saloon, a piano player entertained guests who hadn't yet made it upstairs or, having come back down, were in no hurry to leave.

Major followed Joshua and Robert, wagging his tail in anticipation of the scraps Madam Mamie usually gave him. As they approached, he ran ahead, inside, and up the stairs to the landing where Mamie surveyed her realm. She bent over to scratch behind the dog's ears before coming down to greet them. "Well, if it isn't Doctor French!"

Joshua felt himself blush. Maybe he should go ahead and grow a beard, if he couldn't break himself of blushing. Madam Mamie had saddled him with that nickname because of his insistence on using French letters to keep from getting the French pox. Joshua had no wish to spread it to any of the prostitutes not already afflicted. And if, after all, he were ever to marry, that was one gift he would not be giving his bride. He'd been trying to convince the madam that her customers might have similar qualms, but he'd made no headway so far.

Mamie steered Robert toward the bar and ordered the barkeep to keep him generously supplied, then turned back to Joshua. "The room you used last time is occupied, but just head the other way at the top of the stairs and take the first room on the left. I'll send the girls to you. I believe you'll need to dose four of them, but you'll be able to do your own count." She cocked her head and winked at him. "Which one should I send in last?"

Joshua looked around at the bevy of smartly dressed ladies. Not for the first time, he wondered what the proper women of Cowbird Creek thought of them. Did a woman like Clara Brook catch sight of one of Mamie's girls in the street and wonder how she had come to this? Or, perhaps, instead, try to imagine her life and how it seemed to her? If any respectable woman would do so, it might be she.

But Mamie was awaiting an answer. Some of the girls were tending to customers upstairs, but one of his favorites was chatting up the driver of the Wells Fargo stagecoach at the end of the bar, her auburn curls hanging almost as low as her inviting cleavage. "I'd take it kindly if I could finish up with Coraline."

He gave the lady in question one more long look before heading upstairs. Business, of a kind, before pleasure.

When he made his way downstairs, the piano player was pounding out some dance music. So he stayed for some dancing, and had more drinks than he usually allowed himself, enough that it seemed like a good idea to show the ladies of the house some new magic tricks, but also enough that the tricks didn't all go quite as they should. Abandoning magic, he headed back upstairs with the new girl, Adeline, who had come from a house back east and brought along her own sophisticated bag of tricks.

It was dark and the moon high when he and Robert made their way down the street arm in arm, keeping each other upright, Major trotting behind. Robert peeled off at the pharmacy, bowed with an extravagant flourish, and climbed carefully up to his rooms. Joshua planned to do the same.

Until he saw the man pacing back and forth in the street near his rooms, who ran forward gabbling about his little girl before Joshua could properly hear what he was saying.

Joshua took a deep breath of the cool night air. "Just give me a moment, and I'll be ready." Without waiting for an answer, he cut through the alley to the pump and stuck his head under the spout, running the cold water to shock the fog out of his head. Then he ran up to his rooms for his bag.

The man had ridden into town, so Joshua would have to ride out. It was a good thing Nellie-girl would follow any horse in front of her. He should be able to hang on, so long as he didn't have to steer.

The following afternoon, Joshua went to see Mrs. Blum at her home again. She'd sent a boy to ask him to come look at her teeth. But he didn't guess her teeth had as much to do with the summons as the gossip around town.

All right, so he'd fallen off his horse. He'd still managed to get the little girl's shoulder back in its socket, even while her screaming made his head throb until it felt like it would fall right off.

Sure enough, she waved him into a kitchen chair and handed him a cup of hot tea with honey. When he started to gulp it down, she protested. "What's the rush? Is the room on fire? Or your pants, maybe?"

That startled a laugh out of him. He took a slower sip of the tea while she bustled around the kitchen and then set a plate before him with some sort of rolled-up cookies. "Eat up, put some meat on your bones. So skinny, how can you keep up your strength?"

She hadn't met his father. Joshua would be plump enough in twenty years, if he lived that long. He was in no hurry to acquire that shape.

He let her press one of the cookies on him — and it was delicious, rich and sweet and filled with some sort of seed paste — before putting his cup down with a firm "clink" on the table. "Now you sit down, and I'll look at your teeth."

She thumped down into one of the kitchen chairs and opened her mouth. Hmmm. She did have some tooth trouble, at that. "That molar should come out. And that premolar, as well."

He pulled back his hand in a hurry when she started (of course) to talk. "Come out! Doctors, always doing nothing or doing too much. Can't you just give me something to take until they feel better?"

"You could take laudanum. But those teeth will only get worse."

"Enough of that." She dismissed the supposed reason for his visit with a wave and a sniff and got back to her feet. "Would you like to see a picture of my Samuel? So when I talk about him, you should know what he looks like."

Like many widows, she talked as if her husband were still hanging about somewhere. "Mrs. Blum, I have other patients to see —"

"Oh, it'll just take a minute. And you can have another —" She threw out a confusing hash of syllables that must have been the name of the cookies. Sure enough, she waved him back into his chair and pushed the plate toward him, disappeared into the sitting room, and reappeared with a large, very fat book that when opened, proved to be a photograph album. She plunked it down on the table and opened it in front of him. "Here, my Samuel in his store." He was surprised to see that the tall man in the apron, his foot on a barrel, was not much wider than Joshua himself. He must have had either a will of iron, or a constitution that burned up everything he ate.

"And here we are on our wedding day. Samuel looked his best that day. Not exactly handsome, not like my beaus before him, but the way he stood tall and proud and happy, you'd hardly notice." She sighed, then went on cheerfully, "I made the dress myself. Before the year was out, I'd made four more just like it, almost, for other girls."

In the photograph, Mrs. Blum, as she had just become, looked very much as she did now, minus a few of the pounds and the second chin. And while not even Mrs. Blum could hold a smile long enough for a photograph, the look on her face suggested she'd been thinking of something other than dresses, that day.

He was looking for a decent way to extricate himself when a woman's voice sounded behind him. "Dearie, are you home? I've brought back the sifter you lent me." Joshua stood and moved toward the sitting room, where a woman he'd met once or twice stood in the doorway. Rebecca Wheeler had come to town about six months ago and opened a boardinghouse. She opened round brown eyes and a pretty mouth. "Oh, *excuse* me, Freida! I didn't know you had *company*. Doctor Gibbs, isn't it?"

The hell she hadn't known. Joshua knew a setup when he saw one. But he bowed. "Miss Wheeler."

Miss Wheeler really did have a sifter to return, though it might well have been borrowed for that purpose. Mrs. Blum advanced to take it and pulled out a chair for her. "Sit, sit!"

Miss Wheeler sat. Their hostess fetched another teacup and plate; Miss Wheeler picked up one of the rolled-up cookies and admired it. "You *must* give me the recipe for these."

"We-ell . . . . I suppose. Your guests would appreciate them, I'm sure." Mrs. Blum actually winked at Joshua. "Doctor Gibbs here does." Then she paused and snapped her fingers, something Joshua had never seen a woman do before. "And what an idea I just got! Rebecca, you should have Doctor Gibbs over to dinner at the boardinghouse. He travels so much, sees so many people, he could tell them what a wonderful —" ("vun-derful") — "cook you are, and how happy your guests are at your dinner table."

Miss Wheeler looked shy all of a sudden, even though the two of them had obviously, so to speak, cooked this up between them ahead of time. The shy look dampened his resistance to the conspiracy. And she was pretty, with a curvy but slim figure, and honey-brown hair tied back in a rolled-up bun that reminded him a little of Mrs. Blum's cookies. And she must be a good cook, or Mrs. Blum wouldn't have aimed Joshua at her table, matchmaking or no.

So he looked at both women and said, "If I were to receive such an invitation, I'd naturally be honored to accept."

Three days later, Joshua made his way to the boardinghouse, dressed in his freshly laundered best and trying not to expect anything but a good dinner. As he passed the open meadow near his destination, he saw with a mixture of nostalgia and pain that some schoolboys were playing baseball. When he was their age, it had been mainly a sport for high society, but it had spread rapidly during the war as soldiers seized on it for exercise and diversion, while their officers encouraged it as a way to build morale and accustom the soldiers to working together. Joshua had discovered himself to be a powerful hitter and reasonably skilled pitcher. He thoroughly enjoyed the game until the day he was invited to take part in a match on a battlefield, so recently the scene of carnage that not all the corpses had been removed. The ball had landed in gore more than once. He had not played since.

Emerging from the memory, Joshua found himself at

the door of the boardinghouse. He rang the hanging brass bell outside; Miss Wheeler met him at the door herself, in a violet dress that he would have bet Mrs. Blum had made for her. "Come into the parlor." (The term raised unfortunate associations. Someone had better alert Miss Wheeler to the local usage.) "The other guests are there, except a couple of stragglers, and dinner will be ready in just a few minutes."

He had not, though he should have, anticipated the need to make small talk with a roomful of strangers, nor to satisfy their understandable curiosity about his presence. He stammered out a summary of Mrs. Blum's cover story and turned the conversation to where the various guests had come from and how long ago. They included, he learned, a man looking to buy some real estate and checking out the possibilities; a circuit-traveling judge who stayed at the boardinghouse whenever he swung through town; the newest deputy sheriff; an evasive fellow whose slicked-back hair and oilier manner might identify him as a card shark; and a spinster, sister to a local farmer and working at the bank. Joshua had not thought to find an unmarried woman living here, other than the proprietress. Did a woman like Miss Brook, apparently less than contented with life on her family's farm, ever consider such an alternative?

Miss Wheeler was indeed a good cook. The guests even had a choice, fried chicken or roast beef, along with corn pudding and puffy rolls. Mrs. Blum's rolled cookies appeared as dessert, though they were somewhat less of a hit than Mrs. Blum had predicted. Miss Wheeler urged everyone to eat hearty, though she tactfully stopped pressing the cookies on those who declined twice.

Joshua found eating more relaxing than chatting, and contemplated trying for some arrangement where he could eat here more often. But thanks to Mrs. Blum, his hostess would take that as signifying more than his approval of her table.

Which would be a problem, because, pretty as she was, as good a cook as she was, he wasn't really interested.

Even if he'd felt ready to welcome a woman in his life, he didn't need any more mothering than he was getting from Mrs. Blum. In fact, he could do with less. And though Miss Wheeler was Joshua's age at most, she seemed like the motherly type. That no doubt made the boardinghouse a natural fit for her. But it didn't make her a good fit for him.

He escaped after dinner, despite the hostess's urging him to stay and listen to the card shark play the piano. And coward-like, he snuck around a back way to reduce the chance of anyone seeing how early he came home.

Joshua had not, by the next morning, come up with a suitable explanation of why he would not be courting Miss Wheeler. So when he saw Freida Blum a block away, he ducked into Li Chang's laundry to escape being questioned. He had not looked inside first, and so was startled to hear Clara Brook's voice, and more surprised that she was speaking something that sounded like Chinese. Neither she nor Li Chang was in the front of the laundry; he moved toward the back and found the two of them, too engrossed in conversation to have noticed his entrance.

The Chinaman was laughing. "That is not right, miss! I will not tell you what you actually said, but you would not be saying it. At least not to me. Try again." He recited a stream of Chinese syllables, more slowly than his usual speech. Miss Brook repeated it, and apparently did a better job of it, as Li Chang smiled broadly.

It was Miss Brook who noticed Joshua's presence first. "Doctor! Welcome to our language lesson."

"I am impressed at your progress, Miss Brook. Is this your first attempt at speaking Chinese?"

Li Chang answered for her. "Yes, very first time, and she is doing well, as you see."

Miss Brook laughed and said, "In that case, sir, it is your turn. 'You look lovely this evening.' Mind the l's."

Li Chang put up his hands and shook his head. "Ah, no, I must get back to work. I must wait for another time. Doctor, you come for your collars?"

Joshua had forgotten, when he sought refuge in the laundry, that he had an actual errand there. Relieved that he would not need to invent one, he replied, "If they are ready. I am in no hurry for them."

"Yes, all ready. I go get them." He headed farther into the back.

Joshua tipped his hat to Miss Brook. "Ma'am. I hope I find you well."

Miss Brook's mouth twitched. "Why yes, Doctor. You need have no fear of my following you to your office and requiring your services."

Joshua, casting about for a response, came up with nothing but his curiosity. "How did this language lesson come about?"

Miss Brook looked him in the eye. "I have never, until now, met anyone from China." Her chin lifted in something like defiance. "Do you not think we should take advantages of such opportunities to expand our knowledge?"

Her challenging air took him aback somewhat. He said quickly, "Indeed, there is much to be said for it."

Miss Brook studied his face, and apparently found sufficient signs of sincerity. Her expression shifted toward what might have been approval. But before either of them could speak again, Li Chang was back, collars in hand. Joshua, after a moment's uneasiness that he might have no coins in his pockets, found the one he needed and handed it over. He turned toward Miss Brook, unsure whether she would welcome an escort to her next destination; but she was already waving to them both and walking out the door.

Chapter 5

THERE WERE some patients that felt deprived at the thought of being tended by "only" a small-town doctor, and could be unpleasantly vocal about it. For such annoying folk, Joshua had reluctantly ordered what the vendor called a pulsometer. There might be gadgets with that name that actually helped a doctor calculate the patient's pulse, but from what he gathered, they were unobtrusive and unimpressive. This supposed pulsometer commanded attention. A glass container shaped like a dumbbell held liquid of a vivid purple color. When the device was activated, a stream of bubbles would rise up and perturb the liquid. The doctor had merely to turn the device on as he handed it to the patient, and the patient could fondly believe that his or her pulse controlled the bubbles in some way the learned doctor would decipher.

The bank manager was one of these pompous patients. Joshua, standing in the man's richly furnished and excessively decorated drawing room, watched the man's eyes widen, though he soon caught himself and assumed an expression of calm, almost bored satisfaction.

Using the pulsometer always made Joshua feel a little soiled, even as he also experienced some malicious pleasure at gulling those who thought themselves sophisticated. As soon as he left the house, he thrust the device deep in his bag and headed for the nearest saloon to drink away the emotional aftertaste.

But in the street in front of the saloon, he came upon first a crowd and then the reason it had gathered. A wagon, its horses groomed to within an inch of their lives, stood in the street with posters tacked all over its bonnet, proclaiming the life-saving, potency-enhancing, and teeth-strengthening powers of Dr. Burnside's miraculously versatile patent medicine. The words "Dr. Burnside's Elemental Elixir" were painted on the wagon itself in bright orange and green letters full of curlicues. The pitchman stood on the seat of the wagon, wearing a long-tailed coat, frilly shirt front, and shiny top hat, repeating every fraudulent promise on the posters in a sonorous bellow.

As a child, Joshua had seen a medicine show in one of Philadelphia's theaters, and had been enthralled by the juggling and rope-spinning and magic tricks and fire-breathing, innocent of the dubious purpose behind it. He traced his interest in magic to that show. Now, he looked at the posters and listened to the charlatan's pitch, and felt the weight of the pulsometer in his bag dragging him down almost to the pitchman's moral level.

As Joshua stood staring, people in the crowd noticed his presence and turned to watch him expectantly. No doubt some of them were waiting for him to come forward and purchase some of this marvelous medicine to use in his practice — in which case they could save their money for the present. But if he failed to take advantage of this opportunity, they would plunk down their coins themselves, and dose themselves with the potion over and over while their symptoms grew worse and more difficult to treat. And given the time to do it, the pitchman might soon be telling these people that their local sawbones, while no doubt a well-meaning sort, hadn't had the sort of success that this medicine would produce — guaranteed! . . .

Joshua's hands gathered into fists, and he started

pushing through the crowd toward the wagon, only to have his progress slowed by a hand on his arm. It was Robert, no doubt just as disgusted, and certainly as well aware that the potion would be useless at best, toxic at worst. But he was trying to keep Joshua from grabbing the thief standing on the wagon and shaking him until his teeth rattled. "Let go of me!"

Robert grimaced. "I know, I know. But do you think these folks want their doctor to be a fellow who brawls in the street?"

Joshua shrugged off Robert's hand. "They should want their doctor to protect them from any son of a bitch trying to take their money for snake oil!"

"Think, Josh. They'll see you as trying to drive away the competition. It's the same for me, or I'd go up there with you and help you take him apart."

The competition. Maybe the fellow would pull out a pulsometer and demonstrate it. . . . "I'll go up there without you, then. Don't try to stop me. I don't want to fight you."

Robert heaved a dramatic sigh. "All right, I'll come with you. We'll bluff."

They squirmed and shoved their way to where the long-suffering horses stood. The pitchman saw their approach, and no doubt their expressions; he paused in his oratory and looked down with a smirk. "Now, who do I have the pleasure of meeting? I would wager —"

Robert whispered to Joshua, "Give me a boost," and approached the seat on which the pitchman stood. Joshua made a step of his hands; Robert grabbed hold of the wagon frame and hoisted himself up, landing within inches of the startled salesman. Joshua strained to hear, over the muttering and exclamations around him, what Robert was saying through gritted teeth in the scoundrel's ear. "If you . . . switch over to whatever act . . . won't break every last . . .

Peddle . . . somewhere else . . . ."

The pitchman's face flickered back and forth between indignation and uncertainty. Joshua took hold of the bridle of the nearest horse and glowered.

The pitchman spoke rapidly to Robert under his breath; Robert hesitated, then nodded. Abruptly, the pitchman turned back toward the crowd and proclaimed, "And now it's time for Sadie and her banjo to play for you all — and after that, my Injun associate, Jumping Arrow, will risk his very life eating actual fire!"

Robert climbed down and took Joshua's arm again, pulling him away. "He's going to pretend he only has a dozen bottles of the stuff to sell. And he'll say that after the elixir cures them, they should make a point of having their esteemed physician check them over."

Joshua's face hurt from scowling. He yawned to relax it. "But what do you get out of it?"

Robert let go of his arm and clapped him on the back. "I get out of a fight that might leave me needing your services. And I do a friend a favor. He's done a few for me."

Joshua took a deep breath and blew it out. "You're a good man, Robert. Now let's get to the saloon before I pound the man after all. I need a drink."

That evening, dragging himself up the stairs to his rooms, he found Robert's earlier words returning to mind. "A friend." Robert had called him a friend. And it was true enough, he supposed.

Joshua opened his door, returned Major's fond greeting, found the dog a good bone to chew on, and fell into his easy chair, his head in one hand, thinking about friends.

He had, one way or another, lost so many. First when

he headed off to war, leaving many of the boys he had known all his life, with no conception of how drastically the war would change him. Even if he had stayed in Philadelphia when peace came, those innocent friendships would never have survived. And then, one after another of those who went with him to fight were killed, or so maimed and broken as to be nigh unrecognizable; and the same fate overtook the new, more intense friendships, almost like the ties of brothers, he had formed with fellow soldiers. He had done his best — no, to be honest, something less than his best — to stay in touch with those who had survived, but in leaving for the West, he had forfeited the chance to maintain those friendships, or to build new ones with other veterans in Philadelphia based on their common experience.

And now, without his noticing, Robert had become a friend. Could Joshua be a friend in return? Or had that capacity been blasted or drained out of him? Did he dare?

* * * * *

As he opened himself to socializing more with Robert, Joshua realized he had a potential difficulty to address. Joshua was not infrequently ready to relax with a beer, but for Robert, the frequency was somewhat greater. Rather than imbibe whenever he or Robert sought each other's company, he started steering them toward the ice cream parlor. On this day, one of the warmer spring days so far, the thought of ice cream was welcome enough that the task was easy, though Robert did toss off one comment about how beer could be equally refreshing.

Their conversation wandered among topics with no real direction, a mere backdrop to the pleasure of shared masculine company, until Joshua brought up a subject that had lately come to occupy his mind. "Have you any idea why Mrs. Blum dislikes Miss Brook? I have never known her to dislike anyone else. Though 'dislike' may be too strong a term for what I observed when I mentioned Miss Brook to her."

"The daughter out at the Brook place? Well, I might have heard a bit of gossip about it." Robert paused to slurp melted ice cream off his plate. "According to Rebecca Wheeler, the two ladies got along well enough at first, until Mrs. Blum offered to make her a fancier dress. I suppose she might have been less than tactful about what Miss Brook was wearing at the time."

Joshua doubted that Miss Brook would take offense so easily. "And?"

"I gather Miss Brook said no, she liked plain ones just fine. Mrs. Blum didn't take it kindly, Miss Brook rejecting her offer like that."

It could be that Mrs. Blum had misconstrued Miss Brook's straightforward manner as intending to give offense. Or there might have been a deeper misunderstanding between them. Miss Brook must have little in the way of spending money, and might have assumed Mrs. Blum's dressmaking services to come rather steep. Though to do Mrs. Blum justice, she probably had not intended to charge much at all . . . .

But Robert was gazing at him, bemused. "Where have you flown off to? Did I say something especially interesting? Or are you wishing we'd gone for that beer?"

Joshua turned toward the window in case he was blushing. Once he could be sure of his countenance, he turned back and said, in what he hoped was a casual tone, "Just meditating on the human condition and how much trouble we make for ourselves over nothing much. Got room for any more ice cream before we both get back to work?"

Chapter 6

MRS. BLUM stopped by during Joshua's office hours with some gingerbread, no pretense of needing medical attention, and a mission to interrogate him. "You had a good time with Rebecca, didn't you? Such a lovely girl. And you must have enjoyed her cooking, everyone does, so much better than you're used to! So when will you be seeing—" ("vill you be seeink") — "her again?"

Joshua tried without success to refuse the gingerbread, and did not do much better at deflecting the questions. As soon as his office hours were over, he fled next door and waited impatiently for Robert to finish serving a customer. As soon as the door shut behind the wife of the man who owned most of Cowbird Creek's saloons, he burst out, "She won't give up! What am I going to do?"

Robert raised an eyebrow. "She? Do?"

Joshua blew out his breath in frustration. "Mrs. Blum, of course! She's determined to marry me off. As soon as she's convinced I'm not interested in Rebecca Wheeler —"

"Why not? She's pretty and lively and a good cook. Which of those doesn't suit you?"

Joshua contemplated pulling his hair. Or maybe Robert's. "Not you too! If you like Rebecca so much, court her with my blessing! But that won't help me any. Mrs. Blum will find someone else to shove my way." And so far, her ideas of what woman would suit him were somewhat wide of the mark.

Robert didn't even try to hide his grin. "Tough break, Doc. Can't you think of some way to distract her?"

"Like what? All she seems to care about, besides dressmaking and feeding people, is —" The idea that struck him might not be genius, but it felt like it. "She cares about romance, and weddings. What if I take my turn at matchmaking? Find a nice solid gentleman to get her attention?"

Robert's grin grew even wider. "Matchmaking in self-defense! I like it."

"But you'll have to help me. You've lived here far longer than I have. You know everyone for miles around. You can come up with good candidates."

Robert gave a modest shrug. "I might have a suggestion or two, once I give it some thought. How are you going to do this without her knowing what you're up to?"

Joshua imagined talking to Mrs. Blum with a hidden agenda on his mind. He could picture himself, tongue-tied, even blushing, damn it. "Maybe I don't have to."

It might be best to startle her somehow, to jolt her out of her current way of thinking. So he stopped by the baker and bought a cherry pie, the very thought of the fruit carrying his imagination through spring to summer. When she opened her door to his knock, he thrust it toward her. "With my thanks for the gingerbread."

Her eyebrows shot upward. He added quickly, "I'm sure it won't be as good as you'd make. But maybe it'll be better than nothing."

She stepped back to let him in. "I'll give you some, and you tell me. *And* you can tell me about you and Rebecca. Such a sweet girl!"

He bided his time until she had cut a giant slice of pie

for him and, at his urging, a smaller one for herself. When she had actually taken a bite, he waited until just after she swallowed — he didn't want her to choke — and said, "I have a proposition for you."

"A proposition? That's not like a proposal, I hope!" She laughed heartily, her large bosom bouncing with the movement.

"Not . . . exactly."

That got her staring.

"Mrs. Blum, I'm not going to court Rebecca Wheeler. But I'll let you keep trying to find the right woman for me, just as long as you let me try to find the right man for you."

It was her turn to blush. But she waved her hand as if shoving away the idea, and said with something of a forced laugh, "Such an idea! Who would want an old lady like me?"

Joshua put down his fork and leaned forward on his elbows. "Anyone who wants a woman with experience, a woman who knows something about life, who's also a good cook, and smart, and funny, and has a heart as big as the prairie."

Mrs. Blum gazed at him like a favorite son. "Such a dear boy. And so earnest! I'll have to find you a girl who likes earnest."

"I'm serious, Mrs. Blum."

"As for my heart, is that a good idea, a heart so big? Maybe it's true, and no wonder I have palpitations."

"Stop changing the subject." Though he would need to examine her again soon. Had she been short of breath when she opened the door?

She gave him a long look. "I find you a bride, you stop trying to find me a husband."

"All right — if you really want me to stop. But I wager I'll find your husband first. And then you stop trying to marry me off."

She laughed, a true laugh this time. "A wager! We shake hands on it."

Which they did. And then she picked up the remains of the pie and snorted at it. "Tonight I make you a better one."

* * * * *

Robert had been busy replenishing his stock, even traveling to cities with pharmaceutical houses for the purpose. He had, to Joshua's chagrin, given little thought to the matchmaking project. "But soon, I promise."

Soon? Soon, Mrs. Blum would have found the next prospect to send Joshua's way. He had better get started on his own.

Mr. Blum had been a shopkeeper. A prosperous one? Joshua wasn't sure, though the quality of Mrs. Blum's clothes and furnishing suggested it. He had better start at the top of the shopkeeper ladder. The owner of the general store was married with four children, but the man who owned the dry goods store had lost his wife to scarlet fever just before Joshua got to town.

Though Mrs. Blum must know him already, if she bought her cloth and sewing supplies from him.

Joshua made his way to Mrs. Blum's house the next morning, stern expression and stethoscope at the ready, to check her heart. Her usual protests overcome, he was relieved to find her condition largely unchanged, allowing him to focus on his true mission. "You shop at Mr. Todd's dry goods store, don't you?"

She sniffed. "That man! I tell him he should get better quality linen, and he tells me I don't know what I'm talking about! Now I order in what I can, and go there when he's out. His assistant, now there's a nice girl. Hmmmm . . . ."

Joshua would have to wait for Robert's assistance, after all.

Joshua and Robert took a table in the corner of the saloon, far from the player piano and the rowdy fellows singing around it. It should provide sufficient privacy for their plotting.

Robert brought their drinks from the bar and sat down. "How about Thaddeus Spencer? The telegraph operator?"

Joshua pondered what he knew about the man as he took another swig of beer and let the glass thud back on the table. Thaddeus was tall and skinny, stooped like a heron, with a long coat that flapped a little like wings. Mrs. Blum might enjoy fattening him up.

Robert drained a shot of whiskey and went on. "He's a widower, so there's no question of him being a confirmed bachelor. And his wife was a battle-axe, so he probably isn't still pining over her."

You never knew. Joshua had known some couples who did nothing but fight, and then when one died or went off to the war, the other fell apart as if the battle had kept them going. "Does he ever talk about her?"

Robert looked to be consulting his memory. "Not often, I think. And generally with a shudder."

"So will you talk to him, ask him if he's interested?"

"Whoa, boy! This is your project. I'm just your expert consultant. *You* talk to him."

"But *you're* the one recommending him." Joshua fished a three-cent nickel piece out of his vest pocket. "We'll flip to see who does the job." He added, grudgingly: "Your call."

"All right, fraidy-cat. Heads, you talk to him; tails, I

do." He seized the coin and flipped it high, then snatched it out of the air and slammed it on the table. When he lifted his hand, the lady Liberty gleamed in the lamplight.

Joshua cussed for a full half a minute. Robert laughed so hard he almost choked on his whiskey.

Joshua ambled into the telegraph office two days later with Major at his heels, holding an order for medical supplies. "Afternoon, Thaddeus. Send this for me, would you? And here, have a hunk of cornbread." He held out half a loaf. "My patient Mrs. Blum — you know, that nice widow lady — sent me home with it. Damn, but she's a fine cook."

A week later, Joshua stopped by to listen to Mrs. Blum's heart again. (No worse. But she was wheezing from time to time.)

He let her tell him about her latest chat with the friendly assistant at the dry goods store, who had such a good eye for color, "and what a homemaker she would make!" When he could get a word in edgewise, he asked her straight out, "What about you and Thaddeus Spencer who runs the telegraph?"

She shook her head solemnly. "So timid! If I said boo, he'd jump out of his boots. A man should be a man, not a mouse, don't you think?" ("Doon't you tink?")

He managed to get out without promising to call on the assistant. But he knew his reprieve would be a short one.

Chapter 7

THE FARMER stood in Joshua's doorway twisting his hat. "It's been more than two days, and the baby's not come yet. She's had three before, and no trouble. She didn't want to send for you, said it's women's business, but . . . I finally told her I was coming to fetch you."

Joshua gulped down the cold coffee he always kept on hand. He would need all his wits about him this night. "You go on back to your wife and tell her I'm on my way."

Heading to the livery stable for his horse, Joshua ruminated on the ironies of his practice where babies were concerned. Some families, generally the wealthier ones or those determined to show how modern they were, would call him in when the woman's mother and sisters or a midwife could handle things perfectly well. Others, like this farmer's wife, resisted the idea past the point of reason, sending for him only when things had become desperate.

He had delivered one dead baby. That had left him with a wholly different nightmare his brain could use to torture him. But so far, he hadn't lost a mother.

The coffee had cleared his head enough for him to notice his surroundings. He led Nellie-girl out into the balmy spring night and imagined the farmer saying, years from now, to a little boy or girl, "It was a fine night like this one when you come into the world . . . ."

Nellie-girl hadn't been out for three days, so she had energy to spare, frisking about and then cantering along at a good clip. They got to the farm only a few minutes after the farmer. An older woman waited in the yard as Joshua rode up, a shawl wrapped around her and her arms crossed tight on her chest. "My daughter's upstairs. We've sent the young 'uns to my sister's. I think maybe the baby's turned wrong way around."

Joshua followed the woman so close that he almost tripped on her heels. "Did her water break?"

"This mornin'."

Joshua cursed silently to himself. There was some chance of turning the baby, but it would have been a bigger chance if her water hadn't broken. Whatever her mother had noticed that clued her in, it was a damn shame she hadn't noticed it sooner.

A hoarse cry, like a grunt but louder and longer and higher, came from down the hall as they reached the second floor. A woman in labor, if she made noise at all, could sound like nothing else Joshua had heard or imagined. It sent prickles down his spine. And if he didn't school his imagination, he would be picturing women he knew, girls at Mamie's or shopkeeper's wives or the usually self-contained Miss Brook, in the throes of such suffering.

Just before he entered the room, the older woman clutched his wrist and faced him, with all the fear she must have been hiding from her daughter writ plain on her face. "Can you save my baby? Can you bring her baby into the world?"

Maybe, by the time he'd been a doctor for twenty years, he'd have a better feel for whether to lie. He could hardly say, "I have no idea." Even "I hope to God I can" was probably not enough. So he said, "That's what I'm here to do."

If he failed to do it, she could curse him later. He moved around her and headed for his patient. His patients.

He plunked his bag on the floor and pulled out his smock, shrugging it on. Even an easy birth was a messy business. Then he approached the bed. The laboring woman seemed oblivious to his presence until he bent to take her hand. "I'm Doc Gibbs. I'm here to help."

She lay there pale and sweaty, the bedclothes under and around her all rucked up from her thrashing about. She squeezed his hand so tight he thought another contraction was starting, but her face showed only exhaustion and worry, no pain. She said hoarsely, "Ma thinks the baby's coming out wrong. Is it?"

"I'll find out." He gently moved the bedclothes away from her. "I'm going to be touching your belly now." She nodded weakly.

He ran his hands over her, pressed lightly here and there. "Your ma appears to be right." He hesitated. "I'd like to take a look down where the baby's coming, to see how far along you are in opening the way. And I may need to touch you there, to be sure."

She turned away, her face contorted in protest — or in pain. Another contraction was starting. The pillows muffled her words, but he could hear. "Must you?"

"I should. I really should. I need to know how much time we have to get this baby turned around."

She gritted her teeth and nodded. A moan, almost a wail, escaped her as he squatted down and examined the birth canal. She was almost fully dilated. Not much time, then.

He stood back up and bent over the woman. "I'm going to be pressing on your belly where the baby is, to get it head down." He had been concentrating too hard to notice who else was near, but now he looked around and found the woman's mother hovering in the doorway. "Do you have any wine or spirits? It would relax her and help me with what I need to do."

The mother turned and called an order to some unseen member of the household. While he waited, Joshua told his patient, "It'll probably take a few minutes. And it may hurt some of that time. I'm sorry about that."

The woman actually chuckled. "Well, won't that be a change. This has just been a picnic so far."

He smiled back as best he could. Just then a boy came up to the woman's mother with a glass of dark red wine. Joshua retreated while the mother brought the glass to the bed, helping her daughter sit up enough to drink. "Take it slow, now," Joshua cautioned her. It'd do no good for her to vomit it up again.

She got most of it down before another contraction started. He waited while she moaned and panted. When she finally relaxed against the pillows, he stepped forward and got started, feeling for the hard smoothness of the head and the narrower bump of the buttocks. It was hard to make himself push firmly enough, knowing it was hurting her, but there was no way around it.

She let out a cry and then grabbed a handful of blanket and stuffed it in her mouth. Joshua pressed steadily with both hands, trying to push exactly as hard with both.

"There we go!" He could feel the baby starting to change position. But damn! There came another contraction. If the cord was in the wrong place during it, the contraction could squeeze it shut . . . .

The seconds might have dragged even more slowly for Joshua than for the moaning woman in the bed. When the abdominal muscles finally relaxed, he got to work again, pushing harder, terrified of the next contraction.

Slowly, slowly . . . and then a little faster . . . the baby yielded to his efforts. As it turned more crossways, the woman let out a shriek. But in a moment more, the baby was moving toward vertical again, this time with the head down where it should be.

Now he had to see whether the baby would stay in position. This process didn't always take. Sometimes, for whatever reason, maybe the same reason the baby had been breech in the first place, the baby turned butt-down again. But that was the one good thing about this happening so late, with contractions coming every couple of minutes. The baby wouldn't have much room or time to maneuver itself back into danger.

And twenty minutes later, Joshua got to see a purple head with just a wisp of hair appear, and recede again, and finally crown.

Downstairs again, Joshua collapsed in a kitchen chair while the older woman fixed him a sandwich. He had already removed his smock and rolled it up tight, clean side out. He'd rinse it as best he could once he got home, then take it to Li Chang later in the morning.

The new mother was weak from her ordeal, and her vital signs could have been more reassuring. The baby had been quick to cry and pink up, but its movements were on the sluggish side. He couldn't say either patient was out of the woods just yet, but all he said to the family was to come get him right away if the mother started bleeding much or either of them came down with fever. He'd come back tomorrow evening, after all concerned had gotten some sleep, to see how things were going.

There were still a few stars overhead when he pulled himself back aboard Nellie-girl and turned her toward home. All over, for now, until the next time. . . . A thought struck him so sudden that he pulled up on Nellie-girl's reins, startling a neigh out of her. He patted her neck in apology and loosened the reins again. The next time, if Mrs. Blum's schemes actually came to anything, it might be his own wife lying in a bed, moaning and screaming and tossing around, trying her hardest to bring their baby into the world.

Did every husband, every father-to-be, wonder if it was worth the risk?

Would he be even more terrified than he had been on the battlefield, or assisting the doctors afterward, trying to keep yet one more soldier from dying?

And if the worst happened, would he ever forgive himself for putting the woman he loved in that fatal danger?

When he finally stumbled up the stairs to his rooms, he no longer cared enough to bother with the smock and planned to fall straight into bed. But instead, he found himself looking for the letter he'd gotten from his mother the week before, and reading it over, and kissing her signature.

She had been through all that, or at least something like it, for his sake. And he'd never thought to thank her for it. If he had had the strength to hold a pen and produce recognizable words, he would have written her right now. Instead, he laid the letter on the table where he ate his breakfasts, so he couldn't possibly forget.

* * * * *

It would have been awkward enough if only Mrs. Blum had shown up, just four hours after he got to sleep. But she had apparently had enough of his stalling about the dry goods store assistant. *Both* of them were there at his door, Mrs. Blum beaming to match the morning sun, the younger woman a step behind and considerably shyer.

At least Mrs. Blum looked embarrassed when he

opened the door partway, in nightshirt and cap, and peered blearily at his inconvenient visitors. He hadn't been sure she knew how to look embarrassed. "Oh, I'm sorry! We'll come back —" ("ve'll koom back") "— later on. But here!" She placed a basket in his hand. "We brought you some crullers. Eldora made them herself, such a clever girl, such a good cook, she makes me jealous!"

He could smell the fried dough. It made his mouth water. "Thank you, ladies." He managed to smile. "Now I know what to have for breakfast." He eased the door closed, leaned against it, and stumbled to the stove to make fresh coffee.

An hour later, his mouth coated inside and out with grease and sugar, he made a wager with himself about when Mrs. Blum would return. Another half an hour, perhaps. And probably alone — he doubted the young woman would have the nerve, after that reception.

He was wrong on the first point, right on the second. An unusually timid knock came not ten minutes later. This time he opened the door all the way, dressed properly from collar to boots. The widow looked him up and down, but still seemed less than satisfied. "Sit, sit, before you fall over! You must have been out half the night. At that farm to the north, with the baby?"

Of course she would know all about what everyone in and around town was up to. "That's right."

She followed him as he headed for his easy chair and settled himself in it. "And mother and baby are well?"

He rubbed his eyes. "They were well enough when I left. I couldn't say how either of them'll fare. It was a hard birth."

You still have that tea I brought you?"

He simply shook his head, too weary to deal with her ministrations.

"Eldora, she had to go to work, or she'd have come with me."

Maybe so, maybe not. Just the mention of that fresh-faced lady, youthful health and energy radiating from her, made him imagine how she would look with that happy glow extinguished, sweat and exhaustion and pain in her face, an unearthly wail coming from pale and bitten lips . . . . He hid his face in his hands.

He heard a creak as Mrs. Blum settled into the wicker rocking chair, and then the rumble of the rockers on the floor. When she spoke, her voice was gentle, coaxing. "You'll rest up, you'll feel better. It was a hard birth, you say, but still, a baby born! Such a miracle! And one day, it'll be your own miracle, a joy like no other . . . ."

He let himself drift in the wake of her persuasive voice, imagining holding his own babe the way he had finally held the baby last night. Rocking his little girl to sleep. Taking his little boy fishing, late afternoon sun gilding the trees as the boy proudly carried home his very first catch.

And then, a shadow falling over the picture, the shadow of the angel of death, a woman stretched the length of a bed and gasping her last breath in a darkened room, and himself crumpled in a chair with little hands grasping and pulling at him, and a newborn babe whimpering from a nearby cradle. He gasped, and choked on a sob.

The sound of the rocking chair had stopped. He opened his eyes to see Mrs. Blum leaning forward, elbows on knees, looking solemnly in his face. She spoke softly, the melody of her speech subdued.

"I lost a little one, when I was a young woman. The pains came before time. It was so tiny, the poor little thing. Samuel was so unhappy, I never saw him like that before or since . . . . And I couldn't have more, afterward."

So that explained why she never talked of a son or

daughter back in New York. "I'm sorry."

She took a deep breath and shrugged. "Nu, that's life. Life, death, all written in the book, and we watch the pages turn, and go on."

She started rocking again, the rhythm soothing as he leaned back and shut his eyes again. After a while, still rocking, she spoke. "A good man like you, you'd be such a good father. But . . . not every woman wants to have a child."

What woman wouldn't? A widow with children already, he supposed. He waited, weary, for her to put forth the name of a Mrs. Somebody, still young, still lovely, only three children, he could be a father to them . . . .

But when he peeked up under his eyelids to see what she was doing, he spied an unexpected, mysterious smile on her face.

Mrs. Blum hauled herself up from the chair, setting it rocking vigorously from her movement. "I'll stop by later and bring you some leftover stew I made. You need something solid, you should get your strength back. And I have someone I want to talk to."

"*Who??*" Joshua wondered which of them had lost their mind, the respectable older widow beaming at him or himself.

"Mamie! She's hardly older than you at all, just a year or two maybe. She knows about life, no just-hatched chick, a woman of experience. A good head on her shoulders, responsible, smart. And not counting on having children, but not dead set against it, so you have options. Not to mention she knows how to please a man, you can't say that isn't a good thing."

"Mamie. Madam Mamie." Madams almost always

started as prostitutes. How many men had she been with?

Well, how many whores had he been with? How was that any different, really?

And Mamie had always treated him with respect, and given him a straightforward, friendly welcome.

He imagined walking into church on Sunday with the notorious Madam Mamie on his arm — and he spluttered in laughter. He seized Mrs. Blum's arms, almost picking her up to swing her around before thinking better of it, whirling her around where she stood. "Mamie. You amazing woman. All right, what have the two of you come up with? Where do we start?"

* * * * *

Joshua had never seen this room before, a small dining room with furnishings, wallpaper, and even tablecloth as excessively ornate as the main parlor where guests waited their turn. It made sense, now that he thought about it. Some of Madam Mamie's wealthier patrons would want to have supper parties for a few friends, complete with a girl for each. But this evening the table was set for only two, with covered dishes and a bottle of wine.

Mamie led him in and expertly deployed a corkscrew, then poured him a large glass of white wine, full to the brim. "I figure it can't hurt to start relaxing you."

Joshua found himself relaxing at once, even before his first sip of the excellent wine. Mamie poured herself a glass, just as generous, and waved him to a chair, uncovering the dishes and serving both of them with a feast more like dinner than supper: creamed corn, mashed potatoes and butter, and rare roast beef. "Folks say you shouldn't drink white wine with beef. But you can guess how much I care what folks say."

Joshua raised his glass in a toast. "To white wine with beef, and to hell with 'em!"

Over supper, they traded first histories, then anecdotes. He steered clear of the grisly aspects of his war experience, which left not much, but he dwelt on such topics as the absurdities of command and the deliveries of ridiculously useless supplies. And he managed to remember a few oddly peaceful interludes. "There was one time, maybe three years into the war, a few of us got separated from our company with a blizzard coming on. We found a hut, something someone must have used for a hunting shelter, and almost as soon as we stumbled inside, about the same number of Rebs found it. We just looked at each other, and then me and the other boys stepped aside to let 'em in. We shared our rations and played poker with twigs for chips. And when the weather cleared up, we looked the other way while they vanished." He gazed into the candle on the table. "Always feared we'd come upon 'em in a fight, but it never happened. A bit of mercy, that."

Mamie poured him more wine. "Must have been around that time that I set up here. Speaking of poker, would you believe it, I won this house, or what it was then — a smaller place, I've built it up since — in a poker game, right across the street at the saloon? Damn fool didn't think a lady could bluff. And the first girl I took on — she's moved on since, but she was a corker. Used to be a fancy shooter, showing off her shooting from one town to the next, but her fingers got to troubling her, some sort of rheumatic trouble. She was pretty as all get-out, and knew how to dress up and get attention, and was used to handling menfolk. A real natural, she turned out to be."

And back and forth, on and on, through supper and a couple of hours after, through the bottle of wine and a sweet, thick liqueur to follow. The openness with which

Mamie discussed all manner of subjects reminded him of Clara Brook. Though he had the impression, even with their short acquaintance, that Miss Brook's conversation would cover a wider range of topics.

A pause in the talk, possibly arising from his wandering thoughts, lingered and turned into a portentous silence. What now? If he were here as a customer, he would know what came next, but surely this evening came with no such expectation. He must, above all, show a proper respect for his companion . . . .

Mamie drained her glass, put it down with a decided thump, and folded her hands on the table. "Joshua, I've enjoyed our time tonight, and I'm grateful to Freida for suggesting it. I hope we'll stay acquainted, after this. But whatever it may take to touch my heart, if such a thing could happen, it'll need a different sort of fellow to do it. Someone older, and tougher, and stranger, and at least a little meaner, I'm thinking."

Joshua's jaw dropped; he hauled it back into place and cleared his throat. "Well, then, ah . . . ."

She patted his hand, her cut glass ring twinkling in the candlelight. "I suspected as much. But you know Freida. It's easier to go along when she has an idea. And I was curious to get to know you better, after just doing business for so long." She tilted her head and studied him. "No hard feelings, I hope? Me and the girls count on you to take care of us. And there's several of 'em would miss you more personal, should you stop coming by."

Joshua shook off embarrassment and confusion and a bit of wounded pride, and gave her a little bow from where he sat. "No more than I'd miss them. I'll be by in two weeks, as usual."

"Good." She gave a decided nod. "Now let's have a little coffee, and some brandy in it, before you go."

Half an hour later, she opened the door, stuck her head out, and called out, "Shoo!" Joshua heard giggles and skittering feet. Of course the girls had been curious as all get-out, and lingering to see what might be going to happen.

Mamie turned back toward Joshua. "Would you like a visit with one of the girls before you go? On the house. A thank-you for a pleasant evening."

Joshua had the feeling he should decline and make a dignified exit. On the other hand, that would leave him going home to his empty rooms, more than a little drunk, trying not to feel foolish or even sorry for himself. "Thank you kindly, Mamie. I think I will. Would you see if Adeline is free?"

Chapter 8

JOSHUA came awake to find Major's muzzle nudging him insistently in the ribs. He groaned and rubbed his eyes; the dog licked his hand, whining.

He must have had another nightmare.

Sometimes he remembered details for some minutes, or worse, found himself floundering between sleep and waking, unsure whether he lay on a battlefield in mortal peril with death on every side. Other times, as now, the dream dissolved and fled the moment he awoke. That happened more often when Major was near enough to sense Joshua's distress.

He rolled over and stroked the dog's smooth warm head. "It's all right, boy. I'm awake. You woke me. *Good* dog. What a good dog you are."

Sitting up and breathing deep, he looked around and saw it was morning. That was a blessing. He would not need to choose between trying to sleep again, not knowing whether the nightmare would reclaim him, or lighting a lamp and sitting for hours until morning came. He petted Major one more time and got out of bed to dress.

As he knotted his tie, he was glad to hear a knock at the door heralding some occupation. He called out "One moment!" and quickly grabbed a couple of cold biscuits and stuffed them in his mouth, washing them down with yesterday's coffee. That swallowed, he went to open the door.

The tall young man standing in the doorway had a familiar look to him. As he started explaining that his father was feeling poorly, Joshua realized why. The boy's straight hair and green eyes made it highly likely Joshua was looking at Clara Brook's brother.

Joshua always tried to respond promptly to such a summons, but he might have saddled Nellie-girl a little faster than commonly. He could not deny some curiosity about the Brook farm, and the family that had produced the rather singular woman he was getting to know. And his relief that Mr. Brook had presumably asked to see him, rather than the barber, made him eager to arrive in good time.

The boy had apparently walked; Joshua offered him, and he accepted, a ride behind himself. Nellie-girl should be able to carry them both for this short a distance.

Miss Brook, and a woman almost as tall as she but considerably more stout, awaited them on the front porch. Joshua studied Miss Brook's face for clues as to just how "poorly" her father might be. She seemed calm, but that told him little.

While Joshua took off the horse's saddle and bridle and found a place near some grass where he could tie the reins, Miss Brook handled the introductions, keeping them short, and let her mother explain her father's symptoms. They had thought he had nothing more than a cold, but instead of being on the mend by now, he had begun coughing more and more.

Joshua followed the women into the house and had one foot on the stairs when he heard the coughing up above. He paused and looked at Mrs. Brook. Could she have failed to recognize that sound? But she looked away, obviously embarrassed. "He didn't sound like that before. It just sounded like regular coughing. It's the whooping cough, then?"

"It certainly sounds like it." Joshua headed on up the stairs to confirm the diagnosis and check for complications. Should he try to keep the family at a distance? But no, they had all been exposed already, and the patient would need tending. He waited for Miss and Mrs. Brook to join him and asked, raising his voice to be heard over the coughing, "Has either of you had whooping cough in the past?"

It was Mrs. Brook who replied. "Clara did, something awful, when she was a girl." Joshua glanced at Miss Brook, who gave a slight nod.

"Then it might be wise if Miss Brook took care of her father during this illness. She is unlikely to come down with the disease again."

"Oh, it's mostly been Clara taking care of him already. She's handy with sick folk." Mrs. Brook gave her daughter's hand a little pat. Looking toward Miss Brook again, Joshua saw neither a nod nor any disagreement, but a look of unutterable weariness. It vanished so fast he doubted that he had seen it; and when he went on into the sickroom, Miss Brook followed and stood in a posture of attention. Her mother waited in the doorway.

Mr. Brook's thin frame lay almost flat, his head propped up by two pillows. Joshua turned back to ask for more, if any were available. At once, Clara said, "Ma, you can take mine. And we can put a folded blanket under that."

Mrs. Brook's expression softened. "That's my good girl." She hustled away as Joshua bent over his patient. There were already a few red spots on his face, and on the portion of his chest showing above his nightshirt.

Joshua pointed to these and explained, "Those aren't anything to worry about. They're from blood vessels breaking from the force of the coughs. You can expect nosebleeds, too, and maybe even bleeding from the eyes." This warning was likely to dismay any family member, but Clara's only reaction was a moment of especial stillness as she looked at her father and then back at Joshua. Clearly, her mother was right about her ability to deal with illness.

Mr. Brook was seized with an especially violent fit of coughing. When it subsided, Miss Brook asked, "What else can we expect, and what can we do for him?"

Joshua picked up a pitcher of water by the bed, poured some into the waiting glass, and handed it to Miss Brook. "You must make sure he drinks as much liquid as possible. That is, he should drink plenty of water. If he tires of water to the point of refusing it, you could give him very weak tea, or cider much diluted with water. Liquids that cause him to pass too much water would be worse than none."

Miss Brook gently lifted her father to sitting position, held him through another burst of coughing, and helped him take a few sips before laying him down again. Meanwhile, Joshua added, "He may vomit." He looked at her dress, a lighter fabric than he had seen her wear before, though plainly cut as ever. "You may want to wear an apron, or even one of your father's or brother's shirts, to protect your clothing."

She looked down at her dress and gave a small, wry smile. "That is practical advice."

Joshua cleared his throat and went on. "The vomiting is a reason to give him only a small amount of water at a time, as you did, so he will lose less of what he's drunk when he vomits. Frequent, small amounts are what you should aim for."

Mrs. Brook came back with the pillow and blanket. Joshua took them from her, while Miss Brook put her arm around her father's shoulders once again and said softly,

"One more time, Pa, so you can rest more comfortably." Joshua set the blanket on the pillows already in place and the third pillow on top of it. The patient would still need to be lifted in order to drink. Clara appeared to have the same thought, glancing toward the pitcher of water. Joshua poured a little water into the glass; Clara held it to her father's lips and said, in a coaxing tone, "Here, another little sip. One more? That's good. There you go." She laid him down again.

What else should he tell her? Oh, yes. "Give him cod liver oil. A little at a time, like the water. It seems to help whooping cough sufferers stay otherwise healthy."

Miss Brook headed out of the room, her mother stepping aside to let her. "I'll send my brother to town for some."

Mrs. Brook, who must have been in considerable suspense, put a hand on Joshua's sleeve as he followed Miss Brook out of the room and asked, "How long will it take him to get better?"

Joshua suppressed a frown. If she meant how long it would be until the farmer was up and working, it would be long indeed. At least planting season was weeks away. "He may keep coughing for another few weeks, or it could be only a few days. After that, though, he'll still need to rest as much as possible, and to stay away from anyone with any kind of cold or cough. And don't let any children, let alone babies, anywhere near him until he's altogether recovered."

Joshua headed downstairs, Miss Brook behind him, Mrs. Brook lingering just outside the door where her husband lay. When the two of them reached the bottom of the stairs, Clara asked, "What do we owe you for your help today?"

He was relieved at her thoughtfulness. So many families, distracted by worry for the patient, forgot about payment until days or weeks later. "I recall you mentioning your chickens. I'd welcome some fresh eggs."

Clara's shoulders tensed, and she narrowed her eyes and cocked her head. "I should think you would prefer coin. We can manage that."

He might have fibbed, but fortunately, he could tell her the honest truth. "In fact, I've had a mighty hankering for fresh eggs lately. With all the food offerings Freida Blum brings me, eggs haven't yet been among them."

Seconds later, it occurred to him that bringing up Freida Blum might have been unfortunate. But apparently, whatever Mrs. Blum's feelings might be, Clara Brook had no hostility toward the older woman. She simply relaxed her shoulders and said, "By the time you and your horse are ready to go, I'll have a basket for you."

A week later, Joshua had run out of eggs, and had heard nothing about Mr. Brook taking a turn for the worse. It was probably time for him to visit the patient, though he could hardly in good conscience ask for so substantial a payment again if all was well. He was halfway to the stable when Miss Brook hailed him from the edge of the street.

She looked even thinner than usual, and paler. Her father's coughing might have kept her from sleeping, or she might be spending her strength on nursing him and doing the work her father could not. He was tempted to express some concern, but he had no remedy but time to offer her. He simply asked, "How is Mr. Brook doing? I was just on my way to see him."

She gave a quick shake of her head. "There's no need. He is doing as well as we could expect. We've managed to keep him drinking water, and he's kept most of the cod liver oil down."

"Excellent." Though she could have taken proper credit, rather than saying "we" as if she had not borne most of the burden.

"And I brought something you should have taken before." She reached through the slit in her dress and removed something from her pocket. Coins. "I must insist."

He could think of no polite way to refuse. Silently, he held out his hand and let her pour the coins — thankfully, not many — into his palm.

* * * * *

Once again, Joshua consulted Robert about a match for Mrs. Blum. Sooner or later, they must have better success.

Robert spoke over his shoulder while restocking his shelves. "How about a lawyer? Older women respect professional men, don't they?"

Joshua shrugged. "The only older woman I know besides Mrs. Blum is my mother. And she's never had many dealings with lawyers. Anyway, don't they all travel a lot?"

Robert finished his task and came back to the counter. "Most of them ride the circuit, sure. But apparently we're an established enough town now to have one lawyer actually in residence. He just put up a sign last week."

Joshua took a tour of town in his memory. "Guess I saw a new sign and didn't bother to read it. I've been pretty busy." And tired, from working all hours and not sleeping all that well when he finally had the chance.

"Well, I think he's about her age. Comes from somewhere back east. Maybe he wanted to be top dog for a change, professionally speaking." Robert paused and studied Joshua. "You're looking a little peaked. Who doctors the doctor, huh?"

Joshua ignored the question. "If you think the lawyer

is a good prospect, how about you talk to him? It's your turn to inquire."

Robert looked glum at the prospect. "Lawyers don't like to talk to anyone without getting paid for it. And this fellow hasn't been out west long enough to get frontier-friendly."

Joshua wasn't going to let Robert off that easily. "So teach him how to be friendly! Buy him a drink or something."

Robert narrowed his eyes. "You paying for it?"

"Oh, all right. Seeing as how you're so broke and I'm rolling in wealth."

Robert allowed him a smile. "All right, you've made your point. I'll invest the price of a drink in your matchmaking hobby."

"And I'll tackle Mrs. Blum. Wish me luck."

"A lawyer?" Mrs. Blum sighed. "You think? Well, I'll give it a try. Just to oblige you. ("Choost to obli-ch you.")

"That's the spirit!" Joshua sighed in relief. "And I am, indeed, much obliged."

Mrs. Blum and the lawyer had agreed to share dinner at the tavern. Joshua struggled with temptation for two days ahead of time and then surrendered. At the appointed time, he was seated at a table behind a post, his hat over his eyes, hoping to go unnoticed while gathering some sense of how the encounter was going.

It seemed to be going well, at first. Conversation looked animated, though Joshua could hear none of it. But by the time the serving girl brought their pork ribs and turnips, he noticed a disquieting pattern. The lawyer seemed to be doing almost all the talking. With Mrs. Blum present, that was an impressive feat. But he doubted it was one well calculated to endear the lawyer to his partner.

Mrs. Blum finished well before the lawyer, who apparently preferred talking to eating. Joshua took a peek at his watch to see that she had been sitting in front of her picked-clean plate for a full fifteen minutes. As he looked up again, he was momentarily distracted to see Clara Brook walking by with her arms full of sacks. The sacks looked heavy.

By the time Joshua looked back at Mrs. Blum and the lawyer, Mrs. Blum was leaning across the table and saying something. Whatever its nature, it caused the lawyer to sit back abruptly and snap his mouth shut.

Joshua left his payment on the table and snuck out before either of the two actually got up.

"That man!" Mrs. Blum bustled around her kitchen with even more energy than usual, cutting the apple pie, pouring his coffee, setting out cream he could use with either. "Such lungs he must have! All that talking, and I never saw him stop to breathe."

Joshua laughed, though reminded of the late Mr. Blum's similar observations about his hostess. "I must find a way to examine him, then, and write him up as a medical miracle. I could make a name for myself in the profession."

Mrs. Blum chuckled also, but slapped his plate of pie down with unnecessary firmness. "If I'd bothered to remember, I could tell you a dozen cases he had and how brilliant he was, how the juries loved him, how grateful the clients were, how the judges came up afterward to tell him he was such a great lawyer. I'm a patient woman, wouldn't you say? But oy, by the time I was done with my food, I was wishing I had something left on my plate, that I could stuff his mouth with."

Joshua almost asked just what she had said to bring the man's boasting to a stop, before realizing it would betray his spying on them. Fortunately, she could not resist sharing that tidbit. "Finally, I told him, I said, 'You'll have to excuse me, Mr. Famous Lawyer. I would be ashamed to take up any more of your time, when you could be preparing for another grand performance.' God be thanked, he didn't know what to say to that."

Joshua had a sudden vision of Mrs. Blum in a courtroom, making one of her inimitable comebacks and shutting down the other lawyer. Or even the judge. The legal profession was the poorer for her absence.

* * * * *

It was time for Joshua to check on Mrs. Blum again. She had, to be sure, stopped by his office just the other day with a tin of cookies and the inevitable reminder about Mr. Todd's assistant, but she had managed to evade Joshua's suggestions that he examine her before she left. If he visited her at home, he would have logistics in his favor. And he could bring her the welcome news that the woman with the breech birth and the baby were both doing well — though with Freida's ability to gather news, she might already know as much.

When he knocked on her door, Mrs. Blum called out something he had trouble understanding. He entered in a hurry, concerned she might be in some sort of difficulties. But she turned to him and shrugged apologetically, her mouth holding the blunt ends of several dressmaking pins. She inserted them into a garment on a dress form in the middle of the room.

As soon as her mouth was free of pins, Mrs. Blum gestured grandly up and down the dress form, saying. "Almost ready, a bridal dress for the mayor's oldest son's young lady, such a lovely girl!"

The garment was truly impressive, stylish (as far as Joshua could tell) without being fussy. He could easily imagine a bride wearing it. "The young lady is fortunate to have such a dress for her nuptials."

Mrs. Blum beamed. "I do my best, such an honor, such a joy to dress a bride. This is my second one this month. For now, I make the dress how they like, what they're used to, but I hope soon, the young ladies here will let me go a little fancier, like what we see in the magazines, why should the oh-so-proud ladies in England have better than our good girls here in America? . . . Just make yourself at home, I'm almost finished."

It must be satisfying for Mrs. Blum to make such dresses, not only because she so heartily approved of weddings but because of her evident pride in her craftsmanship. If Clara Brook had not rejected Mrs. Blum's offer, his hostess might well have been able to create a garment that would soften Miss Brook's appearance. Though Miss Brook might have been telling the simple truth about not wishing anything of the kind. Perhaps it would require a special occasion, even a wedding, before she would consider wearing the sort of garment that would accord with Mrs. Blum's sense of fashion.

Meanwhile, Mrs. Blum was rattling on as she adjusted pins and took stitches. "I was so happy to find this print, it'll look so good with her coloring. Such hair! Never did I have such beautiful hair, even when I was young and Samuel used to . . . well, never mind an old woman and her memories." She turned away, possibly to hide some less than festive expression, before straightening up and smiling at him. "And it turned out I have extra, I can use some in my next quilt!"

It shouldn't surprise him that she quilted. And helped run the library. And made dresses. And tried to find him a wife. No wonder she was short of breath sometimes — she never slowed down. "How long have you been making quilts?"

"Only since I moved here. Back home, what did I know from quilts? But so many women here make such beautiful ones, I was ashamed not to learn." Mrs. Blum patted the dress form and then bustled toward her bedroom. "I'll show you some, you can find one you like and take it with you, you should have something to keep you warm at night. There's one on the kitchen table, you can look at it if you're curious."

Given this broad hint, Joshua went to the kitchen to see the quilt in progress. Its border was made of squares with light blue trim against white, and blue six-pointed stars, hollow triangles one atop another, formed from darker blue material. Squares farther in showed a many-pronged candlestick in gold and a shape something like a gate with a shape floating beside it, tapered on both ends.

"That one, I just started." Mrs. Blum had come up behind him, puffing a little with her arms stacked high with quilts. "That one, I'll keep."

Joshua relieved Mrs. Blum of her burden and managed to extract one hand to point at the candlestick, asking, "Do these mean something special?"

Mrs. Blum looked, for once, almost shy. "To me, they're special. To goyim — excuse me, to Christians, not so much. There, that's a menorah. We light the candles on —" The name of the day, or the holiday, started with a sound like getting ready to spit. He made sure to repress any hint of a smile. "One candle the first day, two the next, all the way to eight. Because the sacred oil lasted for eight days, only enough for one, a miracle!" She paused and gave him a sardonic look. "Or so they say, I wasn't there, naturally, and maybe someone had put a little oil by for emergencies, it would be smart to do."

"And this one, the shape like a gate?"

"That's a letter, the first letter of the word for 'life.'" She paused, reflecting. "Maybe I should start adding that to quilts for brides, and for babies. It couldn't hurt, so appropriate, they don't need to know. But I'll fold this up so you can look at the others." Pulling the partially completed quilt toward her, she paused and put a hand to her bosom. He took the end of the quilt from her and asked, "Mrs. Blum, are you all right?"

"Fine, fine, don't start with the doctoring. And we've known each other this long, shouldn't you call me Freida? 'Mrs. Blum' this and 'Mrs. Blum' that, I feel like I should curtsy, or maybe stand at attention."

"Um . . . ." He'd been raised to respect his elders. And he certainly respected her. He tried changing the subject. Putting his armful of quilts on the edge of the table, he said, "I'll just fold this up, shall I?"

She made no protest, which Joshua found worrisome, though she did watch closely as if supervising. Once the quilt was folded as neatly as Joshua could manage, she picked it up and put it on a chair while he moved the other quilts to the center of the table. There were five or six of them, all different color schemes, each one harmonious.

Mrs. Blum elbowed in and took charge, partially unfolding the quilt on top. "Your rooms, they're so bare, you need something to liven them up. How about this one? Just the color would keep you warm, reds and yellows, like autumn leaves."

Joshua stood very still. He had memories associated with autumn, and they would not help him sleep at night. She looked sideways at him, and whatever she saw was enough for her to lay the quilt aside and move to the next. "Or this, greens and blues, like spring leaves and blue sky, and actual leaf shapes. It'll match the view out your window some of the time, and it'll do your heart good on winter nights."

It might at that. "It's beautiful." He felt the soft thickness. "Are you sure you don't have another use for it?"

She mock-glared at him. "Such a question! As if keeping my friend the doctor warm and cozy weren't enough. No, you take it, and when you're my age, you'll remember the old Jewish lady who wanted the best for you."

"Well, if you're sure. Thank you very much, ma'am." He lifted the quilt and put it on another chair, restoring the autumn-colored quilt to the pile and picking the pile up. Maybe she would let him stash them away in whatever chest they had come from.

But no, she firmly retrieved them and headed for her bedroom, talking as she went so that he was obliged to follow. "'Ma'am.' That's no better than Mrs. But I'll have you saying Freida, sooner or later. Now tell me, when will I be dressing your bride? Not Mamie, so who will it be? I've been neglecting you, so busy with this and that, but I need to find her while my hands are still good for sewing, they ache sometimes, especially when it's cold, a good thing winter is so far off."

He might be able to help her with that, if she was willing to try an Indian remedy. Willow bark tea could relieve some of the pain, and even the swelling that might develop. "Mrs. — Freida — I may be able to keep you sewing for years to come." And thereby put off her next attempt at matchmaking? Probably not for years. Probably not even for weeks. He stifled a sigh.

Chapter 9

TRY AS Joshua might to keep his trousers and frock coat clean, his smock didn't catch every mess that came his way. At least his misfortune was of benefit to Li Chang. The laundryman greeted him with a wide smile. "No problem, Doctor Gibbs — I get these all clean, very soon."

"You're cheerful this morning, Mr. Li." (Early in their acquaintance, the laundryman had politely corrected Joshua's assumption that "Chang" was his surname.) "Good news come your way?"

The man clasped his hands together. "Oh, yes, very good news. I start building a new house, very soon now. When I finish, I will have plenty of room for my mother and my wife. I send them money. Then they sail to America, take the train, join me here. My wife will help me with the work, and we will take care of my mother together."

Joshua wasn't sure Li Chang had adopted the custom of shaking hands, so he contented himself with saying heartily, "That's wonderful! Congratulations." He would have to think of the right sort of housewarming present to bring a Chinese fellow. Maybe Robert would know.

He heard the door open behind him, and then a firm tread that sounded familiar. Li Chang smiled warmly at whoever was behind Joshua. "Miss —" The name that followed must have been Li's attempt at "Brook," though the "r" sound was less than clear. "You bring me aprons?"

Miss Brook came up beside Joshua and held out a

bundle of cloth. "Aprons, yes, and a skirt. I was unable to avoid kneeling in the pigpen yesterday. But what did I hear as I entered? Is your family finally joining you?"

"Yes, yes! I will be so happy to introduce them to you." Li Chang took the bundle as he spoke and carried it to a nearby table. Miss Brook waited for him to return before saying, "I hope you will let me show your wife and mother around town when they arrive, and introduce them to any townspeople we encounter."

Did Li understand what a generous offer Miss Brook was making? That she would be tying her standing in town to that of not just newcomers but foreigners? From the moisture that glimmered in the laundryman's eyes, Joshua thought he did.

Joshua followed Miss Brook out of the laundry. She appeared to be headed for the general store, and he accompanied her, figuring he could go on to the tobacconist. Before he could ask about her father, she volunteered an update on his convalescence, going almost as well as Joshua could have hoped. Then, before he could think of another topic, she said, "Your mention of Freida Blum, when you came out to tend my father, brought a question to my mind."

Joshua almost flinched. Was she going to ask what Mrs. Blum had against her? But instead of any such alarming question, she went on, her tone thoughtful, "Do you happen to know how she came to arrive in Cowbird Creek?"

In his relief, Joshua wished he had more information to offer. "I'm afraid I know only that she left New York after the death of her husband."

Miss Brook took that in, saying nothing more until they were close to the store. Then she stopped and faced Joshua as she said, "I admire her courage. Even a younger woman, with a constitution well suited to enduring a long journey, would find the prospect daunting." Her face lighted with one of her infrequent smiles. "But I suppose I should not be surprised at anything Mrs. Blum undertook. She is a remarkable person, and you are fortunate to have her as a friend."

Joshua had no idea how to respond. Was Miss Brook acknowledging that her own relationship with Freida Blum was something other than friendly? Before he could think of anything to say, she had nodded a farewell and gone into the store.

Joshua picked up his pace, to arrive at the tobacconist the sooner. He needed a peaceful smoke to settle his mind.

* * * * *

Joshua's only hope of postponing Mrs. Blum's — Freida's — next candidate for his affections was to return to his own scheming. So far, Robert had not been of any great assistance. What would help Joshua do better?

Of course. He should have thought of it sooner. Freida's first marriage had apparently been happy enough. What had Samuel been like? What interests had they shared?

Now he just had to turn the conversation in that direction before Freida could start in on him. He could think of no subtle way to accomplish it. Instead, he started talking as soon as she'd opened the door and welcomed him inside. "All this time, Freida —" She preened at his obedient use of her name. "— you've never told me many details about Samuel. Do you have other friends here you can talk to about him?"

He'd taken her by surprise. Sadness crossed her face before she chased it away. "Why should I bother people about the past? This is a new country, people should look ahead."

"All the same, I'd like to know more about him."

Freida arched an eyebrow that might indicate suspicion of his sudden interest. But she dropped onto her love seat with an audible "huff" and started in as soon as he had sat as well. Or as soon as she could catch her breath.

"My Samuel, people thought he was just a shopkeeper, until they got to know him. Meek and mild, they thought. Polite, good manners, considerate, so they guessed I walked all over him. But Samuel knew how to stand his ground. Me, I couldn't respect a man who didn't do that much. He had plenty to say for himself, I didn't have to do all the talking."

Joshua recalled his most recent matchmaking debacle. "But — that lawyer did plenty of talking, and you didn't . . . appreciate it."

Freida sniffed. *"Samuel*, when he talked, he had something to say! Not all, 'I this, I that.'"

He had derailed her train of thought, and must try to get it back on track. "So Samuel had interesting things to talk about."

Freida relaxed and smiled again. "My Samuel, when he wasn't at work, he had more on his mind than buying and selling. He followed the news of the day, and he would tell me about it, no 'This is men's business.' And my Samuel was an actor."

"A *what*?" A moment later he realized he might have offended her. Actors had never been part of his social circle. Or any circle above his.

"Not a professional. He didn't have the time, and he believed in financial security. Not something an actor has! But he would read plays to me, and play all the parts, even the women, it was a wonder what he could do with his voice. And he knew so much poetry, that man, all by heart, he could recite it for hours."

Joshua had a hard time picturing Samuel, or any man, holding the stage, so to speak, for hours without Freida interrupting. But just the possibility increased his admiration for the departed Mr. Blum.

Freida sat lost in thought, or memory, for a minute or two. Joshua took advantage of the lull to do some thinking of his own. Based on this history, Freida should appreciate a man who knew his literature. But Rushing, the next town over, had a male schoolteacher. Not quite Freida's age, Joshua thought, but not so much younger, either.

Before he could escape to explore the idea, he must perforce listen to Freida read a letter from her niece back in New York. "Such a lovely girl! She envied me when I told her I'd decided to go west, she's a lot like me, too restless to live all our lives in one place. I've told her she should visit." No doubt Freida's next plan was in the making.

Alton Farley, schoolteacher in Rushing, greeted Joshua with hospitality and curiosity. The teacher was a large man with something of a slouch, but well-groomed, with curly brown hair just starting to go gray. His face shifted easily from one expression to another, and there was something of a twinkle in his eye through all of them. If Joshua had been a middle-aged widow lady, he thought he'd be intrigued. Though Freida would be likely to nag about the teacher's posture.

Joshua managed to put off explaining himself until they were drinking Alton's coffee in Alton's small kitchen. Looking around, Joshua tried to imagine both Alton and Freida in the space. It would be a tight fit. Maybe they could find or build a house together in Rushing — or better yet, between Rushing and Cowbird Creek.

Alton chewed thoughtfully on his lower lip. "I can't say I've never thought about female companionship, and having someone to come home to. But I get along all right on my own. Always have. I don't know how I'd shape up as a husband. And your friend sounds like —" His mouth twitched in a crooked smile. " — like something of a force of nature. Not sure but that I'd get bowled over."

Joshua fumbled for ways to persuade him. "She loves books, the way you do. Did I tell you she's setting up a social library? And she and her late husband used to read plays and poetry together." Well, Samuel had read plays, but that was close enough to accurate. "And she would make any house a home. You'd find out just what you've been missing."

Alton tipped his chair back, gazing over Joshua's head, probably running pictures in his mind. Then he thumped back down, planted his hands on the table, and declared, "I'll meet this lady if you're of the party, at least the first time."

Would Freida mind? Joshua thought not. In fact, she might feel more comfortable at first, having Joshua there to ease conversation along. And if the attempt fell flat, he could be the one to put a tactful end to things. "It's a deal."

Since he'd emphasized Freida's homemaker qualities, Joshua arranged for her and Alton's first meeting to be at Freida's home on a Sunday afternoon. That made it easy for her to greet Alton with a warm smile and an enormous slice of apple cake. He made an immediate good impression by consuming it with obvious delight. "So good to see a man enjoy his food!"

Alton smiled broadly. "Enjoy your food, you mean.

This is wonderful."

Freida cut another slice, almost as large, and shoved it at Joshua. "And you, still too thin, here!"

Joshua took the plate and peered at Freida. "Aren't you having any?"

She shrugged. "I'm not so hungry. I can make more when I want it. Whatever's left today, Mr. Farley should take it with him. A big man gets hungry at night, no?"

When they had demolished their slices of cake, Alton took the initiative. "Doctor Gibbs told me of your interest in literature, and your work on the library. Do you have many books of your own here, or wasn't it feasible to bring them west?"

Joshua had left behind most of his books along with the rest of his life in Philadelphia. Reading so little these days besides medical journals and magic trick instructions, he had never thought to notice whatever books Freida might have. Under the circumstances, he was relieved to see her sit up and announce with pride, "Every book I could carry, I left half my wardrobe behind to make room. I could always sew more dresses, not so much write more books! Over here, you can look." She cocked her head coyly. "And I have more in my bedroom, but I'm not showing you in there."

The books not off limits filled a bookcase near her front door where opening the door hid them from view. Alton leaned in to read the titles. "Oh, *She Stoops to Conquer*! I've always enjoyed that." He turned his head to see Freida while still bent toward the bookcase. "Doctor Gibbs tells me you like to read plays. If I can recruit him, how about the three of us read this one?"

Freida took a step back, a rare uncertainty on her face, as Joshua silently cursed his earlier fib. "Oh, I don't know . . . ."

Alton straightened up and turned toward Joshua. "Doctor Gibbs, help me persuade our hostess!" Then, to Freida: "I promise, I'm no critic. Remember how I spend my days. I am sure that compared to my students, you'll be a shining example of the dramatic arts."

Freida shot an accusing stare at Joshua and then planted her hands on her capacious hips. "Well, all right then, just remember, you shouldn't expect too much."

"Bravo!" Alton pulled the book from the bookcase and carried it back to the kitchen table. "Let's see. You'll read the ladies, naturally. Joshua and I will divvy up the gentlemen. It's too bad we have only the one book to share, but we'll make do."

Before they got started, Freida pushed a second slice of cake on both men, and to Joshua's relief took one for herself. Alton opened the book with a flourish and read, "*She Stoops to Conquer; Or, The Mistakes of a Night,* by Oliver Goldsmith. Prologue. Hmmm. The prologue is on the long side, so we can take turns reading a few lines apiece." He cleared his throat and intoned dramatically, "Excuse me, sirs, I pray—I can't yet speak—I'm crying now—and have been all the week. . . . ."

When Freida's turn came, she spoke haltingly at first, but soon gained confidence. Joshua plugged away at the task, knowing himself to be a mediocre performer and not much caring. Alton, he thought, had some promise as an actor.

They made it through the first act before Alton drew out his pocket watch and shook his head. "This has been delightful, but I'm afraid I should be getting back. I have lesson plans to finish."

Freida stood up and bustled about packing up the remains of the cake. Alton, to Joshua's amusement, made no polite pretense of refusing it, but beamed and bowed as she handed him the parcel. "Thank you for this very useful reminder of a lovely afternoon."

Joshua had used the livery stable buggy to fetch Alton and now drove him back again. As they headed out of town, he said as casually as he could, "That went well, I thought."

"Agreed! I would enjoy more gatherings like this, the three of us reading plays or just talking — and eating." Alton grinned and licked his lips.

Joshua had to agree. But a trio wasn't what he'd set out to achieve.

A week later, Joshua picked Alton up again and deposited him at Freida's before noon, but this time declined to join him there. "You'll get to know each other better without me in the way. I'll be in my office, over there." He pointed, then turned the buggy toward the livery stable without staying to be persuaded otherwise.

An hour and a half later, Alton knocked at his door. Joshua had hoped for longer. He invited Alton in, waved him to a chair, and opened his desk drawer where he kept his whiskey and glasses. "Care for a dram before I drive you home?"

"Don't mind if I do. It'll wash down that good-sized dinner Mrs. Blum forced on me."

Joshua grinned. "I'm sure you fought valiantly against it." He poured for both of them, though less for himself, seeing as how he'd need to get Nellie-girl to Rushing and back. Though she could probably make the latter part of the trip just fine, however impaired Joshua might be.

They drank without talking for several minutes. Then Alton drained his glass and said quietly, "I like your friend the widow lady just fine. She's good company, and every bit the homemaker you said she was. And I think she likes me well enough, in a friendly way. Whether she's open to more, I'm not as sure."

Joshua took one more sip and left the rest in the glass, standing up and heading to the door. "It's early days yet. Are you willing to come again? I could join you this time, try to form my own impression."

"Certainly. We have yet to finish the play."

Alton rode his own horse over next time, to spare Joshua the trouble of conveying him. And he brought a few books for Freida to borrow, if she was so inclined. She thanked him extravagantly. "So thoughtful! Maybe, you set up a social library in Rushing, and the two libraries can lend books back and forth."

Alton tapped his chin. "I'm surely embarrassed I haven't already started one. You're a good influence, Mrs. Blum."

They finished the long second act of *She Stoops to Conquer*, all joining in on the song that closed it, and gave themselves and each other a round of applause. Alton broke the slightly awkward silence that followed. "When we finish this play, there are some good possibilities in one of the books I brought. But they have even more parts than this one. Does either of you have a friend who might want to join us, maybe next time I come?"

Joshua stayed stubbornly silent. That was *not* the direction things were supposed to go. But Freida said cheerfully, "Doctor Gibbs, your good friend the pharmacist, might he be willing? A nice voice he's got, and higher than either of yours, he would add variety."

As Alton headed to his horse, bearing a well-wrapped parcel of roast chicken and cream pie, Joshua took a deep breath and faced Freida. "I'll ask Robert. But wouldn't you like to spend some time with just Mr. Farley?"

Freida chuckled and patted his arm. "You and Mr. Farley, that I can see, the two of you fit together like butter on bread. I'm glad you're making more friends, a man needs to spend time with other men, especially working as hard as you both work, you need to unwind. But what you want to happen, him stealing my heart? I don't see it."

Damn it all, Alton had been right.

At least, if they were enlarging their reading circle, he could conceivably suggest adding Clara Brook to share the female roles. Just as the thought crossed his mind, Freida reached into her apron pocket and pulled out a somewhat battered envelope, extracting the letter inside. "My niece that I told you about, my next older sister's girl? I'm still hoping she'll come out to visit me, I haven't seen her in so long! Let me show you her picture." She fetched her overstuffed photo album and leafed through it, muttering to herself. "Cousin Hymie, such a whiner, he complained the whole time . . . Mama, didn't she look nice that day . . . ." She looked up in triumph. "Here she is! Just look, isn't she lovely?"

Dutifully, Joshua looked. The young woman did indeed look quite pretty, if a little awkward at being photographed.

Freida peered at him. "Wouldn't you like to meet a nice girl like this?" Apparently he did not look sufficiently enthusiastic at the prospect, for she wagged a finger at him and added, "Anyone would think you don't want to have a real home, someone to look after you."

Anyone would be at least partly right. But maybe Freida's niece would be less interested in mothering (or smothering) him. Though the likely alternative, a lively young woman eager for entertainment, made him tired to contemplate. Was he getting old before his time? He mentally snapped his suspender buckles so they thumped against his chest. He needed to give Freida's niece a chance — if she indeed came to town and had any interest in giving him one.

Lost in thought, it took Joshua a moment to notice that Freida was holding onto the chair opposite Joshua, panting a bit. Certainly she'd been talking a good deal, but she always did. He couldn't remember her panting like that before. "Mrs. Blum — Freida — have you been especially short of breath lately?"

She waved a dismissive hand at him. "Doctor, I'm an old lady. My joints ache, even when it isn't raining, and I have palpitations, like I've told you, and even my hair, it breaks in the comb, Samuel would cry to see it. But I can still breathe."

Joshua didn't have his bag with him, but he did have his stethoscope in his vest pocket. "Would you let me listen to your lungs? It's been some time."

She heaved a dramatic sigh. "Doctors, always busy, always worrying! All right, if it'll make you happy, but first, finish your pie."

He ate the pie as quickly as he could manage without choking, and then coaxed her to sit down, and to breathe on command. He was glad she was not in a position to see his frown.

It could be any number of ailments. And some of them, he would be helpless to arrest.

Chapter 10

THE NEXT time Freida dropped by during Joshua's office hours, he expected her errand to concern her niece's imminent arrival. He was, he soon learned, half right. Dropping heavily into a chair with an exhalation of relief, she looked up at him, her expression unusually apologetic. "I had so looked forward to you meeting my niece Rachel, such a charming girl and so eager for the adventure of coming west, but her parents, they wouldn't allow it."

She shuffled her feet around in a restless fashion, giving him a glimpse of a definitely swollen ankle. He was pondering how to ask her for a more prolonged look when she said sharply, "You have nothing to say, you didn't care about meeting my niece, just another girl, hardly worth your trouble?"

Discussion of Freida's ankles could wait while he mollified her. "I'm so sorry, I was distracted by — by concern for a patient. I regret that I won't have the opportunity to meet your niece. Did her family consider the journey too hazardous?"

Freida sighed. "Not hazardous like you're thinking, train accidents and robbers and whatnot. No, they didn't want her to . . . to meet, to maybe want to marry . . . . Well, they want her to marry a Jewish boy, natural enough, but she hasn't met one she likes enough, they should let her be an old maid instead?"

Joshua had somehow failed to appreciate the flaw in

Freida's latest matchmaking scheme, but once she pointed it out, he could understand her family's way of thinking. ""If your niece had come here as you hoped, and if I had somehow gained her affections, what did you expect us to do about religious matters?"

She shrugged, looking down at her feet. "I hoped, a gentleman like you, you wouldn't drag Rachel to a church, at least not too often, and you would let her light Sabbath candles and say blessings like a good Jewish girl."

Very likely he would have done. But as this prospect had now gone from unlikely to impossible, he could at least try to soothe Freida's disappointment. "Your niece looked quite young in the photographs. How old is she?"

Her face softened in a fond smile. "Just twenty-one, such a lovely girl she's become." Her mouth drooped. "Just right for a good man like you."

The idea of such youth made him wince. "Just right for the right young man, someone who could join her fresh hopes to his. Your niece deserves a man with an open heart and a bright future. Not an old fellow like me, several years past thirty." A man with too many memories and too many scars.

Freida sniffed. "Not so old, a girl's husband should be older, he can steady her, help her understand life. I find you the right young woman, you'll see, it'll work out just fine!" Then a thought obviously came to her. "Though she doesn't have to be quite that young . . . ."

Joshua had to smile. No disappointment, it seemed, could restrain Freida's matchmaking fervor for long. But at least he could change the subject. "And now, I would like to examine your feet and ankles. I have some concern about their condition."

In the following days, Joshua took pains to give Freida what attention he could spare. Unsure what to do to improve her health, and with early summer making the outdoors a pleasure before the summer humidity set in, he thought to give increased fresh air a try. After a mix of coaxing and demands and something close to nagging, he got her to accept a buggy ride in the country, the canopy pulled partway back to let the breezes through. Naturally he had not the leisure for such a trip unless combined with his duties, but she sat in the buggy while he dropped off medicines and did a couple of quick checkups on convalescing patients.

Freida did indeed seem livelier as Nellie-girl pulled them toward home, with cheeks reassuringly pink and plenty of energy to whisper her updates about or (more rarely) opinions of the people they passed. As they reentered town under the orange and purple clouds of sunset, he slowed Nellie-girl to a walk. Something had attracted a crowd in the street. Joshua gritted his teeth, remembering the last time he had seen the like. "It might be another one of those —" He held back the various curses that came to mind. " — those medicine shows."

Freida wrinkled her brow. "A show for medicine? Is this a man like your friend Robert who goes from town to town selling? But why would all these people want to listen?"

So somehow, the pernicious practice had escaped her notice. At least it gave him the opportunity to warn her. "They're not pharmacists — far from it. They're crooks, pure and simple. They get people's attention with dancing girls and magic tricks and what all, and then tell them that no matter what ails them, all they need is some miraculous elixir made of Lord knows what — snake oil, some call it, and it can even be true, or worse. Sometimes they call it a 'tonic' to make it sound especially wholesome. People can poison themselves and pay handsomely for the privilege." He restrained the impulse to spit.

Joshua could hear the pitchman's voice now, though not his words. He had a good voice for the task, projecting a long ways, and not as obviously whiny or slimy as some Joshua had heard. All the more dangerous, then. Even Clara Brook, he was indignant to note, was standing and listening, though to her credit, she appeared more amused than enthralled.

Joshua could see only part of the wagon's bonnet, but the curly purple letters on it spelled out a name that might be *Professor Kennedy*. He snorted his derision of the honorific and tried to ease Nellie-girl around the crowd, but there was little room for the buggy, and she balked. They would have to wait for the crowd to thin. Freida, meanwhile, leaned forward to inspect the pitchman as he worked the crowd. Joshua followed her gaze. The fellow was a large, well-looking man, dressed up fancy as they always were, but with more taste than some. His whiskers were trimmed, but not waxed, and his hair was curlier than Freida's, its golden color lending the man an incongruous aura of innocence. He had established an easy rapport with the crowd, answering questions, even listing ingredients — though not, Joshua noted, by any recognizable names.

Freida looked at Joshua. "This is a crook?"

"Bound to be. What, you don't think he looks like one?"

"What should I know, crooks come in all shapes and sizes." But she sounded less than convinced by her own words.

Just then, the pitchman turned and looked right at

Joshua — and then at Freida. "Gentlemen and ladies, won't you come a little closer and let these good people through? That horse isn't getting any happier. That's right. Thank you! And now, without further ado, let me introduce my associate Hercules, who will perform stupendous feats . . . ."

Freida murmured something under her breath. Joshua couldn't hear every word, but he did catch the word "considerate." He would not have thought Freida's standards for consideration to be so low.

Nellie-girl was pulling away, none too soon. Joshua clucked at her to step lively. But Freida turned back and watched a while longer as they drove on toward the stable.

A couple of days later, Clara Brook's brother came in during Joshua's office hours and asked Joshua to come out to the farm sometime soon. From what the boy said, the family had been trying to hold Mr. Brook back from working as hard as usual, accepting a few neighborly offers of help with the plowing and planting, but the farmer was growing increasingly obdurate as his health returned. The family wanted to know whether to offer any further resistance. Joshua doubted anything he might say to the man would make much difference, even if the farmer's recovery was incomplete, but he agreed to make the visit.

Mrs. Brook had not, as Joshua had earlier feared, been the next to fall ill. Perhaps she had had a mild case of whooping cough in the past, without even realizing it. Or perhaps it had been Clara Brook tending her father from the beginning, even before Joshua had been summoned. When Joshua rode up to the farm, Mrs. Brook was hanging sheets on the line and humming a little tune. From the wife's demeanor, the husband was probably hale enough to work to his heart's content.

Now that he had come, however, he had better examine his former patient. Mrs. Brook sent her son out to find his father, while Joshua whiled away the time stroking Nellie-girl and listening to birdsong.

Clara Brook emerged from the house with more laundry to be hung. When she saw Joshua, she set the basket at her mother's feet and came to join him. The sight of her reminded Joshua of the last time he had seen her, among the crowd surrounding the wagon of the medicine show. The sour taste of that memory must have shown in his face, for Miss Brook stopped a few paces away and said in her straightforward way, "I hope I am not the occasion for that frown."

Joshua did his best to smile. "By no means. At least, it was not any conduct of yours that troubled me. I was simply remembering that the last time I happened to see you, that detestable medicine show was in town."

His disclaimer was not entirely truthful, and Miss Brook immediately cut to the heart of the question. "I would wager you wonder why you saw me watching."

Without confirming or denying it, he replied, "There is usually the prospect of entertainment, before or after the pitch for whatever noxious substances the show is there to sell."

"Yes, and I was curious what it might be. And also curious to see what claims the man would make for his product, and whether the people listening would believe them."

Joshua found himself curious as well. "What did you discover?"

Miss Brook took on the faraway look of someone remembering. "The claims the man made were less ridiculous than those of the few other pitchmen I've heard.

As for his audience, I had the impression — which you may find reassuring — that the men were chiefly interested in the promise of dancing girls. As for the women, I believe some of them were admiring the pitchman's face and form, more than listening to him."

Joshua had started to unbend, but Miss Brook's final words brought back forcefully the favorable impression the pitchman seemed to have made on Freida Blum. He was more than ready to end the conversation. Looking around, he saw, to his relief, that the boy had returned, Mr. Brook walking with long easy steps at his side. Joshua gave Miss Brook a hasty bow. "If you'll excuse me, I must examine your father."

He followed the farmer and his son toward the house. As he reached the door, he took one quick look back, to see whether his abruptness had caused Miss Brook any offense. But she stood near her mother, pinning up laundry, and he could not see her face.

Chapter 11

WELL, THAT was a first. Freida had come bearing gifts, generally edible, and she had come to him or asked him to come to her when she felt poorly, but never had she asked him for an actual favor. "One of my customers, a widow, so sad, still so young. She's been so eager for her new dresses, hers are worn to rags, but the neighbor who was going to bring her into town, he got too busy, I hate to make her wait. Would it be too much trouble, you could take me there tomorrow morning, maybe you have a patient to see on the way?"

He could in fact go see the old woman with a leg abscess, which shouldn't take too long to drain and bandage. Her son's place was considerably farther away than the young widow's farm, but Joshua could deal with the abscess first, and then swing by to deliver the dresses on the way back to town.

Freida took her knitting along — "It's a lovely day, I'll be all right in the buggy, finally I'll get some work done on this shawl" — and they set out, a well-rested Nellie-girl taking them quickly out of town. Freida hailed almost everyone they passed, calling out questions about their news and well-being even though those greeted had little time to answer before they were left behind. She did not, Joshua noticed, greet Clara Brook, apparently out for a walk on the outskirts of town; Joshua took it upon himself to wave instead, tipping his hat and receiving a grave nod in return.

Soon they were out in farm country and passing corn growing tall and green, with tassels stirring in the breeze, and here and there the vivid red flash of a Summer Tanager, all accompanied by the sweetly varied chirps of meadowlarks. Freida kept up a stream of chatter, with the rumbling buggy wheels as counterpoint. Quite a bit of it concerned the customer in such need of new clothing. Joshua's vague sense that Freida was up to something soon yielded to the glum conviction that the whole errand was orchestrated to bring Joshua and the customer together. Joshua paid as little attention as he could manage, determined to form his own opinion.

The old woman's leg was more swollen, the old bandages more saturated and odorous, than Joshua had hoped. She had probably ignored his instructions to stay off it as much as possible and keep it elevated. He repeated the orders she had already flouted, drained and cleaned the abscess again, bandaged the leg, and left with a dour sense of futility.

Back on the road, the fresh breeze and birdsong helped put him back in a tolerably good humor by the time they pulled up to a neat little farmhouse with flowering bushes lining the front. It did not look familiar. If the husband had taken ill after Joshua came to Cowbird Creek, it was possible they had called the doctor in Rushing for some reason, or that Joshua had been on one of his infrequent trips out of town.

Joshua helped Freida down and then retrieved the large linen-wrapped bundle that must contain the dresses. As they approached the door, Joshua could hear the murmur of a woman's voice, the steady rhythm suggesting she was reading aloud. At Freida's firm knock, the murmur ceased, and shortly afterward, the door opened to reveal a woman holding a little girl in her arms.

The woman was of less than medium height and seemed entirely composed of curves, from the loose curls allowed to escape and hang around her face, to her arm holding the child, to what he could see of her figure, to her gently welcoming smile. He must have seen her before, and probably more than once — in fact, she looked vaguely familiar, more than, say, Clara Brook had at first — but he had never noticed her face and figure. Perhaps he had encountered her only in winter, when she had been muffled in an overcoat.

She looked up at them, her round blue eyes lighting up as she stepped back to allow them inside. "Oh, thank you! I feared it might be days or even weeks before I could be decently dressed again." Then she looked up at Joshua and said, "I'm Mrs. Arden. Thank you so much for bringing Mrs. Blum. Do come in."

Joshua kept to himself his thought that the gray-blue dress she wore, from what he could see of it, was decent and even flattering. He followed her directions and laid the bundle of dresses on what appeared to be a sewing table, given the sections of gingham fabric that lay on it already. Clothes for the child, most likely.

All this time the little girl was studying him with a surprising solemnity. Freida moved closer to him and said in what she might have considered a whisper, "Poor child, her father and little brother died of a fever last year." The little girl continued inspecting him and then, apparently satisfied, put out her hand. Joshua took it and bowed over it, asking, "Might I know your name, mistress?"

The child giggled, then turned shy again and hid her face in her mother's shoulder. The mother shook her pretty head and said, "This is Hope. Hope, say good morning to the lady and gentleman."

The little girl turned back and murmured, "'Lo, Missus Lady. 'Lo, Mr. Gentleman."

Joshua bit his lip so as not to reveal his amusement. Freida bustled forward, holding out her arms. "Such a darling! May I hold her? You can look at the dresses, they're nothing much, I hope you like them."

Mrs. Arden had a whispered exchange with Hope and then transferred the child to Freida's greedy grasp. Hope nestled against Freida's bosom, appearing pleased with the comfort of it. Meanwhile, Mrs. Arden turned her attention to the linen bundle, untying the twine around it, opening it, holding up the dresses one by one. "Oh, how lovely! Oh, they're just what I needed!"

When all the dresses had been displayed and admired, Mrs. Arden disappeared for a moment and returned with a small leather bag, which she offered to Freida. "Here's what we agreed, and really not enough for all the work you put in."

Freida gave the little girl one more snuggle, sighed, and handed her back to her mother, taking the bag of coins at the same time. "My pleasure, so gratifying to dress such a pretty woman, still so young, you should look your best."

Mrs. Arden glanced at the mahogany grandfather clock standing in the corner. "It's almost dinnertime. Will you stay and eat with us?"

Joshua looked to Freida for clues. She put up her hands and waved them a little. "So kind of you, such a nice gesture, but I really should be getting back, so much work waiting for me. But maybe the doctor could come back another time, you young people should get to know each other."

Mrs. Arden blinked at Freida's boldness, but said prettily, "We would be honored, indeed, if you could join us whenever your work allows you. Would next Tuesday be too soon?"

Joshua was well aware that Freida had managed the entire encounter. But he was not inclined to balk this time. "I am sure I could make it, if I wouldn't be intruding."

Mother and daughter beamed at him with almost identical expressions. "We will be so looking forward to it."

Freida followed Joshua out of the house after a bewildering sequence of repeated farewells. Her praise of Mrs. Arden and Hope began flowing before they even reached the buggy, and continued half the way back to town. "Such a sweet child, she takes after her mama. A girl needs a father. Such a father you would make! And Mrs. Arden — did I tell you her, what do you call it, her Christian name is Dorothy, Dolly for short — such a good homemaker, she really didn't need me to sew for her, she sews so well, but the little girl keeps her busy, you know how children go through clothes."

Joshua could vaguely recall his mother's weary resignation concerning how often he outgrew his shirts and trousers, and her ire if he tore or otherwise spoiled them while they still fit. It was hard to imagine Hope tearing her dresses.

That evening, Joshua studied himself in the small mirror hanging near his bed. His hair could use a trim. He would make time before Tuesday for a visit to the barber. Hopefully it had been long enough since their last set-to that he could trust the man to wield a razor near his throat.

Mrs. Arden opened the door dressed in one of her new dresses. Hope, by her side holding her hand, wore a gingham dress that might have been the unfinished project

Joshua had seen on the sewing table during his previous visit.

The aroma that wafted from the interior made his mouth water. Could it be? With all the bountiful meals he had enjoyed with Freida, she had never served him his favorite pork chops. He had a vague notion that Jews might not eat pork.

With the pork chops and mashed potatoes and peach preserves — he suppressed the urge to put the preserves on the pork chops, a childhood vice he had not entirely outgrown — he was almost too full to move when Hope invited him on a tour of the house. But he hauled himself upright and let her take his hand and tug him around. It was a good-sized house, well built and appointed. The late Mr. Arden, whatever his origins, had left his widow well provided for as to habitation, at least. There was a pleasant sitting room with fireplace and easy chairs, and one small bookcase. The kitchen would have been snug for a woman like Freida, but was spacious enough for his petite hostess.

Hope next led him up the stairs to a cozy room with a large bed in it, looking out into a large silver maple tree. Both the room and the size of the bed came as something of a surprise. He heard first footsteps and then Mrs. Arden's soft voice behind him. "Mr. Arden had modern ideas. He thought married couples should . . . have their privacy. He built this room and made the bed for all our children to share." She caught her breath in what might have been a sob.

Hope started down the hall as if intending to show him another room, but Mrs. Arden intervened. "That's enough, Hope. Take our guest back downstairs to the sitting room so he can let his food settle." Hope pouted briefly, but obeyed. Joshua surmised that the forbidden portion of the tour would have included the widow's own bedchamber. A vision came to him, unbidden, of a bed with a carved headboard painted white, with pastel comforter and fluffy pillows, and — He jerked his imagination back into line and focused on the little girl descending the stairs ahead of him, looking back at him frequently as if to ensure he was still there.

When Mrs. Arden deemed Joshua had had time to digest his dinner, she let Hope take him out to the sunny yard he had seen from the child's bedroom. The maple tree had a swing suspended from a sturdy, low branch; Hope hopped on the swing and begged him to push her. Joshua obliged, smiling to see her struggle with the (to her) complex and mysterious task of pumping herself higher.

Joshua looked at his watch, sighed, and let the swing slow to a stop. "I've got to be going, little Hopeful." The nickname surprised Joshua as well as the child. She ducked her head in a return of her earlier shyness, but then smiled at him, hopping down from the swing and dipping into a creditable curtsy. As she bobbed back up, she said in apparent imitation of her mother, "*Do* come again."

Mrs. Arden, watching from the doorway, added softly, "Yes, please do."

"Thank you kindly, ma'am." He bowed first to Mrs. Arden, then to Hope. "I'd be most happy to."

He found himself smiling and humming "O, Susannah" as he rode Nellie-girl back to town.

Joshua hesitated to encourage Freida by reporting how much he had enjoyed his visit with Dolly and Hope, but upon reflection decided he owed it to her. She crowed over him as much as he had anticipated. "I knew it, such a lovely woman, such a sweet child, just what you need in your life, and dear Dolly, she needs a strong, reliable man like you . . . ."

Joshua was not sure he merited either adjective. There was a side of him Freida knew nothing about, or so he hoped. But he let her continue spinning out his probable future, which evoked a longing he had not thought himself to have within him.

Except for that dinner at Mamie's, it had been a long time since he had called on a lady — or rather, given just how long, a girl — in other than a professional capacity. And times had changed, though he was not sure in what way or direction. He consulted Robert about what would be proper. "Should I bring her flowers next time?"

Robert, amused at his ignorance, informed him that his question was far too general. "You'd have to make sure you picked the right flowers. There are I don't know how many books telling ladies just what to read into the choice of this flower or that."

Joshua gulped. "Why so many books? Don't they all say the same thing?"

"Not all of 'em."

Joshua blew out a long breath and shook his head. "Never mind flowers, then."

But as he rode to Mrs. Arden's on a fine summer day, wildflowers all around him, he decided to take the chance. He pulled Nellie-girl to a halt, jumped down, and gathered as varied a bouquet as he could manage. Hopefully, if they conveyed any message beyond scent and beauty, it would be varied and confusing enough not to land him in any irretrievable difficulties. He managed to mount again, ride the rest of the way, and dismount without dropping any of the impromptu bouquet in his left hand.

He was not sure whether to be disappointed or relieved when Hope ran out to meet him and exclaimed, "Are those for me?"

Mrs. Arden, joining her daughter, scolded her gently. "Don't be forward, Hope."

Joshua extracted a purple coneflower from the bouquet and handed it to Hope. Gathering his courage, he held out the remainder to her mother. "I saw these on the way and thought you might like them." That explanation might make it less likely that she would read any deep meaning into the gift.

Her smile added warmth to the sunshine. "How kind of you. Let me put these in water, and then we can sit on the porch swing for a while until the roast is ready. Hope, you can finish setting the table, and then work on your sampler until I call you."

The little girl hustled indoors. Mrs. Arden settled lightly on the porch swing and looked up at him expectantly. Feeling three kinds of fool, he studied the portion of swing left to him and sat in the middle of it, leaving about a foot of space between them.

She did her best to put him at ease, though her innocent questions did not always have that effect. How he had become a doctor, for example: he had to tug the truth well out of shape, dredging up memories of the doctor who had tended him as a child. This sunny front porch, the pretty woman at his side, did not bear soiling with the filth and blood and anguish of a wartime medical tent, the dogged courage and endurance of the doctors who had humbled and then inspired him. And his family back in Pennsylvania . . . He couldn't talk about the two grandparents who had died a year before he had made it home. But he could at least interest and amuse her somewhat with talk of his father, who after a lifetime buried in books had decided to write one and was apparently finding it a daunting task. As for his mother, he managed to say something superficial about what a fine woman she was. He could not talk about her at any length without showing how much he missed her.

When Mrs. Arden hopped down from the swing and announced that dinner must be ready, he followed her inside with relief.

Dinner helped to relax him. The pot roast was tender, the green beans a deep green in color and just the right side of crisp. And the pie — "Is that blackberry pie?"

"Yes indeed! We have plenty of blackberry bushes in that field yonder." She pointed northwest. "Hope helps me pick them, don't you, Hope?"

Hope nodded vigorously while chewing her first bite of pie.

Joshua bent down to speak to her more easily. "You know, I used to pick blackberries with my mama and sisters, when I was not much older than you. They had me pick the berries lower down on the bushes."

Hope beamed at him. "That's what Mama and I do!" She bounced in her chair, drawing a rebuke. ("Sit like a lady, now.") Hope stopped bouncing, changing the subject with a question. "Can we go pick blackberries now? With Mister Doctor?"

Joshua was seized by a rare impulse toward silliness. He turned to Mrs. Arden and clasped his hands dramatically. "Pleeez, can we?"

Hope let out a high-pitched peal of laughter. Mrs. Arden followed suit in a tuneful soprano. "All right, you two. Hope, go get your apron. Doctor Gibbs, do you have anything with you to protect your clothes?"

He had had no reason to bring his bag, with the smock tucked away in it, so often covered in much less savory substances than berry juice. The thought punctured his giddy mood, but he tried to hide the fact. "Not with me, I'm afraid." He reached for silliness again. "But I could borrow one of your aprons. No doubt Hope would find me most fetching in it."

Hope giggled. Mrs. Arden shook her head, wavy locks bouncing. "The pair of you! I have something more suitable, I believe. An old shirt of my husband's. You could wear it back to front, if you don't mind being a bit untidy."

"That'll do just fine, ma'am." He could hardly withdraw from the plan at this point, not without disappointing the child and being rude to her mother.

The sunshine and the smell of blackberries, together with Hope's delight in the project, helped Joshua focus on his mission. He challenged Hope to a berry-picking contest, making a point of losing. They collected enough fruit for several future pies before Mrs. Arden called a halt and led them back into the house.

She relieved Joshua of his bucket, put it in the kitchen, and held out her hands for his improvised smock. As she took it, he saw, and pretended not to see, a shadow of sadness pass over her face. The memory of her husband clearly still carried some pain.

Dolly sent the child off to wash her hands. When Hope returned, Joshua squatted down and reached out his own hand, heedless of the traces of water on Hope's. "Shall we shake hands goodbye?"

Solemn now, the child put her hand in his. "Goodbye." She paused, her expressive little face warning him before she said, "I wish you weren't going."

Joshua swallowed the lump in his throat. "I've had a lovely time."

Mrs. Arden put a hand on her daughter's shoulder. "As have we."

When he got back, Robert saw him ride in and came

by for a report. Joshua confessed having collected flowers after all.

"What kind?"

"Coneflowers in three colors — I gave a purple one to the little girl. And black-eyed Susans."

Robert's mouth twitched in amusement. "I had a feeling you'd do something like that. I went by Mrs. Blum's social library and subscribed, just so I could look for a book on flower language. Let's see what you were saying, shall we?" He pulled out a book bound in dark red leather embossed with vines and leaves. "Coneflowers, let's see . . . Well, you lucked out there. They mean 'strength' or 'health' — very appropriate for a doctor. And black-eyed Susans . . . ." He leafed through, stopped, and started to laugh. "Well, my boy, those mean 'encouragement.' If she's set her cap for you, you told her she's welcome to do so."

Joshua put a hand to his forehead. "Oh, brother."

But he didn't necessarily regret it.

Chapter 12

JOSHUA SAT in his office after what he hoped would be today's last patient. He had not slept well the night before, waking several times with the fragments of disturbing dreams in his head, and he was ready for a lazy evening in front of the fire with Major at his side and a glass of whiskey in his hand.

He groaned out loud when someone knocked on the door, but then relaxed and sighed in relief to see Dolly and Hope. Or was their visit professional after all? He hurried to the door, opened it, and looked at mother and daughter for any sign of illness. But both were rosy-cheeked, and as they stepped inside, neither of them winced or stumbled or otherwise looked pained.

They did, however, seem stirred up about something. Hope was especially wriggly, and Dolly too distracted to notice and reprove her. He was trying to phrase a question when Hope answered it. "We're going on a trip! On a *train!*"

"Indeed?" Joshua turned to Dolly for confirmation and enlightenment.

Dolly nodded, her face going solemn. "When my husband died, he was buried here, near us. But he was his parents' only son, and they've been wishing they could visit his grave regularly. They've offered to pay our fare to bring his body home. They also said something about investments in his name. They want me to talk to a banker about it,

though I'm sure I won't be able to make head or tail of it."
She fluttered her eyelashes as if to emphasize her inability
to comprehend financial matters. "Of course, I couldn't
leave Hope for so long, and this way she can spend time
with both sets of grandparents."

Joshua was somewhat startled to realize that he would
miss the pair of them. He took refuge in practicalities. "Do
you have anyone to assist you with . . . the details of
disinterring your husband?"

She looked up at him with a tremulous attempt at a
smile. "Oh, yes. The undertaker is handling it. And if the —
" She swallowed and paused before going on. "If the coffin
isn't in the condition necessary for it to go on the train, Mr.
Arden's parents sent money to have it repaired or a new one
made." She looked down at Hope and sighed, then peeked
back up at him. "Such a long way to go! I must admit I quail
at the thought of the journey."

It was too bad her in-laws had sent no one to assist her.
It occurred to him that he could volunteer to go with her.
But he could hardly leave his practice. And traveling with
him, an unmarried man not related to her, might even
compromise her reputation. Besides, Dolly was probably
level-headed enough to cope with the most likely difficulties,
and certainly appealing enough to attract chivalrous
assistance.

He contented himself with saying, "I hope you will
have an easy journey, and that your time in — where is it
you are going?"

"Baltimore."

"I wish you a fruitful stay in Baltimore. When will you
be leaving?"

Hope, apparently feeling left out, stepped in front of
her mother and answered, "Not for a *long* time. Next week."

Joshua fought back a laugh. "I'm sure the time will pass swiftly, with all the preparations you and your mother will be making. You'll help her, won't you?"

Hope stood up at her tiny tallest. "I will!"

Dolly patted Hope's head and said prettily, "I do hope you won't mind if I write to you while we're away. It would make us feel closer to home."

The notion took Joshua somewhat by surprise, but he gave a small bow and replied, "I would be honored to receive letters from you, and undertake to answer them, though I cannot promise to meet any high standards of composition or penmanship."

Dolly wagged a playful finger. "Silly man! I'm sure they'll be lovely. Now we'd better be going. As you mentioned, we have a great deal to do."

"Safe travels, Mrs. Arden, Miss Hope."

He watched as they left, and stood in the doorway to watch a little longer as they trotted down the street. Then he grabbed his hat, locked up, and headed for Major and home.

* * * * *

Joshua had managed to persuade Alton to come to town for a few beers. Their talk covered everything from Nebraska politics (inspiring, if only of cynicism), to local squabbles (including Joshua's ongoing battle with the barber, lately moving toward open warfare), to Alton's students (who actually included a few likely lads and lasses). And of course, they came around to their mutual friend Freida.

"I've tried a shopkeeper, a telegraph operator, a lawyer, and, Lord knows why, a schoolteacher." Joshua waited for Alton's snort at that last and then went on. "Should I just give up? Who haven't I thought of?"

Alton raised an eyebrow. "How about most of the men in these parts?"

Joshua puzzled over that hint and finally got it. "Farmers?"

"Yes, farmers!" Alton wet his whistle and expounded on his theme. "They need wives more than most men, to help with the animals and keep things running, keep the hands fed, raise youngsters. Freida can't, I assume, produce any more children, but she could do the rest of it and do it well. Just her cooking should get many a widowed farmer fellow interested."

Well, maybe if he wasn't too fond of pork chops, or bacon. Or maybe she'd be flexible about cooking such.

The next afternoon, Joshua made a point of helping Freida with her errands, carrying her purchases, listening attentively to her gossip and her inevitable concern about his health, weight, and marital status. Once he escorted her home, he could broach the question of whether she could see herself as a farmer's wife. In the meantime, to the extent he could spare attention for it, he ran through his patients, comparing the widowers and assessing their suitability. He was not confident of his ability to rate male attractions, but there were several with no obviously repulsive aspects.

He did allow himself a breather when they reached the dry goods store, where the objectionable proprietor was apparently absent and Freida could work with the assistant to examine every bolt of cloth in painstaking detail. Leaning against the hitching post outside, wondering if he had time enough to fill and smoke his pipe, he failed to notice Clara Brook approaching until she spoke. "Mrs. Blum doesn't look quite well. Are you concerned about her?"

He jerked his head around to face her, eyebrows

shooting up. The barber with his claims to medical know-how was a known nuisance, but Joshua had hardly expected such second-guessing from this quarter. He had of course had his concerns, and had been watching Freida for any significant deterioration in her health. But how would this woman, hardly an intimate of Freida, think she knew enough to comment?

Joshua froze. There was one way. And it fit with everything he had observed about her.

Miss Brook appeared to have taken his silence as a sign he was offended. She stood stiffly, her chin up, her face a little flushed. She started to say what would probably be something sardonic, but he interrupted. "Were you a nurse?"

She looked at him a little warily. "I was."

He had gone for a soldier at the age of twenty, and Miss Brook was surely several years younger than he. "You must have been very young."

Her mouth quirked in a half-smile. "Younger than they thought me, at least. Being tall helped."

She did not seem inclined to say much more. And Joshua could hear the floor of the store creak under Freida's heavy tread as she made her way outside. He muttered a quick but sincere "Thank you" as he turned to offer Freida his arm.

She looked at Miss Brook's retreating figure and sniffed. "That one, what did she want?"

Joshua was not fond of fibs, but he could hardly tell the truth. "Just a friendly greeting."

Freida rolled her eyes. "Friendly! You must be special." Then her manner softened and she squeezed her hand on his arm. "But of course, so special a man, everyone knows it."

When they had reached Freida's house and she had

put away her purchases, Joshua steeled himself to insist on examining her. Her heartbeat was not as he would want to hear it, and her calves and ankles were definitely swollen.

He would start with the less intrusive questions. "Are you still having palpitations?"

She smiled a little. "At my age, they should stop?"

"Have they gotten any worse?"

She shrugged. "I have time to count how many times?"

Always a question back at him instead of an answer. "And how has your appetite been lately?"

She shrugged again. "I've been busy, I can't always take the time to cook for just one."

An answer in form, finally, but an evasive answer that suggested the true one.

"Have you felt dizzy at all?"

She hesitated. "As much weight as I carry, I wobble a little and it makes me feel dizzy, maybe."

"When you go to bed, when you lie flat, do you have any trouble breathing?"

Another hesitation. "Maybe a little, now and then. I don't sleep so well, I worry about things, I don't know about the breathing part."

Now he must venture into really treacherous territory. "Mrs. Blum, I know this is a personal question, but have you been needing more trips to the necessary lately? Or using the chamber pot more at night?"

She looked away from him. Was that embarrassment because of his intrusive inquiry, or because she knew he had a reason for asking and could guess roughly what it meant?

"Mrs. Blum — Freida — please tell me."

She tossed her head. "All right, so I have to go more than when I was a young slip of a thing!"

It all added up. Her heart was weakening.

Which meant the last thing she should do was take on

the long hours of hard work that were the lot of a farmer's wife.

"So tell me, doctor, what is it you're thinking?"

Many doctors found ways not to answer such questions. He was generally more inclined to tell patients what he thought. But it was rarely easy, and certainly not now.

"I believe, based on my examination and your symptoms, that you're suffering from dropsy. Your heart is not doing its job as well as it should, and that causes fluid to back up in your lungs and elsewhere."

He saw her take that in, absorbing its seriousness, and then don a mask of unconcern. "So now that you think I have this dropsy, such a name, like a game for children, 'Dropsy, whoops!' — what should I do any different?"

"I'll want you to drink some tea I'll bring you. It'll help you get rid of some of the fluid —"

She frowned. "So I should trot back and forth to the necessary even more often?"

"You can drink it in the morning, not at night, so at least you won't have your sleep disturbed any further. And I have some medicines that may help your heart more directly." Foxglove, for one. He would consider mercury as well. Some doctors would try bleeding, but as so often, he was dubious about it doing any good.

Freida hoisted herself out of her chair. "All right, Doctor. I'll drink your tea, I'll even take your medicines. But now I get you something to eat, you should put some meat on your bones."

* * * * *

"You've got a letter."

Joshua frowned. Dolly must still be on her way to

Baltimore. It could be from his mother, although she had written only the week before. Was something wrong at home?

But the handwriting on the envelope was unfamiliar. He stashed the letter and put it out of mind until that evening, when he finally made it back to his rooms. Opening the envelope with his pocket knife, he held the letter close to the oil lamp and tried to decipher the irregular scrawl.

His correspondent proved to be Calvin Grey, one of the childhood friends with whom he had enlisted. Joshua had lost track of him not six months afterward when the man was wounded. Joshua had not been present, and only knew the wound was serious and likely to be mortal. But somehow Calvin had survived, and must have used their common acquaintances to track Joshua down. He appeared desirous of reviving their connection, and to do it by means of filling Joshua in on most everything that had happened to him after taking that musket ball to the chest.

The doctor assigned to tend me considered me a lost cause, and went on to patch up those who'd been wounded in more dispensable places, such as could be sawn off and thrown away. But there was an angel of a nurse that watched over me like a very guardian angel, fetching another doctor from somewheres and pushing him to try whatever he could. She fended off the chaplain that kept wanting to get me ready for dying and write down my last words. And then she kept me in clean bandages, and washed me head to foot when I couldn't move, making nothing of it; and she read the letters that came for me, and wrote my answers; and even laughed at my jokes, or told me more when I was inclined to brood over my chances or over all those good men who'd gone where I expected to go, if not necessarily the same direction. And on that score, she fetched me a Bible when I wanted it, and read it to me when I couldn't, and told me she was sure our heavenly father would be welcoming, and that the blood I'd shed would join with our Savior's in washing away my multitude of sins.

Joshua found the paper shaking in his hand and had to lay it down. Too many memories were rushing in upon him. And even the bold courage of his fellow soldiers, and the fortitude of those left suffering long after the heat of battle, could not make those memories welcome.

As for nurses, they were more often found in hospitals of some kind, rather than at the front lines. He had had little experience with them. How many of them would merit such gratitude and praise? Many, no doubt, but this one above most.

He leaned over the table to read the rest.

I've thought of angels different since that time. As a boy, I always pictured them golden-haired and blue-eyed, and lovely beyond mortal ken. But now, I reckon they're just as likely to be plainer-looking, with straight hair and long limbs, and with eyes as green as the spring prairie.

Joshua shoved his chair back from the table.

Could it be? Had the nurse beyond compare, the nurse who had saved his friend, been the same woman who had made bold to ask him about Freida's health, and whom Freida regarded with so little favor?

He needed to see Miss Brook again, to study her with new eyes. He would have liked to ask her whether she remembered a patient with a chest wound, whose life had been despaired of, and who had yet survived. But he remembered her face as she acknowledged having been a nurse. Her memories might be as painful as his own, even if she had helped more men in that field of slaughter than ever he had done.

* * * * *

The foursome were almost done reading *The School for Scandal*. They could have pushed on to finish today, but none of them was feeling especially ambitious. Next time would do. Instead, they relaxed and devoured the crullers Freida had recently learned how to make. ("I liff out vest, I chould learn how to make somethink fried.")

They passed around the news of the day: the sheriff's plan to challenge the mayor in the next election; the growth of Alton's social library, flourishing somewhat more than the one Freida and the minister were trying to nurture. Robert contributed a bit of gossip. "Saw that tall woman from Brook's farm the other day, sending a telegram. She and Thaddeus seemed to have a lot to talk about."

Joshua tried to imagine the intense Clara Brook finding subjects of conversation with the awkward telegraph operator. He supposed they had a few things in common, besides simply being thin. Neither was much for telling jokes, for example. Although — if his friend had been writing about Miss Brook, and not some other green-eyed Army nurse, she had once been able not only to laugh at the rough humor of soldiers, but to join in.

Robert went on, "She's an odd woman. I wouldn't normally have thought to say Thaddeus was a braver man than I, but if he's sparking that one, I have to tip my hat to him."

Freida nodded agreement. "He could do better."

Joshua coughed. "I seem to remember a time you didn't add him up quite so kindly."

Alton looked curious; Freida made a pushing-away gesture. "So I didn't see him as the answer to an old woman's prayers, I should wish him with that crosspatch?"

"Mrs. Blum! That seems quite unfair. We none of us know her that well, well enough to condemn her character. And I can't say I've ever seen her be cross with anyone."

Freida and Alton joined in staring at him, while Robert sat back and smirked. Joshua sputtered, "She might be quite pleasant, when you get to know her!"

He did not care to say, in the face of this variable scrutiny, that he had found her — most of the time — an enjoyable companion. And he was certainly not ready to share his speculations about what she might have been like before the prolonged calvary of war.

Freida broke the awkward silence that followed, getting up and fetching the teapot. "Here, we could all use some more tea. And I have three crullers left, just enough for the three of you, they shouldn't go to waste."

* * * * *

Grasshoppers were hardly unknown in Nebraska, either before or since it achieved statehood, but rumor suggested that some counties to the south, or west, or both had been invaded by hordes far greater and more destructive than before. Travelers passing through town most often came with nothing more than stories; and some of the storytellers so obviously relished describing calamity that the truth of their tales could reasonably be questioned. Even the occasional newspapers brought in by a salesman or lawyer or coach failed to settle the question, as their accounts varied to a bewildering extent.

Joshua said as much to Robert over supper one evening. "Where one paper suggests that practically the whole state has been eaten down to the ground, another scolds rival papers it claims are grossly exaggerating. Some say false doomsday claims are deterring settlers, others say the crisis is being downplayed to lure settlers hither. What should we expect the next month, or the next wind, to bring?"

Robert peered over his mug of beer, studying Joshua with unsettling shrewdness. "Your worry does you credit, as showing your good nature and concern for your fellow man. Or is there some more particular cause?"

Joshua took a gulp of his own brew. "Need I have some other cause, when this plague could devastate so many of my patients and neighbors? When, if some of the reports prove true, we might see the town reduced painfully in size, as farmers abandon their holdings and flee to the East?"

If the thought of one particular family leaving town, of Clara Brook's tall figure climbing aboard a wagon and vanishing beyond the horizon, gave him a peculiar twinge, he was hardly obliged to say so.

Chapter 13

WHEN THE owner of the general store held out a letter addressed to Joshua in a dainty feminine hand, the man's expression bordered on a smirk. Joshua felt a flare of temper, but managed to take the letter with a bland word of thanks and tuck it away.

He waited until he got home that evening, somewhat the worse for a long day, and then until after he had scraped up some supper before finally opening the letter.

Dear Doctor Gibbs,

I apologize for not having written sooner to assure you of our safe arrival. We had few problems on our journey, and those few made easier by the kind assistance of a gentleman traveling in the same carriage.

It was good she had found someone to help her cope with the challenges of the journey. Of course it was.

The visit began with the sad business of conveying to the bereaved parents the body of their son, followed the next day with his burial in the cemetery where previous generations of his family already rested. But from that point, my hosts have endeavored to make my visit agreeable and entertaining. They make much of Hope and are in a fair way to spoil her. But I suppose grandparents always do!

Joshua had a sudden vision of his father allowing a little girl Hope's age into his library, even letting her touch the books. It gave him an unfamiliar ache in his chest.

I have had one very welcome surprise. Evidently Mr. Arden

had investments of which I knew nothing, and which his father managed for him. They waited to tell me until the process of transferring the assets into my name had been completed. It is not a great sum, but I will have some little income from it, which will make my and Hope's lives easier, and serve as something like a dowry should I ever think of marrying again.

That must have come as a relief. It was surely hard enough to be a woman alone, raising a child, without the added stresses of straitened means.

Life in the city provides much distraction, but I still find myself missing the familiarity of home. Please write and tell me all the news.

Surely one of her female friends would be a better source of gossip. Perhaps he should ask Freida to write to her.

Hope sends greetings, and wishes me to tell you that she looks forward to picking blackberries with you again. I have explained that the season for blackberries will be over before we return, and that it will be some months before they are ripe again. She does not want to believe me.

Joshua chuckled, imagining Hope's little face screwed tight in a stubborn expression.

I must end this letter, as we are going to tea at my sister-in-law's house.

Yours with esteem,

And the signature, so full of curlicues he could barely read it, must be her full name.

He would write back. After all. she had asked him to write, and it would be unfriendly to ignore the request. He could always suggest that Freida do so as well.

It took Joshua longer than it should have to start a letter to Dolly, and then to finish and send it. He did not write many letters, except to order books or equipment, or too rarely, respond to his mother's correspondence; nor did he have any particularly interesting news to include. When he finally completed the task, he half expected Dolly to take as long to send any reply. But when the assistant at the general store waved him down, it could not have been more than two weeks after his letter would have arrived in Baltimore.

He had no real need to go to his office just now, but it was closer than home. He tried to look busy as he made his way inside. Once safe from any observing eyes, he sat down and opened the letter.

Dear Doctor Gibbs,

Thank you so much for your very informative, newsy letter . . . . But I mustn't tease you. Men never write such long letters as ladies, do they?

Joshua raised an eyebrow. He could easily imagine Alton, for example, writing a long, interesting letter if he had occasion to do so. And his father, if he made time to write a letter at all, would probably produce something the length of a medical journal.

We have been in something of a social whirl lately, especially compared to life at home. My late husband's parents — it no longer feels quite right to call them my in-laws — have had friends to tea or to dine several times, and we have gone out to two art exhibitions and to a reception at the mayor's mansion. I have already written to tell Freida how grateful I am for the dresses she made me, which have been much admired at the more casual occasions, and my hosts have been so kind as to provide me with a suitable gown for formal wear.

Joshua winced, imagining Freida's reaction to being told that her creations were suitable only for casual use. But Dolly was no doubt being realistic, given the different society in which it appeared she was moving during her visit.

The meals I am served, with my hosts and on our various excursions, have been so bountiful as to threaten to make my various dresses and gowns grow tight. We have had pheasant, quail, turtle soup, and other such fare, along with more cakes and crudities than I can describe.

Joshua found himself yawning. No doubt such details would hold his attention better if Dolly was telling them in person, with her smiles and bright eyes to enliven them.

I had not realized the extent to which my daily responsibilities have weighed upon me and dampened my buoyant nature, until this respite, where so little is demanded of me. I hope I will return home refreshed and strengthened to resume the little burdens of life as a widow with a child.

It must, indeed, be hard for her. At least her husband's financial legacy would relieve some of her day-to-day anxiety.

Hope has been well, except for a time or two when the richer diet has troubled her little tummy. She has been slow to learn from such experiences, and pouts when I restrain her from overeating.

Joshua smiled, picturing Hope's indignant complaints. Perhaps, when Dolly and Hope returned, Dolly would allow him to buy Hope some sort of treat from the candy store. He should probably ask when they were likely to be back in town. Dolly might even have expected him to inquire earlier.

I sometimes have difficulty remembering that the luxury and diversion of this visit is not my usual lot, and that I will be returning to a very different mode of life.

Dolly must feel something like Cinderella at the ball. Would she meet a prince in Baltimore? How would she view a plain country doctor when the clock struck midnight and the magic was dispelled?

Joshua took greater pains, this time, to collect local news for his reply to Dolly. He sought Freida's aid, which pleased her not a little. "So kind, to send Dolly news from home, make sure she doesn't forget us!"

Joshua's letter recounted the mayor's latest speech, a fire in the blacksmith's yard (soon extinguished), Major's feud with one of the cats that roamed the town, the advance of autumn, and even which eminent town ladies had lately engaged Freida to make dresses. He thought of mentioning the continued reports of severe grasshopper damage in the western counties; but such news was probably available in Philadelphia, and moreover, would hardly fulfill her request for reminders of home.

He read the letter over with something like distaste before sealing it and dropping it at the general store, doing his best to conceal embarrassment behind a haughty air that the young woman behind the counter appeared to find humorous.

He expected, as his just reward for attending to Dolly's reproach, that she would write at least as promptly as last time. But three weeks passed, and then four, and he heard nothing. Perhaps Cinderella had found her prince.

Chapter 14

HEADING BACK to his office after a hurried dinner at the nearest saloon, Joshua was turning over in his mind the uncertain diagnosis and prospects of a patient when footsteps by his side drew his attention. Glad of the distraction, he looked over to see Clara Brook matching his stride. Seeing that she had drawn his attention, she smiled in a manner somewhere between cordial and friendly. "Good afternoon, Doctor. Your knitted brow suggested some puzzle to be solved, but I both hope and expect you will solve it in due course."

Taken aback and yet comforted by Miss Brook's observation, he smiled and said, "You are precisely correct. I have a patient whose symptoms puzzle me."

Miss Brook looked at him with attentive expectation, so he went on. "A young man has lately begun having fits, falling into a faint or thrashing his limbs about, biting his tongue. It resembles an epilepsy, but he has suffered no head trauma, and no one in his family is similarly afflicted. In a young woman, I might suspect hysteria."

Miss Brook's gaze was intent enough to make him slightly uncomfortable. "Do you believe, then, that hysteria is exclusively confined to the female of the species?"

Looking at her, hearing her firm footsteps, and especially remembering her history, he did not dare to suggest that the female constitution might be intrinsically more frail, more easily disturbed by emotion, than his own. Indeed, his not infrequent nighttime ordeals suggested otherwise. "I believe I should, after all, consider that diagnosis. I will inquire whether anything particularly disturbing has lately occurred in the young man's life."

They strode on in pleasant companionship until they reached his office. He could think of no appropriate words of parting, so he simply tipped his hat and went on inside.

* * * * *

Yellow Spring, a few miles north of Cowbird Creek, had no doctor. When folk there needed doctoring, their kin were likely to come fetch Joshua. There was a creek to cross in between; usually that was no problem, as Nellie-girl was more willing than many horses to cross moving water, but she had gone lame the day before.

Fortunately, the young man had shown up at Joshua's door wearing thigh-high rubber boots and carrying an extra pair, big enough to fit almost any man — though therefore too big for steady footing. Joshua popped next door to ask Robert to rent the buggy and give him and the young man a ride to the creek. Of course, there might or might not be a similar arrangement on the other side; and when he finally made it home, he would likely have a long walk ahead of him.

He wrapped his bag in a tarpaulin, secured with rope, for at least a little protection should he drop it in the creek. It was a near thing. He did drop it once, but caught it just as it reached the surface of the water.

Two sisters greeted them, eyes red and cheeks wet. Joshua followed one of the girls into the somewhat ramshackle house, to where the mother was lying on a large and sagging bed, propped up on pillows, flushed with fever and tossing restlessly about.

The daughter told Joshua through her tears, "She's been coughing something dreadful. And she hasn't been able to keep anything down, not even water. And her fever just keeps going up."

Joshua took the woman's hand and felt her pulse: fast, uneven, weak. He didn't think she had long. "Has anyone sent for a minister?"

The girl nodded. "But he was out seeing to people some ways away. I don't know whether —" She didn't manage to finish the sentence, but the message was clear.

The woman moaned and muttered something. Her daughter leaned over to listen. "Yes, ma, the doctor's come."

The woman struggled to sit up farther and looked at him — studied him, Joshua thought. She appeared to come to some decision, turning to the girl and saying, just loud enough for Joshua to hear, "You go out to the others. I need to talk to the doctor alone."

The girl turned to Joshua, stricken. "Is she . . . will there be time . . . ."

"I don't think she's about to leave us. I'll call you and your siblings straightaway if anything changes. Is it just the three of you?"

She nodded. "Our pa died three years ago." She bent to kiss her mother's forehead and then slowly, dragging her feet, left Joshua alone with his patient.

He looked around and found a stool, dragging it to the bed so he could lean forward to hear her without looming over her. He took her hand again, this time for whatever comfort he could give rather than to confirm what both of them already knew.

The woman's rasping voice came again, barely audible. "Is my daughter gone?"

"Yes — at least, she's left the room. It's just you and

me here."

She took a few shallow breaths and coughed a rattling cough before she spoke again. "The minister . . . not here yet?"

"I'm afraid not. I'm sorry."

"No . . . not sorry . . . need to tell someone something . . . not the minister . . . ."

This was taking him into far deeper waters than the creek. "I'll listen to whatever you want to tell me. But what good — wouldn't it be better to tell your family, or the minister, anything important you have yet to say?"

"*No!*" It was almost a shout. He wouldn't have thought she had the strength for it. And indeed, the effort exhausted her. She lay back panting, and said nothing more for at least a minute. Then she managed to go on in a hoarse whisper. "Don't want to leave this earth without tellin' someone. But not them, any of them. . . . Doctors have to keep secrets, don't they? . . ."

"Yes, ma'am. Ministers, too, I'd have thought. But we do."

"The minister . . . He's known me and Nathan since we moved here. Known the children all their lives, baptized 'em. I couldn't bear him knowin'. . . tell you instead."

He took a deep breath, which only reminded him that she could no longer do the same. "Whenever you're ready, ma'am. I'm here listening."

She waited another minute or so, till he was afraid she would never manage to say whatever it was she needed to. But finally she gripped his hand tight and said, with many a stop to gasp for breath, "Nate and me . . . Nate and me, we lived as man and wife for more'n thirty years. But we never . . . it were never legal. . . . He'd had another wife, when he was barely more'n a boy, and she left him. . . . Never knew where, never got free of her. . . . Wasn't free to marry me.

We lived just as if we were married. . . . But nobody knew, not ever. . . . Not until now."

Another pause, before she went on. "And then Nate died and left me alone with knowin' . . . . I miss him so much, and all the while were living in sin . . . ." She looked up at Joshua, face screwed up in defiance. "And I'm not sorry for it! He was a good man and a good father . . . ." She shut her eyes, and tears leaked out and down her face. "The children, they're all of them . . . natural, and don't even know it. Can't no one know, never."

Joshua moved her hand into both of his. "Not ever, ma'am. Not from me. Rest easy, if you can."

She opened her eyes again, opened them wide, searching his. "Do you think . . . will the Lord let me find Nathan? Will he forgive us?"

Joshua bit his lip, but he couldn't stop his own tears from coming. "I'm no preacher, ma'am. And I'm not so good a man as to claim to judge others. But we're told he's a God of love. And you and Nathan loved each other. I have to believe he'd want that love to go on." He added, maybe too quiet for her to hear: "Eternity's no place to be alone, not when there's someone you could love."

Her hand started to loosen in his. Panicked, he let go and ran to the door, calling. "Come now! Come quickly!"

The three of them ran in, almost running him down. And they made it, if without much time to spare, kneeling by the bed and telling their mother they loved her, as she murmured a few faint words of farewell and slipped away.

Joshua offered to find his own way back. "You all need each other, now. And the minister will be coming." All Joshua wanted was to be well away before the minister showed up.

The young man wiped his face with a rough drag of his sleeve. "No sir, Doctor. My sisters can see him. And they can tend to Ma, get her ready. She'll be here still, and made decent, when I'm done taking you home."

Neither of them spoke on the long walk to the creek, or sloshing back through it. He had time to think, instead. What would the minister have done, if the woman had had the courage to confess to him? Was she right to carry the secret with her, unshared except with a stranger who had no power of blessing or forgiving? Had she chosen the only way to protect her children's future?

What would Freida say, if she heard of such a case? Or Dolly, with her own marriage to mourn, and her own child to protect? He found he didn't know her well enough to hazard a guess.

And what about Clara Brook? He had an odd notion she would have understood; that she would have been glad of Joshua's answer.

Robert, bless him, was waiting on the other bank. He must have been driving back and forth all evening. Joshua bade farewell to the young man, glad for once that a family member was too distracted to think about paying him. He would not have felt right taking money for this night's work.

But when Robert had driven him home, and he stumbled up to his rooms, he realized that he had forgotten to return the borrowed boots. So he had that payment, whether he wanted or no.

Chapter 15

WHEN DOLLY finally wrote again, there were signs that Joshua's premonition about her forming an attachment might have been correct. The letter was shorter than her previous ones, as short as his first supposedly inadequate attempt. And a few coy mentions of a Doctor Brent, who had been so kind as to escort her to a play and to join her host family for tea, and had such a lot to tell her about the exciting advances in medicine, might have been designed to make him jealous. Yet he had no claim on her attentions, let alone her affections, that would justify such a feeling.

And what was behind that reference to the possibility of a pension? Only a veteran's death or disability due to wartime experience would provide his widow with such a benefit. Mr. Arden had died of some sort of fever, Freida had said, eight or nine years after the war had ended. Joshua could think of no fevers a man could initially survive and then succumb to so long afterward.

But a doctor seeking to worm his way into a naive widow's heart might be willing to raise her hopes in the process. Joshua's fist clenched around the letter. Should he write to warn her? If he took such a liberty, would she discount it as personal resentment against a rival?

It was none of his affair. And indeed, he had no cause to jump to the conclusion that this doctor was dishonorable. While Joshua did his best to keep apprised of interesting medical discoveries, he had nowhere near the time or resources to do so comprehensively. The man might know something Joshua did not about the aftereffects of Mr. Arden's ailment, or about that ailment itself.

Disgruntled, he left the letter on the table and stoked the fire before settling down in his easy chair to brood. He had no idea what Dolly expected, or wished, him to write in response, so he would refrain from writing at all. If she had more to tell him, she could do so whenever she pleased.

Dolly's unanswered letter lay on Joshua's table reproaching him for his lack of response until he stuffed it away in a drawer. When the owner of the general store waved him down with another missive bearing Dolly's handwriting, he stood goggling at the man for several seconds before reaching out to take the letter.

He again waited until he made it home hours later, drenched and shivering from the freezing rain that had caught him on the way, before extracting the letter, now slightly damp, and reading it with his easy chair pulled close to the fire.

Dear Doctor Gibbs,

I am almost too mortified to take up my pen again, after the foolish fancies that prompted the contents of my last letter.

Doctor Brent, who had visited my hosts often enough during my stay that they and I had considered him attentive, has now made plain — without, it seems, realizing that we were misled — that he was principally interested in exploring the history of my late husband's health, as part of his work consulting for the authorities who administer the Pension Act. On his last visit, he thanked me very courteously for my assistance, promised to inform my late husband's parents if I should prove eligible to receive a pension, and wished me a safe voyage home, as if he could think of no reason to see me again before that time.

Joshua's heart softened at the thought of her embarrassment, even as he could not help thinking that Dolly's apparent interest in himself seemed to have revived in the absence of a more glittering prospect.

Do write to me, dear Doctor Gibbs, and tell me that I am not such a fool as I feel myself to be — or else reproach me for being such in truth.

He would write, yes, and even apologize for his delay in doing so. But he would not comment on her error, either to condemn or to excuse. He had no right to the former, and still little impulse toward the latter.

* * * * *

The winter had begun with cold, wind, and more than the usual amount of snow. But the bleakness was now relieved, and the discomforts easier to ignore, with the approach of Christmas. A large fir tree had been brought from the woods and erected in the middle of the town square, while not a few of Joshua's patients had smaller trees of their own in their sitting rooms. Madam Mamie had one in her parlor, decorated with the very latest in delicate glass bulbs in many colors and intricately cut tin shapes — though it was not, he noted wryly, topped with the increasingly popular Star of Bethlehem. The other trees Joshua saw bore mainly homemade decorations, such as strings of popcorn or beads, carved wooden figures, and folded paper chains. This year, the children in town and those coming for market days had begun bringing their own contributions to hang on the public tree, with the result that its lower branches were crowded with a peculiar assortment of ornaments. Major at first showed an inconvenient interest in those that smelled edible, but after a few sharp commands from Joshua, he refrained from approaching them.

Joshua was even invited to two Christmas parties, one at the mayor's house and the other at Madam Mamie's. He attended both, the former out of a sense of obligation and in the hope that his host was not aware of the latter. Freida, he was happy to see, had been invited to the mayor's party, and spent much of it urging her fellow guests to enjoy the refreshments, admiring the ladies' outfits, and praising the beauty and cleverness of those children present.

Mamie's food and drink were bountiful, and the available entertainment included that in which the establishment specialized. Joshua declined, telling himself that such goings-on were hardly the way to celebrate the holy season.

Clara Brook attended neither party. The mayor, presumably, could not be troubled to include any farmers but the most prominent among his guests. And of course she would not set foot in Mamie's establishment. Though when he imagined the two women face to face, he quite unaccountably pictured them smiling at each other.

Musing along these lines while walking slowly home from his office, he caught his breath, embarrassed, to hear Clara's recognizable firm tread coming up behind him. He turned and tipped his hat, searching her face for any sign that she had noticed something amiss. If she had, he saw no indication of it. The brisk air had brought unwonted color to her cheeks, and she greeted him with noticeable good cheer. "How now, doctor, are you headed to some holiday gathering?"

He could do nothing to stem the blush that heated his face, but he could hope to distract her from it. "You may regard me as a hopeless stick-in-the-mud, trudging homeward as usual. And yourself?"

Her expression faded toward its usual sobriety.

"Homeward bound as well. A good evening to you." She nodded and strode past him before turning onto the road out of town. Feeling the weight of the long day, and of his accumulated years, he walked heavily on. At least, with luck, Major would be there to greet him.

* * * * *

In light of the decorations and festivities, Joshua chose to regard Dolly's next letter as a sort of Christmas present. Arriving only three weeks after he had sent his own, it continued her tone of timid apology, particularly as she announced her news and asked a favor.

Hope and I will finally begin our homeward journey not long after the New Year. My hosts have been so kind as to say they will pay for us to stay at two hotels along the way, so that we need not travel day and night for the entire journey. I was reluctant to accept such generosity, but will do it for Hope's sake.

And no doubt for her own, given how exhausting it would be not only to travel such a long way without respite, but to do so with a child. She should not shrink from admitting as much.

I am hoping to arrive on January thirteenth by the afternoon train. If nothing delays us, in which case I would send a telegram, would you by any chance be able to meet us at the station? I am sure both of us will be weary, even if Hope is at her most well-behaved, which after my hosts' indulgence of her I am not sure I can expect.

Of course, if you are too busy, I will understand.

It was in fact hard to predict whether he would be available. His practice was comprised as much of emergencies as of more routine matters. But he could write and tell her to look for him at the station, and promise to let the stationmaster know if he was prevented from coming.

It would be good to replace Dolly's letters, which — aside from the inconsistent contents — he must confess to having found somewhat lacking in originality or wit, with her living, breathing, charming presence. And his life had been sadly lacking in contact with children, except those in pain or fear or the misery of illness, during Hope's absence. He took a deep breath as if inhaling the ineffable scent he always noticed when Dolly was near.

He would do his very best to meet the travelers at the train.

It took Joshua some exertion of will power to set the farm hand's arm with sufficient care and patience. The time that task required left him with the choice of running in the street or possibly being late for the train. He compromised by walking fast and looking stern and purposeful, as if hurrying to the aid of a patient in need.

Passengers were disembarking as he came within sight of the platform. He looked around for Dolly and Hope without finding them. Had they been first off the train, and given up on him, or were they still to come? He had not seen them leaving the station, but he had been in too much of a hurry to look around. He waited, on tenterhooks, for at least five minutes.

Finally, to his relief, he saw Dolly making her careful way down the step, assisted by the conductor, who then held out his hands for Hope and jumped her down to the platform. Joshua should have known Dolly would take her ladylike time reaching the door and descending.

Both travelers looked about them, but Hope saw him first. "Mister Doctor!" She took off running in Joshua's direction, heedless of her mother's embarrassed cry of "Hope! Manners!"

Joshua crouched down and caught Hope, swinging her up in the air. She giggled wildly. When he set her back on her feet, she turned and called to her mother, "Oh, mama, Mister Doctor is *strong!*"

Dolly hustled up, followed by two crew members burdened with a trunk and multiple suitcases. "Oh, Doctor Gibbs, thank you for meeting us, and please excuse Hope's heedlessness. It has been as I feared — she has nearly forgotten how to mind her mother. She nearly drove me to distraction on the train."

Dolly did not look driven to distraction. She looked charming as usual, clad in an elegant coat (what would Freida think of what must be a new purchase?) and a velvet bonnet, the bonnet sitting far enough back that it could scarcely keep her head warm. "It's good to see you both, and I am sure Hope will adjust promptly to the habits and routines of home."

The crew member cleared his throat. Dolly looked up at Joshua with trusting eyes. "Where should the man take our things?"

Like a fool, he had forgotten about their luggage — and would have underestimated its volume had he remembered. "I'm afraid I have no suitable conveyance. But if you will wait over there —" He waved a hand toward a nearby wrought iron bench. "I should be able to hire the necessary transport." There was at least one wagon at the livery stable. And a barouche, but Joshua could hardly afford that carriage, not without time-consuming haggling at the least and probably going into debt.

"Of course. Hope, come here." Dolly perched on the bench and patted the space next to her. Joshua waited to make sure Dolly needed no assistance and then strode off even faster than he had entered.

He reached the livery stable still undecided. Dolly

would probably consider a wagon a crude means of travel even under normal circumstances, and now she was fresh from Philadelphia and the luxuries she had enjoyed there. But he had never yet owed money in town beyond his tab at the general store, and hated to do so now.

The hostler came up to greet him, asking, "Need the buggy? It's here."

"No, not this time. I need something bigger, with room enough to take a woman, a child, and multiple cases from the railroad depot to the Arden place." Joshua moved toward the wagon as he spoke. It would be heavy for Nellie-girl, but he could manage the hire of a sturdier horse. He could not resist one longing look at the stylish barouche nearby. It looked spotless — the hostler might have just finished cleaning and polishing it.

The hostler took that in, and a knowing smile spread over his broad face. "The Arden place, is it? Well, since you're looking to oblige the lady . . . I could let you have the barouche over there for less'n usual." He named a price that would leave Joshua short of coin for weeks, but he could make do without tobacco and a few other indulgences . . . .

But no. To appear at the depot with a barouche — to play fairy godmother with a shining coach for Cinderella — would give Dolly a false impression as to his resources. He could never maintain such a standard.

And with all that luggage, even the barouche might not have room.

Joshua had not driven a wagon since the war, rarely even then, and never as fast as now. Either his speed or the sight of him driving a wagon at all had several passersby turning to stare. One, he was momentarily abashed to realize, was Clara Brook, on whose face he glimpsed both surprise and amusement. What would she think about the cause of his haste? He attempted to dismiss the question from his mind as he reached the station and tied the horses to a hitching post.

The train had of course left by this time, leaving Joshua to transfer the luggage from platform to wagon. Hope jumped to her feet and offered to assist. He fought to keep his smile consistent with polite gratitude. "I thank you for the offer, Miss Hope, but I would fear to jostle you with the larger bags I will be carrying. Please stay and look after your mother instead." Hope preened at the assignment and turned to Dolly, patting her hand and adjusting the lay of her skirts as Joshua lumbered away with two large suitcases.

There were two more after that, plus two smaller cases presumably belonging to Hope, but he finally got all the cases stowed. He escorted mother and daughter to the wagon, doing his best to ignore Dolly's hesitation as she approached it. He had determined he would not apologize, but found himself saying, "The buggy could not have accommodated all the cases, and — "

Dolly valiantly rallied, saying, "Of course you had to find something larger, and on such short notice. I only wish we had not needed to put you to the trouble."

Hope's pleasure — "look, Mama, we get to ride in this big wagon, with such a big horse!" — helped distract him from any further thoughts of Dolly's dismay. He helped Dolly up to the driver seat, tucked Hope into the nest of blankets he had hastily contrived, and set off. He should attempt to make conversation, but nothing came to mind. He had some reluctance to ask for details of their sojourn in Baltimore, given those of which he was already aware, and his own doings during the same period were largely a collection of the uninteresting, the distasteful, and the grim.

His continuing acquaintance with Miss Brook was an exception, but not a topic he found himself wanting to introduce.

When they reached Dolly's house, he helped Dolly descend, lifted Hope out, and carried the luggage again, though this time Hope positively insisted on carrying one of her own suitcases and Dolly allowed it. Once the suitcases stood in a neat row near the front door, he went out to throw a blanket over the horse in case his departure was for any reason delayed. Returning to the house, he saw that Dolly had shed her coat to reveal an equally elegant and unfamiliar dress. Courteous as ever, she insisted on taking his hat and coat, saying, "Please allow me to offer you some refreshment after all your hard work!"

He was, in fact, thirsty, and somewhat too warm despite the chill in the long-unheated house. "Thank you kindly. I could use a glass of water, or even cider, if you have anything of the sort available so soon after your return home."

"Of course. Hope, run down to the cellar and fetch the cider." The child hurried away on her errand, and Dolly waved Joshua toward the sofa, waiting for him to sit and then seating herself at the other end. Some sort of scent, like the citrus trees he had encountered in the South, wafted from her. He tried to enjoy the odor and banish its associations.

The new dress, a delicate floral print in lilac and pale blue, seemed to bring out the blue of her eyes. He caught himself gazing into them and looked away, feeling the hated blush in his cheeks. Where was Hope with his cider? He listened for her footsteps, but heard nothing. He cast about for a benign subject. "I hope you will soon recover from the fatigue of your journey."

Dolly smiled sweetly. "I am sure I shall. Is there any

regimen or tonic you would recommend to ensure it?"

He suppressed a shudder at the word "tonic," which called to mind the idea of medicine shows and their worthless products. "Only that you not over-exert yourself in your desire to unpack your cases and set everything to rights." Though with only Hope to help her, it would be hard to avoid such exertion. "Please feel free to call upon me for any services that would ease the return to your routine."

Dolly's smile grew positively dazzling. "I hope I shall not need to take advantage of your very kind offer, but I will certainly remember it."

Hope reappeared at long last, holding a pitcher cradled in one arm. Dolly jumped up and took it from her, setting it on a side table and fetching a glass from a kitchen. He started to get up to take the glass, but she pouted and gestured imperiously for him to stay seated, bringing the glass to him before resuming her position on the sofa. Hope lingered near him, watching closely as he took a sip, so he made it a large one and beamed in appreciation. "Just right!" Hope's smile shone back at him.

Hope then squeezed herself between him and Dolly on the sofa. Joshua avoided looking to see how Dolly took the change, focusing alternately on Hope, now running on about the excitement of railway travel, and on his drink. As soon as he finished, Hope hopped down and put her little hand out for the glass. He handed it to her with a seated bow and then got to his feet. "I'll leave you ladies to get settled in. Thank you again for the cider."

Dolly gave a ladylike snort. "Little enough to do in return for rescuing us and all our cases from the station! Thank you so much."

He let an eyebrow twitch at the thought of himself as a rescuer, but bowed again, retrieved his hat and overcoat, and made his way out to the patient horse. He retrieved the blanket, climbed back into the seat, wrapped the blanket around himself, and made his way home. For once, he didn't mind the chill of the January evening, glad of the way it helped clear his head of the cider-induced fog.

The clopping of the horse seemed notably quiet after the visit. He both enjoyed the peace of it and missed the duet of womanly and childish voices. Was man ever satisfied with his lot?

Chapter 16

NOW AND again, Joshua found himself restless, impatient with the familiar faces all around him, the square and the livery stable, the walk between rooms and office and back again. Sooner or later he would find or invent an errand that took him elsewhere, to Rushing or further afield. On this day, his excuse came from a temporary shortage of cheap tobacco. The tobacconist in Rushing might have some, or so he told himself as he rode Nellie-girl out of town.

The tobacconist, he soon discovered, carried nothing as inexpensive as the leaf with which Joshua usually contented himself. Rather than return empty-handed, he purchased a more expensive variety and left the establishment disgruntled. If he had planned better, he could have sought Alton's company, but Alton would still be at the school. For lack of a better alternative, he took himself to the tavern for an early dinner.

A pork belly sandwich and glass of beer were beginning to soothe him when, to his disgust, he spotted a familiar golden head atop broad shoulders. The pitchman he had seen months ago in Cowbird Creek, and in whom Freida Blum had taken such unjustifiable interest, was finishing his own meal while telling some tale that seemed to captivate a crowd of locals. Finishing with a flourish and accepting the laughs and cheers of his audience, he stood up, draping his velvet-lined greatcoat over one arm, and headed right for Joshua's table. Standing over Joshua, legs apart and smiling broadly, he asked, "Did I not see you some months back in Cowbird Creek, driving a pretty little mare — a Missouri Fox Trotter, if I'm not mistaken — and with a charming older lady by your side?"

Joshua would have been sufficiently annoyed by either the man's particular (and accurate) attention to his mare, or the insinuating reference to Freida. The two together were insufferable. He shoved his chair back, put his glass down on the table with a clunk, and said stiffly, "I recall the occasion."

The pitchman could reasonably have taken offense at Joshua's manner, but he apparently preferred to ignore it, holding his smile as he said, "Please be so kind as to convey my greetings to that lady, when the occasion arises."

Joshua stood, his chair rattling behind him. "I cannot undertake to comply with that request."

The confrontation had attracted some attention, and some of the men the pitchman had been entertaining looked ready to come to his defense. He waved them back, however, and faced Joshua again, his smile a little forced but still in place. "In that case, sir, I can only hope the future brings me an opportunity to wish the lady well in person. You may finish your meal — I have no intention of troubling you further." He tipped his hat, swirled the greatcoat around his shoulders, and left the tavern, pace steady and with a roll in his step.

Joshua, on the other hand, sat back down with his stomach roiling and took only one more bite of his sandwich before donning his overcoat and walking stiffly out the door.

He had intended to linger in Rushing until Alton was free, but now he faced a dilemma. Alton was a friendly and sociable man. What if he, like the fellows in the tavern, found the pitchman a diverting companion in spite of his deplorable profession? Of course, Joshua could simply avoid mentioning the encounter, but he was sufficiently ruffled, not to say angry, that he was not sure he could manage it.

In the end, he rode home, urging Nellie-girl to a rare gallop on an open stretch of road, careless of the cold bite of the wind.

Back at the livery stable, Joshua checked Nellie-girl's legs for any swelling or tenderness. "My apologies," he muttered, stroking her neck. "You had the burden of my temper as well as the rest of me, this day." The mare blew at him, stirring his hair and tickling his ear.

Somewhat eased by the interlude, he still made straight for the pharmacy to tell Robert the pitchman had turned up again. Robert, busily grinding and measuring and pouring, lent an ear to Joshua's complaints, grimacing and cussing when appropriate, but it struck Joshua as friendly indulgence more than genuinely shared indignation.

The cold outside air blew into the pharmacy as the door opened. Clara Brook came in, cheeks pink from the cold, and smiled pleasantly at both Joshua and Robert as she approached the counter. "We've finally used up our supply of bandages. The same quantity as before, please."

Joshua, who had not bothered to remove his hat, did so now. He looked Clara over as much as he could do without rudeness, seeing no injury. "I hope the hurts that used up your supply have been minor."

Clara chuckled. "Indeed. My own skill, such as it is, served to tend them." She studied Joshua in turn. "Forgive the observation, but as I entered, I thought you did not look entirely pleased with life. I hope nothing is seriously wrong."

He could well imagine that he had looked annoyed, at best. He opened his mouth to deny any cause for her concern, and then thought better of it. They had, after all, discussed the pitchman once before — though not Freida's reaction to him, which the pitchman must have been acute enough to note. In as level a tone as he could manage, he described the morning's encounter, and after some hesitation, added, "I fear the man will take some advantage of Mrs. Blum's generous interest in him. I would sooner know him across the country than so close as Rushing."

Clara cocked her head. "You know Mrs. Blum better than I do, but I suspect you do her wrong in thinking her so easily deceived. She strikes me as perfectly able to read a man's character, without some other man stepping in to do that office."

Joshua felt some of the stiffness leave his neck, only thus realizing how tense he had become. "I bow to your perception, ma'am."

He suited the action to the word; she laughed again before producing a coin, handing it to Robert, and picking up her bandages. "Good afternoon, then, to both you gentlemen — and Doctor, I hope I leave you in better humor."

As indeed she had.

Chapter 17

JOSHUA had not encountered Dolly and Hope since their return to town, but as he took an early afternoon stroll to settle his dinner, he saw Freida shepherding mother and daughter toward an unfamiliar building near the church. He yielded to curiosity and followed them.

It turned out Freida was taking them to the social library the minister had established. Dolly perused the shelves while Hope stared wide-eyed at the mysterious volumes. Joshua greeted the three of them, then squatted down by Hope. "Would you like me to find something you might enjoy?"

She grabbed his hand and pulled on him so that he landed on his rump. Dolly turned around at the thud and exclaimed, "Hope! That wasn't ladylike!"

Joshua smiled at the child. "Maybe not, but seeing as I'm down here, I may as well set a while." He scooted closer to the shelves and pulled out a volume with a red cover and gilt lettering on the spine. "Oh, this is a wonderful story. It's about a girl, a little older than you, who goes to a magic place full of funny people." If that left out the more frightening aspects, no matter. "Would you like me to read you the beginning?"

Hope answered by crawling over and climbing into his lap. Seeing Dolly about to intervene, he gently lifted her back off again, hoisted himself up, and held out his hand. When she took it, he led her to a sofa, lifted her onto it, and sat beside her. "Ready?"

She nodded vigorously, and he began.

Alice was beginning to get very tired of sitting by her sister on the bank, and of having nothing to do.

He skipped ahead a bit, to get to the real beginning of the story.

So she was considering in her own mind (as well as she could, for the day made her feel very sleepy and stupid), whether the pleasure of making a daisy-chain would be worth the trouble of getting up and picking the daisies, when suddenly a White Rabbit with pink eyes ran close by her.

He turned to Hope. "What do you think of that?"

Hope looked disappointed. "I see rabbits all the time. Maybe I even saw a white one once."

"That's what Alice thinks, at first — but wait and see."

There was nothing so very remarkable in that, nor did Alice think it so very much out of the way to hear the Rabbit say to itself, "Oh dear! Oh dear! I shall be too late!"

Joshua commented, in the tone of one sharing a confidence, "You know, I think I'd be surprised to hear a rabbit talk. Would you?"

Hope tilted her head to the side, considered carefully, and finally said, "Yes."

But when the Rabbit actually took a watch out of its waistcoat-pocket and looked at it and then hurried on, Alice started to her feet, for it flashed across her mind that she had never before seen a rabbit with either a waistcoat-pocket, or a watch to take out of it, and, burning with curiosity, she ran across the field after it and was just in time to see it pop down a large rabbit-hole, under the hedge.

"What do you think she did then?"

Hope pursed her lips in and out, thinking hard. "I think she chased it!"

"That's absolutely right!"

In another moment, down went Alice after it!

Joshua became aware that both Dolly and Freida were standing in front of him. He put his finger in the book to mark the place and closed it, looking up. Freida's gaze rested softly on the little girl, but she spoke to Joshua. "Mrs. Arden is going to check the book out, so maybe you read more of it later."

Joshua asked Hope solemnly, "Would you do me the honor of continuing our reading at some future time?"

Hope smiled graciously, ruler to subject. "Yes, Mister Doctor."

Joshua handed the book to Dolly and got up. "Then I'll see you two ladies on that happy occasion, if not before."

Dolly and Hope headed home, Hope now allowed to hold the precious book while Dolly carried several others presumably meant for her own reading. Joshua asked his remaining companion, "May I escort you somewhere? I am headed for the general store, but am in no particular hurry."

"The general store, why not? I can always use some flour, so many things I can do with it."

As they walked, Joshua wondered what simpler books the social library might have. Perhaps, if there were such, he could try his hand at giving Hope a reading lesson . . . .

He became aware that Mrs. Blum was talking, and he had failed to take in whatever she was saying. "I beg your pardon. I was lost in thought."

"Naturally, why should you listen to an old lady rattle on? You must be thinking about important subjects, new treatments, medicines to invent."

He shook his head laughing. "Nothing so monumental." He explained his musings; she beamed.

"Such a lovely thought! And you and Hope, so sweet together, just like a father and daughter. And Dolly, didn't she look lovely? I admit I made the dress she was wearing, but I can do better, just wait until I make her wedding dress . . . ."

"Mrs. Blum!" Joshua did his best to sound stern. "I do hope you haven't said anything of the sort to Mrs. Arden."

Freida in her turn, pretended offense. "What do you think of me, you should say such a thing?"

What he thought, in fact, was that she had probably made just such a comment, and most likely more than once.

Joshua's next visit to Dolly and Hope was scheduled for the following Saturday afternoon. He made time the day before to visit the library. He found just what he had been hoping to find.

When he arrived, Hope was industriously polishing Dolly's Sunday shoes. When Dolly opened the door for him, Hope cried out, "Mister Doctor! I can polish your boots!"

Joshua took a quick glance at Hope's work in progress. She appeared to be doing a decent job. He took off his hat, hung it up, obtained Dolly's permission, and sat in the chair to which Hope directed him.

When his boots were clean and gleaming, he extracted the somewhat battered little volume from his inner vest pocket and showed it to Hope. "I found another book at the library for you. It's not a fanciful story, like *Alice's Adventures in Wonderland*, but I liked it when I was a boy first learning to read."

Hope's face expressed a mix of interest and caution. "I don't know how to read yet, Mister Doctor. I just know my letters."

Joshua opened the book to a page with detailed drawing of insects and animals. In the corner of his eye, he saw Dolly shrink in delicate distaste at the sight of the insects, but

Hope craned forward. Encouraged, Joshua pointed to the cat on the right-hand page. "Knowing your letters is a very good start. With that knowledge, you may be able to find which of the words next to this picture is the word for 'cat.' I could help you."

Hope brightened right up, but Dolly made a "tsk" sound and said, "Oh, Hope is too young for reading. It can hardly be good for her to task her brain so."

Thus quelled, Hope sank back in her chair. Joshua laid the book on her lap and stood, facing his hostess. "If I cannot be of use as a teacher, perhaps you have some chores I could attend to, jobs for which you would otherwise need to hire help."

Dolly looked down at her hands. "I wouldn't want to trouble you —"

He cast about for supporting argument and found only a white lie. "I have had insufficient exercise this week. You would be doing me a favor."

She looked up again and twinkled at him. "Well, in *that* case, as a gesture of Christian charity, I could ask you to bring in some more firewood."

"With pleasure, ma'am." He donned his coat and hastened outside to the woodpile.

Dolly thanked him profusely when he returned with an armful of logs stacked up to his nose and dumped them where she directed. "It's not often we have a strong man here to do such things."

Joshua wondered wryly just how feeble he would have to be before she would hesitate to call him strong. But he gave her a little bow, and asked for another assignment. A few chores later, she could think of nothing else. "Let me give you some tea. I have some biscuits made just yesterday, and strawberry jam."

He should really be going. But the lure of strawberry

jam weakened his resolve. "Well, just one biscuit, maybe."

As she set out the food and poured the tea, she chatted about the opportunities becoming available to a man in this state, now that the struggles over statehood were well behind them. He was ill acquainted with some of the industries she described, and was not altogether sure that she knew them a great deal better. But he did his best to hold up his end of the conversation, all the while wondering how the topic had arisen. Did she imagine him to be ambitious for high position? She might, he realized, if she assumed he had graduated from one of the eastern medical colleges, instead of just hanging up his shingle and studying his way to as much competence as possible.

Three biscuits later, and after the educational experience of seeing just how much strawberry jam could end up on one little face and how efficiently a good housewife could wipe it away, he finally took his leave.

When he stopped off to bring Freida some more diuretic tea and dose her with essence of foxglove, he mentioned his latest visit with Dolly. To his surprise, she shook her head at him. "So many visits and nothing coming of them, people will start to talk. A man should make his intentions known."

"Intentions? Can't I be intending to enjoy her company and get to know her better? And to make myself useful now and then?"

"Useful, he says. A husband is useful! A father to the little girl, that would be useful! Setting the town to talking about her, not so much."

"Freida. Be serious with me, please. Based on what you've heard, am I already compromising her reputation by spending time with her? Should I stay away from her, if I'm not ready to . . . go further?"

She scrutinized his face like a gypsy reading a palm. "You're not ready? You think you keep looking, you'll do better?"

"It's not that! Dolly is a wonderful woman. But . . ." What could he say? Suddenly he remembered how all this had started. "I wasn't looking for a wife! I don't know that I am, even now. Nor that I'm not. I don't know . . . I don't know what I want. So how much time do I have to figure it out, before I need to shy off for Dolly's sake?"

Freida sighed. "Am I a fortune teller?" He started a little at her echoing his thoughts; she looked quizzically at him, then went on. "But you want serious, I'll try. Seriously, I think you should figure yourself out before too much longer."

He did run into Dolly again three days later, but without contriving to do so. He had determined to winnow out such of his books as he didn't plan on rereading, and brought the resulting stack to the social library. Dolly was already there, returning the books she had borrowed — along with, he was sorry to note, the *McGuffey* reader — and looking for new ones. Under the circumstances, he was somewhat relieved to see that Freida was absent.

She looked at his armful of books. "May I see?"

He held them out for her inspection. "They're mostly history and medicine. And a Latin dictionary that helped me when I was learning what medicines were made of."

She looked daunted at the idea of Latin. "Maybe the history. This one looks interesting. I don't know as much as I should about our War of Independence, given how many of my family fought in it."

The minister's wife wrote down the title, while Joshua

glanced at the volumes Dolly was returning. Besides the reader, none of them looked familiar. "Novels?"

She blushed a little. Joshua hoped she did not think he was the kind of old stick who considered novels unsuitable reading for a woman. "Some of them are quite absorbing. The one I just finished was so sad! A woman finds out that the man she married, the man she loves, already has a wife, and she has to leave him. It was so hard for her. But of course, she had no choice, did she?"

Joshua busied himself with handing the minister's wife the rest of his books. He was afraid his secret, or rather, the secret he was bound to keep for another, would be written on his face. Along with his thought that the fictional woman's choices hardly seemed so straightforward to him.

He made sure to find an errand in a different direction from where Dolly appeared to be heading. But before they parted, she said, in her pretty voice, "Will you be attending the meeting next Friday? Our own congressman will be speaking."

The congressman had not graced the town with his presence since he had managed to get elected. Having voted for the other fellow, Joshua was tolerably curious about what the man might have to say. "I daresay I will."

Chapter 18

JOSHUA TIED off the bandage around the young prostitute's wrist. (What was her name? Bessie? Betty? She had arrived shortly before his last visit, and he had never spent time with her.) "Keep that clean, and send for me if it gets seriously soiled. Otherwise I'll be back in three days to change it. And I'll tell Madam Mamie you must be excused from further attempts at cooking until that time."

The young woman cackled. "Just as well I'm not making my living as a cook, ain't it? I'd be bandaged from head to foot in no time." She winked at him. "Though if you were to do the bandaging, I might enjoy it at that."

Joshua gave a short smile at her banter. Flirting was a tool of her trade, and she may as well practice it.

As he packed up his bag, he noticed that she had dropped her professional manner and was gazing at the bandage. "This brings back memories of when Mama and I and my sisters scraped lint and packed it up, and tore up her old petticoats for bandages and rolled them. I loved the lint – it was like snow that didn't chill my fingers." Her look went mischievous again for a moment. "And I did enjoy tearing up the petticoats."

Joshua had seen such makeshift bandages often enough. It was just possible that he himself, or Clara Brook, had handled the very bandages that innocent child had rolled so carefully.

He could picture the woman (June? *Jenny*, that was it)

as a little girl, with the dark brown hair whose roots showed beneath her brassy blonde, rolling up strips of white cloth, her lower lip stuck out in concentration the way Hope's sometimes did. "That was very good of you and your family. I can assure you the doctors and those assisting them appreciated it. Did you write notes, as some children did?"

"Once or twice. I remember once, after Mama told us some sad stories of wounded soldiers, she helped me write that I wished I could kiss their hurts and make them better. She kissed me, on the top of my head, when I asked her to help write that." Jenny bit her lip and swallowed what must have been a lump in her throat. How long had it been since she had seen her mother?

Joshua looked away for a moment to let her collect herself. But he had a most inappropriate urge to kiss the top of her head.

* * * * *

Joshua had often thought of asking Clara Brook about his old friend's letter, and as often hesitated to do so. But as he left the general store, where he had stopped to drop a coin in the collection box for grasshopper region relief, he saw Clara passing by and felt for no clear reason that the time had come. Once they had exchanged greetings, he took a somewhat deeper than usual breath and said, "If I may make so bold, ma'am, a letter from a man who was with me in the Army made me wonder about something. Did you ever, in your nursing, have a patient by the name of Calvin Grey?"

Clara frowned as if searching her memory. "That name doesn't call anyone to mind."

"You might remember him by the wound he had, a

sucking chest wound, in the first year —"

She interrupted him, her face brighter. "A chubby fellow, with a round face and a gap in his teeth that made him whistle when he talked? If that's your friend, I do remember him. A fighter, for all you mightn't think it to look at him. At least, he knew how to fight to live. That's the kind of fighting I came to admire most."

"That's the very man, ma'am. He remembers you most kindly. He had no idea I might know you, but he told me about the nurse who stood by him when the doctor despaired of him, and kept his spirits up even as she held body and soul together."

Clara's eyes glowed, and she stood very straight. He had touched the core of pride in her, and she was unwilling, in that moment, to deny it.

The moment was broken by the approach of light footsteps. Clara's expression shifted in an instant to closed and wary. Joshua turned to see Dolly and Hope, Dolly holding one of Hope's hands while the girl held a stick of striped candy in the other. Hope called out gaily to him. "Mister Doctor! I have candy! I was a good girl, so Mommy bought me candy!"

Joshua raised his hat to mother and daughter. "I'm very glad to hear you were a good girl, Miss Hope."

He heard heavier footsteps retreating behind him, and glanced backward. Clara had left without a goodbye to him or a word to Dolly. He looked back at Dolly to see her looking after Clara with no very friendly expression. Whatever might be between the two of them, he would rather not know it. He turned his attention back to Hope. "Do you think that if I went to the ice cream parlor, the man might let me have one of those sticks? Or would your mommy have to tell him I've been good, first?"

Hope's giggle mingled with the somewhat more

refined titter of her mother. Too late, he realized his words might have been taken as flirtatious. Conversation with females was fraught with peril, it seemed, even the pint-sized variety. He excused himself, no doubt with less than the aplomb he might have preferred to display, and retreated to the safely masculine comforts of the saloon for a restorative glass of beer.

* * * * *

Joshua had learned over the years to assume a calm and reassuring manner, whatever the condition in which a patient presented himself. Such a demeanor calmed the patient in turn, giving confidence that the doctor could cope with whatever mishap, or even calamity, had occurred; and a calm and confident patient would be easier to deal with.

But it took a positive effort of will to avoid any sign of alarm when Hawkins, of all people, banged at the door of Joshua's office, pushed it open, and entered with Clara Brook leaning on his arm, shivering and pale.

Even as Joshua stared, Clara straightened up and looked about her in evident dismay. She muttered something under her breath; Joshua could not catch the words, but it had the rhythm of a curse.

Hawkins led her to a chair and pressed her into it before addressing Joshua. "I was passing by the town square when I noticed Miss Brook sitting on a bench nearby. I tipped my hat and said good morning, but she didn't say nothing back to me. Well, that wasn't like her, seeing as we're acquainted, so I looked closer, and I saw she looked poorly, as you'll have noticed when we come in. Well, I may know a thing or two —" Hawkins paused and thrust his chin up and his shoulders back, then slumped down again. "But I don't rightly know what to do when a young lady gets the vapors. So I thought, may as well bring her over here and see what you could do for her. But looks as if she's going to be just fine, without no special treatment."

Indeed, as much color as Clara usually possessed, if not more, had returned to her face. A moment more, and she stood up, her posture almost aggressively straight. She took the barber's hand. "Thank you for assisting me. I am only sorry to have caused you concern."

"Weren't no trouble, miss. And I'm right glad to see you looking better. I'll be on my way." He smiled at her before releasing her hand, nodding stiffly at Joshua, and taking his leave.

Clara shook her head as if dislodging unpleasant images. "I hope you will believe that I am not often afflicted with what Mr. Hawkins calls 'the vapors.'" She paused and went on more quietly. "Or at least, not for such causes as are traditionally attributed to delicate females."

Joshua would have very much liked to inquire as to other likely causes for her symptoms, now or in the past, but her manner made all too clear that any such question would be unwelcome. He could not force his diagnostic efforts on her. "Are you feeling quite well again?"

Clara lifted her chin in a gesture echoing Hawkins' defiant posture. "Perfectly. You'll have no need to rummage for smelling salts or other such remedies." She forced a smile, an expression that sat poorly on her face and troubled him more than a frown would have done. Then some thought evidently crossed her mind and gave rise to a look of more genuine amusement, or even mischief. "And I defy you to hold so firmly to your low opinion of Mr. Hawkins, after he has demonstrated such gallantry."

As more than once before, she left him stammering for a reply. She awaited none, but turned and fairly marched out the door.

Chapter 19

THE DAY of the meeting where the congressman would speak, Joshua was called to a farm off near Rushing, and then Li Chang flagged him down as he was riding back. The Chinaman had burned himself with an iron in a moment of inattention, and felt quite foolish about the uncharacteristic accident. "My fault. I was thinking about my mother's letter. They decide what to bring on the boat. So little room!"

By the time Joshua made it to the meeting hall, the band was playing and most of the seats were taken. With such a mass of people, the room was warm enough that Joshua soon shed his overcoat and draped it on his arm. He took a moment to admire the place, transformed by as much bunting as if election season were still in full swing. Grabbing one of the many pieces of cake set forth on the refreshment table, he managed to find a seat near the back of the hall. Looking around, he saw Dolly in the third row. Freida had not chosen to attend — or was she too unwell to venture out on a winter evening? He would have to call on her tomorrow.

The band launched into "My Country 'Tis of Thee," at least half the crowd singing along with surprisingly harmonious results. After the ringing conclusion, the band packed up and joined the friends who had saved seats for them, and the mayor took their place. Joshua tuned out the words and listened to the mayor's speech as if to another musical instrument. So regarded, it was pleasant enough, rather like a bassoon. After a couple of minutes, however, he realized that something was amiss. It was not, after all, the congressman who had come to town. Congress was in session, and he could not absent himself merely to meet with those who had elected him. Instead, the mayor was introducing some sort of aide. Dolly had been misinformed. Joshua wondered whether the mayor had been as well, and if so, before or after he had organized this circus.

The mayor finally reached the end of his introduction, and the aide came down the aisle, shaking hands with the men left and right in as condescending a manner as the congressman might have displayed, bobbing his head at the ladies, sweat shining on his round red face.

Joshua tried, this time, to take in the content of the speech. After all, in less than two years, he would have to decide whether to do his one-vote best to boot the man's employer out of office. However, he soon realized that in order to make that decision, he would have to busy himself with finding out the truth about all the splendid things the congressman was supposedly doing in Washington. He would never find the time.

" . . . and your representative has added his support to the Page Act, which will protect our shores from the yellow tide of strumpets, brought hither by nefarious petticoat pensioners to tempt and poison our men and offend our virtuous wives and mothers with their presence . . . ."

Joshua whispered to Thaddeus the telegraph operator, sitting next to him, "What in the Sam Hill is the Page Act?" Thaddeus, he knew, read the out of town papers and might have an answer.

Thaddeus whispered back, "It's a law to keep Chinese women from immigrating, unless they prove they're not whores. I don't know more'n that."

"But — but why Chinese? I don't know a single Chinese lady at Madam Mamie's. Who says China's planning to send us whores?"

Thaddeus shrugged. Joshua returned his attention to the speaker, who had moved on to the congressman's plan to bring more settlers to Nebraska and even make it a site for tourists to visit. Joshua let his mind wander again. It settled, uncomfortably, on the memory of Li Chang, burning his hand as he contemplated the arrival of his wife and mother. Did Li know about this Page Act? Would it pass before his family could board their ship and leave?

Joshua got up, maneuvered his way through the row of seats, and walked out.

Thaddeus was, albeit with some difficulty, able to get Joshua the text of the bill. It made for difficult reading. He puzzled over it, trying to match up the words with what the congressman's aide had claimed. It seemed to be about making sure that anyone who took ship from the Orient hadn't somehow ended up agreeing to involuntary servitude. Except it mentioned a law that already did that. This was about one kind of servitude, for "lewd and immoral purposes." The law would put some penalties on United States citizens that tried to get away with bringing people in for such. That didn't sound like a bad idea.

He stopped by the inn where lawyers usually stayed when the circuit brought them to town. He was lucky enough to find one, and lucky again that the lawyer was bored and saddle-sore and in need of a drink. For the price of a couple of whiskeys, Joshua got a lawyer's-eye view of what all the verbiage actually meant, or would mean once it was a law and people started acting on it.

"You see, no one is going to get in trouble for stopping

Chinese women from coming. The only way they get in trouble is by letting them through. And you've got all these people encouraged to throw their weight around. First the U.S. consul at the port they're leaving from, and then the officials at the port where they show up. And if those officials decide some Chinese woman is here to be a prostitute, they can keep that woman, or maybe any 'alien' — it's unclear — from leaving the ship. That puts the ship's master in a bind. So whether any of the women who want to take ship are prostitutes or not, plenty of shipmasters will just say no to Chinese women passengers."

Joshua ground his teeth. "So even an old lady like our laundryman's mother, not to mention his wife, might not be able to join him here."

The lawyer drained his glass and thunked it down. "Free legal opinions are worth what you pay for 'em. And whiskey, however welcome, is close to free compared to what I charge for words I have to stand by. But that's how I see it."

Words he would have to stand by. That was an apt phrase for what Joshua was attempting. He had never mixed much in politics, even locally — and here he was planning to raise a stink about what people were up to in far-off Washington City. But it was going to matter right here.

When he stopped by to examine Freida — whose symptoms had not gotten appreciably worse, so she might actually be taking her medicine — he hesitated when she asked him what was new in his life. She was probably fishing for some update about his intentions toward Dolly. It was that thought as much as anything that led him to tell her what he was actually up to, that he planned to write a letter for the local paper to publish. It took a while, first to explain what the Page Act was, then to explain how it would affect Li Chang and others like him. To his relief, she was indignant for Li, and also — and this should not have surprised him — on Li's mother's behalf. "A man with a family, with a wife, and they want him to keep living all alone! And keeping an old lady from her son, how could they, what would their own mothers say! Is this the latest thing, old lady prostitutes? You want I should sign your letter?"

That would almost certainly entail letting her change what he wrote. "No, thank you. But . . . I might have another idea."

First, he wrote the letter and dropped it by the newspaper. He did, in fact, add Freida's thoughts to what he had already written.

This proposed Act, while claiming to stem the flood of foreign and coerced immoral labor, has not been justified by any proof that this flood is lapping upon our shores . . . . It will, instead, condemn honest Orientals already present to continued loneliness, deprive their wives of the marital companionship to which they are entitled, and condemn their mothers to unsupported old age . . . .

The editor greeted Joshua with raised eyebrows. "This is new. We usually have the same folks over and over." From his expression, he might as well have said "the same old cranks." "I'll be interested to see what's got you fired up."

Joshua thought of leaving before the editor could make that discovery. But sooner or later, especially with his new scheme in mind, he would have to actually talk to people on the topic. So he lingered while the editor glanced at the letter, then read it more closely. After what seemed to Joshua a rather long time studying it, the editor looked up. "Well, that's not how I've seen anyone look at it."

"You'll print it?"

Another too-long pause. "I guess I will. Anything that gets people talking might sell more papers. You'd better be prepared for that talk."

Joshua tipped his hat in thanks for the warning and headed back to the office. He would have little leisure for the rest of the day, but by evening he should be able to give some thought to the next step in his campaign.

The newspaper included Joshua's letter in its next edition two days later. He bought a paper, noting with a sense of irony that the editor was already proved correct: Joshua usually bought the paper only twice a month if that, and he had bought one the previous week.

His morning was spent traveling to several farms, at none of which anyone mentioned the letter. Most likely the paper had not made its way to them, if it ever would. But when he rode Nellie-girl back into the livery stable, the hostler was waiting for him, with a disturbing expression, something close to a leer, on his face. As Joshua handed him the reins, the man said with a wink, "Not wantin' those government johnnies to spoil the fun, eh? I wouldn't mind some of them Chinee girls over at Madam Mamie's. I hear they've got special ways none of the local calico queens ever learned."

Joshua bit back the retort he longed to make and forced a smile. He would have to deal with this man almost every day for the foreseeable future, and Nellie-girl's comfort was in his charge.

The next comment came from Madam Mamie, who

stuck her head into his office as he was writing up his notes on his morning patients. "'Immoral labor'? I'll be sure to tell the girls what you think of their profession."

"But — but —" After his first embarrassment, he saw that she was twitting him, and relaxed enough to be able to answer. "That's what they're claiming, which is what I said. And I wanted those who have that view to listen to me."

Her expression combined cynicism and something darker. "We sure see plenty of men with that view, as you put it. See 'em over and over, as a rule. But anyhow, I'm glad to see you sticking up for our Li Chang. He's never been anything but a gentleman to me and my girls."

Joshua had a quick dinner at the nearest saloon, and then it was off to see more patients. As he left the saloon, he was rattled to see Dolly approaching. Since Freida had chided him about her, he had been somewhat avoiding her, but it seemed she was not avoiding him. "Good afternoon, Doctor. Out on another errand of mercy?"

He wriggled inside at her phrasing. "I'm going to see Li Chang, to check how his burned arm is doing."

He could have answered her without mentioning the laundryman, but he was curious to see how she would respond. Her faint blush and shifting gaze supported what he would have guessed, that she had seen, and had not meant to mention, his letter. Half curious, half resigned to her disapproval, he pursued the subject. "Did you happen to read the paper this morning?"

She did not pretend to ignorance, but said, still looking to one side, "I did, and saw your letter. I was — surprised, I suppose. When the congressman's aide described the bill, it sounded . . . sensible. A way to protect those Chinese girls, as well as the men here who might . . . ." She blushed more deeply. ". . . who might suffer unfortunate consequences if those girls are brought to our shores."

He had said what he had to say in his letter. He would not further defend his opinion to her, standing in the street. After a supremely awkward silence, she finally looked straight at him and said, in a voice whose cheerful tone seemed forced, "But it's important for a man to get involved in the issues of the day. I'm sure your family would be proud of you for doing so."

Now that she had turned away from disagreement, he found himself perversely wishing she had continued to disagree. It would have helped him understand her better, and possibly to examine his own opinions and test their merit.

Li Chang was agitated as Joshua had never seen him. "I don't understand. What is this Act? What is Page? This Congress wants to keep my wife and my mother in China? How can they do that?"

Joshua could say little to calm him. He was no great expert on Congress, and what little he knew would not be encouraging. But he said, as he changed the dressing on Li's arm, "It may not happen. The speaker was trying to make his boss look important — this bill may not pass after all. But . . . if your wife and your mother have any way to come sooner, it might be a good idea."

"Yes, yes. I will write to them. I will tell them to leave what they can't sell, borrow from my uncle, do whatever they can."

It might give the man some bit of comfort to know what Joshua planned to do next. "I'm going to try to get folks here to sign a petition to Congress, asking them to vote against this bill. We'll see what we can do."

Li Chang grabbed Joshua's right hand and shook it hard enough that it must have made his burned arm throb.

"You are a good man, Doctor. I thank you. My wife and my mother will thank you."

Joshua returned the handshake with some embarrassment. "I look forward to seeing them here, and when they are, they can thank me if they've a mind to." He went on his way as soon as he could decently manage it.

The lawyer who had advised him was gone, riding the circuit. Another had turned up in the meantime, but Joshua was unlikely to get his advice at bargain rates. He studied his accounts and confirmed that he simply couldn't afford to hire anyone to help him word the petition. But the mayor had seemed friendly with the congressman's aide. Maybe he would be willing to share some thoughts about what phrasing might be effective in Washington.

The mayor, however, was far from willing, either to assist or to give Joshua the time of day. How dare Joshua challenge their very own representative about matters of which Joshua was so entirely ignorant! Did he think himself the intellectual equal of such a man? What business did he have interfering? Did he want to see more men infected with the noxious diseases of the Orient? Was he, perhaps, trying to ensure an influx of patients?

Joshua went from gritting his teeth to clenching his fists. He managed to leave without pounding the fellow's face in and hurried over to Robert's, there to pour out his indignation. "So good Americans are supposed to crawl on their bellies to anyone with a fancy chair in the capital? I suppose he imagines himself in Congress next, and wants to make sure all of us at home are properly mealymouthed once he gets there! He probably thinks himself above us already, from being the mayor. And him without the wit to tell a bull from a steer!"

Robert snorted at Joshua's fulminations and then reached for a bottle on his shelf. "Here, old son. Captain Worthingson's Potent Potion, sure to calm your inflamed liver, soothe your fevered brow, and knock you flat until you wake up forgetting all about it."

Joshua was distracted, as Robert no doubt intended. "Where did you come by that swindler's piss?"

"Oh, we had a medicine show come by the other day. Reckon you were out seeing to farmers."

Joshua abruptly remembered the last such invasion. "Was the pitchman a yellow-haired man, good-sized, with whiskers but no wax on 'em?"

"No, he was a runt of a fellow, with slicked-up whiskers about as wide as he was tall."

"And you bought a bottle as the price for speeding him on his way."

Robert grimaced. "Not one. Three. And stood by as four of my customers bought one apiece. And paid for his dinner at Mamie's, and a round with one of Mamie's girls. He drove a hard bargain."

"Glad I wasn't here. I have enough aggravation."

That night, the oil lamp pulled close and his tired eyes stinging, Joshua scratched out yet another line of what would be the petition if he ever finished it. What would make a difference to a congressman? What motivated them? Reelection, for one. But he could hardly claim that voting against prostitution, or in favor of foreigners so unlike most of their constituents, would cost them votes. Or could he? He could repeat and expand upon the theme Freida's comments had suggested, for what was more fundamental, more moving, than motherhood? What politician worth his salt would vote against it? And marriage was almost as sacred. . . .

We, citizens of the State of Nebraska and proud Americans,

protest against the legislation proposed, to deprive our Chinese brothers of the companionship of their wives waiting faithfully on distant shores, and yearning for the freedom and prosperity for which their menfolk left home and entrusted their futures to our country . . . And further, we entreat our Representatives to honor the bonds of kinfolk and the respect due to sacred motherhood, as this cruel bill would forever part mothers and sons, and leave those who bore those sons alone and destitute in their declining years .
. . .

He stumbled to bed after midnight, with little idea of what he had written. But in the morning, reviewing his draft by sunlight, he thought it would serve.

Joshua paid the town clerk to write out three fair copies of the petition, not trusting his own handwriting for so important a purpose. He posted one copy on the signpost in the town square and another on his office door. He would have liked to post the last one on the notice board at the church, but the preacher practically kicked him out the door at the suggestion. He took the copy to the social library during Freida's hours there and asked diffidently, "Could you see your way clear to letting me post this? I'll understand if you'd rather not risk upsetting your subscribers."

Freida snorted and plucked the paper from his hand. "Give it here, I'll put it up near the history books. People who read about history, they should be less afraid of the world and the people in it, wouldn't you think? And if they don't like it, they can try to find books somewhere else, good luck to them, they'll have a hard time." She stumped over to the desk in the room and retrieved a pen. "Here, I'll put a pen on this table, very handy." She held the pen in her hand, pondering it. "The ladies, they can't vote, can they sign this petition?"

"That's a very good question." Joshua considered the matter and picked up the pen, drawing a line down the middle of the paper and writing *Gentlemen* and *Ladies* at the tops of the columns. "The bill's sponsors claim to be protecting our womenfolk and our families. Seems fitting to have wives and mothers tell them they're wrongheaded in how they're doing it."

A new voice came from the doorway. "I'm glad to hear you say that." Clara Brook stood in the doorway with two books in her hand. She came in, handed the books to Freida, and held out her hand for the pen. "Let me be the first to sign in the 'Ladies' column." Then she hesitated, with first a troubled and then a sardonic look on her face. "At least, if you'll allow those of us who are neither wives nor mothers to sign."

"I wouldn't dream of objecting." He was heartily glad that she wanted to do it. It was balm to his spirit, after Dolly's failure to see things his way.

Clara took the pen and wrote on the paper, her signature full of bold diagonals and firm strokes, but entirely legible. "These politicians dream up a problem so they can puff out their chests solving it, and never mind who gets hurt in the doing."

It occurred to Joshua that he could inquire where she was going from here, and possibly escort her. But Freida's earlier lecture about Dolly rang in his ears, reinforced by Freida's presence. He had better watch his step. He contented himself with thanking her, and with looking out the door after her as she went her way.

Joshua had little grasp of how things worked in Washington. He didn't know how long it might be before what kind of votes on the Page Act. That made it hard to decide how long to wait for signatures before taking down the petitions and sending them — where? He did not even know that. His own congressman was unlikely to pay them any mind. They could end up used to line bird cages, or even in some congressional outhouse.

Back he went to Thaddeus. "Who's the head man in Congress?"

"For which party?"

"The Republicans, I guess. They're in charge, aren't they?"

"For now. And that would be James Blaine, in the House at least."

Joshua put Blaine's name on the envelope, got the address from Thaddeus, and filled that in as well. He would wait three days in the hope of getting more signatures.

During that time, every footstep outside his office, every creak of the door, took on a possible new meaning. It might be a patient, or Robert coming over for a chat, or the wind rattling the door as it often did. Or it might be someone reading the petition, deciding whether to sign. The window in his office did not give him a good view of anyone standing right next to the door. If footsteps approached, stopped, resumed, and faded away, it could be a nervous patient who had changed his mind, or someone who had read the petition and signed it, or someone who had read it and simply walked on.

On the second afternoon, he heard heavy steps and then the door rattling. Holding his breath, Joshua thought he could just make out the scritching of a pen on paper. He moved near his window, where he could see the street, and saw the burly frame of the barber walking away. He waited until the man had turned the corner and then opened his door. There it was, the large signature taking up more than its share of paper.

Joshua whistled to himself. You just never knew.

None of the copies had filled up entirely by the time Joshua took them down. He took one more look at the names before stuffing the copies in the envelope. He did not know whether to be amused, gladdened, or annoyed to see Dolly's careful, rounded handwriting at the end of one.

* * * * *

Joshua timed his errand according to the weather. He would prefer not to have too many people wondering why he was visiting the barber with a paper sack in his hand, and possibly lingering nearby in the hope of a confrontation. A sudden squall, complete with sleet, cleared the street well enough for his purposes. He fastened his overcoat and made his hunched and shivering way to the barbershop, slipping in without, he thought, attracting attention from anyone but the barber and his customer. Both turned toward him, the barber wary, the customer — an unfamiliar traveler, perhaps a salesman — only curious. Joshua breathed a sigh of relief. He could simply sit down as if waiting his turn, and with luck, no one else would brave the weather for a haircut or shave.

During the few minutes he had to wait, he idly studied the silvery tools sitting ready for the barber's hand and the ceramic jar full of brushes. Once the door shut behind the traveler, Joshua stood up and proffered the sack. "I brought you something. The bartender down the street tells me you like Scotch whiskey." He need not add that Clara Brook had said something similar, months before.

Mr. Hawkins's heavy brows moved slowly upward as

he took the sack. "What's the occasion, Doc?"

Joshua cleared his throat. "I mailed off the petitions concerning the Page Act yesterday. Naturally, I saw your signature."

The barber gave the basso chuckle Joshua had rarely had occasion to hear. "Would this be a thank-you, then?"

"It would."

Hawkins studied the sack in his hand, pulled out the bottle, and lumbered over to the door. He flipped the sign from Open to Closed and hung his smock on a peg. "Care to join me for a drink, then?"

Whiskey would warm him up nicely. "Yes, thank you."

The barber kept glasses in a cupboard, it seemed, and pulled out two. Joshua wondered whether there was already a bottle in there as well. Hawkins poured generous amounts for both of them, handed one glass to Joshua, and settled himself in his red leather barber chair, swiveling it around to face the room rather than the long low mirror. Joshua pulled one of the chairs in which customers waited so it faced the barber's and settled in to enjoy his drink. One taste told him that he and Hawkins had one more thing in common, their taste in whiskey. He toasted his host. "To a warming drink on a cold day."

Hawkins lifted his own glass and then took a gulp. "Good of you to come out in this weather. Appreciate it."

"And I appreciated your signing the petition."

Hawkins looked into his drink as if seeing visions there. "It's not right, what they're doing. I thought, what if it was my ma? Or my Katie?"

They nursed their drinks quietly for a few minutes. Then the barber said, "I've noticed something."

Joshua cocked his head.

"I've noticed you don't seem to like false teeth too

much."

How had the man come to that deduction? He waited. Hawkins finished his drink and poured himself another, then held the bottle out toward Joshua. Joshua held his fingers a small distance apart; Hawkins poured him a smaller amount than before, put the bottle down, and went on. "You'll pull a couple of teeth, and wait, and then pull another, before you give up and pull 'em all."

"Sometimes two teeth — the bad one and one next to it — is all they need pulled." Joshua looked into his glass and decided to wait a while before getting any nearer to emptying it. He put it down and waited for the barber to get to the point.

"I thought it might be you don't much like Waterloo teeth. Having served and all."

An astute guess, and Joshua had felt just that way when he first thought about becoming a doctor. Waterloo teeth, so named for the battle when the first human vultures thought of raiding the bodies of the dead for the teeth in their jaws, selling the teeth for dentures. Joshua's own teeth gritted at the thought of corpses still unburied, mouths gaping open, teeth missing. Recollecting himself, he glanced up at the mirror to check his expression. To his relief, the anger that had surged up in him did not show — or was no longer showing — in his face.

The barber went on, swirling the whiskey in his glass. "I wasn't never called up. Waterloo teeth wouldn't bother me." He took a drink. "You can send folks to me for 'em, if you want. If you tell me where to order the teeth."

How to honor his intention while correcting his error? "It's a thoughtful offer. But these last few years, there's something better and less expensive available. Some clever fellow invented porcelain teeth a while back, and now there's a way to set them in a kind of rubber. That's what I order, when pulling just a few teeth won't do."

Hawkins looked crestfallen. He might have been hoping to use false teeth as a wedge to get hold of other patients, but the offer could well have been in good faith. What could Joshua offer as a substitute olive branch? What tasks did he dislike, that would be within the barber's abilities?

Well, there was bloodletting. Patients still asked him about it, despite how rarely he believed it worthwhile. If he sent them to Hawkins, they might seek him out for other "treatments" Joshua considered useless. He would lose out on their fees, but it might be worth it in reduced aggravation, at least if Hawkins stopped actively trying to divert other patients his way. A significant *if*. "You know how to bleed folks, and I don't often hold with it. If I send you folks who insist on being bled, will you try to get them to look for you for all their ailments? And tell their friends to do the same?"

The barber grinned. "Guess we might still tussle over some folks." The grin faded. "But I won't seek anyone out, for bleeding or anyone else, if you send folk to me from time to time. You might not think it, but I want you to stay in business. I might need doctoring someday."

"So you might." Time to be diplomatic. "As good as you are with a razor, even you might get cut now and again. Or get sick like anyone else." Joshua held up his almost-empty glass. "Shall we toast our truce?"

The barber lifted his own glass, topped off both, and clinked his glass against Joshua's. "To our bargain, then." He and Joshua both drained their glasses, and Hawkins reached for the bottle. "One more?"

Joshua put his glass on the table and stood up. "Best not, or you might be needing me soon, and I'll be too drunk to tend you."

Leaving the barbershop, Joshua found that walking required somewhat more attention than usual. He should perhaps have taken one glass fewer of that whiskey.

He found himself wanting to tell someone what he had — or hoped he had — just achieved. Robert? He would almost certainly be interested. But he was also likely to express some skepticism about the arrangement. Who might welcome the news while refraining from pessimistic predictions?

The image of Clara Brook floated to mind. She would likely understand how draining the feud had been, how glad Joshua would be to leave it behind him. And she would appreciate the solution he had come up with. He was just about sure she shared his views about bloodletting as a cure-all.

But she would also be well acquainted with the signs of inebriation. Whatever her opinion of him, he did not want to lessen it by approaching her with an unsteady gait and (probably) reddened eyes, to say nothing of whiskey on his breath. He sighed and headed home to tell the tale to Major. Major would thump his tail on the floor, and Joshua could take that as approval.

Chapter 20

JOSHUA LAY lazy in bed on a Sunday morning and contemplated going to church. He didn't go as often as he probably should, to reassure his neighbors if for no other reason. And he had plenty of time yet to get dressed and have some breakfast first. But after a long, trying week, he needed to sleep more than to spend time praying. And scandalous as the thought might be, he'd never known praying to do much for him or anyone.

He had just decided to let himself go back to sleep when, as if to punish him for it, there came a pounding on the door. Major jumped off the bed barking; Joshua rubbed bleary eyes and called out over Major's noise. "Hold on! I'm coming!"

He cracked the door open and saw a boy, maybe thirteen years old, with eyes so wide the whites were showing, no room for pride in being chosen to come. This one was going to be bad. Joshua's stomach sank to somewhere near his knees as he opened the door wider. "Come in while I get ready."

Major eeled out the door as the boy came in. Joshua considered putting some scraps on a plate outside his door, then decided against it. He'd probably end up feeding either strays or rats. Major was good at cadging scraps from the butcher. He'd be all right, even if Joshua didn't make it home before evening.

While Joshua dressed, the boy stammered out what he

knew. His older brother had managed to let the plowshare, propped up for cleaning, fall on his leg. He was in the barn. Their pa had told the boy to come fetch the doctor. His brother was hollering so loud, the boy had trouble getting the horse to hold still for him to mount up.

Joshua jammed his boots on, grabbed his bag, and stopped. He had better bring the bone saw. Cursing under his breath, trying not to let the boy hear, he dragged the saw in its case down from the shelf, threw it in his bag, and banged down the stairs ahead of the boy, running for the stable.

Joshua's horse and the boy's were both winded when they arrived at the Barlow farm. Joshua paid little mind. The horses would, he feared, have plenty of time to recover before Joshua would need his own again. But he did tell the boy to put a blanket over Nellie-girl before striding toward the barn to see his patient.

To his considerable surprise, Clara Brook emerged, her head bare, and came to meet him. Her pallor fit with all the other discouraging signs. She explained briefly that the patient's mother had come to fetch her, seeing as she lived a good deal closer than town and might be able to help somehow until the doctor arrived. Joshua gathered that was pretty much a quote.

He looked her in the eye. "How bad is it?"

She held his gaze. "I'd rather let you be the judge of that. I might be making too much of it."

Clara might still have some hope that the man would keep his leg. Joshua couldn't muster much of the same.

He stopped short in the barn doorway as the patient came into view. The groaning, tossing figure, lying on a rough, torn blanket atop the straw, was barely more than a boy. Just around the age of all the men or boys Joshua had seen on blood-soaked tables, an Army doctor standing over them with a saw in his hand.

He staggered and might have toppled sideways if Clara had not been there, grabbing his arm and steadying him. He turned toward her and saw her read, and then reflect, the anguish in his face. Her grip on his arm went from support to a more frantic clutch. She said under her breath, "You can get through this." And after a long, shaky breath: "I'll get you through it."

But her hand was trembling on his arm.

He whispered, "I'll do the same for you."

He heard multiple footsteps behind them and turned around. The boy, his parents, a sister, all looking at him with various mixtures of hope and terror. He turned back to his patient, approached him, knelt beside him. "What's your name, son?"

The young man looked up at him, straining as if he could hardly focus. "Tom. Are you the doctor?"

"That's right. So I'd better take a look at you." He turned back the cloth someone had laid over the injured leg.

He saw at once that there would be no saving the entire limb. It was crushed, mangled, a few inches below the knee. That left the grim question of whether to try for a below-the-knee amputation, and risk having to cut again higher after seeing what was left, or cut above the knee to start with and be sure of cutting only once.

He could ask the parents what they wanted him to do, but that would be craven of him. They had no way to know what was best, even as much as he did.

Clara had crouched down beside him. He said under his breath, "How many amputations have you assisted?"

She answered in a monotone. "Too many. And saw the results of many, after."

"What think you? Above or below?"

She looked toward his bag. "Your saw — is it good and sharp?"

He so hated the sight of the thing, it had been some time since he sharpened it. But he couldn't remember using it since — and he would have remembered. He fished the case out of his bag and inspected the blade, testing it with the forefinger of his left hand. It should do. "You're thinking I can cut close enough, save the knee?"

She said very quietly, "If it were mine to decide, which I'm thankful it isn't, I'd be choosing so. If it's the wrong choice, you can cut again, and by tomorrow it'll make little difference. If you cut higher, there's no going back from it."

Joshua swallowed the bile in his throat and nodded. Standing, he approached the huddled family group and said, "I'm afraid much of the leg has to go, or it'll mortify and kill him." He waited a moment for them to absorb that blow and then went on. "I'm going to amputate below the knee. But I must warn you, I won't know for sure if that's good enough until I try it."

He stood there awkwardly, as if waiting for absolution, and then returned to the barn. A sudden doubt assailed him: did his bag still contain the secondhand Army Surgeon's Field Companion, with its tin of chloroform and sutures? He hurried over and threw the bag open, gasping in relief to find the kit there at the bottom, along with a sponge to use. He retrieved the kit and sponge, along with his case of scalpels. Returning to the family, whom he had left staring, he asked, "When was the last time he ate anything?"

The mother answered. "He just took a little biscuit and coffee to sustain him while he did the morning chores. I was making him a big breakfast when — when —" She buried her face in her apron.

It could be worse. If the injury had occurred after the boy had had a chance to eat that big breakfast, using chloroform would risk him vomiting and choking, and Joshua would have had to choose between that risk and using only morphine. He took a deep breath and said with as much command as he could muster, "While I'm getting ready, I'd appreciate it if you could fetch plenty of clean cloths and hot water."

The mother and sister ran toward the house. Joshua beckoned the father and drew him away from the boy. "I don't think your other son needs to see this. And I don't want any distractions I can avoid."

Rather than invite further discussion, he went back to his patient. The chloroform would render the young man insensible for the operation itself, but Joshua would need to administer morphine for the awful pain after. He pulled out his clean handkerchief, filled up his hypodermic syringe, and laid the syringe on the handkerchief.

Blood was still welling up in the wound and dribbling out onto the straw. He needed to get to work. Standing and striding back into the yard, he demanded, "Where's that water and the cloths!"

The father, now standing alone, clenched his fists. "I'll go see to it." He strode off.

Joshua knew he had spoken harshly, but he had no mind to spare for such things. In fact, mind, a clear head, was getting hard for him to manage, harder by the second. Was that the rumble of a cart he heard on the road, or the wheels of cannon being rolled into position? Why was he standing in a barn instead of a tent? Why the odor of blood mingled with that of fresh straw instead of stale?

He started as a nurse — she looked familiar — shook his shoulder. "Doctor Gibbs!"

He gasped for breath and came to himself. "I'm all

right. Thank you."

She pointed toward the patient. He had somehow missed seeing one or both women in the family return and leave again. "The water and cloths are ready."

Joshua pulled out his smock and put it on, then knelt back by the soldier — no, the farm boy — and dipped a cloth in the water. The nurse took it from him and swabbed away the blood around the wound, then let the cloth fall into the gash and soak up more. The young man moaned.

Joshua opened the tin of chloroform and carefully poured a small amount onto the sponge. He handed the sponge to the nurse; she held it over the man's nose and mouth, murmuring to him, "Just breathe in. That's right."

The man said something Joshua could barely understand, his voice twisted with pain and muffled by the cloth. "My leg . . . Can you save it?"

The man spoke to the nurse — Clara, that was her name — but this news was Joshua's to deliver. "I'm afraid not. We have to take it to save your life. We're going to try cutting below the knee."

The man tried to sit up. Joshua pressed down on his shoulders as Clara held the cloth in place. The man moaned, and a single tear leaked down across his cheek and into the blanket below him.

And then, again, as if for the first time, except the voice was weaker: "Can you save my leg? . . ."

Joshua clenched his teeth and waited. As the chloroform took effect, the man's muscles contracted and relaxed again, once and twice. Finally, they stayed relaxed. Clara lifted the man's closed eyelid and said to Joshua, "He's under."

"Keep the cloth on him whenever I don't need you to do something else. Wet it again every few minutes. You know the amount?"

"Yes. Shall I wipe here?" She indicated the point on the

leg where Joshua would have to cut.

He felt a deep thankfulness that she knew not just how to assist, but what questions to ask. "Please. And then stay alert to hold him down if he starts writhing about."

The nurse dipped a fresh cloth in the hot water and wiped in one steady motion. Joshua pulled the correct scalpel from the case and made a swift slashing cut, through skin and muscle down to the bone. He was dimly aware that Clara had added another few drops of chloroform to the sponge and put it in place again. He picked up the saw and with quick circular motions sawed through the bone and then down through the flesh beneath. Clara mopped up blood as he worked.

The surgeons doing this gruesome job during the war had had to work as quickly as possible, and would simply slice on through the limb, leaving a raw stump that could take a long time to heal. Joshua could instead leave some skin from which to fashion a flap and sew it over the stump. It would heal more quickly, as long as he made sure to visit often enough to detect any signs of infection.

When the lower leg was fully detached, Clara lifted it away and put it somewhere close by, then handed him a needle she had already threaded with silk thread. Joshua used a rasp to scrape the protruding piece of bone smooth at its end and edges before he trimmed the flap of skin, pulled it across the stump, and sewed the patchwork closed, leaving only a small hole for fluid to drain from. Then he slumped back on his heels, shuddering, as Clara deftly bandaged the stump.

Where had he put the syringe? He fumbled for it, forced his hand steady, and injected the morphine into the man's nearest upper arm. "You can take away the sponge now and let him come to."

Their patient came back to consciousness babbling,

almost as if drunk. Joshua forced himself to stay by the man's side as he surfaced. But the morphine kept the man dulled, peaceful. By the time he was able to rage and weep and despair, Joshua would be on Nellie-girl and heading for home.

A hoarse, choking sob came not from the patient, but from somewhere behind. Joshua rose, joints protesting, to his feet and looked for the source. The man's father was standing just inside the doorway to the barn. He might have been there the whole time, unable to do anything but witness the cutting off of his son's leg and who knew how many of his hopes. Now he was staring at Joshua's blood-soaked smock. Joshua pulled off the smock and threw it behind him.

A rustling of straw came from the vicinity of the patient. Joshua turned back to see Clara sprawled on the straw next to the bloody blanket. Had she fainted? No, her eyes were open, staring upward, at the heavy wooden beams above or at some inward vision. He went to her and supported her into a sitting position, fumbling for and squeezing her hand. It took a worrisome few seconds before she squeezed back and said, "Help me up, if you would."

He pulled her upright and then dug in his bag for the other morphine, the powder. He approached the father, making as much noise with his feet as he could to give the man warning and a chance to collect himself. The father looked up at him, face working in sorrow. Joshua held out the can of powder. "If you should need to change the bandages before I return or between my subsequent visits, dust this on the stump. Keep it handy for me to use, as well. In the meantime, whenever the pain gets bad, give him laudanum." Did the family have any, or know where to get it? Did they have bandages? He could not think about any of that now. He could not think about anything but leaving this place. But he would have to come back, tomorrow and the next day, to see to his patient. And then his patient would be able to tell him just what he had done.

But at least he would not be back in this barn. Just another few minutes to pack up his things. Clara, during his brief talk with the father, had cleaned his saw and needle with the remaining water and wiped them dry, and rolled up his smock with the bloody side in. All that remained was Clara's abandoned bonnet, the blanket as bloody as a battlefield, and some blood spatters on the straw nearby. Clara looked at the barn floor and back at Joshua before saying, "I'll clean that up before I head for home."

She was pale and shivering. "Not by yourself. I can help you."

"The family can help me, if I need it."

"I'll help. And then I can get you home. Nellie-girl can carry us both."

In another few minutes, he was standing by Nellie-girl and staring at the mare's back. Of course he had no side saddle. He asked Clara, resting against a tree stump with her bonnet back on, "Do you think you could sit astride the mare, if I assisted you?" If not, he could walk beside the mare and try to steady Clara sitting sideways.

Clara managed something like a smile. "I have done, and with no one assisting me, when someone needed a message sent or help summoned in a hurry during the war."

He gave Clara a leg up and made sure she was secure sitting astride the puzzled mare. It then took him two tries, and the aid of the tree stump, to mount up behind her. Clara showed him where to go, Joshua not having approached the Brook farm from this direction before, and he let Nellie-girl set the pace at an easy walk. Clara might have been falling asleep, her body slumping forward, her belly soft beneath his encircling arm.

Clara's brother came out to meet them as they approached, looking a little puzzled. The boy and his father had probably expected Clara home hours earlier. Joshua pulled Nellie-girl to a halt, dismounted, and stood back for the man to help his sister down, saying to him, "She's had a long day and a hard one."

The brother supported his sister in an awkward side embrace while looking at Joshua. "She was able to be of some help, then, in whatever you were doing?"

Joshua put his hands hard against his sides to control their shaking. The fury sweeping through him was not, or barely, to do with the youth standing before him. "She was of great and much needed assistance." And to her, though he was not sure she could hear him: "Thank you. I am deeply in your debt."

He thought he could feel the youth's blank stare at his back as he rode away.

Only as Joshua struggled to stay on the mare's back did he realize that he had eaten nothing all day, and that it was past noon. If he had been less exhausted, and less shaken, he would have stopped at the saloon for a sandwich. Instead, he dragged himself up the stairs to his rooms, sat down to remove his boots, and looked at the bed he had abandoned what seemed like half a year ago.

He was still staring when a knock, a soft one this time, roused him. He hauled himself to his feet and shuffled to the door in his stockings. It was Freida, holding one of her pots, and Major whining at her feet, then tangled up in Joshua's feet, rubbing against his legs, tail drooping. Joshua dragged his gaze back up to Freida, who said in her usual rush, "I saw you come in, so tired, I thought you might have been too busy to eat, you should have some soup, beef and potatoes, some carrots, some onions. May I come in?"

He stepped back wordlessly and let her set the pot on the table, find a bowl, fill it. He fell into a chair and stared at the bowl until a spoon landed beside it. With an effort like lifting an anvil, he picked up the spoon and ladled some soup into his mouth.

He looked up at Freida long enough to see the motherly concern on her face and then dropped his eyes back to the bowl. He kept eating, with a stubborn determination like something in a dream, until he heard the door open and close again. There was still some soup in the bowl. He set it on the floor for Major, let his head fall into his hands, and sobbed like a broken-hearted child. Or like a young man, barely more than a boy, waking up with only half a leg.

Chapter 21

IT TOOK four days, longer than Joshua had expected, for the news to spread. Maybe the Barlow family had been too busy tending the young man to come into town, or hadn't needed anything enough to take them from his side. And Clara Brook — he hadn't seen her since he left her leaning against her brother, but even if she had come into town, he doubted she would have said a word about the job they had had to do together.

He went out to the farm twice during that time. His patient had not, so far, shown signs of infection, a stroke of luck Joshua had hardly dared to hope for. And whatever Tom's reaction had been at first, he met Joshua's return with resignation. He had little to say, but did volunteer, as Joshua was leaving after the first visit, "I don't blame you, Doc. You did what you had to." Which was almost worse than blame would have been.

Joshua attempted to comfort his patient, or himself, by telling him about the modern prosthetic limbs available. "You'll be able to walk on it just about like a regular leg, with practice." The lad at least affected to believe him.

After those four days, as word got around, people started making their comments. From most, it was a quiet word about how that was a hard thing he'd had to do. A few of them had said what a shame it was, for a young man to be crippled, and not even in the war. A couple had started to say something about whether there might have been some other way — but his freezing glare cut such speculations short.

The veterans understood best. It would be a rare man who came through the war without seeing the piles of severed limbs, or a fellow soldier learning to use crutches as he left for home.

Meanwhile, Joshua had his other patients to see. He found himself driven to prayer, after all, pleading for a respite, as long a time as he could have before the next maimed man or dying woman. And whether due to the prayers or no, the woman whose husband had come for him from Rushing, that town's doctor being away, needed little more than some time over steaming hot water with pine oil to get her breathing easier.

By the time he left, the sky was darkening well before its expected hour. Alton, sticking his head out of the schoolhouse, invited him in to wait the weather out, but Joshua had his mind set on home and his own easy chair. And while Major could find shelter if necessary, the dog would be more comfortable indoors by the fire. He pushed Nellie-girl as hard as he could to beat the storm.

He almost made it. He was less than two miles from the edge of town when the sky opened up on him, pelting him first with gouts of cold water and then with wind-driven sleet. He had trouble seeing his way, only Nellie-girl's horse sense saving them from riding into first an ice-burdened tree, and then an abandoned and ruinous shed. He pulled her up under another tree, trying to get his bearings. The livery stable was on the other side of town from here, but he was only about fifty yards from Dolly and Hope's house and barn. Nellie-girl was wet and shivering; she needed shelter, and soon. He would have to make for Dolly's, but he could go into the barn without troubling her.

That resolve began to weaken almost immediately.

In the dim light, he could not find a blanket to put over Nellie-girl, nor anything to wipe her down with. And the barn was not weather-tight enough to keep out all of the winds that seemed to be increasing in strength. His wet, cold clothing clung to him as if he were drowning in it.

Reluctantly he left the mare in the barn and shivered his way to Dolly's door. She did not answer right away, and he wondered whether she could be away somewhere or whether the wind was drowning out his knock. But after the third and somewhat more emphatic knock, she opened the door and stared wide-eyed at him. Hope stood behind her, peeking around her mother's waist.

Joshua took off his hat, sending shards of ice to the ground, and said, "I'm very sorry to trouble you. My horse and I were caught in the ice storm, and I've put her in your barn. Might I ask the favor of a blanket for her?" He did not quite have the nerve to ask for one for himself, but he trusted her good heart to prompt the offer.

Dolly threw the door open wide. "You come right in! I'll fetch a blanket for your horse in a jiffy, and then we'll see about you. Hope, say good evening to Doctor Gibbs while I go for that blanket."

Hope did her little curtsy. "Good evening, Doctor Gibbs. You're wet."

He had to smile. "I surely am, mistress. It's raining and sleeting out there. It gladdens me to see you and your mama so cozy and dry."

Small as she was, Dolly could still move quickly. Almost as soon as he had stepped inside, just barely out of the weather, she was back with a large close-woven blanket in some sort of plaid. She would have gone right on outside with it if he hadn't stopped her. "I'm already wet, ma'am. I'll take it to her."

"At least take a lantern, so you can find what else she'll

be needing. There are cloths hanging up, and a bag of oats in the corner farthest from the door. And when you come back in, I'll have some dry things for you to change into."

"Thank you kindly, ma'am." He took the blanket and the lantern she handed him, turned, clenched his jaw, and headed back out into the storm, which felt even colder and windier than a few minutes before. He found what he needed for Nellie-girl, took off her saddle and tackle, and did what was necessary for him to leave her with a clear conscience. Dolly had kept the door open and waved him inside. "You poor man! I've put some of Mr. Arden's things on that stool there, and a towel. You peel off those clothes and get changed while Hope and I make you some tea — or would you rather have coffee?"

Joshua considered the choice. Coffee would do better at keeping him awake when he went back out, but it would also make him jittery and maybe keep him up when he was ready to collapse into bed. Tea would warm him, and help a little in staying alert. "Tea would be wonderful, ma'am."

She beamed at him as if delighted to be fussing over a dripping uninvited guest. "Come along, Hope." She whisked herself and the child away, leaving him free to shuck off his clothes as fast as he was able and then spend a luxurious few minutes drying off before getting dressed again. The clothes smelled of starch, soap, and just a whiff of another man's odor. He felt a bit as if he were borrowing a dead man's skin, and muttered an awkward word of gratitude.

He left his wet things in a pile near the door and made his way to the kitchen. Hope, at her most domestic, was setting out a cup and saucer for him, as well as a plate. Dolly poured the tea as he was sitting down and put a basket of biscuits in front of him, along with a jar of her peach preserves. He let out a huge sigh. "Ma'am, I believe I just took a wrong turn and ended up in heaven."

She shook her curls at him. "As cold and wet as you were, you might almost have done that very thing. Why didn't you stay wherever you were?"

He supposed her hospitality gave her the right to scold him, so he answered meekly, "An error in judgment, ma'am." Then he applied himself to tea and biscuits and preserves.

Dolly sipped at some tea; Hope was allowed a single biscuit, but no more. "Not until supper."

Joshua had neglected to transfer his pocket watch to his borrowed clothing. He only hoped it had not gotten wet enough to need repair. He looked around for a clock and only then noticed the friendly ticking of a clock on a shelf near the stove. "When will you ladies be having supper? I'll be sure to be out of your way by then."

Dolly frowned, somehow keeping the expression charming. "And get drenched and frozen again? That storm isn't letting up before nightfall, and I'd guess for hours after. No, you'll stay for supper, and stop the night here if it's still wild out."

"I wouldn't want to impose on you — "

"Nonsense! I call it positively providential, having a man here on a night like this, instead of a woman and child all on their own. We'll be a sight less frightened."

He couldn't quite see the logic of it. He was hardly endowed with the ability to affect the fury of the storm, or to keep branches or even trees from falling under the burden of ice. But he supposed he could be of some help in either event. Besides, seeing the light in Hope's eyes, he could believe that his visit might prove a distraction any thoughts of danger, and from the howl of the wind.

"If you're sure, ma'am, then I'll accept your very kind invitation."

She nodded briskly. "Good! Now I'll fetch those wet clothes and get them drying by the fire."

Warming his hands by the fire — even the smell of it seemed warming somehow, if somewhat tainted by the odor of his drying clothes — he looked around for a suitable place to sleep. There was the floor, of course, which would be tolerably comfortable with the addition of a blanket or two. Compared to the rocky ground or mud in which, a few years ago, he had often snatched what sleep he could, it would be positive luxury. But he might be able to scrunch himself up small enough to fit on the love seat along the wall.

Over a supper of bread and butter and cold bacon, he asked whether Dolly had any preference as to these two choices. To his surprise and discomfort, she scorned both of them. "Put a guest on the floor? What do you think of me? And that sofa wouldn't fit but half of you."

Hope interjected, "Mama, he can have my bed! It's longer than the sofa, and I can sleep with you."

Dolly looked sternly at her daughter. "Don't interrupt when adults are speaking." She apparently considered that sufficient answer to Hope's suggestion.

Joshua wrinkled his forehead. What alternative was there? He could bed down in the barn, but that didn't seem to be how her thoughts were tending.

Dolly noted his bewilderment and smiled, head tilted to one side, eyes crinkled. "We'll do what folks used to do all the time. We'll bundle."

Joshua's eyebrows shot up before he could catch them. Bundling was still sometimes practiced when folks were traveling, or when young people were courting. In the latter case, they might be sewn into bundling bags, or sleep with

a board between them, not that either always stopped the
carrying-on it was supposed to prevent. . . . Well, he
supposed he was traveling, in a way. And as bone-tired as
he felt, he didn't know as he had the strength of will to turn
down the chance of an actual bed under him.

He wasn't sure what to say, but she seemed to take his
assent for granted, bustling about clearing away the supper
dishes and humming a little tune. Hope pouted a bit, but
soon enough went to help her mother.

Joshua hoped his clothes would be dry by the time
they retired for the night. He would feel more than a little
peculiar, sleeping next to Dolly in the bed she had shared
with her husband and wearing the man's clothes to boot.

Back in his own shirt and trousers, he stood in the
doorway of the room where Hope slept, watching Dolly
tuck the little girl in bed. The domesticity of it gave him a
queer, lonesome feeling in his chest. One of his sisters was
younger than he, and he had often seen his mother tuck her
in, before tucking him in not long after. But whatever he
was feeling, it wasn't some lost moment of maternal
affection.

He declined the offer of another cup of tea and made a
dash through the rain to check on Nellie-girl, with his still-
damp coat and the already-damp blanket over him for
protection. When he came back in, he did not see Dolly
away. She might have already retired for the night.

He found her bedroom where, from his early tour, he
had expected it, and there found her. Rather than wear all
her things to bed, she had stripped down to her petticoats,
and was sitting on the bed waiting for him to show up. She
was a fine enough sight sitting there, her arms and
shoulders showing in the light of the bedside candle. He

had left his boots by the door, intending to sleep in the rest, but now it might look like a comment on her choice, or even a rebuke. Turning away, he stripped down to his smallclothes and slipped under the covers as quickly as he could. The mattress yielded beneath him, softer than his own. He heard her blow out the candle and slide into the bed beside him, only inches away. The warmth of her body reached him, teasing him with her nearness, seeming to wriggle right into his brain and conjure pictures of the soft curving flesh under the thin layers of fabric.

He had lain with plenty of whores, some of them on winter nights like this where a body's warmth would be welcome. But he had never lingered in those beds, or drifted toward sleep with soft breathing beside him and the sweet scent of woman carried on the air.

He rolled to the side to keep his back toward her. He would not do anything to encourage the twitching in his loins, but if he stiffened on his own, she'd know no sign of it. For now, as he drifted toward dreaming, what came to him were not images of grappling and lust, but a sort of phantom copy of the bed where he lay, a dream of future days where he shared such a bed with a woman who had a claim on him, and who claimed him in return.

The screams of men already pierced by the metal shards of artillery shells mingled with the shrieking of more shells overhead. Accompanying this shrill chorus came the bass rumble of cannon, and of Union forces firing their artillery in return. All the while, Joshua found himself sinking into the mud, as soft and deceptively welcoming as a feather bed. He thrashed about, trying to free himself, knowing that even if he did, there was nowhere he could hide.

A shell burst, so close by that he howled in pure animal terror —

The bloom of a candle nearby. Softness beneath him, but dry, not clammy. And a cry, but not the agonized screaming of the wounded — the sobbing wail of a child. Joshua sat up to find himself confined by something heavy. A shroud? Was he alive or slain?

"Joshua — Doctor Gibbs! What is it? Hope, darling, it's all right. Doctor Gibbs?"

A woman's voice, soft but clearly frightened. A soldier's wife come in search of her husband? But this was no battlefield. Too slowly, the confusion lifted, and the world formed around him: a bed, a room, candlelight, and a woman in petticoats, holding a trembling child close to her bosom.

He stood up, pulling the blanket with him and wrapping it around him. "Mrs. Arden. I seem to have had a nightmare. From the look of things, I'm guessing I made some noise."

Hope's sobs subsided, and she twisted around to stare at him, her face shining with tears in the candlelight. "You made a *lot* of noise. You shouted. And then you *yelled*."

"I'm very sorry, Miss Hope." The nightmares had been less frequent of late; he had even dared to hope they were gone for good. What had set him off? The unfamiliar surroundings, the disconcerting softness of the bed? Those small strangenesses, and perhaps the wailing of the wind, might have been enough. And there had probably been some sudden loud noise, like a branch falling on the roof . . . .

Hope's face shifted from fright to indignation. "I never heard a man yell like that. I don't think they're *spozed* to." Dolly opened her mouth as if to correct the child and then closed it again. From the look on her face, she felt much the same way.

Joshua breathed deep to calm himself. "The late Mr. Arden was in the war, as I recall . . . ."

Dolly stood up straighter. "He served, of course. As the corps' quartermaster."

"I see." Little chance of those experiences troubling his dreams.

Joshua dropped the blanket back onto the bed and stooped to retrieve his shirt and trousers. Holding them, he gave a little bow. "If I may, Mrs. Arden, I think I'd best spend what's left of the night on that sofa after all."

Dolly's face clouded with distress. "Oh, you needn't do that. It's quite all right." And then, after a pause: "I do understand."

She did not, nor would she ever. Joshua shook his head and made his way around the woman and girl, holding his clothes in front of him like a shield.

He did not try to sleep. He would not risk another nightmare, though he thought it unlikely. He got dressed and tiptoed into the kitchen to look at the clock. Only another two hours or so until dawn.

Looking out the window, he could see trees waving their upper branches, but the wild wind had eased. No rain or sleet hit the glass. The storm had blown itself out, a little too late.

He lit the oil lamp, found the notebook in his bag, tore out a page, and spent the hours until daylight composing a letter to Dolly. Then he crumpled it up and stuffed it in his pocket before leaving the house, closing the door gently behind him, and saddled Nellie-girl to take him back where he belonged.

Chapter 22

JOSHUA went to bed in the early morning and awoke hours later with a miserable cold. He dragged himself to his office, put up a DOCTOR IS SICK sign, and dragged himself back to his rooms again, there to spend the rest of the day coughing, sneezing, blowing his nose, and cursing everything about the day before, from the weather to its disastrous results.

Freida, of course, insisted on bringing soup — chicken again. "The best thing for a cold! You watch how it helps, then you'll know, you can tell your patients." When she had finally left and he was sitting in his easy chair eating (and, he had to admit, feeling strengthened by) her soup, she returned with one of her quilts. She would have tucked it around him if he had not lost his temper and shouted hoarsely at her to leave him in peace.

She dropped the quilt on top of him, narrowly missing the bowl in his hands, and thrust her considerable chest out at him. "I'm leaving, I'm leaving! God forbid I should bother you, a big important doctor, busy feeling sorry for yourself." She closed the door with force just short of a slam.

Of course she didn't know what had happened. She would have been more forbearing if she had. . . . A sudden thought made him jump out of the chair, tripping on the quilt and dropping the bowl with a clatter. What if she went to talk to Dolly? To complain, to seek advice, to send someone to him that he would be less likely to treat rudely?

He knew Dolly would not come. He could only hope that she would not tell Freida why.

Freida brought him soup again two days later. When he apologized, she shushed him. "You were sick, naturally you got cranky. So you need to take care of yourself, get better, then you'll be able to keep your temper. A hot compress on your chest, it'll loosen up that phlegm, you'll see."

He laughed out loud, which made him cough again. "Yes, Doctor Blum. Whatever you say."

She gave him a stern look down her nose. "There have been doctors how long, compared to old women? And somehow people survived long enough for doctors to come along."

When Joshua recovered enough to get around again, there was so much work waiting for him that he overexerted himself and relapsed. Freida came to scold him, and he suffered it humbly: he should have known better. This time he paced himself, seeing only the patients who needed him most urgently. The first day that he made it to evening without struggling to stay awake for supper, he declared himself well.

Freida must have agreed. She stopped by the next day, caught him up on events, and asked, so she said, a favor. "Rachel, my niece, she's coming to visit! Her parents, they found her a Jewish man to marry, a little older, but a good provider and worships the ground she walks on, my sister says, and they're getting married this summer, so she wants to come see me while she can, one of her cousins has business farther west and can escort her, then he'll come back for her in a couple of weeks." She stopped for breath and went on, "So I'm going to meet the train, I could use some company while I'm waiting if you're not busy, who knows if it'll come on time, and if it wouldn't be too much trouble, you could bring the buggy, Rachel will have luggage."

Joshua wondered what else Freida might have in mind. Had she discovered the change in his relations with Dolly, and meant to get to the cause of it while he was distracted and off guard? Or while he was in a public place and would be constrained as to his manner of protesting?

He would take preemptive action.

As they drove to the station, Nellie-girl pulling the buggy at a sedate pace, he told Freida, "You mustn't ask me about Mrs. Arden."

He was aiming for uninformative firmness. But he could feel a jaw muscle twitching in his cheek. Freida opened her mouth and then closed it. She said, quietly for her, "You say don't ask, I don't ask. Would I stick my nose into your business?"

Joshua burst out laughing. Freida made a brief attempt to look offended, but after a few seconds she gave up and laughed with him. The baker, the barber, and two farmers stopped in the street and stared at them, which made them laugh harder as they reached the station.

They were early — an eastbound train would be coming through before the westbound train brought Rachel and her businessman cousin. Two passengers stood near the track, a well-dressed older man with a valise and a woman with a larger trunk —

Joshua exclaimed, "Clara!" without intending to do so. Freida looked at him in surprise, but he paid her no heed, joining Clara and the older man. Both had turned toward him, the man with a vaguely censorious expression, probably due to his use of Clara's given name, and Clara with no expression beyond a dull weariness.

He had wondered, in stray moments when he thought of anything beyond his own miseries, how Clara was faring, whether she had suffered any lingering impact from that day at the Barlow farm. It had even crossed his mind to go see her. But Freida's strictures about endangering the reputations of women, or low spirits, or shyness, or a mixture of them had kept him from actually doing it. And here she was, seemingly ill or in distress, and bound on some journey.

Joshua suppressed his embarrassment at intruding and introduced himself to the man with Clara. The man reciprocated, briefly. He shared Clara's last name. An uncle, perhaps. But where was he taking her? And "taking" appeared to be the right word, from the demeanor of both.

Before he could decide whether or how to question either of them, the train appeared around the bend. The uncle took Clara's arm as if to steer her. The train pulled in, puffing and grinding; the uncle gave Joshua a short nod as the conductor descended the stairs and called, "All aboard!"

As her uncle towed Clara toward the stairs, Clara turned and looked Joshua in the eye, in a sort of solemn farewell.

Joshua returned to Freida's side and tried to pay attention to her report of Rachel's fiancé and impending nuptials. He suspected his efforts would have fallen short, but Freida was apparently too excited by her niece's imminent arrival to notice his distraction.

The westbound train arrived in due course, and the travelers disembarked with Rachel's single suitcase. Freida thanked the cousin profusely, saw him back onto the train with a kiss on the cheek, and enveloped her niece in a Freida-sized hug before holding her at arm's length. "You must be exhausted, but you look so well, let me look at you!"

The young woman's slim nose and pointed chin were familiar from the photograph; her hair, a surprising shade between copper and auburn; her eyes, a warm brown. As soon as Freida released her, she turned toward Joshua, smiling warmly. "You must be Doctor Gibbs. Thank you so much for meeting the train. Oh, and do call me Rachel."

He refrained from mentioning that Freida had failed to tell him her surname. "Certainly, if you wish it. How was your journey?"

She replied at some length and with a quickness of speech that reminded Joshua of her aunt. He found it impossible to attend to what she said to the degree politeness required; but fortunately, Freida's eager interest and frequent interjections disguised his neglect. When his failure to contribute became too glaring, he managed to smile and say, "I would wager that your aunt's kitchen is overflowing by now with all the dishes she's made to welcome you."

Rachel gave a rueful little laugh. "It's a good thing Auntie is a seamstress, because I won't fit any of my clothes by the time I go home." She turned wide, appealing eyes on him. "Please come with me and eat some of what she's made!"

He replied quickly, before Freida could chime in repeating the invitation. "I'm afraid there are matters I must attend to, but it has been a great pleasure to meet you." By now they had reached the buggy, so he could concentrate on assisting both women inside. It took little time, though it felt longer, for them to reach Freida's, where he helped them out again, carried Rachel's case inside, and said his goodbyes. Then he was finally free to return to the buggy and dwell on his thoughts, which were increasingly troubling.

Where was Clara going, and why did she, or her kin, think she needed an escort to go there?

He hesitated for a couple of days, knowing her family would be puzzled and possibly offended at his making inquiries. But the morning of the third day, he rode Nellie-girl out to the Barlow farm, examined Tom, replenished the family's supply of laudanum, and headed from there to the Brook place.

Clara's family were, as he had expected, bewildered at his stopping by. Joshua explained to Clara's father, "After she assisted me so well in such a difficult case, I wanted to thank her once again, and make sure she had suffered no ill effects in the aftermath." He would probably learn more and meet less resistance if he pretended ignorance of her leaving town.

Mr. Brook wrinkled his forehead and goggled at him. "What case? Assisted? How? Our Clara isn't a nurse no more."

Had she told them nothing? Had her brother not mentioned Joshua's praise? "I would have had serious difficulty dealing with young Tom Barlow's crushed leg had she not been there, doing so much for me and for that poor lad." He owed it to her to say more. "It was a hard thing for both of us, and she helped me immensely."

The man shook his head. "Well, I wish the lass had said more about it. We knew Tom's mother had come, though not exactly why, and Clara went off with her. And she came back looking mighty wrung out, her brother said. We didn't make much of it at the time. But I figure that's when she started being so poorly."

Joshua hung onto his patience with difficulty. "Can

you tell me more about how she was?"

Clara's mother had come up and took her turn answering. "She got awful moody. Hardly talking, except once in a while to snap at someone, which wasn't usual. She's always been a good-tempered girl. And then she didn't eat much at all. She's thin enough without missing her meals."

The father took over again. "We didn't know what to do for her, so I wrote to my family back in Kentucky. And my brother, he reckoned that what she needed was treatment for nerves, such as she could get in one of those hospitals back east. So he came and got her, and that's where she'll be now."

It obviously hadn't occurred to them to consult the local doctor about their daughter's condition. To be fair — which he was having trouble being — he had never done much to encourage people to think of him as someone who treated nervous conditions. Nor could he claim to have the latest knowledge on such things. But he suspected the "latest" was as likely to include treatments that would be useless or worse. Someone had patented a machine twenty years ago that subjected patients with "nervous diseases" to electricity, a thought that had made him shudder as if subjected to it himself.

"I would like to write to Miss Brook to see how she's getting on, and to convey the thanks I'd hoped to convey in person. Do you know the name and location of the hospital?"

The father was obviously unsure whether to help Joshua take such a liberty. But the mother, perhaps more tender-hearted or more in tune with her daughter, said, "I believe I have it written down somewhere," and hurried off into the house. She returned with a slip of paper and handed it to Joshua with a somewhat defiant air, looking at

Joshua rather than her husband.

He bowed and tipped his hat. "Thank you kindly, sir, ma'am." He mounted Nellie-girl and rode away at as fast a pace as he could set without looking positively suspicious.

Joshua had not thought of asking for the uncle's name and address. But remembering the man's manner, he doubted there was much to be gained from writing to him. He would try the hospital first. If he bluffed, if he claimed to be Clara's treating physician, they might be willing to respond and even provide some information.

Or they might not. And he would have lost a worrisome number of days in the attempt.

Joshua returned to his office sunk in profound gloom. If Clara Brook needed assistance, and if there was any way he could provide it, he would almost certainly have to do so in person. But how could he take the train so far, all the way to New England? He lived as much on the payments he received in kind as on cash money. His account at the bank was so small that he sometimes imagined the banker snorting with laughter at the sight of him approaching to make one of his infrequent deposits.

As a boy, like any child reading fairy tales, he had idly imagined being rich, but he had never longed for wealth. And never until now had he regretted leaving behind the possibilities Philadelphia might afford for attaining it. But wealth would have given him the means to come to Clara's aid.

Though if he had remained in Philadelphia, he would never have met Clara, let alone know she might need his help.

He half hoped a patient would come to distract him from his thoughts, and half feared he would be unable to pay a patient sufficient attention. When he heard a familiar knock, he forced himself to the door and opened it, as expected, to find Freida standing there, evidently overflowing with updates about Rachel's visit. If all he had to do was listen and act interested, he could probably manage it. He escorted her to one of the chairs that would hold her, pulled another chair near it, and assumed an attentive expression.

Either he overestimated his acting ability or underestimated Freida's powers of penetration. After a mere ten minutes or so of wedding details, she stopped in mid-sentence, leaned closer, and put her hands on her substantial hips. "So what's wrong?"

He was reluctant to confide in her, given her almost unfriendly comments about Clara in the past. In his present mood, if she repeated any such sentiments, he would find it hard to restrain his temper. But it would probably prove impossible to evade her questioning for long. He surrendered. "I am concerned about Miss Brook. I have made some inquiries and discovered that her family has sent her east to be hospitalized for some nervous disorder."

To his relief, Freida had nothing critical to say, but wrinkled her forehead in concern and replied, "Poor girl, a shame, she's always seemed healthy. And you worry about everyone, no wonder, it's part of what makes you a good doctor."

He managed a quick twitch of a smile at the compliment. "I am uncertain whether it might not be helpful for me to travel to the hospital myself. But such a journey is wholly beyond my means."

Freida tilted her head and raised her eyebrows. "You want to go there why? A hospital full of fancy doctors isn't enough, she needs one more who has patients right here? Not that you aren't every bit as good a doctor, don't get me wrong, but to me this makes no sense."

Except for Clara's parents just now, he had told no one of Clara's part in the amputation. He should have done. She had been more than helpful, more than competent; she had been invaluable, and might well have saved him from failure and dishonor. Well, he could remedy the situation now. What Freida knew, others would know shortly. "I have knowledge her doctors lack, and which may make a material difference in her care. Her condition did not come upon her as mysteriously as her family believed, and I am in part responsible for it. On the day I was summoned to tend an injured farm lad . . . ." He told her all of it, how Clara had helped him withstand the assault of his own memories even while struggling with her own.

Freida listened without a single interruption. When he had done, she reached out and patted his hand. "Like a knight in armor, you'd be, riding to the rescue."

Joshua had to laugh. "A poor battered knight I would make. And whether she would want rescuing, and whether I could help her if she does, I can hardly predict. But it makes no difference. A knight may ride his steed to the rescue, but this distance would require the railroad."

She sat back and nodded a little as if in agreement with her own thoughts. Finally she leaned forward again and looked him in the eye. "You maybe know, my Samuel left me well provided for."

He put up his hands as if to fend off whatever might come after. She waved the gesture away and went on. "You spend so much time on me, and you never charge enough, I would be happy to help you do something that matters so much to you."

He was shaking his head almost violently before she

finished. "It is a kind and generous offer, but I could never take money from you for anything but your care —"

"Men! So proud, always! Call it a loan, then, if it makes you feel better."

This one time, he would out-stubborn her. "I cannot see any prospect of repaying such a loan. I thank you, but this must be the end of it. Now, shall I examine you before you go?"

She stood up, tossing her head. "No examining, I didn't come here to have you fuss. You won't let me help you, I hope you find some way to do your good deed." She turned and opened the door before he could reach it, surging through with majestic displeasure. He caught the muttered exclamation, "Men!" as the door closed behind her.

He had two patients after Freida left. The first, a farmer's wife in town for provisions, wanted a rash looked at. He had seen such rashes often on women who spent much of their day washing and scrubbing, and had an ointment to give her. Then, when he was already flipping the sign on his door, one of Madam Mamie's bartenders hurried up, full of apologies, with cuts from broken glass on the palm and forefinger of his right hand. Joshua tried unsuccessfully to stifle a sigh and fetched what he needed to clean and stitch and bandage them.

When the job was done, the bartender inspected the bandages, stood up, and said, "I'd shake your hand to thank you, but I reckon you'd tell me I shouldn't. Come back to Mamie's place and have a couple of beers on the house instead. Mamie won't mind."

Given the tenor of his thoughts, he could not help wondering when he would receive some more substantial payment. But beer would, if not actually drown his sorrows, at least blur his vision of them. Off to Madam Mamie's they went.

But once he was sitting at the bar with the glass in front of him, he found he had little interest in drinking it. He took a couple of swallows and then left it there, collecting condensation, watching the drops trickle down and form a ring.

A familiar voice jarred him from his brooding. "Something wrong with the beer in my place? Or something wrong in your world?"

Joshua looked up at Mamie and mustered up the closest he could come to a smile. "The beer is as fine as always. I was contemplating an intractable dilemma."

"I know. Freida Blum told me."

"My God, already?" The exclamation burst out of him before he could frame a more temperate response. And then, of course, he blushed.

At least Mamie was used to far franker language. She chuckled and patted his shoulder. "I'm glad she did. I may have an answer. I've been paying you fifty cents for each of my girls for each visit, right?"

He held himself back from speculating on where she was headed. "Yes, and welcome it is, too." It was, in fact, the top of his range of fees, because both of them knew she could well afford it. "Of course, that's not counting the, uh, other payment."

"That's right. And you know I usually have around a dozen girls at any one time. And you check them over once a month, and tend to any with a particular need in between, that not being a rare occurrence."

It was true enough. Girls that chose to be, or ended up as, prostitutes didn't tend toward careful habits or quiet living. He couldn't count how many bruises and lacerations he'd treated due to fights between them — though Mamie allowed only one such, followed by a stern warning, before letting a girl go for a second offense. And once in a while a customer would get rough, which usually meant Joshua had another patient after Mamie's boys got through with him. And then there were the hangovers and drug overdoses.

"And of course the 'other payment' you mention takes time a girl could spend with another customer or two. Time being money, you could say, that adds up some."

Somehow he managed not to blush a second time. "And you're reckoning —"

"I reckon that over the course of a year, we pay you enough, one way or the other, to take care of that train ticket you're wanting. East and west again."

She couldn't know that he might need two tickets west. But if he used the cheapest possible type of railroad travel, he could save money for something better on the way home, if somehow events fell that way.

"So what do you say, Doc?" Perhaps reading him as more easily bothered than usual, she spared him the usual nickname. "I'll pay you in advance for your services over one year, as best we can figure it. And you can go take care of another lady first."

Joshua stood up, the better to grasp Mamie's hands. "If you are sure this arrangement is fair to you, I gladly accept."

She gave their joined hands a shake and let go to slap him on the back. "That's settled, then! I'll go to the safe and get your money. And you drink that beer!"

Striding to his rooms, cash tucked in his vest pocket, he ran through everything he needed to do before he could depart. Along with making arrangements for his patients during his absence, he would need to tell Freida what had happened, awkward as that task might be —

The thought that came to him stopped him mid-stride, so that he almost tripped over his own feet. Had Freida known what Mamie would propose? Had they even discussed it?

He shook his head as if he could dislodge the image of such a conference. He could only hope that if it had taken place, Freida would refrain from telling him as much.

He especially hoped she would not comment on how the new regimen would eliminate his private enjoyment of Mamie's girls. Unless, of course, he paid for their time out of pocket. But it was hardly likely he would have the cash to spare. Besides which, the thought had somehow, lately, grown less enticing.

Later that afternoon, he rode over to Rushing and visited the town's resident doctor, a scholarly-looking man with half-glasses and an ancient but well-maintained frock coat. When the doctor offered Joshua a glass of some sort of amber liquor from a flask in his desk, Joshua considered it politic to accept. Sipping the potent liquor cautiously, he broached the reason for his visit. "I am obliged to make a journey of perhaps two weeks, possibly more, and would like to leave as soon as possible. Would you consent to see those patients in Cowbird Creek who most urgently need a physician until I return?"

The doctor flashed a saturnine smile. "With a good will. But I do not promise to deliver them back to you afterward, if they are pleased with my services."

Next, Joshua went to see Robert. He filled him in on

Clara's departure and its disturbing circumstances, asked him to direct those needing medical attention to the doctor in Rushing, and then made the request perhaps closest to his heart. "Would you look after Major until I return?"

"That's as easy an ask as none at all. Major looks after himself, generally. I'll give him my scraps and a place by my fire, most happily. But just what do you propose to do?"

Joshua twisted his hat in his hands. "That depends on what I find. If she's being ill-treated, I can try to remedy it. If she didn't go there of her own free will . . . well, I would try to do something to gain her release, though I confess I've no present notion how. And at the least, I can give the doctors the information they lack as to what went before."

Robert filled and lit his pipe. "Are you planning to introduce yourself as her doctor? I hope you won't take it ill my mentioning the fact, but you've no curly-lettered sheepskin hanging in your office, handed out by some college. Will those Eastern doctors treat you as one of their fraternity?"

"I don't take it ill. I've been pondering that very matter. But Miss Brook has never been my patient. I can present myself as friend and witness, and whether they see me as a doctor or no, I can try to get them to listen."

His final call on Freida proved uneventful. Rachel greeted him prettily, exclaiming about her enjoyment of the local landscape and the friendliness of the townspeople. Freida, possibly due to Rachel's presence, refrained from embarrassing him with any revelations.

He of course examined her, removing with her to her bedroom for privacy. With some anxiety, he inspecting her extremities, listening to her heart and requiring her to breathe for him. To his relief, the tincture of foxglove and the diuretic tea seemed to have slowed or even arrested the progress of her symptoms. "May I rely on you to keep to the regimen I've prescribed while I'm away?"

She pretended to scoff. "Regimen, such a fancy word for taking drops and drinking tea! But I'll do it, I wouldn't want you to worry while you're busy."

As he packed up his bag, he could see out of the corner of his eye that Freida was studying him, a disquieting look in her eye. He did not want to know what was behind it. He had final preparations to make, and then a train to catch.

Chapter 23

THE HOSPITAL was deep in New England. Joshua had not taken a long train ride since the several trains that carried him to Nebraska. He was underslept enough to worry that he might doze off and miss one of the stops where he had to change trains, but the discomforts of the journey helped him to stay awake. He had brought two blankets, one for warmth in the unheated railroad car and one to pad the bare wooden seat, but they did not substitute for a fireplace or a mattress. Nor did the chugging and clacking and rumbling, the vibration beneath him, and the occasional varying hoots and shrieks of the whistle make slumber easy. How soft he had become, after so often falling asleep in moments on rocky ground, with nothing but a thin blanket wrapped around the tattered remains of a uniform, and in spite of the constant tumult of orders and laughter and cursing and the roar of not-always-distant cannon.

It was strange and novel to have nothing in particular to do for hours on end. He could have used the time to plan his approach to the hospital, if he had any idea what he would find there. Lacking the same, and having managed to grab a seat near a window, he read the only book he owned that discussed nervous disorders, in the hope of finding either information that might help Clara or jargon that might make him more acceptable to her doctors. When he had finished it, he gazed out at snow-covered fields, farms, barns, cattle, when smoke and steam did not obscure the view; or tried to catch, over all the other noises, the irregular tapping of sleet on the window of the car. And all the while, he pondered what little he knew.

If only he had a better sense of her uncle's character, he could make some reasonable guess as to what sort of hospital the man had chosen for her. Would it be a grim asylum with barred windows and shrieking inmates? Or a spic-and-span modern facility?

Freida had insisted on sending him off with provisions, a roasted chicken and apples and some of her rolled cookies. This bounty did not last as long as she might have imagined, Joshua feeling it right to share it with the passengers beside him. Once it was gone, and except when a news butcher boarded the train to sell stale sandwiches and other sundries, Joshua perforce joined the other passengers in besieging the sandwich vendors at depots during the train's brief stops, except when the call of nature had priority.

The first change of trains meant a farewell to the seat by the window, with the silver lining that he felt no need to leave one of his blankets as a place marker and risk the loss of it. The change meant less time during the day when he could read, and more time to brood about what awaited him.

What he found, when he had reached the final station and walked a mile, was a pastoral setting and a stone structure pleasing to the eye. As he approached the front walk, a uniformed nurse was escorting a man around a pond, encouraging him to keep up a good pace. Other patients were seated on benches here and there, bundled up against the chill and presumably so placed for the value of fresh air.

No one seemed particularly surprised or alarmed to see him strolling up. Inside, another nurse sat behind a large desk. A nook to one side held a smaller desk and a man, in garments of a somewhat more martial character. Behind the nurse was a large lobby, and sounds came from beyond it suggestive of a dining hall, the clinking of cutlery on china, the murmur of voices and shuffling of feet. A large spiral staircase rose from the lobby to one or more upper stories. Clara's immediate family might be simple farmers, but either her uncle or some other connection must have sufficient means to keep her in such an establishment.

But he could not stand about gawking. Doing his best to assume a confident air, he approached the nurse and began his inquiries.

It was a doctor who led him to a small sitting room where Clara would shortly be brought. He studied Joshua as if trying to piece him into a puzzle. "After your visit, I would much appreciate it if you would come see me in my office." He pointed to a closed door in the corridor through which they were passing.

All the better, so long as he was allowed to do more than respond to interrogation. "I would appreciate that opportunity as well."

The room looked out on well-maintained lawns and paths. The sunshine that had graced Joshua's earlier walk was yielding to clouds. The gloom suited his apprehension. Would he be granted enough time with Clara to assess her state of mind? Would the doctor heed what he had to say? Would he be allowed back for a second visit, or a third?

What could he hope to accomplish, and what failure could he withstand?

Then a nurse was escorting Clara in. "We will, of course, leave this door open. I'll return for the patient in thirty minutes." The heels of her sturdy shoes click-clacked as she headed back down the hall.

Clara was indeed too thin, painfully so. But she had color in her cheeks, and her expression was not so haunted as Joshua had expected. Maybe this place had been what she needed, after all. Maybe his journey had been not just quixotic but utterly unnecessary.

Still, she held out her hand to him with something like eagerness. And she spoke first. "I thought I wanted to see no one from home. But I was thinking of family. I'm glad to see you."

He returned her firm hand clasp — he could hardly do otherwise — and then let go. He gestured to the two easy chairs by the window; she took his suggestion and sat, as did he. "You look . . . less unwell than I had feared."

Her smile had some bitterness to it. "I scarcely dare to be unwell, with all my uncle is paying for me to live in luxury." Then she shook her head as if in self-reproach. "I do believe the serenity here, and the absence of obligations, has lessened the turmoil in my spirit. What is that new word? I am on vacation, and somewhat the better for it. . . . So your diagnosis is encouraging?"

He pursed his lips, considering his answer. Her frankness suggested she would not easily take offense. "I would like to see you less thin."

"So would the doctors and staff. They do their best to fatten us like princes. You should see the meals — meat three times a day, eggs, cocoa . . . . And fresh vegetables, which I do appreciate, whether or not I actually consume them. I'm sure you remember how hard it was to come by anything of the sort, during the war."

Joshua shuddered in recollection. "I remember all too well what we were given instead, sometimes — the desiccated vegetables issued to us, that tasted and smelled like something ladled out of the latrines."

Had he offended Clara by speaking so bluntly? Apparently not — she grimaced in agreement before returning to her account. "And all the drink they urge on us! Rum, sherry, port, stout — some medical authority has apparently decided that disordered nerves are best addressed with large quantities of alcohol. And morphia." She shuddered. "I resisted the morphia. Forcefully. It made for rather an unpleasant scene."

Given her likely associations with the drug, he could well understand it. "But the meals? You resist them as well, it seems. Why?"

Clara hesitated. "It is not so much deliberate resistance as . . . I look at the bountiful repasts, the clean table linen and sparkling-clean tumblers, and see as if overlaid on it a muddy field drowning in rain, and cold rations in my hand. The same can occur without warning when I take my prescribed walks on well-raked paths or close-mown grass. I hear nothing but the murmur of distant voices, birdsong, breezes in the trees, and I am disoriented by the absence of other sounds, of gunfire and artillery and the anguished shouts of men."

His conscience smote him. She would not be suffering to this extent if he had not drawn her into a scene so much like her wartime experiences. Though she had answered the summons before he received his own, and had not refused it . . . . "Do the doctors know your history?"

Her eyebrows lifted, and her mouth twisted in what was barely a smile. "I do not recall them troubling to ask me for it. They spoke to my uncle at some length, but I was not privy to the conversation."

Disdain of highly credentialed doctor for mere patient? Or of man for woman? "Would you allow me to enlighten them?"

She laughed outright. "Only if you inform me, after, of

whether they appeared chagrined at their ignorance."

She turned to look out the window, then back at him. "What feelings does this place inspire in you?"

He gazed out the window at the bucolic landscape. "The peace of it is soothing."

"And if you had the opportunity, as it appears I have, to stay here for weeks or months, would that proposal appeal to you?"

He considered the matter. "A week, perhaps, or even two. But I believe I would then repine. The idleness of it would make me restless — and perhaps increase the difficulties I myself face from time to time."

Her eyes widened briefly — not, he guessed, at the fact of his condition echoing her own, which she had had the opportunity to observe, but at his admission of it.

The approach of purposeful footsteps heralded the nurse's return. Both of them arose. Joshua said, bowing, "I will visit again, if I may."

She caught and held his gaze. "I hope you will."

"Should I fail to do so, please believe that the indulgence of your . . . caretakers has diminished, rather than my own will."

Clara gave the nurse no very cordial look, then appeared to consider the imprudence of showing hostility and instead assumed a blank expression the nurse seemed to take for granted. As the nurse led Joshua away, he asked her to convey him to the office previously shown to him. The doctor, however, was elsewhere. The nurse installed him in the straight chair opposite the doctor's desk and went in search. Joshua would have liked to get out his pipe, but for all he knew the doctor disliked smoke. Instead, he sat and fidgeted.

After what might have been ten minutes, the nurse reappeared, doctor in tow. He nodded at Joshua with no apologies for his absence and sat down behind his desk. "I wanted to discuss your . . . friend's diagnosis."

Joshua sat up straight. "As did I. Would you permit me to begin that discussion by providing some information of which Miss Brook's family are unaware?"

The doctor narrowed his eyes and said curtly, "Proceed."

Wondering at the almost-hostility in the doctor's manner, Joshua summarized what he knew of Clara's wartime experiences and the events that would have called them freshly to mind. He decided to leave unmentioned his own claim to physician status, which was not, strictly speaking, relevant, and might have moved his listener to be contrary.

The doctor did, as Clara had predicted, look somewhat nonplussed. When Joshua had finished, he leaned back in his chair. "Miss Brook's uncle had provided us with a somewhat different explanation of her melancholia. Or, according to you, her neurasthenia. He had believed her to be suffering from a disappointment in love. And his description of the man who had spoken to the patient just prior to her departure is a tolerable portrait of yourself."

Joshua felt himself flush, and flushed more from the annoyance of it. "I did indeed speak to Miss Brook at the train station, and to her uncle as well. But our acquaintance has never been . . . tender in quality. I respect and admire her abilities, and find her a pleasant conversationalist. And the lady has never shown any signs of any particular interest in me."

The doctor smirked. "And are you reliably perceptive as to the nature of a lady's interest?"

Joshua clenched his fists as if they held his temper. "I cannot say, sir. But I hope you will consider the possibility that Miss Brook's uncle, coming on the scene but shortly before he conveyed her here, and utterly unacquainted with me, may have been forced into conjecture, given that he had no way to know what I have just told you." He waited for some response; none came. "Do you have other questions for me?"

The doctor set his chair to rocking back and forth, the chair legs in front periodically hitting the floor. "I had thought to confirm Mr. Brook's account, or else inquire what other gentleman might be the cause of Miss Brook's distress. As you deny the likelihood of such distress, I have nothing else to ask."

Joshua had. "May I inquire whether Miss Brook would be free to leave this establishment, should she choose to do so?"

The doctor leaned forward, the chair landing with a thunk. "That would depend on the reason for her wish, and the situation for which she intended to depart, as well as the desires of the family that entrusted us with this patient."

Joshua found lodgings near the train station and returned to the hospital the following morning. He had promised Clara a report on the doctor's reaction, a promise that now held unexpected potential for embarrassment. But perhaps her uncle's misunderstanding would amuse her.

Unless . . . could there be any kernel of truth in the uncle's conclusions? Did Clara actually hold him in particular esteem?

He could not consider himself worthy of her affections, but if there was the slightest chance that she had bestowed them, he would not for the world venture anywhere near that subject. He compromised by editing the doctor's response in the direction of generalities. This time the nurse had enjoined him to guide Clara on one of the prescribed walks, circling a placid pond; as soon as they had achieved enough distance for privacy, he said to her, "I believe your physician was somewhat disconcerted to receive information from such a quarter, and I cannot say with confidence that he is willing to credit it."

She let out a low growl in evident frustration. Then her mood shifted, and she said quietly, "It may be as well if he does not have cause to examine me with more accuracy as to the nature of my indisposition."

They passed a paddling of ducks, making their way in determined fashion toward the bank of the pond. Joshua briefly regretted having no crumbs with which to reward them. Clara, looking at them, seemed to have thoughts along similar lines. "If only I could provide them with some of the bounty set before me this very morning! But I had no convenient means of concealing any."

As Joshua searched his pockets, finding nothing useful to the ducks, Clara added, "Mentioning bounty reminds me of a question I had, though the answer is hardly my business."

"Please ask. I am unlikely to object to answering, but if I do, I will tell you so."

"Thank you. It will be easier if I ask in plain terms — how did you manage to make this journey? I have some idea of the expense involved, and I would be unhappy to think you had gone into debt for the purpose."

Joshua smiled ruefully. "Little danger of that. I am not the sort of customer of whom bankers dream." Though he had gone into debt in a way, if not as she meant it. How could he explain without indelicacy? "An establishment that employs me on a regular basis heard that I wished to take the railroad a considerable distance, and was so kind as to pay me for my services in advance."

Clara took that in. From the quirk of her mouth, Joshua

suspected she knew just which employer he meant. But all she said was, "This establishment obtained its information from . . . I would venture to guess your friend Mrs. Blum was responsible. You confided in her? Did she not attempt to dissuade you?"

"Not once I explained that I thought I might be of service to you. In fact, she wished to fund the journey herself, as a gift. I did not feel I could accept."

Clara's eyes widened. "That was generous of her. And I admit, I did not think her opinion of me would move her in that direction."

He could hardly confirm, but nor could he deny, the opinion of which she spoke, though he thought Freida might have softened toward Clara since she last expressed it. He compromised on saying, "She said nothing during this discussion to suggest any ill will or disapproval."

He had been more honest than he intended; Clara gave a quick bark of laughter. "During this discussion. I see. But I apologize. I am making you uneasy."

They walked in silence for a minute or two, while Joshua's mind returned to something she had said to him the day before. "You said, when I came, that you had not wished to see any of your family. Would it be amiss for me to inquire why that should be?"

She looked away from him, toward the pond but not, he thought, actually seeing it. They walked on a few paces before she said, her voice almost too low to hear, "I had another brother."

He walked, and waited.

"I went to be a nurse because of him, because he was going off to war. I traveled with him and was let to work for his company, until he was sent off, and I — stayed for a while, before moving to a hospital." A long pause. "The family was told he had died in battle. And I the only one to know, to understand, what that means. The others imagine something swift — a bullet extinguishing him in an instant. They never saw, or heard, or — or smelled the things that let me imagine what he likely endured. And that is just part of what makes me feel like . . . some different kind of creature, pretending to be like them, to be one of them. To be the daughter and sister I used to be. Someone I scarcely remember being."

Joshua understood all too well. "I lived in Philadelphia, before the war. When I returned home after all those years of war, they thought I would be the son I had been, the man I was becoming. But he — he died, almost. I left him behind, on some muddy, bloody field, or in a medical tent."

She stopped and looked straight at him with her keen eyes. "So you left your family and headed out to start over. Which I have not found the means, or perhaps the courage, to do." She gazed out at the pond again. "And yet whenever I may return to them, it will be just the same. I will be with them and yet apart from them; and they will know it, and be helpless to amend it."

The idea that struck him, with the force of a revelation, would not be suppressed. It came spilling out. "If you could live differently, near them but seeing them only when it would bring comfort to you all, and you were able to use the skills that have cost you so dearly . . . would that be a better path?"

She looked at him with a mixture of confusion and something sharper. He explained. "It would add much to my practice if I had a skilled assistant. I believe I could increase my fees in consequence, and pay such an assistant a wage sufficient for support." And if that left him living lean, he had survived worse. "Miss Wheeler's boardinghouse is a respectable dwelling for a woman. You could take a room there."

She said slowly, enunciating each syllable, "You are offering me a position."

He found himself smiling. "I am."

She waved her arm in a broad gesture, encompassing the hospital and all its grounds. "And you believe I can take such a position without . . . ill consequences?"

He had, and suppressed, the urge to step closer to her. "Before, you were among those who could not possibly understand. If we were to work together, we would neither of us be alone in that way. If it proved too much for you, you could move back with your family —" She flinched violently. He winced in response, but made himself continue. "Or you could survey other opportunities. They exist, for a woman of your intelligence and will. I am sure of it." Now he, too, swept his arm across the landscape. "Or you could remain here, making the acquaintance of patients and doctors and ducks. Will that be better?"

He had startled a snort of laughter from her. It seemed to ease her. She located a nearby tree and leaned against it, facing him. "Should I decide your offer has more benefits than difficulties, do you think I would be free to accept it?"

He recalled his interview with her physician. "That would be easier to accomplish if we were able to convince your uncle to endorse it — one or both of us."

She gave him a sidelong glance. "I don't believe my uncle trusts you overmuch."

Damn and blast, the man must have said something. He could only be glad that it had not prevented Clara from treating him as a friend. And her frank and open manner probably meant that she harbored no such feelings as her uncle had so rashly supposed.

He did not pursue the fleeting sense of loss that followed this realization. Instead, he pondered the immediate problem. "What did he think of your going for a nurse?"

Her jaw went taut. "I didn't consult him. He would have thought me too young, if nothing else. As did my parents, but the thought of someone being of use to my brother overcame their concern." Her expression softened. "When my uncle found out, he was afraid for me. He's no daughters of his own, but he has always tried to look after me." She shifted back to her more usual sardonic look. "As you see."

"Besides the danger and your youth, did he think it proper? Did he approve of you learning such skills?"

She considered the matter. "He liked that I learned quickly in general. As to nursing, I believe he thought it might have its uses when I came to have a family."

Whatever thought crossed her mind next, it stole any remaining softness from her face. He needed to know that thought, if only to dispel it if he could. "What is it?"

She said in a tone devoid of emotion, "If he were convinced that I would never marry, he might consider my having a way to keep myself as a suitable alternative to remaining with my family, a lamented spinster. It would be truth, most likely."

"I'll not have you saying such a thing!" His outburst startled the both of them. She tested him with the blade of her glance as he cast about for a more rational response. "He would believe it to be your melancholia talking, and take it as a sign that you needed to remain for further treatment."

She gave a short sniff of agreement and then turned back toward the building. The nurse was approaching to herd her indoors again. Clara rolled her eyes. "It must be time to stuff me like a capon. Shall we both ponder the question until tomorrow?"

Then, as the nurse laid a hand on her arm to direct her inside, she turned toward him with sudden mischief lighting her face. "'Virtue is bold.'" And with that cryptic reference, she walked obediently back to her keepers' care.

Joshua slept less than soundly. Whenever some noise pulled him to the surface, the creak of bed springs through the wall or boots outside or the hoot of an owl, he lay in bed puzzling out what Clara might be planning. A little before dawn, he came up with one idea, and spent the remaining hours trying to decide what he felt about it. Which would be a waste of time and worry, if he had it all wrong.

A different nurse brought him to a larger and more finely appointed sitting room than before. Clara was already there, sitting demurely on the sofa. She looked better, brighter. Something seemed to pass between her and the nurse, an almost conspiratorial exchange of glances. And contrary to the rules as told to him before, the nurse shut the door almost all the way as she departed.

He stared after her and then asked Clara bluntly, "What's going on?"

She beamed at him. "Why, good sir, I'm just a happy girl this morning. Your visits must be doing me good. I'm sure the nurse thinks so." And then, with another flash of mischief: "I may have eased her way to taking that view."

It took only a moment to see how this could fit with his early morning speculations. "You're thinking you should depart without leave, and are preparing them to think we — eloped?"

"Nothing quite so particular. But I believe we can give them an impression that'll satisfy them — the doctors and my uncle both. See what you think." She twisted away, reached into her bodice, and turned back holding a rolled-up piece of paper out to him. The procedure distracted him, but he shook it off and reached for the paper, unrolling and reading it.

I apologize for my failure to seek permission for the step I have taken. But my circumstances have changed materially, and in such manner as has restored me to myself so much that I do not, in conscience, believe I should any longer divert the attention of this establishment from those in greater need, nor further postpone my transition to future ties and responsibilities . . . .

Joshua looked up to see her intently watching him read. He handed her back the paper, looking politely away while she hid it again, and stroked his chin, trying to assess their chances. His conversation with Clara's doctor might make the man less likely to be believe what the note implied, but he would rather not explain as much. "I am not sure the personnel here would be fully satisfied. But they would most likely take the time to consult your uncle, by which point we would be at some distance. And he might be sufficiently gratified at having his suspicions confirmed, if he does not think me a complete villain."

Her mouth twitched, probably at the picture of Joshua as a villainous cad. Then her face grew momentarily sober before she said, with an overly casual air that must mask some uncertainty, "This presupposes that your offer of employment remains open. Have you repented of it?"

"No, indeed. My only concern is that your reputation is likely to suffer if we are known to have traveled together without any sort of chaperone."

Clara set her jaw. "I have considered that fact, and am willing to live with such damage." She stopped and sighed before saying quietly, "I would spare my family their share of any scandal, but I do not believe I can put their feelings in the matter above my own."

As always, she had seen to the heart of a question and spoken accordingly. "We are agreed, then." As for the finances of their arrangement, she was apparently willing to believe his somewhat optimistic words the day before. It was up to him, then, to live up to them. She would need to be paid in coin, for the boardinghouse; but he could live on the payments in kind he received, if coin stayed scarce. "How do you purpose to leave here unobserved?"

They spent the remainder of the visit plotting. The nurse, Clara confirmed, was well pleased at the thought of furthering a romance, and would bring her to a path bordering a less conspicuous road than Joshua had been using. Joshua had noted the location of a livery stable not far from his hotel; he would hire a buggy and drive them two towns over, there to catch a less obvious train.

When they heard the nurse approaching, Clara reached out her hand. "It would be well for her to see us comfortable together, I think."

He took her hand in both of his, feeling the warmth of it and the strength of her fine, long fingers. He was rather loath to let go and be escorted out.

Chapter 24

AS JOSHUA checked out of his hotel, the clerk handed him a letter. "This just came for you by express, sir. It almost missed you."

Joshua opened the letter and unfolded it enough to see Robert's signature at the end. Robert must have had a considerable task to find out the name and direction of the likeliest hotel for him to be staying at. The letter must concern a matter of some importance. But he had barely enough time to pick up the buggy and make his rendezvous. He stuffed the letter in his vest pocket to read it later.

Clara was walking, or rather pacing, up and down the path when he pulled up. He did not see her trunk, but only a somewhat smaller case placed next to the path. The nurse must have procured it for her.

Clara waved at someone (presumably the nurse) concealed in the nearby trees, patted the chestnut gelding's sleek neck, and took his offer of a hand to hoist her case and help her in. That last, he suspected, was for the watcher's benefit — she could easily have climbed in unassisted.

He urged the horse on as soon as she was seated. The train was due not long after they could hope to make it to the station. They left the buggy at the livery stable and hurried along, Clara carrying her own case, despite his offer to do so, and making nothing of the weight.

They had a hasty argument about what class ticket to buy. Clara adamantly refused to accept a second class ticket. "I will not strain your resources so far, when a sturdy bench is available. After all, I have just come from many days of restorative rest. But you should get a proper seat this time."

Of course, Joshua refused to sit in comfort Clara denied herself, and they ended up in emigrant class, only to have another quarrel as to the disposition of blankets. Joshua prevailed only in that they shared the blankets covering them and padding the bench, rather than Clara foregoing both. There was just enough room on the bench for the two of them. At least their close contact fit their story, should anyone notice and remember them, and also allowed them to discuss the future without being overheard so long as they kept their voices to a murmur. Joshua could not help noticing the warmth of her thigh so close to his own — first pleasing, and then an unwelcome reminder of the disaster at Dolly's weeks before.

The color was high in Clara's face, and instead of the near torpor he had observed on his first visit to the hospital, she was more restless than he had ever seen her. He made so bold as to cover her hand with his own. "I hope you are not regretting our 'bold' decision."

A smile flickered across her face at his reference to her quotation, which he believed to be Shakespeare but had not identified more specifically. She glanced down at their hands; abashed, he removed his from hers. She continued looking down as she said softly, "I am not so much regretting it, given the alternatives, as unsure of its practicality. You are well respected as a physician, but our region is not inhabited by many who can pay what your services are worth. I am concerned that I may deplete your resources without adequately supplying my own."

Joshua could not completely reassure her, but he shared his reasons for optimism. "You may have heard the maxim about presenting the appearance which you intend to make a reality. A doctor with an assistant must be successful, and is therefore the more to be valued and sought after. Your addition to my practice may well generate more than enough additional income. And there may be other possibilities. My friend Robert, the pharmacist, could perhaps use some skilled assistance in preparing his medicines. I am sure you could learn how."

Clara frowned, probably at the idea of soliciting work from someone not already committed to the scheme; but speaking of Robert had reminded Joshua of his unread letter. He extracted it and smoothed it out, saying, "I hope you will excuse me. This came by express just before we left, and I have not yet looked at it."

It opened with apologies for troubling Joshua while he was, in Robert's words, "on a mission of mercy." Joshua took care to keep the paper turned away from Clara's view.

But the meat of the matter, when he reached it, banished such concerns from his mind. In fact, he cursed aloud before recollecting his surroundings and his companion. From the corner of his eye, he saw other passengers turning his way with expressions varying from disapproval to surprise to amusement. Clara only looked concerned. "You have troubling news?"

Joshua ground his teeth. "Robert writes that a medicine show, the one you saw and which Mrs. Blum and I had occasion to notice, has returned. I did not mention to you before the sympathetic interest Mrs. Blum showed in the pitchman. That interest has apparently not waned, and Robert sees signs that the pitchman is at least as interested in my friend. In fact, he describes the man's behavior as close to pitching woo."

Clara's mouth twitched at the phrase, and possibly at his unintentional pairing of "pitching woo" and "pitchman." But she moved quickly to addressing his question. "In what ways might this pitchman have engaged Mrs. Blum's interest? Does he have particularly winning ways, or pleasing features?"

"She didn't think he looked like the crook he must be. Men like him have a nose for a mark's weaknesses. He must be using her sympathetic nature as a way of disarming her."

"But why? Is she wealthy?"

Joshua considered the question. "She told me her late husband left her well provided for. He owned a shop, so it is plausible. And I have never known her to be in hardship. From my knowledge of her, if he were not a good manager himself, she would take over whatever responsibilities would enable the enterprise to prosper."

"When did Robert write?"

Joshua looked for a date and found none. "He says at the start that he had not anticipated writing to me so soon after my departure. This must have occurred within days after I left town."

Clara bit her lip. Her earlier pallor had returned. "I hope that your impulse to . . . come to my rescue will not have unfortunate consequences for someone so close to your heart."

Her words lingered in his ear, raising some internal echo, stirring thoughts and feelings he had not faced or acknowledged. He sat in silence as his world rearranged itself. What should, what could, he say? Finally, as the silence threatened to be worse than speech, he stammered out, "I would not have you think that I value your friendship less than any other."

She started, a flush chasing away the pallor from her face. He held his breath, awaiting a response. But she appeared as much at a loss for words as he.

His heart had sunk nearly all the way to his boots by the time she said, in her forthright manner, "I am glad of your friendship, and of your affirmation of it."

There was more he could have declared, had he the courage. But he retreated to contemplating Freida's possible peril. Clenching his fists, he muttered, "If only I could know what is occurring as we crawl toward home!"

Clara's rare smile brightened her face. "You do our trusty conveyance wrong, I think."

He chuckled and nodded his acknowledgment. But he wished, absurdly, that the train were a steed of flesh, and that he could dig his knees in or cry commands to speed it on its way.

At the next change of trains, as they stumbled sleepily up the steps to the third class car, a voice behind Joshua divided his attention. The conductor was hurrying along the platform, calling out over and over, "Is there a doctor? We need a doctor!"

Joshua leaned against the side of the train and carefully waved one hand to attract the conductor's attention. "I am a doctor, and this lady is my assistant."

The conductor hurried over, speaking almost too fast for Joshua to understand him. "Our fireman is hurt — a nasty cut on his shoulder — it needs stitching up and whatever else, and we don't want to leave him here for whatever doctor we could find, and we aren't supposed to hold the train for long — can you tend him?"

He did not wait for an answer, but maneuvered himself ahead of them and led them to the dark, smoky cab at the front of the locomotive, with its looming furnace and multiple pipes and dials running every which way. The fireman was collapsed on a bench, gritting his teeth, sweat shining on his face in spite of the cold overpowering the heat from the furnace. A bowl of red-stained water sat beside him, and the engineer was wiping at the fireman's shoulder with a blood-soaked cloth.

Clara briefly studied the engineer and the conductor and chose the latter. "More water, please. Warm, if you can manage it."

The conductor stood staring at her, looking flummoxed. Had he not heard Joshua's naming Clara as his assistant? Joshua cleared his throat and stepped closer; the conductor started to attention and then headed off, either to fetch the water or to be bewildered somewhere out of reach. Joshua retrieved the apron in his bag — he had not thought to bring two — along with a clean cloth and gave both to Clara. She seemed about to refuse the apron, but then looked at his clothes and her own and accepted it. She put the clean cloth aside, using the already stained one to apply firm and steady pressure to the wound. Joshua fished out a spare shirt and turned it backwards, tying the sleeves around his neck for a makeshift apron, and prepared his needle and sutures.

By the time Clara said the bleeding had slowed, the conductor had returned, somewhat to Joshua's surprise, with a large basin of clean water. He set it down and said awkwardly, "It's warm. Sir. Ma'am." With that, he retreated as far as the limited space allowed, leaning against a wall and watching with furrowed forehead.

The fireman refused Joshua's offer of an injection of morphine, but accepted the alternative of whiskey and took three deep gulps before Joshua began stitching up the wound. When the wound was closed, cleaned again, and bandaged, Joshua stood up, stretched his aching back, and rubbed his strained and blurry eyes. By the time he looked over at Clara, she had finished with any similar motions and was shaking out the wrinkles in her skirt. At almost the same moment, they took off their aprons, actual and improvised, and tossed them on the bench next to the fireman. The conductor stepped forward to pick them up, along with the two blood-stained cloths. "I'll bundle these up for you." He was gone before they could reply.

He returned, carrying a tied-together sheet, just as Joshua was wondering where they might find a seat. Emigrant class might be full. They could upgrade to second class, after all . . . . But the conductor said smoothly, "The railroad would like to offer you a choice as to compensation. We can pay you cash money, of course, but would you by any chance prefer accommodation in our Pullman car?"

Joshua had hoped Clara would agree to the Pullman car, for her comfort and his own. He had less than usual need of cash, after getting third class tickets west. But he suspected that Clara's assent had more to do with a sense of irony and of mischief. At least, the barely contained merriment of her countenance suggested as much, as they made their bedraggled and weary way past the startled and well-dressed occupants of the luxuriously upholstered seats. Dressed neither like wealthy members of society nor like railroad employees, Joshua and Clara were clearly viewed as intruders.

Under such scrutiny, Joshua had no wish to gawk at his surroundings, but the black walnut paneling, the mirrors suspended from the walls, the ornate chandeliers overhead put the finest drawing room in Cowbird Creek to shame.

What next commanded his attention was the unexpected and welcome warmth of the air. Somehow, this car had heat. It might soon be possible for them to shed their coats. And was the car actually riding more smoothly than those in third class? It certainly seemed so, though Joshua was beginning to wonder whether his imagination had got the better of him.

The conductor accompanied them a short way into the car and then beckoned sharply to a tall colored man in uniform. "George, you take good care of Doctor —" The conductor stopped, eyebrows shooting upward. "My word, in all the commotion, I never got your names."

Clara's friendly smile put him at ease as she identified them. The conductor then went on, as if the colored man would not have heard, "George, this here's Doctor Gibbs and Miss Clara Brook, and they've done the railroad a good turn today. They'll be in this car now. Doc, Miss Brook, George is the porter for this car. Anything you need, you tell him to get it."

Joshua noticed the porter's mouth twitch as the conductor said "George," and wondered if the conductor could have misremembered the man's name. The conductor interrupted Joshua's musings by grabbing his hand and shaking it before tipping his cap to Clara and heading out of the car.

The colored men Joshua saw at home were mainly cowboys. The porter in his pressed and spotless uniform made quite a contrast with the grubby cowboys in their boots and dusters. Another contrasting vision tried to surface: the colored troops Joshua had seen once during the war, their uniforms covered in mud and worse . . . He shook the memory off as the porter spoke. "Doctor, Ma'am, I'll be pleased to help you in any way you require."

Clara replied before Joshua could. "Thank you, George — if that is your name. Did the conductor report it correctly?"

The porter's eyes widened before he reverted to an impassively polite expression. "It is the custom for Pullman porters to be referred to as George, the given name of the company founder."

Clara frowned. "Would you like us to use your actual name?"

The porter seemed, for the first time, at a loss for words. After an awkward silence, he said quietly, "It might lead to . . . confusion. But I appreciate the thought."

Finally able to catch his breath after the flurry of activity, Joshua realized he was hungry. Clara must be as well. He asked the porter, "Do you know when a news butcher is likely to come through with refreshments for purchase? Or must we wait for the next depot?"

The porter spoke as if choosing his words carefully. "Many of the Pullman car patrons . . . dislike dealing with the vendors you mention. Porters like myself, under the supervision of the conductor, make a point of reviewing the vendors' offerings and stocking the most palatable for those passengers who do not have their own supplies. If you will take a seat in the parlor, I will bring you a selection. And I can make up your berths at the same time."

The porter pointed to a portion of the car they had not passed through, visible through an open door, where a selection of armchairs and benches played a variation on the theme of luxury evident throughout. Clara headed through the door, then stopped and turned to watch the porter's activity. Joshua did the same, marveling at the swift efficiency with which the porter folded two facing seats into one bed, attached a headboard, closed the curtains, pulled down the polished and decorated compartment overhead into an upper berth, and whisked sheets and blankets and pillows onto both. He let out a low whistle of appreciation before heading toward a well-upholstered chair, one of two close together, and sinking into it. Clara took the other. When the porter arrived a few minutes later with a selection of quite edible-looking sandwiches, he managed to refrain from snatching the food out of the man's hand, though he did allow himself to gobble it with dispatch. Rather too late, he thought of what his companion might make of his manners, and looked toward her for any sign of displeasure. But she held his gaze, took a large bite of sandwich, chewed with exaggerated vigor, swallowed — and winked.

* * * * *

Both Joshua and Clara chose to sleep in their clothing rather than changing in the limited berth space or attempting to maneuver night clothes and themselves in the even more cramped washroom. That choice reduced the intimacy of sleeping so close together to a level with which Joshua, at least, was comfortable. As he climbed the ladder the porter provided and slid into bed, he said a short prayer that his dreams would not have any embarrassing effects.

His prayer went unanswered.

Joshua came awake to find Clara standing next to the lower berth and saying his Christian name aloud. He was at first disoriented, looking around for the camp hospital, thinking her still a nurse, before the motion and sound of the car's progress along the track brought him to himself. The dim light through the curtains suggested it was the middle of the night or not long after.

Had he moaned or shouted in his sleep? He looked down at Clara to confirm the dismal assumption. She seemed self-possessed, but rather pale. Before he could summon his wits enough to ask, she said softly, "You appeared to be having a nightmare."

He looked away, gritting his teeth. He would have

welcomed even a blush as an alternative to the sickly expression he was sure she saw.

She persisted despite his rudeness. "Would you like to get down and sit quietly for a while?"

He had to bite his lip to keep from snapping at her for the reasonable suggestion. He would have refused, but before he had the chance, the porter appeared with the ladder, his expression impassive. He seemed inclined to linger and steady it for Joshua's descent, but Clara motioned him away and performed that office herself. Joshua could hardly dismiss her without further discourtesy. He waited until his hands stopped shaking before climbing down.

Clara sat on the lower berth and wordlessly made room for him to sit beside her. When he did, she put her hand on his shoulder, moving slowly so that he could see her intention.

Joshua did not shake off her hand. In spite of himself, he found its warmth and light pressure comforting. It was so unlike anything he had experienced in his nightmare, or in the living nightmare that had given rise to it.

He turned toward Clara as she asked, "Would you like me to ask the porter to fetch you some water? Or if you have a flask of spirits with you, you could tell me where you keep it, and I could bring it to you."

Joshua would in fact have welcomed a dram of whiskey, but he would not display further weakness. "Thank you, no. I am very sorry to have disturbed you. I should not have allowed myself to sleep."

Clara's eyes studied him gravely. "Are bad dreams so likely for you, then?"

He could think of no answer that would extricate him from mortification. Clara removed her hand from his back and clasped her hands together. "I would never think less of you for such an affliction, as I share it myself to some extent. And, I would venture to guess, from a similar cause."

Now Joshua did blush, in shame at his self-absorption. He had every reason to know that her wartime ordeal had been at least as traumatic as his own, possibly even more so. As he searched for a proper apology, he found, to his horror, that he was saying something entirely different. "It was a patient. A patient who did not survive."

He snapped his mouth shut; but Clara loosened her hands and reached out to take one of his. "Please go on. I believe it will ease you."

He drew a shuddering breath, searching for strength. "I was acting as an orderly, carrying the wounded to the surgeon. He had no leisure for seeing who had the greatest need of him. We did not, like some units, have an assistant surgeon to perform that task, and it was too early in the war for an ambulance corps. It was left to soldiers like myself to make the best guess we could as to whose need was most pressing."

He could feel his hand trembling again, until Clara grasped it more firmly.

"There was a soldier — I noticed first that he still wore his forage cap and his cartridge box. So many of the wounded had lost or abandoned one or both. I could see some sort of dark stain on his coat, but not whether it was sweat or blood. He sat on a stump, not quite upright, but not slumped low. I thought his injury must be one of the less pressing." Now it was his lip trembling. He forced himself to go on. "I walked by him to a man lying on the ground with a bleeding wound in his leg, and summoned another orderly to carry him to the surgeon, who then pressed me into service assisting him. By the time I could return to the wounded, I did not see the man. It made me uneasy, for some reason I could not — or did not dare to — understand. And then I turned, and saw where some of the — "

He shut his eyes tight, as if he could hide that tears had started there. "I saw a row where some of the dead soldiers had been laid, and were being placed in body bags. He was there, his face not yet hidden, and I could see, now, that his coat was soaked quite through with gore."

He could not remember when he had ever heard anything so gentle as her voice. "And was that what you dreamed?"

He could not stop himself from opening his eyes, reddened as they must be, to see her face. "Only part. That memory, and my remorse for my failure, would haunt me without the aid of my imagination. But sometimes, like this time, the dream goes on. Instead of lying still and waiting to be stowed, the corpse rises to his feet. And stares at me. Saying nothing, only staring, and pointing to his wound."

Clara's face echoed the horror of the dream. "I hardly wonder that you cried out. I would surely have shrieked, and louder." Her voice grew quiet. "And probably have done, when my own ghosts haunt me. It is only chance that your distress woke me, rather than the reverse."

She did not, as he expected, tell him that the soldier's death was none of his doing. She could not know that, nor could he. And she might have known, from her own hard experience, that such attempts at comfort would have little effect — if she had confided to her family the nature of what troubled her sleep.

He had nothing to say, nothing else that needed saying, and she seemed to feel no greater impulse to say more. They sat like that for a few moments longer before she squeezed his hand once more, released him, and made her way out toward the washroom at the end of the car, to let him climb back to the upper berth and at least give the appearance of composing himself for sleep.

After such a dream, he usually lay awake, sometimes for hours. But he found himself drifting toward sleep, with the memory of Clara's gentle voice echoing in his ear.

He had the dream again the following night. But this time, the dead man looked at Joshua with something like compassion, and then set to work helping him carry those wounded still living. When no more soldiers lay bleeding and crying out on the ground or on carts, he bowed to Joshua and faded away like mist.

Joshua awoke, sat up slowly, and looked around the railroad car. No ghosts, no trauma, nothing but Clara sleeping in apparent peace in the berth below him, and curtains growing bright with morning light.

Chapter 25

AFTER THE revelations and fraught emotions of the last several days, Joshua would have been glad to lighten the mood in some fashion. He provided the opportunity without conscious intention. Clara had been looking out the window of the parlor since the porter brought them a passable breakfast, but suddenly turned toward Joshua. "May I ask what you're doing with your hands?"

Joshua had not known he was doing anything with his hands. He blinked, looked down, and answered, "I am repeating elements of magic tricks. Such practice, especially when done more slowly than in actual performance, helps me maintain my skills, such as they are."

Up went Clara's eyebrows, as amusement lighted her face. "Do you mean to tell me you're a magician? How did this knowledge escape my notice?"

"I hope it is not commonly mentioned. I usually indulge the hobby only in the company of a very few friends." His memory inconveniently offered up his most recent public performance, at Madam Mamie's, where the onlookers included some he would hardly so describe.

Clara took a moment to reflect on his confession. "I suppose there might be folk in town who would view such a hobby as inconsistent with professional dignity. Though there might be others, possibly more, who would think it a sign of desirable cleverness — and of manual dexterity that can only add to your qualifications."

Joshua had never considered that possibility. He would have to give the matter more thought. In the meantime, Clara had more to say. "Would it be possible, and would it amuse you, to teach me one or two of your simpler tricks?"

Joshua hesitated and looked around. There were only a few other passengers nearby; if he spoke softly and kept to tricks he could perform with smaller gestures, they might not draw attention to themselves. "I have never taught magic to anyone, and I had no teacher myself. I learned from the few books I could find, and rarely, from observation. But I am willing to attempt it, if your expectations are sufficiently modest." He mentally ran through a few tricks he had mastered early, and another that had become feasible more recently. "Let me show you a few tricks I might be able to teach, and you can choose which I should try to teach. But please keep in mind that even the simplest are likely to require many attempts before one can master them."

Clara sat back in her seat, smiling broadly. "Your audience is ready, sir."

Joshua held up a hand, palm out. "But your performer is not. I must retreat and make a few preparations." It was fortunate he had brought what he needed for a few tricks, having thought he might pass some of the time on his long journey with practicing. That had not happened on the journey east, due to the crowded and uncomfortable conditions in third class, but now his plan proved useful.

Joshua took his bag to the washroom and returned a few minutes later to find Clara once again looking out the window, her expression pensive. She appeared relieved to see him return, and he was glad to have a distraction to offer from whatever thoughts or memories weighed upon her.

He started with appearing to puncture the midpoint

of a dollar bill, folded inside a bit of paper, with a steel-point pen, only to display the bill intact. Clara clapped, but the twitch of her eyebrow suggested she might have deduced the general nature of his method, if not the particulars.

He moved on to card tricks. First he asked Clara to choose a card from the deck, then allowed her to insert it in the deck and to cut the deck for good measure. When he laid his finger across the deck and lifted the finger with her card seemingly attached to it, he won from Clara a small start of pleasure that made him ridiculously proud.

"This next trick can be appreciated from a slightly greater distance." He held the deck face down in his left hand and started pulling cards off the top with his right, holding them there. "Tell me when to stop." When she obliged, he turned over the portion of the deck in his right hand and showed her the visible card, then slid that card onto the seat next to Clara. He turned the remaining cards face down again and fanned them out, showing her that the intricate design on the back of all the cards was blue. Laying the fanned cards on his own seat, he turned over the card whose face he had shown to Clara. The design on the back was a brilliant red.

Clara not only applauded this trick, she actually bounced slightly in her seat, reminding him of Hope. He suppressed the pang of sorrow and regret that came with that recollection, standing up to bow to Clara with a dramatic flourish, careless of any onlookers.

"A last card trick, one that can land the magician in a great deal of trouble if unwisely used." He proceeded to deal her a royal flush, only then thinking to wonder whether she would recognize it for what it was.

To his relief, she grinned. "Now there's a 'trick' worthy of the name. It's good to know you're a man of honor and would never take advantage of your skill."

He gave her a sitting bow with another elaborate flourish, put away the cards, and made a wooden toothpick disappear. For his finale, he nerved himself to ask permission to touch her hair, so as to produce a coin from behind her ear. He could not help noticing the unexpected softness of her hair, and the warmth of her skin. He took his seat again in some confusion of mind.

With difficulty, he dragged his attention back to the subject at hand. "Which of these tricks would you like me to teach you?"

She chewed her lip thoughtfully. "I should perhaps ask, which of these tricks would you like to teach, and which do you believe I may be able to learn in our remaining idle hours?"

"The toothpick trick is relatively easy, so long as you have a ring to wear. But unless you have a ring in your bag, we will have to defer that one, as the ring I use is too large for you."

Clara shook her head. "I am not sure I even possess any rings."

That made sense. She seemed to have no interest in geegaws or finery. And of course, she had no wedding or engagement rings . . . or could he be sure? He knew little of her life before the war. . . . What had he been saying? "Ah. Yes. The dollar bill trick requires only the bill and paper, a pen, and a little preparation. Or would you rather start with cards?"

"I must admit cards have greater interest for me." Her smile had a touch of wickedness to it. "I rather like the picture of myself as a card sharp."

Joshua had to laugh at the image that came to him, Clara in a dandy's suit and eye shade, shuffling cards in a saloon. "Well, then, I believe you would have least difficulty learning the first card trick I showed you, the one with the rising card."

He was not really surprised when she mastered the trick before the train pulled into the station.

* * * * *

Shortly before they were to arrive at the Cowbird Creek depot, Clara said quietly and rather abruptly, "I have a question you might consider surprising and even intrusive." Not only her voice but the set of her shoulders betrayed tension. What could she possibly have in mind?

Joshua looked around to make sure no one was within earshot. "I am confident you would not ask such a question without good reason."

He had hoped to reassure her, but somehow seemed to have the opposite effect. He had never heard her speak so hesitantly. "I have heard it said that you . . . that when you visit Madam Mamie's, it is not only to provide services. That you are also there to . . . to receive them."

Joshua's jaw dropped. As he was hauling it back up, she added hurriedly, "I am only wondering how you avoid . . . unpleasant consequences. I know you would not be ignorant of such, or careless about them."

If he paused to speculate as to her reasons for asking, she would be likely to misconstrue his hesitation as disapproval. Explanations could come later. "There is a simple means of preventing the consequences I believe you to mean." Now that he had begun, he must find a way to go on, and if he blushed, so be it. "There is a, a thin sheath the man can wear that serves to protect . . . either partner against any contagion from the other. It also greatly reduces the chance of the woman conceiving."

To his enormous relief, her face brightened as it usually did in response to intriguing information. "Indeed!

I wonder who first performed the necessary experiments to discover this."

Joshua's mind instantly flooded with various absurd pictures of such experiments. Clara snickered. And then the two of them were laughing together, guffawing, attracting the attention he had taken pains to avoid, and about which he no longer cared in the slightest.

Chapter 26

CLARA WOULD have declined Joshua's offer of an escort to Miss Wheeler's boardinghouse, but Joshua pressed the point in case his involvement would smooth things along. Gossip about his following Clara and returning with her would run rampant in any case.

Miss Wheeler cordially invited him to return the next day for dinner, but Joshua declined. He had been pondering the difficulties before him where Freida was concerned. He could not involve Robert by revealing that Robert had sent word of the pitchman's reappearance and its alarming consequences. More subtlety was called for. It seemed likely that Freida would — if not too distracted — respond to his return with an invitation of her own, which he could accept and use as an opportunity to question her.

In the meantime, he wanted a quiet evening alone with Major. It might settle his mind.

He went to pick Major up, thanking Robert for looking after the dog while bringing him up to date in a summary fashion. Robert laughed heartily at Joshua's account of his and Clara's flight, and listened thoughtfully to the plans for Clara's employment. He made noncommittal noises about the notion of having work for her in his pharmacy before changing the subject to ask, "You got my letter?"

"I did, and have seldom been so shocked by a communication. It's as well I didn't foresee such a consequence to my leaving town."

"Come now, you don't think you could have stood in the way of Cupid's arrow?"

"You must have misunderstood Mrs. Blum's response to this man. He probably presented himself as in need of feeding, to take advantage of her generosity."

Robert shrugged. "If so, he'll take himself off and that'll be the end of it. You'll soon have a chance to see for yourself, I expect."

Joshua shook his head as if to dislodge the thought. "What could possibly attract her to that charlatan?"

"I'm hardly an expert on affairs of the heart, my good man." Robert stopped short. "Though we have a mutual acquaintance who could conceivably shed some light on the subject."

Instead of heading straight home with Major, Joshua stopped by the butcher to get a bone for the dog and left him comfortably worrying it in front of Madam Mamie's establishment. He entered with some discomfort, given the likelihood that his visit would be misconstrued. He was relieved to find Mamie herself first, rather than any of her girls. Before she could ask his business, he blurted out, "May I consult you about a matter that has left me utterly bewildered?"

"Of course, Doctor! Would you like a whiskey while you tell me about it? And does this by any chance concern your recent travels?"

"No, thank you, and no, it does not . . . involve my own affairs. Robert tells me — are you aware, or would you agree, that Mrs. Blum has shown some sort of interest in the fellow running that medicine show?"

"Has she really? I'll have to talk to my girls. They're

failing in their duty to keep me abreast of the local gossip."

"Mamie — what can have *possessed* her? Is this some sort of mania? Can he have practiced upon her with one of his potions? Though I don't know how he would have prevailed upon her to drink it . . . ."

She looked at him with an almost motherly air. "Dear Joshua, it's not so unlikely as you're making it. He's a well-looking man. She's a widow, long accustomed to a man and now long enough without one." She watched Joshua sputter, seeming to enjoy it, and then added, "As a matter of fact, I talked to the man when he first came to town. I wanted to make sure he knew where my house was located — though he never did visit us as a customer."

Joshua would have assumed otherwise. But the pitchman might reserve his attentions for more useful women, older and wealthier.

Mamie read his expression with the ease of an expert. "Whatever you're thinking — and I can't say whether you're right or wrong — I found him an interesting gentleman. And a lonely one, poor fellow."

Of course he would play that card, for Mamie and Freida both. But — if Mamie was so good at reading Joshua, could she be correct about Freida's suitor?

But whether the man were lonely or an opportunist or both, surely it took more than loneliness to attract Freida in more than a momentary charitable way. And the man's profession! Joshua looked at Mamie in renewed indignation, exclaiming, "But a pitchman! I would never have believed that she could tolerate dishonesty in a man, even a friend, let alone a — whatever he's hoping to be."

Mamie twinkled at him in a manner disconcertingly like one of Dolly's expressions. "Maybe they're both hoping to find some enjoyment in each other, without searching each other's souls. Or do you imagine only men do so?"

He could not believe it, not of Freida. But he had no means of refuting the suggestion. He took his leave even less satisfied than he had been when he arrived.

Freida did indeed invite him to dinner, puffing her way up the stairs to his rooms to welcome him back and insist on his accepting. "Such a journey you took, so much must have happened! You'll tell me all about it?"

Joshua had been expecting the question and had an answer ready, though it was harder to deliver than he had hoped with Freida standing there beaming at him. "I am sure you would not wish me to touch upon matters that concern the private affairs of another."

"Pish, you think I'll spread gossip? Who would listen to me?"

He was quite sure she would find eager listeners aplenty. But he turned the conversation to her health. "Exertion such as climbing stairs might be best avoided. You can search me out at my office at the usual times, or ask someone to summon me."

He was surprised and concerned when she failed to push back against the suggestion. "I have some number of breaths left, you think, and I should save them for when they're needed. A smart man, I always say."

Joshua had forgotten to ask Freida whether her niece remained in town, or had returned home to her family and fiancé. The subject troubling him might be even harder to approach with Rachel present.

As he mounted the steps to Freida's front door, rehearsing the manner in which he would approach the matter at hand, he was startled to hear two voices within, but neither of them Rachel's. One, of course, was Freida's. The other was masculine, and rippled along with practiced smoothness. Joshua cursed under his breath. Freida had stolen a march on him.

Freida flung open the door while Joshua was still trying to collect himself. "Doctor Gibbs, welcome! I hope you don't mind, I invited a friend, you two should meet, you have so much in common!"

Joshua's indignation threatened to burst forth. He said through clenched teeth, "I will always be happy to meet any *friend* of yours, after all you have done to be a friend to me."

The other guest was indeed the golden-haired pitchman, dressed not in his medicine show finery but in a more sober frock coat. He had apparently stood up as Freida answered the door, and now bowed to Joshua. "I am most happy to see you, Doctor. After all Freida has told me about you, I have been eagerly looking forward to actually making your acquaintance. She tells me, for example, that you are open to the use of Indian herbal remedies?"

Joshua responded stiffly, "*Mrs. Blum* is correct that I have included some such remedies in my pharmacopeia."

Freida, now in her kitchen, called back, "Never mind the Mrs., by now you can call me by my name, we've known each other how long?" Joshua could imagine the smug little smirk that must accompany her playing such a game with him.

Joshua gave a short nod to the pitchman and went into the kitchen to confront his hostess. "You are of course free to invite anyone you choose to your table, but I believe it would be best if I returned another time."

She planted herself squarely in front of him, hands on hips. "Oh no you don't, Mr. Big Shot I'm Better Than Everybody. You're happy looking down on Mr. Kennedy?" (Oh, yes — the name on the wagon. At least she wasn't calling him "Professor.") "Well, you sit at my table with him like civilized people, if you feel the same way afterward, you can go on your way and despise him as much as you like. Now out of my kitchen, you'll make me burn the roast with your nonsense."

Accepting temporary defeat, Joshua fairly stomped back to the sitting room, hung up his hat next to the pitchman's polished silk topper, and flung himself into the remaining easy chair, Kennedy having occupied the one nearest the door. After a minute or so of sulking, his manners and his sense of justice resurfaced sufficiently to make him both ashamed of the display and ruefully in agreement with Freida's scolding. He faced Kennedy, who was awaiting developments with a patient smile. "How did you come by your knowledge of Indian herbs?"

"I've been through some places that had a lot more Indians than you seem to have around here. Sometimes they're curious about the wagon. I do some trading with 'em, when they know enough English to tell me what the herbs are supposed to do."

"And then what? You just give the stuff to someone and see what happens?"

The man chuckled, obviously used to disapproving medical men. "I generally start with myself. Sooner or later, I'm liable to have a headache or indigestion, or pull a muscle, or whatever. The ones that seem to help, I keep, and put into a potion when I stop somewhere with the necessary apparatus."

Joshua hadn't given much thought previously to how medicine shows obtained or produced their nostrums. It seemed likely there were pharmacists with flexible enough standards to let fellows like this make use of their facilities — no doubt for a price. He caught himself curling his lip and forced his mouth to relax into something friendlier as he studied the man sitting near him. He was older than he had appeared at a distance, possibly close to Freida's age. The golden curls did not match the lines on his face; Joshua suspected the color was regularly and unnaturally renewed.

Kennedy redirected the conversation in an innocuous direction. "Were you born on the frontier, Doctor?"

"No. I come from Philadelphia."

"I, too, am far from my ancestral home. Though that may be too grand a term for the town I was born in, this town's size if that."

Freida appeared in the doorway carrying a large platter barely containing the heaped slices of roast beef perfuming the air. Joshua's mouth watered; Kennedy jumped up, took the platter from her, and placed it on the kitchen table, saying, "What a bounty you provide for us!"

Freida waved a hand in an unfamiliar and coy gesture. "It's nothing, but it'll fill you up, at least. You men seat yourselves, I'll get the corn and the beans and the biscuits."

When the table was groaning under the feast, Kennedy said with a respectful air, "Freida, would you care to favor us with one of your people's blessings?"

Freida's eyes went wide, and she seemed momentarily at a loss for words. Damn the fellow, he knew how to impress. "Of course. Not that I bother with such things so often, Mr. Blum thought it was old-fashioned, but it's good to remember traditions, people had a reason for coming up with them in the first place." She paused for breath and then rattled off a rhythmic string of syllables. "It means 'blessed are you, Lord our God, King of the Universe, at whose word all came to be.'"

Kennedy nodded solemnly. "How very fitting." He flashed a well-practiced smile. "Though I believe much of the credit is due closer by."

Joshua had never thought to ask about Jewish customs.

It brought home just how much he didn't know about this woman who had become a cherished friend, and whose welfare he was now attempting to protect. Speaking of which: "This must be the sort of spread you don't get often, Mr. Kennedy. It would take a direct-from-the-Almighty miracle to get food like this while following the trail in a wagon."

"True enough. That makes it even more of a pleasure, like any fine thing one has gone without for too long."

Just how many meanings did the man intend with that statement? Joshua restrained himself from looking at Freida to see how she had taken it.

Kennedy, seeming entirely at his ease, remarked, "Doctor Gibbs and I were just comparing our origins. He's a big city fellow — not like me. I don't suppose it surprised his kin when he turned out a doctor."

Joshua suppressed the impulse to squirm. Was he obligated to explain the unofficial nature of his credentials? He compromised on an indirect approach to the matter. "It may have surprised them, in fact, because of the way it happened. It was the war, and helping the surgeons there, that drew me to it."

"Now that's mighty interesting. I had studied for a doctor myself, before the war, along with doing my best to improve my mind more generally, but my neighbors had no inclination to take those studies seriously. They'd known me and my family too long, maybe. My folks were good people, and I thank God for them every day, but we were never what you might call upper crust. I worked in a livery stable and helped our pharmacist in the evenings, learning more than he knew and more than the townsfolk would have credited." Kennedy had tensed up now, as if his memories galled him. He took a big bite of roast and chewed it slowly, maybe to calm himself, before going on.

"Well, like I said, studying to be a doctor didn't turn me into one, as far as anyone there saw it. I'd about given up on finding patients. But in the army, no one cared where I came from, or who my kin might be, or how old I was. They snatched me up and set me to work." His face darkened. "And grim enough work it was. As you know."

This traveling swindler had once been a doctor? Could that be true, or was the man preternaturally good at making up a story to suit his company? Joshua searched his memory for any doctors resembling the smooth-talking pitchman sitting at the table. None came to mind. But there had been battlefields and hospitals aplenty, and he'd paid little heed to what doctors looked like when he was busy trying to help keep their patients alive.

"After the war, I thought it might be different at home. But it wasn't. So when my parents passed away, and I was free of family ties — well, with my knowledge of medications and of horses, as well as what I knew of doctoring, I hit on another way to serve the same goal."

Joshua almost choked on his mouthful of roast. Freida took one look at him and spoke before he could get his throat clear. "Some people, they might wonder how having a medicine show is like being a doctor. Even with the word medicine right there to give them a clue."

Joshua thumped his fists on the table. "Medicine! Sir, if you were really a doctor or trying to become one, I cannot imagine how you can countenance encountering those in need of actual medicine, people who might have sought out vital treatment, and persuading them instead to spend their coin on potions that, if not positively dangerous to their health, at best will do nothing to further it."

Even now, the pitchman did not respond with open anger. He gripped the table tight enough for his knuckles to whiten, but his voice remained even and well below a shout.

"Is it not necessary for doctors to examine symptoms and treatments, and allow the facts to govern their judgment? You assume the nature of the medicines I sell, and allow no possibility that they might be . . ." He seemed to search for a word, and finally found it. " . . . efficacious?"

"Tell me then, *Doctor*," Joshua fairly snarled, as Freida looked daggers at him. "Your *expertise* has surely led you to notice our hostess's less than perfect health. What would your *efficacious* treatment be for her condition?"

Kennedy laid his large, well-groomed hand over Freida's, a gesture that inescapably recalled to Joshua his own similar recent action toward Clara. "Given the weakness of her heart, I would provide her with my Doctor Bloomington's Revitalizing Elixir, which includes foxglove as well as an herb to bring water from the body."

Joshua sat dumbstruck, his mouth hanging open before he managed to clap it shut.

The pitchman — the doctor — Mr. Kennedy took advantage of Joshua's silence. "I would imagine, Doctor, that you sometimes find your patients stubborn, and inclined to trust family remedies or a neighbor's suggestion over your advice. As a traveling salesman of miraculous potions, I benefit from this peculiar habit — but my customers benefit as well. I sell some preparations not of my own making, but only those that I believe to be either harmless or of some small benefit. And even these can do more than I can rightly explain."

Joshua cleared his throat. "I have heard the word 'placebo' used to describe this effect."

Mr. Kennedy nodded thoughtfully. "Good to have a word for it. I'll remember."

Freida studied Joshua's face, presumably to see if he had suffered sufficient mortification for the sin of pride. She appeared satisfied, for she said, "Enough talk for now. Both of you eat up, it shouldn't get cold. And then I have apple pie."

Mr. Kennedy stood up. "Thank you, dear friend, but I would be liable to burst if I took another bite. If I might beg a slice of pie to take with me, I'll bid you good afternoon. You and your friend surely have news to catch up on."

"A piece, he says! Let me pack up half the pie, I won't eat but a sliver and Doctor Gibbs can have the rest." Joshua saw her pause and lean on the counter before she rummaged through her cabinets for a plate and napkin.

Joshua followed the pitchman to the sitting room. "Mr. Kennedy. I owe you an apology."

The man's smile had a weariness to it. "I can hardly blame you for jumping to conclusions. I know well enough what most of those in my profession are worth."

Joshua felt a sudden wave of sympathetic feeling. "It must be a lonely way to live, going from place to place and knowing that those you could most respect are unlikely to offer you a like esteem."

Mr. Kennedy's gaze moved to the kitchen, where Freida was now humming to herself, some air as unknown to Joshua as her blessing had been. "It is lonely. And more so the longer I live it." He took a deep breath and regained his smiling composure as Freida emerged with the covered plate. He took the plate and bowed over her hand. "Thank you again for your kindness, and I hope I may call again soon."

Freida opened the door for him. "Keeping an old woman company, it's a good deed. That pie, don't leave it too long, it'll be better warm."

She stood watching him until he reached the street, and then closed the door and turned back to Joshua, looking up at him with something like defiance. "Well? You have something to say, you can say it."

"First and foremost, I ask you to forgive my rudeness and arrogance. My behavior tonight is a poor return for your hospitality and your friendship."

Her face softened. "I knew what you thought, it was no surprise. But now you think different?"

"I admit I am somewhat of a loss as to what to think. I have never conceived of a — a benevolent medicine show pitchman. If he will permit it, I would like to examine his merchandise, with Robert's assistance. But I do not know why he would allow me the liberty."

Freida looked away as if embarrassed. "Seems to me, what do I know, but I think maybe he would like your good opinion."

There was little enough Joshua could do to dampen the townspeople's enthusiasm for the pitchman's products. Joshua could think of only one reason the man might care what Joshua made of him. But before he could attempt to confirm it, Freida turned the conversation back on him. "So tell me already, how did it go in New England? You're back here with Clara, and all of a sudden she's at Miss Wheeler's boardinghouse instead of with her family, so what happened?"

Joshua summarized the plan for Clara to become his assistant, skipping over the means by which he had extracted her — or he had helped her extract herself — from the hospital. He had little hope Freida would overlook the omission, but perhaps she would be merciful enough to leave that subject for a later interrogation.

For now, at least, she was content to focus on the immediate future. "Your business can support an assistant?"

He sighed. "I hope so. We'll find out. If not, I'll endeavor to find her work suited to her capabilities in some other town. I owe her that at the very least, after having persuaded her to return."

It occurred to him that if Mr. Kennedy's medicine show lingered in Cowbird Creek, it would reduce the number of patients in Joshua's practice at exactly the wrong time. "Has Mr. Kennedy been staying continuously since his arrival?"

Freida chuckled. "That man, he's so restless! He goes east to one county and west to another, always moving, coming back for a day or two and then off again."

That was some relief.

"And you and Clara, she'll be your assistant and what else?"

That had been a short respite . . . . "I confess my feelings are in a state of some confusion. I cannot say whether hers are in the same condition."

She studied him and then said with an unconvincing casual air, "If you're just as confused about Dolly, I should maybe tell you that the cordwainer, the one who makes shoes a little too tight, but they say he was good at saddles, he should go back to making them — he's maybe courting her."

He had not expected the news, but he found he was not surprised at it. Looking back at his dealings with Dolly, he could see that she was more than ready to find a man for herself and a father for Hope. It was the thought of Hope, mainly, that saddened him. "How does the child like this cordwainer?"

Freida looked at Joshua fondly. "Maybe not as well as she liked you, with you so good with her, it was something to see. But she likes him well enough, it'll be all right."

Then she gasped dramatically. "The pie, I forgot all about it. You sit right there, there's plenty left, I won't be a minute." She bustled off to the kitchen, while Joshua took several deep breaths and tried to recover some sort of aplomb. At least he knew the pie would be delicious.

Chapter 27

JOSHUA'S truce with the barber appeared to be working. At least, since their meeting over whiskey, no patients had come to him with complications arising from delay and the sheepish admission that they had seen Mr. Hawkins first. So when Hawkins knocked on his office door and thrust his head inside, Joshua welcomed him with more curiosity than wariness..

After the exchange of a few pleasantries, the barber got to the purpose of his visit. "Some of us are getting together a baseball game on Saturday afternoon, and we're looking for players. I don't know if you've ever played the game, but I know that many soldiers did." Hawkins studied Joshua with an unusually alert expression, as if watching for a reaction to Joshua's veteran status. Few townspeople, Joshua realized, ever alluded to his service. He must have somehow revealed, early in his residence in Cowbird Creek, that the topic pained him.

Joshua waited for the weariness and near nausea that references to the war often brought. To his surprise, his reaction was muted, bearable. He swallowed and replied, "I have in fact played baseball, though not since some time before I was mustered out."

The barber's shoulders relaxed. "I thought you might have. And we all know hereabouts that you're tolerable strong, and plenty good with your hands. So we hoped — well, not to put too fine a point on it, I hoped you'd join my team. Not that I'm captain of it — that's the blacksmith."

Given that the blacksmith was somewhat accident-prone, that choice of captain might be unwise. But Joshua had more urgent matters to consider. What would Hawkins make of it if Joshua declined? It was unlikely the barber, who had not — as far as Joshua knew — been a soldier, knew any details of when and where the soldiers had played. He might misconstrue the refusal as excessive pride or remaining hostility. Or an admission of insufficient skill, which Joshua found he did not want anyone assuming.

With a feeling of watching himself act rather than acting, Joshua put out his hand to shake the barber's. "You've got yourself a player. What positions remain open? And when does practice begin?"

He did not mention the upcoming match to Clara, lest she consider herself in any way obligated to attend it. But on Saturday afternoon, as the preliminary practice ended and the crowd of onlookers swelled, he caught sight of her familiar figure among the crowd. And as he approached the pitcher's mound, amidst the varied and rowdy calls of encouragement to an onlooker's favorite team or of challenge to the other, he heard her clear voice cheering him on.

* * * * *

As Joshua made his way through the general store, the storekeeper hailed him. "No mail for you today, but there's a letter for Li Chang. You heading out his way for anything?"

Joshua had no errands in that direction, but he was greatly concerned about what tidings the letter might contain. Among the news items Joshua had missed during his travels was the passage of the Page Act. It had passed weeks ago, perhaps even before his petition had reached Washington City. He had gone to see Li Chang as soon as he heard. Li had not, at that time, known whether his wife and mother had already set sail. Nor did Joshua know whether the Act was already being enforced, either in China or in U.S. ports.

In retrospect, his efforts to oppose it appeared ridiculous, a sign of arrogance and delusion. When Clara asked the cause of his brown study, he burst out, "I was six kinds of fool, to think I could change the course of things. At least Don Quixote brought a lance when he went tilting at windmills, rather than a quill."

She drew in her breath in dismay and then blew it out again, assuming a determined stance. "You know better than that, Doctor. You were a soldier. Can you look me in the eye and tell me that every battle lost was therefore ignoble? That surrender, rather than striving, is always the better course, no matter the cause to be served? When that cause is just, is not any chance worth pursuing? You should be proud of having made the attempt."

In his bitterness, he was hard put not to answer harshly. The best he could do was not to answer at all. But he suspected that once the smart of humiliation had faded, he would grant her the better argument.

The laundryman was somewhere in the back of his shop, busy with his work, when Joshua arrived. Joshua called to him, got no answer, and made his way back, weaving between the padded tables, staying clear of the vats of steaming water, the mangle, and the hot irons. He saw Li and waved vigorously, managing to get his attention after a couple of minutes. Joshua kept the letter in his vest pocket, where it would be mostly protected from the steam, and retreated to the front room.

Li Chang soon emerged, wiping sweat off his forehead, and bowed politely. Joshua did his best to match the gesture and pulled out the letter. "This came for you today."

The laundryman reached for the letter with a suddenly shaking hand. He broke the seal and unfolded it, started to read, and let out a wordless cry of anguish, followed by a torrent of Chinese. Joshua studied his boots until the man fell silent, and then looked back up at him. "I'm afraid I have brought you bad news."

Li had tears in his eyes. "It is my wife who writes. She and my mother tried to board the ship, but they would not let her. They would have let my mother go, and my wife tried to persuade her, but she was afraid to go alone."

"So they are still in China?"

"They are in China, and they will stay in China. My mother had only a little money with her, but she tried to bribe the official. They threatened to arrest her. My mother —" He sobbed aloud, wiped his eyes, and managed to go on. "My mother collapsed. When she was able to stand, the official told them both to get out and not to come back. My wife writes that they have plenty of money now, because they were not allowed to buy their passage, so I do not need to send any."

Joshua clenched his fists in futile rage. "I am so very sorry. I wish there was something I could do."

Li stood up straighter. "There is something I can do. I can go home."

"And leave everything you have built here?"

Li seemed to have aged years in minutes. "I came here to make a better future for my family. Now there is no future for them here. So I will go home."

Joshua looked around the laundry. "I will spread the word that there is a good business here, wanting a buyer."

Li reached out his hand, American fashion. "I thank you, for this and for what you tried to do, writing to your government. Only an American would try such a thing. I did not expect it to work, but I thank you."

Joshua wrung his hand wordlessly and left. When he had reached the street, he vented his feelings in as long a string of curses as he could manage, careless of who might be listening.

As he finally ran down, he heard steady footsteps to his left. He looked over to see Clara. She looked behind Joshua, and her mouth tightened. "Were you visiting Li Chang?"

"I brought him a letter that came for him. You can guess what it said."

Clara took a deep breath and came out with a stream of cussing that would have done a soldier proud. He stopped short and stared at her. She kept walking; he caught up, in time to hear her say wryly, "I learned more than nursing in the war. Sometimes it's good for the health. Wouldn't you agree, Doctor?"

He nodded gravely. "I suppose I do at that." He felt like smiling, but refrained. It felt wrong to smile with Li Chang not far away, standing in the building he was abandoning, his dreams dissolving away like the steam from his laundry.

Joshua spread the news about Li Chang's laundry as widely as he could. He supposed he should have expected that people would come to him to discuss the business, even though Li's English was quite good. The people who had stopped by so far seemed to think that the Chinaman would have to sell for a pittance. Joshua very much hoped that Li would wait for a better offer.

The knock on his office door sounded too vigorous for a patient. He went to open the door and barely avoided a double-take. Silas Finch, the cordwainer, stood in the doorway shifting his weight back and forth, his hat in his hands.

"I come about the laundry. Folks say you're selling it for the Chinaman."

Joshua waved him to a chair and sat back down in his own. "Not exactly, but I am authorized to answer preliminary questions."

"I'm meaning to branch out. I don't figure on spending that much time in the laundry, not with my other business, but I could hire some young fella who's tired of farming."

Joshua had his doubts that such a youngster would be meticulous about cleaning spots and starching collars, but so long as the man was willing to buy Li out for a decent price, Joshua would put aside thoughts of his own future as a customer. "What were you thinking of offering?"

The cordwainer named a sum higher than anyone had previously mentioned. Whether it was sufficient, Joshua wasn't sure. "I'll pass this along and see what Li Chang has to say."

"I appreciate it." There seemed little else to discuss, but the man stayed put. He said abruptly, "Dolly Arden and me, we're getting hitched."

After Freida's warning, the news came as no sort of shock. "My congratulations. She's a wonderful woman."

"She tells me you were sweet on her."

Joshua raised his eyebrows, not sure whether to be irritated or amused. He could hardly protest that she might be exaggerating the nature or degree of his interest. He fell back on self-deprecation. "I always knew that Mrs. Arden was too rare a blossom for a tired old sawbones like me. I'm sure you'll be very happy."

The man seemed a little taken aback, as if he had expected Joshua to make some last-ditch challenge for Dolly's affections. He said with the truculence that such an effort would have deserved, "I aim to be good to her. Her and the little girl both."

Joshua said gravely, "I am very glad to hear it." He stood up. "I'll let you know as soon as I've talked to Li Chang."

The cordwainer shoved his chair back hard enough for it to rattle on the floor, nodded, and stumped out. Joshua stood looking after him and shaking his head.

The man seemed sincere in his intentions. But Joshua would keep an eye on the family, just in case. And maybe, months or years down the road, he could find a way to be friendly with them, and to see Hope now and again.

* * * * *

The arrival of the Wells Fargo stagecoach always brought a crowd. Joshua rarely joined it, but he was hoping Tom Barlow's prosthetic leg would be among the parcels. He was not sure Major was savvy enough concerning wagons and such to stay clear of the wheels, particularly given the distractions of many people and much excitement, so he took the precaution of shutting the dog inside his rooms, wincing as Major whined his objection.

The others waiting noted Joshua's presence, accounting for it with guesses from practical to hilarious. When the stagecoach pulled in, the long narrow package the courier hauled out for him provided enough of a clue for many in the crowd to figure out. He could hear the news passed around in appropriately hushed murmurs.

He lugged the parcel into his office and laid it on his examining table, opening first the parcel and then the case inside. The leg proved to be a handsome object, if viewed as such — ash-brown wood polished to show the grain, shaped in the likeness of a slender limb and foot, with a joint in the ankle and a strap rising from the upper portion to a cuff that would go around the lower thigh.

He had patients with more urgent needs that afternoon, but the next morning he rode out to the Barlow farm, carrying the case by putting one arm through its strap. Someone must have told Tom that the stagecoach had come through, for he hobbled out to meet Joshua with his homemade crutch, looking both expectant and nervous. Joshua hoisted the case; Tom grinned.

"Let's go into the house, and I can show you how to put this on." The last thing Tom needed was to get grit or straw where the prosthesis met the stump.

Joshua directed Tom to doff his trousers and sit in an easy chair. Tom was willing to do so only when his sister had taken herself elsewhere. His mother stubbornly stayed put. "I've seen a lot more of you than that, and you might need help with the thing at first."

Tom was already wearing something like a large sock over the stump. Joshua would have bet that his mother or sister had knit it specially. "That'll do nicely for a start. If you can get something with finer thread, it'll chafe less once you're wearing the leg for longer periods." Tom's mother gave a determined nod.

Joshua opened the cuff, placed the wooden leg in position, and fastened the cuff closed. He handed Tom his crutch and positioned himself to take Tom's weight on the other side. "Let's get you standing up. Easy, now."

Tom wobbled a bit getting up, but Joshua was able to hold him steady. "Rest as much weight on the leg as you can, and tell me how it feels."

Tom shifted his weight accordingly and said in an uncertain tone, "It feels strange."

"It will, naturally, until you get used to it. Do you have pain in the stump?"

"Not much." The boy's grimace suggested otherwise, but Joshua withheld any challenge.

"The skin will toughen up if you don't overdo it the first few days. Let's get you sitting down again. We'll have you stand up again a few more times, and then try walking."

Walking went less well. Tom would have fallen if Joshua had not managed to catch him. The boy looked ready to cry.

"Don't be discouraged. It takes practice. I'd wager you'll be getting around easily with the crutch in a week or so, and without the crutch not long after. Just remember not to have it on for more than ten minutes at a time today, and move to longer times by degrees."

The boy was biting his lip now. Joshua gave him the excuse he needed to sit down again. "Let's get that sock off and see how your stump is holding up."

To his relief, there were no actual abrasions, though the skin had reddened in spots. "I can sand the end down if necessary, but being as it's polished, I'd like to hold off on that."

Tom's father came in just as Joshua was leaving. He turned on his heel and walked out again with Joshua, asking him in a low voice, "What will the lad be able to do?"

"He'll be able to walk around almost like anyone else once the stump toughens up and he gets the hang of it. But he won't be able to stand nearly as long at a time. He'll need to keep dirt and such out of the mechanism and the sock, so his trousers will have to be tucked into his shoes or boots. And the more he has to bend over and straighten up again, the greater the chance of chafing in the stump or where the cuff fits."

The father's jaw tightened. "You've just described a lot of our day around here."

"I'll keep my ears open for anything he could do in town, if you like."

The father nodded glumly.

Riding back to town, Joshua suddenly recalled the cordwainer's plans for expanding his business holdings. Could Tom possibly do the work in the laundry? Joshua rather doubted it, but once he had returned Nellie-girl to the livery stable, he headed to the laundry to talk to Li Chang.

The laundryman was barely visible for the steam all around him. Joshua tried to picture a stool in such a room. Metal would become slick with moisture; wood would deteriorate over time and have to be replaced. Though perhaps the metal could be roughened in some manner — but then, wouldn't it rust?

Joshua had heard several people complain that Li had become less friendly. He had mostly restrained himself from asking how friendly they would be under Li's circumstances. But Li's manner with Joshua remained unchanged, or a little more cordial. Joshua asked him about whether a man who could stand for no more than a half hour at a time could take over his work. Li shook his head. "I stand all day. And still my customers complain that they wait too long for their laundry. If I stopped to sit down, they would complain more."

Joshua moved on to the cordwainer's offer, which he had not yet had a chance to convey. Li's face fell. "I was still hoping for more. But maybe no one will pay more. What do you think?"

Joshua put up his hands, disclaiming expertise. "How much longer are you willing to wait?"

Li's lips tightened. "Maybe one week, maybe two. This country does not want my kind. I do not want to be here any more."

Walking down the street, Joshua considered Tom's remaining options. Was there anything better for him than farm work? In what profession could he spend much of the day on a stool or in a chair?

Some possibilities would require more book learning, or capacity for the same, than Joshua judged Tom to possess. Work with his hands would be the thing . . . .

What about working in leather? Tom must have grown up keeping saddles and horse tackle in good condition, at least. Maybe the cordwainer would be open to having more assistance in his original business in order to spend more time at the laundry — though the disdain with which many white men viewed the job might prove a deterrent. Or he might have a use for Tom even if he found some other farm lad for the laundry work.

He headed for the man's shop to sound him out. As he approached, he was at first disconcerted to see Dolly approaching from another direction with a covered basket. Apparently the cordwainer did not always make it home for dinner, or was not yet dining with Dolly, engagement notwithstanding. But Hope was skipping along by her mother's side. Dolly would refrain from any noticeably awkward conversation in Hope's presence. Joshua doffed his hat, trying to take in both Dolly and Hope in the gesture.

Dolly smiled up at him as if there was nothing at all that might make her do otherwise. Hope started to run toward him; Dolly grabbed her hand. "Manners, Hope!" Joshua supposed that the child needed to learn not to run to adults without an invitation, but he felt a pang at the thought of lifting her and hoisting her into the air.

"Howdy-doo, Mrs. Arden, Miss Hope. Here on an errand of culinary mercy?"

Hope giggled at his multisyllabic phrasing, though Joshua doubted she knew just what he had said. Dolly smiled, though without her once-familiar twinkle. "Silas is working so hard, he wouldn't even eat if I didn't bring his food to him."

Joshua seized on this unexpected opening, despite his qualms about raising his proposition indirectly through the cordwainer's fiancée. "If you think Mr. Finch could use some help in the shop, especially with the likely acquisition of a second business, I know a young man in need of just such a position, who would be grateful for it and work hard to show that gratitude."

Dolly tilted her head, eyes bright. "You may be sure I'll suggest it, even urge it. Would this by any chance be the poor young fellow who lost his leg?"

"Yes, Tom Barlow. I thank you on his behalf. You will be doing both of us a kindness."

For the first time, she seemed self-conscious, looking down at the basket she carried. "I will always be happy to do you a kindness, Doctor Gibbs."

Hope started tugging on Dolly's hand. "I want to show Mister Doctor the cake I made!"

Joshua attempted to forestall any more admonitions by saying, "If your mama is willing, I would very much like to see it. I'm sure it's a fine example of the baker's art."

So urged, Dolly relented and allowed Hope to approach him with the basket. "Hold it carefully, now. It would be a great shame if anything were to fall out."

Hope held the basket out toward him while still clutching the handle. Joshua considered himself as well as the child bound by Dolly's instruction, unwrapping the contents carefully and just enough to expose the slice of moist apple cake resting next to a large chunk of bacon. "I'm sure Mr. Finch will enjoy it greatly."

Hope beamed and carried the basket back to Dolly. As soon as she had handed it over, she started bouncing on her toes. "Mama, when can Mister Doctor come to dinner again?"

Dolly blushed. Joshua waited for her to look at him and then said gravely, "If at some point, Mr. Finch and I become better acquainted, I would look forward to such an invitation. In the meantime, may I hope to see both of you at the social library from time to time?"

Dolly smiled again. "Indeed you may. Hope is always demanding fresh stories for me to read to her."

Joshua had never redeemed his promise to read Hope more of *Alice's Adventures in Wonderland*. Had Dolly done so, or had the book sat neglected until returned to the library?

They had stood there in the street long enough. Joshua tipped his hat again and took his leave, hoping Dolly would remember her promise to speak to her fiancé about Tom. Dolly's charms would make a better advocate than anything Joshua could muster.

Turning, he could hear Hope chattering to her mother as they entered the shop, the cordwainer's rough voice, softened as he greeted them both, and Hope's shrill giggle. The child's future stepfather was fond of her, then, and Hope comfortable with him. Joshua's relief almost outweighed the sense of loss as he walked away.

Chapter 28

JOSHUA HAD by now installed Clara as his assistant. As he had expected, the arrangement, as well as their journey preceding it, had led to considerable public comment, some of it along infuriating lines. On one of his trips to the general store, he heard the owner's wife say to her husband in a stage whisper, "I always knew there was something wrong about her. No decent unmarried woman would spend hours with an unmarried man unchaperoned." As she was pretending she could not be overheard, he had little choice but to pretend not to overhear her. He dearly wished he could afford to place orders for goods by telegraph with eastern concerns and have them shipped, rather than continuing to benefit the couple with his custom.

Others stared goggle-eyed at a woman who, they thought, was holding herself out as almost a doctor. Joshua privately thought she would make an excellent one, but reluctantly discussed with Clara whether it would be worth the expense of procuring a nurse's uniform, "nurse" being a better understood position. Clara, more pragmatic than he, not only thought it sensible, but had saved one of her wartime uniforms with the intention of reusing the fabric. It was badly stained in places, but Li Chang, nearing the end of his time as a laundryman, bleached it so thoroughly as to weaken some of the thread and was able to make it respectable again.

Clara's uncle wrote to her parents, a letter Clara described as combining indignation, hope, and concern. She herself wrote back, but as to the content of her response, she had little to say.

Just as Freida had said, the medicine show had been leaving town for up to two weeks and returning for far shorter periods. During one of the latter, Joshua recalled his earlier intention and asked for samples of the pitchman's potions. He half expected the man to go back on his offer to provide them, but Mr. Kennedy actually helped convey the main ingredients — absent agents used to add brighter color or an impressive fizz — to Robert's for examination. Through smell, heating, dissolution, and very cautious tasting, as well as visual comparisons to various known medicines, they were able to identify not only foxglove but willow bark tea and several other Indian remedies, as well as a powder that, when dissolved in steaming water, appeared to loosen phlegm in the chest. Another resembled one of Joshua's own preparations for settling the stomach. Others would, as best they could determine, have effects either soporific or intoxicating, while still others were likely to have no direct effect whatsoever.

Joshua returned what was left to Mr. Kennedy, with his thanks and acknowledgment that their inspection fully supported the man's claims. Mr. Kennedy was more gracious than Joshua thought he would have been under similar circumstances. The pitchman went so far as to acknowledge that his visits were likely to divert customers not so much from Joshua as from Robert, and suggested a remedy. "I would have no objection to making some recompense, on the order of twenty-five per cent of my revenues from my sojourn here. I would consider it a kindness if you would convey this offer to your friend. I believe he would be more receptive to it if so presented."

Given that Robert had been complaining of just such an impact, Joshua undertook to broach the subject.

The pitchman still seemed to have something on his mind. He was not long in revealing it. "I will be leaving again, and for somewhat longer, having exhausted the sales potential of the neighboring counties. My absence will also give our mutual friend sufficient time to consider . . . that is, I have . . . ."

What could put this man, of all men, at a loss for words? To ask the question was to answer it. "You have asked her to marry you."

Mr. Kennedy faced Joshua squarely and looked him in the eye. "I have. And I have asked her, if she can, to have an answer for me by the time I return."

The many questions that boiled up in Joshua's mind must have occurred to Mr. Kennedy as well, and they had not deterred him. There was no point in raising them. Joshua simply said, "I see." Finding nothing to add, he nodded curtly and left.

Heading back to his office, he told Clara the news. Somewhat to his disappointment, she had no immediate reaction. Soon sensing that he expected one, she asked, "As I recall, you found him less objectionable than you expected. Do you believe them to be incompatible?"

Somewhat at a loss, he could only reply, "I can hardly believe them to be compatible, even if he is not the scoundrel I first thought him."

She regarded him with what he feared might be disappointment. "What do you know of her late husband? What was he like?"

Joshua tried to cast his mind back over the months to Freida's praise of Samuel. "He had, she told me, plenty to say for himself. He would talk to her about a range of subjects. He liked to read plays aloud, and to recite poetry. And he had good manners."

Clara gave a little listening nod. "And does Mr. Kennedy share any of these attributes?"

"Well . . . speech naturally comes easily to him. I can well believe him to have a flair for the dramatic. And he has made efforts to extend his knowledge in several subjects." He could not help recalling the pitchman's request that the crowd let Joshua's buggy pass, on their first encounter. And his suggestion that Freida say a Jewish blessing. "And I suppose he has shown some signs of being considerate."

Clara studied his face as if seeking the answer to a mystery. "Then your objections must lie elsewhere."

His concerns tumbled out in a rush. "Elixir of foxglove is not a miracle cure, whatever claims he may make for it in his pitches. Freida's heart is weak and will remain so. How will exposure to all the discomforts of travel, inclement weather and irregular meals, and a probable increase of exertion, affect her?"

Clara looked at him soberly. "It is not, to be sure, what either of us would prescribe as an ideal regimen." Her mouth twitched into one of her sardonic smiles. "Though I have not observed that Mrs. Blum is given to long periods of inactivity. She is more likely to be found bustling about town, deep in everybody's business. And it would not greatly surprise me if she gives more attention to others' meals than to her own."

Joshua's next thought made him wince inwardly. "I asked Madam Mamie's advice when I discovered Freida's — kindness toward Mr. Kennedy. She suggested that Freida may be lonely. I have been trying for months to find a suitable companion for her, but I could make another effort during the respite afforded by Mr. Kennedy's absence."

Clara's face lit with barely suppressed laughter. "If even Mrs. Blum, with her admirable energy and determination, was unable to find you a proper match —"

Mortified, he interrupted. "You heard about her efforts?"

"My dear doctor, you cannot imagine them to have gone unnoticed in town. As I was saying, your confidence in believing you can be more successful is . . . admirable."

Joshua sighed deeply. "I will once again consult with Freida's and my mutual friend Alton. It may be that some resident of Rushing would provide a less drastic alternative."

Alton poured a dram of whiskey for Joshua and another for himself. They sat at his kitchen table as Alton ran through the town's widowers and bachelors. "There's several farmers, but that's out . . . . There's a bank teller who's unmarried, but he's a dry stick of a man, hardly Freida's type . . . ." He snapped his fingers. "The barber who took over the barbershop last month is a widower. He's a stout fellow, a good match for Freida in figure, and has fine long whiskers."

Joshua frowned. "There's no way of knowing, I suppose, how he treated his wife."

Alton held his whiskey up to the light, admiring its color, and took a sip of it. "You suppose correctly. But he seems good-natured enough. He talks to his customers, and none of them seem to take it amiss. And there's nothing unpleasant about his manner with the ladies in town."

"Think you he's looking for another wife?"

"I believe I've heard him lament the life of a man alone.

I'd say he's your best prospect, given that you're in something of a hurry. The question is, whom do we approach first, our barber or Freida?"

Joshua drained his glass. "Why don't you ask him in general terms whether he'd like to meet a goodhearted woman who loves to cook and take care of folks. Then I'll get Freida to invite you over for another play read. If he's interested, you give me a quick word once you arrive, and then — which of us should mention him?"

Alton grimaced. "I suppose you'd like it to be me. It's my turn, at that. Now how about another whiskey before you go?"

Joshua grinned. "You'd better be saving your whiskey to fortify you for your visit."

Freida was more than willing to host Alton and himself for another reading. She offered Joshua his choice of the plays on her shelves, and he took his time reviewing them, hoping to find something particularly to his purpose. When he found a short adaption of *Sense and Sensibility*, a novel his mother had been proud to discover and had often discussed, he looked no further.

They arrived, per Freida's decree, in time for supper, and Freida served them a hearty and unfamiliar dish, sausage cooked with onions. "Jedidiah mentioned he likes it, so I practice for when he gets back to town, it'll be a surprise."

She had to mean the pitchman. Joshua bit his tongue. Play first, then their own sales pitch.

Alton and Joshua had flipped a coin to see who would play the dashing but unreliable Willoughby, and who the steady, reliable, and ultimately victorious Colonel Brandon. Freida obviously saw what they were up to, and responded by playing up Marianne's passion for the unsuitable choice. When it came time for her to declare her new appreciation for the worth of the quiet, sober suitor, she delivered her lines with an almost comical lack of enthusiasm. Her last line closing the play, she closed the book with an emphatic snap and narrowed her eyes, glaring at Alton and Joshua in turn. "So before you bother telling me about the butcher or baker or candlestick maker I should meet, don't waste your breath."

Joshua opened his mouth; Freida's glare intensified, and he shut it. She took a few too-shallow breaths and went on, "Two grown men acting like little boys who won't take 'no' for an answer, you should be ashamed! Jedidiah comes from nothing and still finds a way to make something of his life, you should be glad! You know by now, he doesn't hurt anyone, he gives them a show for their money and some of them he even helps with his potions. He had to leave home because the people looked down their noses instead of giving him a chance, and now you do the same, you should know better, both of you!"

Joshua gulped. "I must concede the justice of your reproach. But I have other reasons for concern about your evident . . . attachment to this man. The life he leads is hardly one I would prescribe for your condition."

Somewhat mollified, she reached out to pat his hand. "My condition, which you help me with, and I'm grateful. Tell me, my friend the doctor, have I gotten much worse in the last month?"

"Thankfully, no. Which is why —"

She hushed him with an imperious gesture. "So this last month, I've been taking Jedidiah's foxglove-and-whatnot potion instead of your medicine and tea, and look at me, still above ground."

Joshua put his face in his hands, utterly routed. Alton

filled the awkward silence. "I apologize on my own behalf as well for my unwarranted interference. Please believe that I, that both of us, acted out of concern for the welfare of a cherished friend."

Finally she smiled at them. "It's all right, I should know about trying to help, I've stuck my nose in people's business often enough. I'll get the pie, it's cherry this time." Her smile was triumphant. "Jedidiah's favorite."

Alton, who had ridden over from Rushing, left as soon as he had praised and enjoyed the cherry pie. Joshua departed soon after, hoping Freida would shortly retire for the night but not daring to suggest it. As he retrieved his hat, she asked, "So what about Clara?"

Joshua turned back toward her, hat in his hand. "I am not sure I understand. She is well, and a great help in my practice, which so far is managing to sustain both of us."

Freida scoffed. "You don't understand, you're telling me? An old lady like me is about to be engaged, when will you climb down off the fence and ask her?"

Joshua frowned. "Even if, as you suppose, I had formed a tender attachment to Miss Brook, I am now in the position of her employer. I would not for the world wish her to believe that I induced her to enter that position out of undisclosed and self-interested motives."

Freida sniffed. "That's what you don't wish. What is it you do wish?"

Joshua could feel the hated blush rise in his cheeks. "I trust I may answer you in the strictest confidence."

"What, I'm going to go calling out in the street, the doctor is in love? Or go running to Clara, who likes me so much, I don't think, and whisper in her ear?"

Joshua refrained from pointing out that the lack of

friendly relations between Clara and Freida had been due primarily to the latter. "I will trust to your discretion, then, and admit that I do hold a growing fondness for Miss Brook, and greatly desire to win her esteem and affection."

Belatedly he looked at Freida's standing clock. "But it is late, and you require rest." At her indignant expression, he hastened to add, "As do I, I must confess. Thank you for your indulgence in listening to me."

"My pleasure, what else should an old woman do but listen to the young? Let me pack up some pie, you could get hungry in the night."

Next morning, after a night without bad dreams and yet too wakeful, Joshua took advantage of the spring sunshine to go for a walk with Major. He had rather neglected the dog of late.

As Major sniffed and ran about, Joshua heard a high voice hailing him. "Mister Doctor! Mama sent me to the store for some thread!"

There came Hope, clutching a basket and looking very proud of having an errand of her own. Joshua smiled at her. "Do you know where to go for it?"

Hope nodded vigorously. "The dry goods store. Mama and I have been there lots of times. But Mama's talking to Mrs. Blum about her wedding dress, and Mrs. Blum needs more blue thread, and Mama sent me to get it." Just then, Major barked at a suddenly appearing squirrel. Hope's eyes went wide. "Is that your *dog*?"

"Indeed it is. Major, here!" The dog, already in pursuit of the squirrel, hesitated. "Here, I say!"

Major abandoned the squirrel and trotted right over to Hope, tail waving. She laughed in delight as he sniffed her skirts. "He's so *pretty*!"

Joshua allowed himself to grin. "I guess he is at that. He's an Irish Setter, you know."

"He came all the way from *Ireland*?"

"No, no. He was born right here in Cowbird Creek. That's just his breed, the kind of dog he is. You may pet him, if you like."

Hope bent carefully down, still holding the basket tight in her left hand and caressing Major with her right. Major licked her hand; she jumped and then laughed again. "What's he *doing*?"

"He's kissing you. That's how dogs kiss people."

"Should I kiss him back?"

Joshua stroked Major's back. "I don't think your mama would approve. Major doesn't take much trouble to stay clean. But you can pet him again. He likes it."

As Hope followed his suggestion, Joshua heard a familiar clear voice behind him. "I'm glad to see Major is taking you for a walk on this fine morning."

Joshua turned toward Clara smiling and tipped his hat, belatedly wondering if he should have done the same for Hope. "I must give him a bone to thank him. We have been having a very pleasant time."

Clara studied Hope and Major with her measuring gaze. "Hope seems to be fond of dogs." She looked back at Joshua and said quietly, "And you seem to be fond of Hope."

He said equally quietly, "I am. She is an affectionate child, and bright as well. I believe I am fond of children in general, though I have known few of them as well as I have come to know Hope."

Clara searched his face. "I hope the manner in which you came to know the child, and the way events have fallen since, does not give you pain."

He shook his head. "No, indeed. I am content with the

— resolution of that relationship. And glad that Mrs. Arden has found someone with whom to share her life, after her loss and her time alone."

Meanwhile, Hope reluctantly stopped petting Major. "I must go. Mama and Mrs. Blum need the thread. Thank you for letting me pet Major."

Joshua bowed to her. "Major and I both thank you for your attention to him." He watched her run off, making sure she was going in the right direction, and then returned his attention to Clara.

Clara's eyes also followed Hope. Was she avoiding looking at him? "You might, in time, have children of your own. If you should, like Mrs. Arden, find someone to share your life. A young woman, perhaps, who could provide you with a family."

Joshua examined his boots. "It has been my professional observation that women may be blessed with children even when no longer in what most would consider the first bloom of youth."

Now he thought he could feel Clara's eyes on his averted face. She said soberly, "There are also many youngsters orphaned by various misfortunes. We could provide an orphan with a home, to the orphan's and our own great benefit."

He started to nod agreement and then did a double-take, finally looking straight at her. "Miss Brook, what did you just say?"

Her face had a mischief in it. "I said that you need not despair of a family, even if we were unable to produce one in the usual way."

He seized her hands. "I would despair of nothing, if I had your support and comfort."

He would not shame her by kissing her in the street. Nor in their shared office, where anyone might enter, and where she even more than he needed to maintain a professional appearance. The boardinghouse? He dimly recalled a sitting room, with a door that could be closed . . . . "May I call on you this evening at Miss Wheeler's establishment?"

He had never seen this smile before, neither sardonic nor mischievous nor bitter, a smile of simple joy. "I shall be greatly looking forward to it."

Chapter 29

FULL OF his news, Joshua charged up Freida's front walk, barely restraining himself from pounding on her door. She answered his knock holding a piece of paper in her hand. "Come in, come in! You should excuse me, I'm just rereading this note Jedidiah left me. So romantic, that man, he wants I should read it every day while he's gone, so he'll know I'm thinking of him, as if I wouldn't be. . . ." She finished reading and folded the paper back up, tucking it into her apron pocket and patting it gently. When she finally looked at him with some attention, her eyebrows shot up, and she clasped her hands. "You asked?"

He was not sure he had ever beamed so broadly. "Clara has agreed to become my wife." The words lingered strangely on his tongue. He had never said them before, and could hardly believe he was saying them now. He thought it best not to mention that Clara had in point of fact more or less asked him, instead of the reverse.

Freida reached up, pulled his head down, and gave him a resounding kiss on both cheeks. "Your wife! You're getting married! Such wonderful news!" And then, inevitably: "I told you, I was right!"

Joshua reached out to clasp her hands. "You were right, as you so often are."

Freida cocked her head and looked suddenly shy. "So we'll be two brides, your Clara and I."

Joshua kept hold of her hands. "You must know I wish

you every happiness."

"Happy, why shouldn't I be happy? At my age, to see new places, meet all sorts of people, have a companion after all this time, it's a blessing. Who knows, maybe I'll learn to do magic tricks for the show, people won't believe their eyes!"

Joshua let go of her hands as he realized he was still wearing his hat. He took it off and hung it on the hook near the door. "I have a request to make, if your own plans do not preclude it. Would you make Clara's wedding dress?"

Tears glimmered in Freida's eyes before she blinked them away. "Of course, would I let anyone else make your bride's dress, I'd snatch the cloth out of their hands first. She can come for a fitting any time, or I can go to her at Rebecca's, whatever she likes, so exciting!"

Freida would have enough to do, and quite sufficient activity, without crossing town to Miss Wheeler's. "I believe she would be most happy to come here, where you have all your measuring apparatus and samples ready to hand. But what of your own wedding attire?"

Freida snorted. "Why should I need to get fancy, at my age?"

"I cannot allow you to deck Clara in finery while you go to your wedding without. Will you accept the necessary fabric and other supplies for your own dress as a wedding gift?"

She hesitated. "You shouldn't, you'll need your money for your new household, so many things you'll have to get! But . . . you really want to, dear man, I'll say yes."

At least with two fine dresses to prepare, she would perforce be in town a little longer.

Joshua did his best to spruce up before heading to

the boardinghouse, brushing his frock coat and hat, giving his boots yet another polish. From what he could see of himself in his mirror, he looked as good as he was going to. "Major, what do you think? Do I make a presentable gentleman caller?"

Major wagged his tail, eyes bright with delight at being addressed. Joshua bent to stroke his tawny coat. "Wish me good fortune, then." He made his way to the boardinghouse and found himself whistling a dimly remembered tune.

He was not entirely at ease about seeing Rebecca Wheeler under the present circumstances, but she opened her door with an amused smile on her lips and a matching light in her eyes. Evidently his lack of interest in Freida's earlier matchmaking attempt had not left her particularly disappointed. She ushered him in and said, before he found the words to ask, "Clara is in the sitting room. And may I offer you my congratulations? I do hope you'll be very happy."

Joshua bowed. "Thank you. I am already happier than I deserve."

His hostess scoffed. "You both deserve every good thing, after the service you have given this country and this community." Clara must have confided in her. He shrugged awkwardly. Miss Wheeler smiled again and led him down the hall.

Clara was sitting in an armchair leafing through a book when Miss Wheeler opened the door and waved him in. The door closed behind him; Clara put the book on a side table and stood, her hands clasped in front of her. She wore a dress he had not seen before, in some patterned fabric whose predominant green complemented her eyes.

She looked cautiously relieved to see him. Had she doubted that he would come? Even thought he might be regretting their engagement? He must dispel any such supposition at once. He strode toward her and grasped her hands, looking in her eyes. "I am so glad to see you."

Her clenched hands relaxed, and she smiled at him. "And I am glad to hear you say it. Won't you sit down?"

"Not yet."

Clara's eyes widened as Joshua let go of her hands, only to move his hands to her shoulders. "There is a — a privilege I have been longing to exercise."

She looked in his eyes and took a slow, deep breath. He no longer felt tension in her shoulders, but she was just perceptibly trembling. Usually so forthright of speech, she said nothing, only gazing at him. He stood holding her, hesitating. And then she stepped closer to him, her eyes bright, and lifted her face to his. He could not say whether he or she closed the last distance between them as their lips finally touched.

The soft sweetness, the warmth of her lips meeting his, was like nothing he could remember. He had kissed a girl or two in his awkward youth, and he had kissed the girls at Madam Mamie's in the frenzied urgency of passion, but he had known nothing like this tingling sensation spreading through him. He longed to press her closer to him, but refrained. It was only the first kiss. There would be many more.

His heart sung hosannas to Heaven above.

Mr. Kennedy and his medicine show returned to town three days later. Joshua noted with a complicated mixture of feelings the ebullient air with which the pitchman addressed the crowd. Freida must have given him her answer. The show's performance that day was noticeably abbreviated. The performers dispersed, all apparently heading for saloons, while the pitchman disappeared into the back of his wagon. Seized with curiosity, Joshua strolled around to a spot in front of the dry goods store from which he could see into the wagon. He was unsurprised to see Freida sitting on the upholstered bench inside, and only momentarily surprised to see her stand up and open her arms wide, inviting and joining in a hearty embrace and enthusiastic kiss. The man's height and broad shoulders made Freida look, if not small, less bulky than usual, and the strength of his grasp had lifted her to her toes. Was that a muffled moan of pleasure he heard from her?

Joshua's lips seemed to tingle with the memory of his visit to Clara at the boardinghouse. Clara was back at Joshua's office now, dealing with anyone who wandered in while Joshua was absent. It would be imprudent to repeat that delightful experience in such a setting, prior to their marriage. He had already decided so. But how tempting the thought!

The embrace showed no signs of concluding. Joshua backed away, turned, and headed for his office, breathing deep to dispel the alluring visions in his head.

* * * * *

Joshua escorted Clara to Freida's when she went to be fitted for her dress, and was unsurprised to find Mr. Kennedy seated at her table, working his way through a very large helping of sausage and onions. Mr. Kennedy shoved back his chair, wiped his mouth, and stood up as Joshua and Clara entered. "Miss Brook, I hear I am not the only fortunate man in town. My very best wishes, and may Dr. Gibbs here treat you like a queen."

Clara lifted an eyebrow. "I would be most uncomfortable with such treatment, and have sufficient faith in Dr. Gibbs to consider it unlikely. My congratulations to you, sir. And my best wishes to you, Mrs. Blum, and my thanks for taking time for me with everything else you must have to arrange."

Freida rolled her eyes. "So much to do! So much to pack, to sell, to give away. Joshua, tell dear Alton, I want the two of you to take all the books you want, the rest should go to the social library. But listen to me run on, you're here about Clara's dress and I'm excited to make it, you'll look so lovely! Come let me show you some colors that would look perfect on you, you can choose."

Clara followed Freida into her bedroom, leaving Joshua relieved at the warmth Freida now showed his intended. Mr. Kennedy interrupted his thoughts by holding out his hand and saying, "I hope you will call me Jedidiah from now on."

Joshua accepted the handshake. "Of course, and please call me Joshua."

Jedidiah strolled over to the stove. "Appears there's a whole lot more of this excellent dish. Will you join me?"

It struck Joshua for the first time that he had little time left to enjoy Freida's cooking. It was a very unsettling thought indeed. He felt rather like a child looking at a "Closing Soon" sign at the local ice cream parlor. "I will join you, and gladly."

Freida swept back in, Clara in her wake, before he had finished his serving. "Oh, good, I'm so glad you're eating, it shouldn't go to waste, not even Jedidiah can eat that much. You want, I can give Clara the recipe, all my recipes, you can enjoy them after we leave town."

Joshua worked to keep his voice steady as he asked, "Will you be leaving for good, then, rather than circling back as the wagon has lately done?"

"Going in circles, it seems silly with a whole country

to see. Sooner or later, we'll pass back through, so many people I'll be happy to see again, but first, Jedidiah has so much new to show me, so long since I've been anywhere but here!"

Jedidiah added, "Our first goal will be to find a Jewish community in which we can be married. I have hopes of Denver, Colorado, but if Denver lacks a sufficient number of Jewish residents, we will head for Tombstone, Arizona, where there is already a — what is the word? Oh, yes, synagogue." He pronounced the word with almost exaggerated care.

Freida shook her gray curls. "Men, do they listen? I told him, no rabbi will marry a Jew and a Christian, but he knows better, he thinks he can talk anyone into anything."

Jedidiah reached out to take Freida's hand and wink at her. "Do you really doubt it? You must admit that persuasion is one of my well developed skills." His face grew more sober. "Although if it comes to it, I would be willing to embrace your faith."

Joshua stared at the two of them and then caught himself. "Then you will not wed before you depart." He managed not to add the word "together."

Freida snorted. "What, you're worrying about my reputation? We'll have one strong man, two dancing girls, and a lasso-throwing cowboy as chaperones, you can relax."

"Of course," Joshua replied. "I will be sorry not to attend your wedding, but I understand your desire for your own rites."

Freida cast her gaze around her rooms, with all the furniture and knick-knacks she would be leaving behind. "You and Clara, you should both choose something from the shelves to remember me by."

Joshua could not speak for the lump in his throat. Swallowing it, he took both her hands in his. "Freida, dear

Freida, you are in any case utterly unforgettable."

The next time Joshua stopped by, he was surprised to see that very little had changed: Freida's spacious sitting room was still crowded with furniture and books and bric-a-brac. Freida took in his bewilderment, but said nothing about it, instead asking with a casual air, "You and Clara, where are you going to live?"

That question had been troubling Joshua considerably. They could not currently afford to build a house, and he had found no suitable rooms or cottage to let. "We'll make do with my rooms for now. We're both of us used to worse."

"Used to, nothing, why shouldn't you have more than what you used to? I've had an idea, better than the two of you crammed into such a place, you should take this house, and I can leave all the furniture, you sell what you don't want, buy what you like. I won't be needing it, it'll be my wedding present to you, I didn't make you a new suit, this will be better anyway."

Joshua's jaw dropped. He looked around at the kitchen, the sitting room, the bedchamber. He had never noticed the size of the bed. Had she brought it from New York? It was big enough for two. He shook off the image of sharing it with Clara. "That's enormously generous, but we couldn't possibly — you should sell it. If the sale isn't complete before you leave, I could wire you the money —"

She gave an unusually vigorous snort. "Money, what would I spend it on? Jedidiah does well enough, he wouldn't want me offering to support him, I shouldn't think, and what could I buy worth carrying from place to place? You live here in good health, I'll be happy to think of you finally having a kitchen, not even a proper stove you have in those little rooms!"

He swallowed a considerable lump in his throat and managed to say, "I'll speak to Clara, and if she tells me my reluctance is unnecessary, we'll take this house with the utmost gratitude. I'll sell anything we don't need, and I *will* wire you the proceeds, whether you expect to need them or no. And this place will always be here to welcome you."

Freida patted his cheek. "There's a good boy. Now sit down and have some plum cake, a new recipe, Rachel brought it from back east, her fiancé loves it."

* * * * *

Joshua's parents and his oldest sister Beth were able to make the journey to attend the wedding. Clara's uncle would be attending as well. His letter accepting the invitation expressed his surprise at how long it had taken for them to come to the point.

It took little discussion to confirm that Joshua and Clara each felt some apprehension about the arrival of their family members. Joshua proposed that both of them go the station as each set of relations arrived. Clara raised both eyebrows at him. "Did you imagine I would excuse you from encountering my uncle? Perish the thought. I will, of course, have the easier task."

There was some truth in her observation. The unfinished business between Joshua and his family, his failure ever to fully explain why he had left, did not involve Clara, and his parents and sister would know as much. But he thought Clara was understating the degree to which her intelligent empathy would pull her into the emotional currents surrounding the meeting.

As the train bearing Clara's uncle pulled into the station, Joshua took Clara's hand and stood close beside her. But when the passengers began descending from the cars,

Clara squeezed his hand once and stepped in front of him. He had no time to catch up before she stood face to face with her uncle. Their family resemblance, which Joshua had failed to notice previously, was evident as niece and uncle scrutinized each other. Both, it seemed, were soon satisfied. Clara's shoulders relaxed, and Mr. Brook reached out to clasp Clara's hands.

As Joshua rejoined Clara, Mr. Brook released Clara's hands, but did not immediately offer his hand to Joshua. Regarding him with a glance almost as keen as those his niece could command, he said, "I will offer you a pact, young man. If you will bear no grudge for my not entirely trusting you at our previous meeting, I will not inquire as to the role you may have played in my niece's unhappiness at that time."

Clara bristled. "Uncle, that is entirely —"

Joshua laid a hand gently on her arm. "If I may respond?"

Clara turned to him, indignation still showing on her face but soon replaced with wry amusement. "If you like. I must say I am curious to hear it."

Joshua turned back to Mr. Brook. "As I believe your niece was about to say, I do not believe her state of mind during that period was primarily due to any uncertainties she may have had about the state of my affections, nor am I at all sure she desired to win those affections at that time." By his side, Clara stirred as if suppressing some comment. He, in turn, suppressed his curiosity about what it could have been, and went on. "However, I cannot entirely acquit myself of responsibility. I was aware that in assisting me with a medical procedure all too common during the war, she was recalling and to some extent re-experiencing past traumas. Yet I did nothing, in the following days, to ascertain how she was faring or offer any assistance. For that failure, I ask both her and your forgiveness. And if you grant me yours, I will ask for your hand on it."

Mr. Brook studied Joshua for one long moment more and then extended his hand at last.

They had time to escort Mr. Brook to Cowbird Creek's sole hotel before returning to meet Joshua's parents and sister. The warmth and excitement with which his mother and sister greeted both him and Clara, and the prompt and hearty handshake with his father, made for a notable contrast with the preceding more awkward encounter. But by the time they had walked to the hotel, with Joshua, his father, and Clara carrying all the suitcases for the party, the initial babble of conversation had died away. Clara pulled Joshua aside as the visitors dealt with the clerk. "The office has gone unattended long enough, I think. And you and your family will need some private time together."

He had little concern for the office at the moment, but he reluctantly agreed with the latter point. He held her shoulders between his hands, wishing he could kiss her; she gave him a reassuring smile and strode away, leaving him to negotiate the familial shoals alone.

His father assisted by suggesting that the two of them have a drink in the hotel's saloon. It was perhaps early in the afternoon for drinking, but Joshua would not reject the overture, and could in fact use some liquid courage before talking to his mother.

His father, having taken the initiative, now appeared content to let Joshua open any conversation. Joshua waited for their mugs of beer to arrive and then held his aloft for a toast. "To Clara."

His father hoisted his glass with a good will. "To Clara, indeed. I am delighted, not to say relieved, that you have found yourself a bride. Your mother had begun to despair of it."

Joshua could hardly expect otherwise. He took a swallow of beer before replying. "Indeed, I was not in search of one. In fact, I had for some while been resisting friendly efforts to find a wife for me." His thoughts inevitably strayed to Freida, and the parting soon to come. With some difficulty, he held to his jovial tone. "Had I not met Clara, I might well have remained forever a bachelor. It is to Clara my mother owes the relief of her feelings."

His father raised his glass again. "To the end of your mother's laments about her unwed son!"

They clinked their glasses together this time, then sat quietly drinking for several minutes. At a loss for other topics, Joshua finally said, "I would ask you to tell me about your book, but I am certain Clara would want to hear you describe it."

His father chuckled. "If so, she is indeed a paragon, and you are greatly blessed." He drained his glass. "And now, I should return you to your mother and sister."

Joshua gulped down the rest of his beer. "As you will, sir. Lead on."

Beth and Mother had used the interval to unpack and change out of their travel clothes. Joshua was relieved to see the room was one of the largest available. It eased his conscience, which had nagged at him that his family should be staying with him and Clara instead. But it would be difficult to invite them without inviting Mr. Brook, a prospect neither he nor Clara relished; and both of them much preferred to begin their married life in privacy.

Beth ran up to them, stopping to peck their father on the cheek before giving Joshua another hug and then seizing his hands. "You're looking splendid, Joshie! Small town life must agree with you, though I can't understand why."

Joshua obliged with the expected wince at the childhood nickname. Mother stood up from the armchair where she had been resting and joined them. Looking him up and down, she said softly, "Beth is quite correct. I have had my doubts about whether you found whatever you hoped to find, when you left Philadelphia. Your letters did not give me much reassurance. But it has been many years since I have seen you look so well."

How, in Joshua's letters, had she managed to read his emotional state? He could only ascribe it to some mysterious maternal intuition. He smiled at both women. "Small town life has greatly improved of late, for the obvious reason."

Beth peered up at him. He had forgotten that his oldest sister was now so much shorter than he. "I wonder, then, if my new sister is responsible for your new happiness, whether you might consider bringing her back east."

He should have anticipated the suggestion, and prepared an answer. But he found only the words wanting, not the essence. Squeezing Beth's hands, he said with all the tenderness he could muster, "I have missed you, all of you, and hope to see you much more often in future. But I have made a life here, a life with Clara. It is one I would not willingly abandon, even to be closer to the family I love."

The small sound his mother made might have been a sob. Joshua could not force himself to look at her and confirm the possibility. He waited, instead, for her to compose herself if necessary, and then released Beth's hands and pulled Mother into an embrace.

* * * * *

Clara's lilac dress, trimmed with green ribbon, set off her coloring perfectly. Joshua had one suit of clothes he considered suitable; Freida conceded they would pass inspection.

The church was full to bursting with townspeople, farmers, and friends from Rushing, and decorated with flowers blooming in and around town. Clara's hand on his arm, the firmness of her grip, reminded him for a disorienting moment of that day she had supported him at the Barlow farm, when the memories of his Army days had threatened to unman him. He thrust the memory aside, then called it back again. The courage and strength she had shown then were now to be his mainstay, and he would honor and cherish them and her.

Freida and Jedidiah were in the front row of spectators, but as soon as Joshua and Clara had said their vows and the preacher had announced them as man and wife, Jedidiah excused himself to those around him and left the church. A bit startled, Joshua glanced toward Freida, but she beamed at him, untroubled by her escort's disappearance. When he and Clara had made their way back down the aisle and emerged from the church, he found the explanation for Jedidiah's odd behavior. The medicine show had pulled up next to the church, Major circling the wagon and barking enthusiastically. The pitchman stood on the wagon seat, gesturing toward the married couple. "Three cheers, good people, for Doctor and Mrs. Gibbs! And when you've cheered their happiness, the Professor Kennedy Traveling Medicine Show will give its farewell and finest performance to celebrate the joyous occasion."

An idea popped into Joshua's mind — frivolous, possibly unwise, oddly compelling. He whispered in Clara's ear; she grinned and gave him a little shove toward the wagon. Heartened, he approached it and called up to

Jedidiah, "Might the show be in need of a guest magician to perform a few tricks, on this occasion only?"

Jedidiah beamed. "The perfect addition! Ladies and gentlemen, may I present your doctor the groom!"

When Joshua's few, kindly received magic tricks, and then the dancing with veils and feats of cowboy roping, were over, the crowd began migrating toward the boardinghouse where Rebecca Wheeler would host the reception. Freida and Jedidiah came up to Joshua and Clara, hand in hand. Jedidiah shook hands with them both and then climbed back up on the wagon. Joshua stared at him and asked Freida, "You're leaving? Now?"

"We thought, why should we draw it out, have you thinking all night about saying goodbye, you have better things to think about!" She actually winked at them; Clara laughed aloud before Joshua had time to feel embarrassed. "This way, we're all sad for a little while, then you go and be happy, and we get on our way, better all around."

Joshua gazed at Freida for the last time in who knew how long. "You're a wise woman, Freida Blum, and I'll sorely miss that wisdom as I follow my own new path."

She scoffed. "Wise, what do I know, I didn't even find this wonderful woman for you! Not that you did any better, so it's a good thing we're both more lucky than smart."

Joshua put his arm around his wife. "Very, very lucky." She leaned in close to him, her warm side against his.

Joshua let go of Clara long enough to help Freida into the wagon. He stopped just short of it. "You have plenty of Jedidiah's medicine available? And you'll be careful about exerting yourself?"

Freida let out a hearty shout of laughter. "Listen to you with all the questions, you sound like me! Yes, yes, I'll do everything I should, I wouldn't want you worrying. Here, let me give you a hug, I never did so now's the time, isn't it?"

Joshua embraced her, holding her tight against his wedding coat, feeling the beating of her heart and willing it to beat for many years to come. He let her go, eyes stinging, and handed her up to her fiancé. Then he stepped back and held Clara close to him again as the wagon drove away.

He saw that Clara too had tears in her eyes. She smiled through them. "It'll be strange to go back to that house without Freida there. I never knew anyone like her."

"There's no one like her. And no one like you." He whistled for Major; the dog trotted up, wagging his tail, jumping to lick Joshua's free hand. Joshua had already moved Major's dog bed and toys into Freida's — into their house. He gave Clara's waist another squeeze and then took her hand. "Come, we'll put in our necessary appearance at the reception. And then, let us go home."

THE END

Acknowledgments

My profound thanks to cover designer Kelly Martin of KAM Design and her unequaled patience and persistence.

The National Museum of Civil War Medicine provided invaluable assistance in filling in Joshua Gibbs' and Clara Brook's wartime experiences, through their Twitter feed (@CivilWarMed) and their Research Department (accessible via http://www.civilwarmed.org/contact/research/). I owe particular thanks to Terry Reimer, Director of Research.

The Researcher & Reference Services Division of the Library of Congress and the library's Business Reference Services; Adam Burns of American-Rails.com; Patricia LaBounty, curator at the Union Pacific Railroad Museum; Chris Rockwell, librarian, and Jeff Asay, volunteer, at the California State Railroad Museum; Christina Windheuser, volunteer at the National Museum of American History Archives Center; and longtime friend Fred Campbell helped me find railroad timetables, Pullman car plans and schedules, and railroad-related details. Another (anonymous) staff member or volunteer at the Archives Center steered me in a direction that allowed me to find Sandy Stalder, President of the Quad County Museum and Humboldt Chamber of Commerce; Margo Prentiss, Curator of the Cass County Historical Society; Dick Miers of the Seward County Historical Society; Kelli Baker, Certified

Local Government Coordinator for the State of Nebraska; Susan Quinn of the Nebraska City Historical Society; Ed Zimmer of the Lincoln Historic Preservation Commission; Megan Sothan, Museum Administrator for the Gage County Historical Society and Museum; Kathy Woodrell, Reference Specialist for Decorative Arts and Architecture at the Library of Congress; and Jill Dolberg, Deputy State Historic Preservation Officer for the State of Nebraska. All these people provided information about rental housing in Nebraska in the 1870s. Ms. Sothan also alerted me to both the Financial Panic of 1873 and the grasshopper (aka locust) plague of 1874-1875. Andrea Faling, Head of Reference, History Nebraska, provided more information about both. Sarah Williamson, President of the Johnson County Historical Society and Museum; Mary Ann Robertson, Curator at the Heritage Museum of Thurston County; Christine Solomon of the Blair Historic Preservation Alliance; Julie Ashton, Director, and Faith Norwood, Curator, of the Washington County Historical Association; Jane Elske of the Burt County Museum; and Jeff Kappeler, Executive Director of the Dodge County Historical Society, also assisted me in my research into the grasshopper invasion.

Richard Weyand pointed me toward the movie *Back to the Future III* for useful setting details.

My heartfelt thanks to my beta readers: Jennifer Bourgeois, Faith Flores, Lehsa Griebel, Paul Hager (aka my husband), Kimberly Hunt, Steven Karel, Nik Parker, and Dedaimia Whitney.

Paul and my daughters Livali Wyle and Alissa Wyle also gave me feedback on any number of points throughout the drafting and revision process. My love and gratitude to them once again.

Author's Note

As far as I know, there is no Cowbird Creek, Nebraska, and never has been. All my characters are likewise fictional. The Page Act, unfortunately, was as described, and became law in March of 1875.

I have tried — with the aid of some of the very helpful people and organizations listed in the Acknowledgments, and quite possibly others I omitted — to ensure that the medical procedures, wartime practices, and equipment described are accurate for the period. I have also striven to keep to words and expressions already in use by 1874, and otherwise to avoid anachronisms. I am not so optimistic, however, as to believe that I completely succeeded.

One usage issue that arose was how to address a single adult woman and how to refer to her. My research suggests that "ma'am" could be used as a direct address. It also suggested that referring to an unmarried adult woman as, e.g., "Miss Brook" might have been uncommon, at least earlier in the century. The period of my story may have been one of transition as far as this usage is concerned. In the end, I decided the use of "Mrs." for my single female characters would unduly confuse modern readers.

I have used, for African-Americans, the term they preferred at the time, namely "colored." I have Joshua refer to Li Chang as a "Chinaman" and as "Oriental," which I considered likely as well as more polite than the hostler's reference to "Chinee" girls. I have also assumed that Joshua, like most Americans up until a much later period, would use "he/him" to refer to unknown persons.

The sort of "rooms" that Joshua Gibbs inhabits above a storefront were more often occupied by the store's owners, but some were available for rent. I have assumed that such rooms would have a pot-bellied stove for heating, on which Joshua should be able to do rudimentary cooking. His office would have had running water, which he could use for washing dishes, and he might also have had access to some pump or well for the purpose if he did not object to publicly demonstrating the modest nature of his living quarters.

The preferred routes for 19th century medicine shows covered the Midwest and rural South. In eastern cities, the shows were likely to be larger and take place in theaters. I have not been able to confirm that Joshua could have seen such a show during his childhood in Philadelphia.

I invented a dramatic adaptation of Jane Austen's *Sense and Sensibility* for Joshua, Freida, and Alton to read together — though there may conceivably have been such an adaptation of which I've found no mention.

I have not confirmed that a Pullman car was actually available when and where Joshua and Clara encountered one, though it is not particularly unlikely. (They might well have needed to change to a less luxurious car for the final leg of their journey.) As for the porter's ingenious solution to the absence of a kitchen or dining car, it is based on speculation, rather than any reference I've been able to find. Porters were apparently not allowed to handle railroad money, which would have been a logistical complexity.

The sources I consulted differed somewhat as to when cards were first produced with differently colored but otherwise similar designs on their backs. I have chosen to go with the date that served my narrative purpose.

For more information about the magic tricks Joshua performs for Clara on the train, see "Easy Magic Tricks for Beginners and Kids" at https://www.thesprucecrafts.com/magic-tricks-for-beginners-and-kids-2267083.

"The Great Grasshopper Plague of 1874-1875" was often, and appropriately, referred to in biblical terms. In the areas most affected, including much of Nebraska, Kansas, Missouri, Iowa, and other states, the devastation was unimaginable. Clouds of "hoppers" blackened the sky, coated the land, invaded houses, and ate every growing thing and more. Farmers said grimly that the grasshoppers "ate everything but the mortgage." Cowbird Creek, however, is located in one of the more fortunate counties that largely escaped the grasshopper invasion. The story I wanted to tell would not have suited a place and time where farmers as well as their livestock were threatened with starvation, and many were forced to abandon their farms and their dreams and go back east.

Finally, I wanted to note that what we now call post-traumatic stress disorder (PTSD), and doctors during World War I called shell shock, was sometimes, during the Civil War, called "soldier's heart." That fact gives a certain additional resonance to this book's title.

About the Author

Karen A. Wyle was born a Connecticut Yankee, but eventually settled in Bloomington, Indiana, home of Indiana University. She now considers herself a Hoosier. She and her husband have two wildly creative daughters. (Return readers may notice that I no longer claim to have a sweet though neurotic dog. She left us in June 2019. We miss her.)

In addition to writing fiction (science fiction, afterlife fantasy, and now historical romance), Wyle is an appellate attorney, photographer, and politics junkie. Her voice is the product of almost five decades of reading both literary and genre fiction. It is no doubt also influenced, although she hopes not fatally tainted, by her years of law practice. Her personal history has led her to focus on often-intertwined themes of family, communication, personal identity, the impossibility of controlling events, and the persistence of unfinished business.

Connect with the Author

Learn more about Karen A. Wyle by looking her up on her author website, http://www.KarenAWyle.com; her Facebook page, at https://www.facebook.com/KarenAWyle; her Twitter account, for which her username is (predictably) @KarenAWyle; on Goodreads; or on her blog, Looking Around.

Like the book? Please tell readers! Online book reviews are enormously helpful —and old-fashioned word of mouth is terrific as well! (I particularly appreciate Amazon reviews.)

You can sign up for email alerts about new releases and (at your option) other book news at the newsletter signup link on the home page of her author website.